Newcastle
City Council

Newcastle Libraries and Information Service

 0845 002 0336

Due for return	Due for return	Due for return
26/10/18		
19/10/21		

Please return this item to any of Newcastle's Libraries by the last date shown above. If not requested by another customer the loan can be renewed, you can do this by phone, post or in person.
Charges may be mad

D1421134

AMARANTH MOON

Recent Titles by Janet Woods from Severn House

THE STONECUTTER'S DAUGHTER

AMARANTH MOON

AMARANTH MOON

Janet Woods

This first world edition published in Great Britain 2005 by
SEVERN HOUSE PUBLISHERS LTD of
9–15 High Street, Sutton, Surrey SM1 1DF.
This first world edition published in the USA 2005 by
SEVERN HOUSE PUBLISHERS INC of
595 Madison Avenue, New York, N.Y. 10022.

British Library Cataloguing in Publication Data

Woods, Janet, 1939-
   Amaranth Moon
   1.   Dorset (England) - Social life and customs - 19th century - Fiction
   2.   Love stories
   I.   Title
   823.9'14 [F]

   ISBN 0-7278-6248-0

Typeset by Palimpsest Book Production Ltd.,
Polmont, Stirlingshire, Scotland.
Printed and bound in Great Britain by
MPG Books Ltd., Bodmin, Cornwall.

Dedication

To my grandsons, who (shaken and stirred)
provided the inspiration for the Batterby brothers.
Adrian O'Connor
Ryan Bowe-Woods
David Larsen
Brodie Larsen
James Hutton

One

Dorset, 1800

The Batterby cousins were brown-eyed, brown-haired and average in every way. Neither tall nor short, ugly nor handsome, loud nor soft, clever nor stupid; Geneva Tibbetson loved them all, from the eldest, who'd just turned fifteen, to the youngest, whose seventh birthday would be celebrated the following week.

'We're having a hounds and hares game tonight whilst the parents are out visiting. They won't be home until midnight,' Gerald, the eldest of her cousins, informed her.

'What, all eight of you?'

'Seven. No one will take Moth, he's too much of a nuisance. Unless you help out, of course. Myself and Matthew will act as the hounds if you do. It will make it harder if there's two.'

Geneva grinned when Moth offered her his mortally wounded look. 'How much start are the hares being given?'

'Ten minutes. The moon will be full and this will be Edward's initiation . . . Moth's as well, if you care to look after him. Michael has offered to take Edward. You always won the game when we were kids, but now you're grown up . . .' He shrugged. 'Well, most of us can outrun you now. Still, someone has to take care of Moth, otherwise he can't come.'

Timothy was small for his age and had only just survived his early birth. What he lacked in stature, he made up for in spirit. Geneva couldn't ignore the challenge. 'Can you find me some old knee breeches to wear?'

Gerald grinned. His hands came out from behind his back and he dropped a pair on the bed. He'd been that sure of her. 'Thanks Gen, I knew you would.'

'I take it we're using Welford Manor as a rendezvous.'

Gerald nodded as he gazed at the two initiates. 'You might

1

see a ghost at the manor if you're lucky. But don't dare say a word to the parents, else they'll froth at the mouth and forbid us. The pair of you had better come and take the oath of secrecy.'

Edward's scoffing noise was more bravado than conviction, but Moth slid his hand into hers and gazed up at her, his eyes wide open and scared. She dropped a kiss on his cheek and whispered, 'Don't worry, Moth. I'll take my magic stone with me. It will protect us.'

How the atmosphere of suppressed excitement in the house didn't alert the Batterbys, Geneva couldn't understand. But it wasn't long before the carriage taking Reverend and Mrs Batterby away was bowling out of sight. They all exploded into action.

The dusk was a misty purple, the air slightly humid as they gathered at the secret rendezvous behind the stables. Through the trees the moon was rising in all its glory. Moth was trembling with excitement.

Geneva had braided her fair hair, for her curls were of the unruly type.

'Most unfortunate hair, like the fleece of a sheep,' her aunt often told her, which wasn't exactly the truth, but it was certainly difficult to keep tidy when tendrils kept escaping from her braid. Over her breeches she wore a dark bodice and a dark cloak. A pair of scuffed boots adorned the bottom half of her legs.

'Right, you know the rules,' Gerald said when they gathered for the game. Geneva grinned when she saw the pale pantaloons the hounds wore. They would be easy to spot in the dark. Gerald ruffled Moth's hair. 'Those of you in pairs, stay in pairs. If we catch one, we catch both. The first to reach Welford and hang the dust sheet from the window wins the pot.'

The others took off at a run, but Geneva walked Moth across the garden to disappear into the shrubbery. When they reached the stream, she smeared their faces with mud, then they sat in the shadow of a tree, hiding under the cloak until she heard the hounds go by. Taking a pendant from her pocket, she held the stone against Moth's eye. 'Here, take a look at the moon through this and make a wish. It came from a bazaar in Egypt.

If everything turns the colour of amaranth, your wish will come true.'

'What colour is amaranth?'

'It's a purplish colour.'

'It looks blue to me,' Moth said, holding it against his closed eye.

'That means you can have two wishes.'

The man whose house they were about to invade had given Geneva the pendant. She'd only met Sorle Ashby once. That had been eight years previously, when, as a twelve-year-old, she'd attended his uncle's funeral.

It had been a cold day, she recalled. She'd had a slight fever, but Maudine had ignored her complaint and the tickle in her throat had turned into an uncontrollable cough during the service.

Turning a pair of coal-dark eyes her way, Sorle had frowned. Then he'd smiled and, fishing in his waistcoat pocket, had handed her a peppermint lozenge to suck before turning to Maudine to say in a warm, rumbling voice, 'That child has a fever, she should be in bed, not standing in a draughty church.'

The next day, Sorle had come to the house to enquire after her health. He'd found her in the garden, perfectly well again. He'd brought her a gift. The blue stone was set in gold, and it twisted back and forth on a gold chain dangling from his finger.

'I've brought you this because it matches your pretty eyes. I purchased it from a bazaar in Egypt. It has magical properties. If you gaze through the stone during the full moon and the landscape turns the colour of amaranth, any wish you make at that moment will come true. Do you swear to keep this a secret between us?'

His lips had twitched when she'd inadvertently revealed the influence of her cousins by placing her hand against her heart and saying solemnly, 'I do so swear, My Lord. Torture by a thousand bee stings or throwing me into a pit of deadly adders won't make me give the secret away. It's a sacred trust between us for ever.'

'Forever then,' he'd said, and he'd dropped the trinket into the pocket of her apron, probably secure in the knowledge that such events as she'd described were rare to extinct in the

3

small community of Edgley Cross. But then, Sorle Ashby didn't know her cousins!

Geneva had seated herself on top of the gate and watched the young earl ride away, his long legs clad in buckskin breeches as he sat comfortably astride a gleaming black gelding. At his throat was a muslin cravat, and the dark curls of his hair were hidden under a round-fronted hat. He'd seemed a heroic figure to her as he'd turned to wave goodbye.

She'd hidden the trinket amongst her things so her aunt couldn't find it and make her hand it back.

Now, eight years and another two male cousins later, the Batterbys had heard a rumour that Lord Ashby was coming back to look Welford Manor over. He was to decide whether to live in the district, or to sell the estate.

Geneva couldn't remember when she'd become a permanent resident at the rectory. It seemed as though she'd always lived here.

'Geneva is the daughter of my husband's half-sister,' her aunt Maudine was wont to tell people in a suitably lowered voice. 'Her papa was a ne'er-do-well who died abroad and left them penniless. Such a shock. Her mama imbibed too freely of spirituous liquor and followed him into the grave not long afterwards. How convenient that Reverend Batterby's poor relation was looking for a home, just when I'd dismissed one of our maids. The dear girl has made herself so useful.'

And any man who cast an interested eye Geneva's way was quickly informed in a hushed voice, 'Miss Tibbetson has no dowry, poor thing, and no accomplishments. Bad blood in the family, I'm afraid.'

So here she was, Geneva Tibbetson, aged twenty, who looked every inch the impoverished spinster lady that was her future. Required to act as unpaid governess, she was reminded at every turn of Maudine's largesse in the matter. She could barely remember either of her parents.

Sometimes, Geneva felt so trapped she could scream! Sometimes, when she could get out of the house unseen and visit her favourite spot, she stood on the cliff top with her arms spread wide and *did* scream, allowing her howls of frustration to blow away on the breeze!

Thank God for her cousins, who treated her as a sister and

always took her side against their mother, come what may.

Moth shied when an owl hooted in the tree above, bringing Geneva back to the present. 'I wish I was brave,' he said in a trembling voice.

'You are brave, Moth. You're just not old enough to know it yet.' She took the pendant from him and slipped it in her pocket. 'Come on, the hounds have gone, so let's follow after them for a while. They won't expect anyone to be behind them.'

Sorle Ashby, having recently celebrated his thirtieth birthday at the residence he shared with his mother in London, was now ensconced in one of the upper chambers of Welford Manor, deciding whether or not to live in the property his uncle had left him.

He was tired of the London scene – bored of the card tables, the drinking and the womanizing. Here, in Dorset, with only a couple of rolling green hills between the house and the sea, he could ride, fish, hunt and entertain as he pleased. Or not, come to that, for Sorle, with his many interests, found his own company perfectly agreeable for most of the time.

Somewhere on the floor below him was a fine library, he recalled. And if he became bored he could take passage abroad from the harbour town of Bridport, which was not far away. As for his bodily comfort, there was bound to be a house of easement in one of the bigger towns; there always was. Come to that, he could take a wife for himself and breed an heir or two from her. God knew, his mother had tried hard enough to tempt him with a procession of delectable, wealthy and eligible women.

Welford Manor had a hall big enough to hold a ball in, he mused. Once he'd got the house and garden into better shape, he could throw a Christmas ball for the locals, many of whom would have daughters of marriageable age. Ideally, Sorle would like to be in love when he married, but he'd never met a woman yet who could hold his interest in more than a temporary manner.

Once, he'd seriously considered marriage to a widow, one Olivia Wainbridge. But his mind had kept throwing up little questions for him to ponder on. Could he spend evening after evening in Olivia's company when her mind was so

5

preoccupied with the latest play or fashion? Why, she rarely even seated herself in company lest her skirt be creased by doing so. And her empty prattle sometimes took on a carping note, which had begun to annoy him.

Fortunately he'd come to his senses, for he'd remembered Olivia's late husband as being an unhappy, downtrodden fellow. He'd reached the conclusion that instinct had kept him free of any meaningful entanglement with her, and he had great faith in his instinct.

It was now telling him to change his lifestyle and move into Welford Manor. He could put his legal training to use by defending the poor at the quarterly assizes, and live the life of a country gentleman – for he didn't need to earn money other than through his many investments.

As the evening darkened, Sorle's mood mellowed, due, no doubt, to the bottle of fine brandy at his elbow. He'd forgotten his uncle's wine cellar until today. Just as well, for had he remembered it before, he would most certainly have visited Welford Manor sooner.

The outside caretaker he paid to keep an eye on the place had also taken it upon himself to give the many bottles in the cellar a quarter turn on the first of each month. As a result, the corks had remained airtight and the fine selection of wines and spirits the cellar contained had improved in flavour as it had matured.

Gradually, the room lightened as a white moon drifted up from behind the trees. Thank goodness the upstairs windows had been left unboarded, otherwise the room would be stifling. Opening the window wider, he took a deep breath of the summer air. It smelled sweet and fresh, as if the flowers dancing amongst the high summer grasses had released their perfume into the night.

In London, most nights the windows would have remained shut against the unhealthy stench of the River Thames.

He thought he saw something move on the other side of the garden to his left. But when he looked again, he concluded it was only the shadows shifting in the shrubbery.

He returned to his chair and the contemplation of his life, gazing through his glass at the weak light coming from the stump of a candle he'd lit. He doubted he'd be able to sleep tonight, for the ides of the month always kept him alert. But he did, drifting off in the winged chair he was seated in, lulled by the distant sound of the sea, the soft night air and the soporific sense of relaxation it produced.

Soon, the candle began to gutter and smoke.

Geneva saw the hounds part company when they reached the meadow, one going left and the other to the right. Bent double, she and Moth had gone straight on to reach the house, sneaking through the long grass of the meadow on their stomachs for the last stretch. Geneva parted the grass on the edge of the path to gaze cautiously at the manor. The moon lent a pearly incandescence to the upper windows.

There were several ways to gain entrance to the house, despite the boards on the downstairs windows. One board swivelled sideways to reveal a window with a broken latch beyond. You could also climb up the ivy to a balcony over the porch, where a thin blade inserted between the glass-paned doors would gain entry to a large bedroom. The room was filled with wonderful treasures, for it had belonged to the wife of the previous owner. Geneva had hidden the jewellery away in case of robbers. She'd tried it all on first, admiring the way the precious stones sparkled and shone.

Entrance was also possible via terrace doors to the drawing room. The wooden shutters could be lifted off, the doors unlatched in the same way. But Geneva needed none of those entry points, and she knew the hounds would be patrolling them all anyway. Patting her pocket, she grinned. She had her own way in, one the others didn't know about. It was a key to the front door, one she'd discovered years ago, hidden in a crack between two bricks. All she had to do was make sure the coast was clear before they sprinted across the gravel.

Cautiously, she turned her head both ways. One of the hounds was crouched in the shrubbery, his breeches illuminated by the moonlight. She pointed him out to Moth, who was quivering with all the pent-up excitement of a puppy dog hoping for attention. 'We must be as quiet as mice now,' she whispered.

Suddenly, off to their right, came the crack of a branch and a shushing sound. Immediately, the husky bark of one hound signalled to the other. The one in the shrubbery rose. It was Gerald, and he pounded straight past them.

'Now!' Geneva whispered to Moth, and the pair slipped across the carriageway into the shadow of the porch. It took but a moment to insert the key into the lock, turn it and slip into the pitch-black hall inside.

Moth pressed against her side, whispering, 'Will there be ghosts?'

'Shush!' Geneva certainly felt a presence of some sort, but it would have to be one of the hares, for both the hounds were still outside. They must get upstairs as soon as possible if Moth was to claim the prize.

It was a over a year since she'd last been inside Welford Manor, but she still remembered her way around it. Forty paces forward and slightly to her left, her hand encountered a bannister. The stairway curved up to the gallery, where a gleam of light came through one of the upper windows and fell over the dark-eyed visage of Charles Ashby, Sorle's uncle.

'It's only a painting,' she whispered when they reached it and Moth gave a small cry of alarm.

'I don't like it here in the dark, Gen.'

'I know. But think of how proud your brothers will be of you when you win, and you'll have part of their allowance to spend at the midsummer fair.'

Somewhere at the back of the house she heard a scraping noise. 'Quick!' she whispered, taking his hand. 'We don't want the other hares to get there before us.'

The rendezvous was a quick walk around the gallery to a chamber at the front of the house. The door creaked as she pushed it open. Picking up the nearest dust sheet, she flung it over the sill to hang out of the open window.

There was a soft curse, then one of the hounds gave a series of barks. She grinned when her cousins began to emerge from their hiding places.

But realization hit her as soon as she heard the sound of a horse fidgeting. The window shouldn't be open! And the room smelt strongly of a flame drowning in candle wax. In fact, it was still guttering on the mantelpiece. But the vast bed was unmade and still covered by a dust sheet. Geneva's heart began to beat very fast. She had to get them out of here.

8

But Moth was gazing at the chair, his body rigid as he stared at a figure reclining in it. When it grunted, he gave a loud and terrified scream. 'It's a ghost!'

Sorle woke with a start from a pleasant dream of near-naked nymphs dancing in the grass outside his window. Disorientated, his befuddled gaze fell on a figure outlined by moonlight.

'Lucifer's oath!' Coming upright, he threw a punch, his fist connecting with something soft. Air expelled in an agonized gasp. His second blow glanced off the intruder's face as he began to double over. The intruder staggered backwards, hit the wall and slid to the floor, where he curled up and began to moan.

Sorle hadn't hit him as hard as he could have done, but there hadn't been much muscle resistance, he thought. Either the huddled figure had underdeveloped muscles, or was smaller than he'd first thought. A lad who hadn't reached adulthood yet? He was about to stoop to investigate when someone pummelled at his thighs. The high-pitched voice he heard contained all the sobbing terror of a small boy left alone to deal with the unknown. 'Don't kill Gen, you damned ghost, else I'll set my brothers on to you.' The threat was followed by a kick to his shin.

'Ouch!' Sorle grunted. His hand connected with a collar and fisted around it. He hauled the child from the floor and, dangling the squirming creature from the end of his arm, gazed at him. 'Calm down, lad. I won't hurt you.'

'I want my brothers,' the lad quavered, then burst into loud sobs.

The figure on the floor staggered upright, snatched the child from his grasp and occupied the chair he'd just vacated, cuddling the lad close. A voice rasped painfully, 'Stand back, sir. I have a dagger and will stab you through the heart if you venture closer.'

'I've got a sword, and I'll kill you as well,' said the child, catching him under the knee with a well-aimed foot.

'Stop that, you ferocious little tyke!' Guilt flooded through Sorle when he saw the blood on the older lad's mouth. Thank God he hadn't used his full strength. 'Seeing as how both your hands are engaged, I must point out that your threats and your

9

dramatics are without substance. Who the hell are you, anyway?'

The intruder offered him a watery sniff and the minimum of information. 'That's none of your business.'

'Like hell it isn't! You've come into my house uninvited, and I intend to discover the reason.'

'Don't swear in front of Moth. He's only six.'

'Like hell I am!' said Moth. 'I'm nearly seven. I'm having a birthday party next week.'

Sorle grinned at the boy's answer. Holding a fresh candle to the flickering flame, he managed to capture the light of the old before it drowned in the wax. Soon, a sconce was blazing. He turned to the intruder. There was a very feminine curve under the bodice. Wispy curls framed a mud-stained face. His eyes widened. 'Good God, you're a girl?'

'Very observant, Lord Ashby. Where are your manners? Pass me your handkerchief, if you please, for my lip is bleeding. I bit it when you hit me.'

He handed it to her with alacrity, apologizing all the while. There was a bruise purpling on her cheekbone too, and no doubt her midriff was as sore as hell, for she was still breathing in shallow gasps and tears glistened in her eyes.

'You know my name. Have we met before?' What the hell was going on? Hearing scuffling at the door, Sorle strode swiftly and silently across the room to jerk it open. A heap of youths fell into the room under their own pressure, tripping over each other's bodies until they came to rest in an ungainly heap of thrashing arms and legs and a variety of boyish curses.

'May I introduce my cousins?' the girl said drily. 'From tallest down to shortest, Gerald, Matthew, Adam and Simon, who are twins—'

'Though we don't look alike,' the pair pointed out unnecessarily.

'Then comes Michael, Robert, Edward and Timothy, here on my lap, who you've already met.'

'Ah . . . you must be the Batterby boys.'

'You make them sound like a gang of felons, when they're not. Do get up, cousins, so the gentleman can see for himself that you're not what you seem,' she said, and with some asperity.

The cousins began to unravel themselves and eventually stood, forming themselves into a ragged and shamefaced line.

The girl took it upon herself to direct operations. 'This gentleman is Lord Ashby, who is the owner of Welford Manor. No doubt he'll require an explanation of our conduct tonight.'

'I won the game,' Moth said gleefully, smiling proudly at his brothers for approval.

'Well done, Moth,' they said together in various tones of admiration and envy. The older lad's eyes widened. 'What happened to your face, Gen?'

Her eyes were cornflower blue, Sorle imagined, though they were a mysterious purple in the candle glow and saturated with tears as she flicked a reproachful glance his way.

'I punched her,' Sorle confessed.

The two older boys stepped forward, gazing at each other in uncertainty. 'You bully, you deserve a flogging,' one of them said, though neither looked as though they'd be interested in taking him on.

Moth jumped from her lap, his fists raised. 'I'll flog him.'

The one called Matthew, second in line and gangly limbed, pushed his hands down. 'Don't be such an idiot. Lord Ashby would flatten you.'

'I don't care. Gen allowed me to look through her magic stone at the moon and wish. I wished to be brave, and I was.'

'There's a difference between courage and foolhardiness. Pipe down, Moth. Wishing on a stone will get you nowhere.'

'I wished to win the game, and I did,' Moth pointed out. 'Now you've all got to give me part of your allowance to spend at the midsummer fair.'

'It's not fair to use magic,' Edward, the next one up in size, said indignantly.

The girl bit her lip and both hands clutched at her midriff. 'You were very brave in my defence, Moth, but you must apologize to Lord Ashby. We all must. He thought I was an intruder, so his actions are blameless.'

The ones named Robert and Michael, a pair of youths remarkably alike in feature, exchanged a grin. 'Pa will stop our allowances altogether this time, Moth. A quarter of nothing is nothing.'

This only served to increase Sorle's guilt.

'Our domestic arrangements are of no interest to the earl. The apology, please.'

'Well, that goes without saying,' Gerald said, offering his hand. Matthew followed suit and there was a chorus of apologies.

'Now we must go, for it's time the younger children were in bed. Goodnight, My Lord.'

'You can't just walk off like that.'

'We most certainly can, unless you intend to keep us prisoner. No doubt we'll see you on the morrow, when you come to Edgley House to lay your complaints before Reverend and Mrs Batterby. Off you go, cousins.'

'Come over for breakfast,' Gerald offered generously. 'I'll take the blame, of course, for the game tonight was my idea. I suppose I'll get the thrashing for all of us, as usual. My father hasn't got the energy to thrash us *en masse*.' Morosely, he gazed at the girl. 'God knows what Mama will do to you, Gen. You'll probably never hear the last of it. She'll lock you in the cellar for a week this time, instead of just overnight.'

'We don't want to bore Lord Ashby with our domestic details. Let's go home,' she said edgily. 'Good night, My Lord.' She took a candle from the sconce and they filed out, the boys clattering down the stairs after her into the pool of darkness below.

A loud whisper drifted up to him. 'Are you alright, Gen? You look dire.'

'I feel a bit sick. I'll be all right when I get some fresh air.'

She'd held herself together well, but her voice was trembling with shock. Sorle went to the window when the front door slammed behind them. They made it across the carriageway in single file, Moth sitting on his eldest brother's shoulders, the girl bringing up the rear now. He grinned at the sight she presented. She looked good, her buttocks moulded by those tightly fitting breeches. A long braid divided her back. He'd like to see her pale hair hanging loose.

Then she began to slow down, her hands clutched at her stomach and she doubled over, before staggering on for a few steps. Sorle headed out of the room and down the stairs at a run. When he reached the group, the boys were gazing down at her still figure in consternation.

12

'Stand back, give her some air,' he ordered and, falling on one knee beside her, tucked her shabbily booted feet up on his thigh.

'What's wrong with her?' one of the cousins demanded to know.

'She's fainted, that's all.'

'Lucifer's oath!' Moth said, goggle-eyed. 'Only girls do things like that.'

Edward gave him a superior look. 'Geneva *is* a girl, stupid. She's got long hair.'

And quite delightful curves to go with it, Sorle thought, trying not to grin.

Geneva began to come round almost instantly, her eyelashes fluttering. When her eyes opened, she seemed startled to see him. Then the expression was replaced by a smoky intensity. Finally, a rueful smile turned her mouth into a delicious, curving smile. 'I'm so sorry,' she whispered.

Not as sorry as he was for hitting this dainty creature with the muddy face. How could he ignore such a delightful apology, though. 'I forgive you.'

'Hah! May I remind you that it was you who hit me.'

How stupid of him to have supplied her with the wrong answer. How calculating of her to have reminded him of it. His eyes narrowed in contemplation of her. She was less the child and more the woman than she'd first seemed. 'My humble apologies. It was all my fault, of course. I'll hang myself from the highest rafter.'

The husky chuckle she gave made his hair stand on end as she turned his own words back at him. 'There's no need to engage in such dramatics.'

'Dammit, woman! Remind me to put you over my knee when you've recovered,' he growled.

'Please don't curse in front of Moth. He collects them.'

'So I've noticed. Here, put your arms around my neck. I'll carry you home.'

'Thank you, you've given me quite a headache and my knees are wobbling.'

Was that a gleam of amusement he saw in her eyes? But no, even the moonlight couldn't disguise the pallor of her face, and she was trembling with shock. He'd hurt her badly, but

13

she was putting on a brave front for her cousins. She didn't protest when he hefted her up in his arms, just laid her head in the crook of his shoulder and sighed as he strode off across the meadow. She smelt of honeysuckle warmed by a soft summer breeze.

He enjoyed walking through the night with this girl in his arms, her breath fragrant against his chin and the wisps of her hair teasing his cheek. His thoughts wandered to kissing the tantalizing curve of her mouth, just a turn from his own – then further, of lowering this unladylike creature into the meadow grass, spreading that long, pale hair about her and making love to her under the moonlight.

He scowled. It was unfortunate that the Batterby boys were dogging his heels like a pack of silent wolves. Worried, no doubt, about the outcome of their escapade.

'I've decided I won't say anything to your parents about tonight,' he informed them.

As the boys began to cheer and whoop, the girl gave a faint sigh of relief, which was followed by a soft, tentative brush of her lips against his cheek. It felt like a butterfly alighting.

When he turned his glance her way to contemplate her action, her cheeks warmed.

Two

Edgley House was large, but bursting at the seams.
Maudine Batterby, grey-eyed, brown-haired, cushioned and constantly querulous, was relating that fact to her husband at breakfast.

'We are so cramped here. We should take up the lease of Welford Manor if the earl doesn't wish to reside there himself.'

'But, my dear, we can't afford it. Gerald will be going to Cambridge in three years time, and I intend to buy Matthew a commission in the army. Our accommodation will seem more spacious then.'

'The army? With all those nasty wars going on? Whatever are you thinking of, James?'

'It's what he wants.'

'The boys are still children. Matthew's mind can be changed if you would but apply as much of your mind to counselling him as you do to teaching music to the twins.'

The Reverend James Batterby smiled happily. 'Ah . . . but, Simon and Adam will do well at music, for both have a fine ear. As for Matthew, since I know nothing about soldiering, how can I counsel him? Make sure the twins practise whilst I'm absent today. Two hours apiece. My niece, as well. Her playing would benefit from it, I'm sure.'

'You know as well as I that Geneva has very little musical ability.'

'You're wrong,' James said mildly, and rather vaguely, for his fingers were drumming on the table, indicating that his mind was engaged with the cantata he was composing. 'Geneva's playing can be classed as satisfactory, even if not inspired. But since her main asset is a fine singing voice, an understanding of music can only be of benefit to her in the future. If she marries well, such feminine skills can only prove to be an asset.'

'Another thing,' Maudine said and, despite knowing that only catastrophe could tear him from his music when he was composing, insisted on stating what was occupying her mind. 'The constant noise of piano practice is very wearying. If we lived at Welford Manor it wouldn't matter, because it has a fine music room, as I recall.'

A pained expression came into James's soft brown eyes as he recalled the state of the church organ. The concept of having a room reserved solely for music caused him to sigh with pleasure, and it was with regret in his voice that he reminded her, 'My dear Maudine. Only two of our children display real musical talent. The upkeep of the manor would be enormous. Besides, when the church organ is repaired, the boys can practise there.'

'We'll all be in our graves before that happens,' Maudine snorted.

'Trust in the Lord, my dear, he will provide. Didn't he bless us with eight fine sons?' James smiled, indeed feeling blessed when his boys came trooping in. However, the feeling was temporary when he gazed at the small clock on the mantle. His mental cantata came to an abrupt end as unease prickled at the hairs on the nape of his neck. It was unusual for them to be organized into a pack so early in the morning. It meant they'd been up to something. All would be revealed in time, but he hoped he wouldn't have to punish any of them. It was physically draining, and he hated to hurt them, however deserved the punishment was. 'Good morning, gentlemen. You're late again this morning, I see.'

'Sorry, Pa,' Gerald said. 'Good morning, Mama. I ran into Lord Ashby yesterday and invited him to breakfast. We were keeping a lookout for him from the landing. He's coming across the field now.'

Maudine's hand went fluttering to her bosom, her eyes to the maid. 'Oh, my goodness! Set another place, Sally, and take the food back to the kitchen to keep warm. Where's that girl?'

'Geneva isn't hungry,' Matthew muttered.

'Isn't hungry? She should be grateful for the food in her belly and the roof over her head. Someone go and tell her that fact, and to present herself this instant. I'm not well this morning. I need her to supervise the music practice and look after Edward and Timothy. Do put that ham back in the dish, James. There will be nothing left for our guest to eat.'

By the time the earl was presented, Maudine's head was in a spin. She didn't know whether to curtsy to him or not. She gazed slightly askance at him, thinking: Goodness, he'd grown to be a large man since the last time she'd seen him. But a proper gentleman wouldn't present himself looking as if his pantaloons and cutaway had been slept in, nor indeed when his whiskers needed removing. And although his stock was the very latest in fashion, wasn't it a little soiled for visiting in?'

'I hope you'll forgive my appearance, Mrs Batterby,' he rumbled, kissing her hand. 'I hadn't intended to stay at the manor overnight, but I fell asleep and my servant and fresh clothes are still at the inn. The country air is too peaceful and relaxing by far.'

'Where's that slothful girl?' Maudine hissed at the maid,

16

who was trying to do a dozen things at once. She turned to Robert, a glint in her eye. 'Fetch your cousin. Tell her to come this minute, for our guest has arrived and it will be bad manners to start breakfast without her.'

The men relaxed into talk of boring world affairs whilst they waited. Maudine silently fumed as they waited for Geneva. Who cared if King George was insane and was causing mayhem by interfering in parliamentary matters, or whether someone called Napoleon Bonaparte was becoming a popular hero in France, for that matter? Certainly not herself, for she didn't understand any of it. Finally, just when Maudine's patience was at its thinnest, the door opened a crack and Geneva slid through.

'Lucifer's oath!' Moth exclaimed and, for once, Maudine let him get away with it.

There was silence for a few moments, then Maudine said, 'How on earth did your face become so bruised?'

A babble of voices broke out.

'Does it hurt much, Gen?'

'Of course it hurts her, stupid. Wouldn't your face hurt if someone three times your size had punched you?'

'Ouch!' Edward said when one of his brothers kicked him, and they all fell silent again. One by one their gazes were drawn to the earl, as if seeking direction.

Lord Ashby seemed to notice nothing amiss, but pulled out a chair for the wretched girl to sit next to him. 'Allow me, Miss Batterby?'

'Her name is Tibbetson,' Maudine said loudly. 'Geneva is not our child, of course, but an orphaned distant relation of my husband. She had nowhere else to go, so, as one must under such circumstances, we offered her a home.'

'*Noblesse oblige*,' he murmured. 'How very generous of you, Mrs Batterby. Miss Tibbetson, would you care to be seated?'

Geneva kept her head lowered, as well she might, for the girl looked appallingly ill used with her swollen lip and bruised cheek as she mumbled, 'I usually sit next to Moth.'

'You may use the seat Lord Ashby has offered for today,' Reverend Batterby told her, obviously none too pleased at having his day disrupted so early by family matters.

17

'Perhaps you would allow me to talk privately with you immediately after breakfast, Reverend Batterby,' Lord Ashby murmured.

'Of course.' James looked as though he'd been expecting the request, but Maudine couldn't understand why. Men were so infuriating with their private talks, which were usually about money or boring events.

Maudine wished she could command attention from the children so well as her husband, without having to constantly raise her voice and repeat herself. She nodded her head in satisfaction when he said, 'After I've spoken to Lord Ashby, you will attend me in my study, Geneva. You as well, Gerald, I think. As for the rest of you, you will wait on me in the drawing room in case I need to speak to you. Timothy, I'll have no more vulgar expressions from you. You will apologize to your mama, this instant.'

Moth grimaced. 'Sorry, Mama.'

'I should think so.' Maudine automatically offered Geneva a glare. 'It seems that my youngest son has been mixing in bad company.'

James said quietly. 'Enough, Maudine. We have a guest. Allow me to say grace before the food gets cold. Lord, thank you for this bounty on my table. Grant my children humility, wisdom and –' he sent Moth a meaningful glance and sighed – 'the ability to speak only when they have something sensible to say.'

Moth, his hands palmed in prayer under his chin, opened his eyes and bestowed upon his father a smile that was unbelievably angelic. 'Our men and hallejula, Lord!'

Maudine frowned when Geneva exchanged a sidelong glance with Lord Ashby. When he smiled at her, she strangled a giggle. The forward hussy! She was flirting like a milkmaid.

Geneva was not laughing later, when she presented herself with Gerald to her uncle's study. Sorle Ashby was seated in a chair by the open window. He said nothing, but raised an elegantly curved eyebrow and shrugged apologetically.

Beyond him, Geneva could see the shadow of her aunt hovering on the terrace. She was eavesdropping.

18

Her uncle James smiled kindly at her. 'Geneva. Do you require a doctor to tend to your injuries?'

'No, uncle. The bruising is superficial and will heal in its own good time.'

'Good . . . good. Lord Ashby has explained the circumstances of the injuries. Perhaps you would like to tell me exactly what you were doing in his house.'

'It was my fault—'

Her uncle held up a hand. 'Be quiet, Gerald . . . If you please, Geneva?'

'We were playing a game called hares and hounds. We usually rendezvous at Welford Manor and the one who gets there first hangs a sheet out of the window.'

'Usually? How long has this game been going on?'

'About seven years.'

Surprise came into his eyes. 'Seven years? You've been breaking into the manor for all that time and I've only just heard of it?'

'Not breaking in, exactly. I have a key.'

'From whom did you obtain this key?'

'I found it. It was hidden in a crack between two bricks by the front door.'

'So, you stole the key and used it to enter Lord Ashby's house. Did you steal anything else?'

'Certainly not,' Gerald interrupted. 'As if she would. Look, father, it's my fault. I made up the game in the first place. It wasn't just Gen. We all went into the manor. This was Edward's and Moth's first time. But we didn't do any damage or steal anything. If you're going to punish anyone, let it be me.'

The reverend stopped his son's explanation with a raised hand. 'I would be very much obliged, Gerald, if you did not try to dictate the nature of the punishment you all deserve. Geneva, fetch the key. After you've handed it back to Lord Ashby and apologized, you may go and explain your actions to your aunt Maudine.'

Reluctantly, Geneva turned to go, then turned back and pleaded. 'Isn't Gerald a little too old for a birching, Uncle?'

'On the contrary. He's the perfect age. If your cousin indulges in childish pursuits and encourages his younger siblings in the same, he must expect punishment.'

Gerald managed a rueful smile. 'Don't worry, Gen. It won't be the first time.'

By the time she came back with the key, Sorle was outside the study waiting for her. She winced when she heard the swish of a cane, and tears came into her eyes. 'I'm so sorry, Lord Ashby,' she said, holding out the key.

'So am I.' He gently touched her bruised cheekbone, then closed her palm over the key. 'Keep it. You have my permission to go to the manor any time you wish whilst I'm absent. Make it your refuge, if you will. Perhaps you would walk me to my horse, Miss Tibbetson?'

But they were waylaid by her aunt, who was out of breath from hurrying in from the garden. Judging from the gleam in her eye as her elbow stabbed into Geneva's sore midriff, she had heard everything that had taken place in her husband's study.

'To my sitting room, missy,' she hissed. 'I'll deal with you after I've escorted Lord Ashby to his horse.' Maudine turned to talk to him as Geneva walked off.

The sitting room was not far away. Watching them through a crack in the door, Geneva overheard every word.

Maudine's voice was as cloying as honey. 'Rumour tells me you're leaving Welford Manor vacant. My husband and I would be interested in considering a lease arrangement if the rent suits our circumstances.'

Sorle retrieved his hat from the hall table. 'Odd that your husband didn't mention it. As it so often is, rumour is wrong. I like the place, and have decided to move in as soon as I've settled my affairs in London and made arrangements for the house to be staffed.'

'Oh, I see,' Maudine said, clearly disappointed.

'Thank you for the breakfast, Mrs Batterby. It was most generous of Gerald to invite me. I trust you were not put to too much trouble. Pray, do not be too hard on your offspring. Their game was just youthful high spirits. Their cousin seems to be a nice girl, too, and she's already been punished enough at my hands, I feel.'

Maudine's eyes glinted at that. 'You have seen only one side of her, My Lord. Geneva Tibbetson is irresponsible in her

20

duties towards her young charges. Timothy's language is outrageous. She has inherited bad blood, I'm afraid.'

Ears beginning to burn, Geneva felt herself wilt under such condemnation.

'Ah . . .' he said. 'Then I was mistaken in believing that Geneva is your husband's ward. Miss Tibbetson is actually hired by you. I'd wondered why the girl was so shabbily gowned. She is, in fact, a servant.'

Surely he couldn't think that! Geneva's small gasp nearly gave her away, for Sorle's hooded glance flicked towards her hiding place.

'Not at all, My Lord,' Maudine blustered, and Geneva smiled. Ah . . . he had her aunt on the run. 'But she has only a small allowance of her own, and she has grown so quickly of late that I haven't been able to keep her suitably attired.' She steered him towards the door, obviously discomforted by the conversation. 'We were honoured by your company, sir. I hope to to enjoy it again in the future.'

'Be sure you shall, Mrs Batterby. Once I'm settled in, which will be soon, I hope, I shall be arranging a Christmas ball so I can become acquainted with my neighbours. You will be the very first to receive an invitation.'

'A ball!' Maudine trilled. 'How exciting. I shall look forward to Christmas then, and being introduced to . . . *Lady Ashby*?'

Geneva experienced a moment of disappointment when he said smoothly. 'I'm sure Mrs Ashby will be delighted to make the acquaintance of my closest neighbours, Mrs Batterby.'

Tears pricked Geneva's eyes and she winced when one of the younger boys cried out. It sounded like Moth. Gerald had been wrong in his assessment of his father. He'd not taken this as lightly as expected.

Crossing to the window, she watched Sorle ride away, as she'd watched him so many years before. This time, he turned in the saddle, smiled when he saw her standing there and blew her a kiss.

Her cheeks warmed and her fingers went to her mouth.

'You needn't set your cap at that one,' her aunt said from behind her. 'He has a wife at home, and children, no doubt.' Head to one side, a spiteful look in her eyes, Maudine gazed at her. 'What a dreadful fright you look. Now, how shall I punish you? You can scrub the scullery floor, I think. It might teach you to appreciate all I have done for you. The next time something like this happens, I will probably throw you out into the gutter.'

Geneva's chin lifted a fraction and she smiled, shored up by the knowledge she wasn't quite as destitute as she'd been led to believe. 'Then you'd lose my help with the household chores and the children. And my allowance . . . ? I think not, Aunt, for you'd have to pay for a governess, then. How much of my parents' estate was left to me, pray?'

'That is none of your concern, missy.'

'Enough for you to profit from having me here, I imagine. Shall I ask Reverend Batterby about it?'

For her trouble, Geneva received a sharp slap across her bruised cheek. She didn't cry out. She was used to such treatment from Maudine when the woman knew they were not being observed.

'You will not bother your uncle over such a trifling domestic matter. Already his day has been ruined by the results of your exploits. And don't imagine you have something special awaiting you in the future. The payment is only enough to feed and clothe you for a little while. When it runs out I shall turn you out of my house.'

Her uncle James would not allow Maudine to carry out such an act. 'A welcome day that will be for me, Mrs Batterby. I'll miss my uncle and my cousins, though, for I love them dearly and they've made life bearable for me. If you ever have a daughter, I hope you treat her better than you've ever treated me.'

'Ill-mannered and low-born creature, how dare you talk of such personal matters to your elders and betters? You're beneath my contempt. Fetch your apron, then go about your tasks. Be thankful Lord Ashby's intervention has persuaded me to be lenient with you. If you ever cross me again, I'll take a horsewhip to you.'

When Geneva opened the door to her wardrobe, she found Moth hidden in a corner, his face screwed up from trying not to cry.

'Papa caned me,' he hiccuped. 'I hate him.'

'Oh, my dearest.' As Moth came into her arms, tears filled

22

her eyes and she hugged him tight. 'You mustn't hate him. What on earth did you say to him to make him cane you?'

'I only asked him if he was going to froth at the mouth.'

Geneva tried not to grin. 'Oh, Moth. You really must learn not to repeat everything you hear.' Inspecting his palm, she noticed the blood. Her eyes widened. She'd never imagined her uncle would be so unfair to Moth, since the escapade wasn't his fault. 'Your papa has a good heart and just wants you to grow up to be good. I think our adventure tried his patience a little too far.'

Moth's pain was forgotten as he was reminded of the adventure, and a grin lit up his face. 'It was a damned cracking adventure, wasn't it? Can we do it again?'

'I think not, for the secret is out. Besides, Lord Ashby will be moving into his house. We'll have to think of something else to do.' She gently kissed his injured palm. 'I'll find some soothing salve for your hand. And don't say damned. It's rude.'

Sorle's sense of guilt had increased since the night before.

The undercurrents in the Batterby household had been unpleasant, to say the least. The males seemed to rub along all right, but everything pointed to Geneva Tibbetson being resented by Maudine Batterby, a woman he found extremely difficult to like.

And no wonder the girl was resented. It was obvious that, whilst the Batterby brothers tolerated their mother, to a man they adored Geneva. That was just as well, for he believed she might have been treated harshly after he left. Having eight knights in shining armour looking after her would ensure the punishment wouldn't go too far. Not that there was anything he could do about it if it did.

It was a fine morning. Sorle hummed to himself as he cantered through the green-hedged lanes. Apart from the over-supply of self-loathing, he was in fine spirits. Welford Manor was nicer than he remembered, the countryside pretty.

Geneva intruded on his thoughts again. How badly dressed the girl was, and how exquisite of feature, if one looked past the damage he'd done. The gown she'd been wearing was so old and patched, his sister would have been too ashamed to donate it to the poorhouse for rags!

He berated himself for succumbing to the temptation of blowing Geneva a kiss. She was a country girl, not a sophisticate, and was bound to get the wrong idea about him. She came from bad stock, Mrs Batterby had said.

'Tibbetson . . . ?' he mused out loud, tipping his hat as he passed a woman with a child. He remembered his father taking him to a meeting of the Royal Historical Society, where they'd listened to a talk by an archaeologist named Tibbetson who had presented Egyptian artefacts to the company. The man had been invited back for dinner and had woken an urge in Sorle to see the place for himself. But it would be too much the coincidence to suppose Geneva was his daughter.

He cantered over the stone bridge into Edgley, which couldn't make up its mind whether it was a large village or a small town. The area was populated by people of means who were mostly spread about the countryside on small estates. A row of commercial premises had been established along one street. One end accommodated the church. The other end supported the Black Dog Inn, with the smithy opposite.

Straggling along the road between them was a variety of shops, including a baker, a butcher and a dressmaking establishment which incorporated a haberdashery department. There was a pretty blue muslin gown and a straw bonnet trimmed with ribbon and flowers on display in the window. The building next to it served as a school and a meeting hall. Owned by the church, it was run by a schoolmaster and his wife, who lived in the upper level.

A small stream trickled along the road verges, then, after meandering under the bridge and winding through the grounds of Edgley House and Welford Manor, it became part of the English Channel.

Leaving his horse to be attended to by the stablehand, Sorle strode into the inn, nodding to the landlord. 'We'll be leaving early in the morning, have my account ready, would you?'

'Certainly, Lord Ashby. I'll be up early to serve you breakfast. Shall I ask my woman to pack you some food for the road? She's famed in the district for her pork pies, and she's just made a fresh batch.'

'Thank you. I'll be moving into Welford Manor soon. Could you advise me where I'd be likely to engage some local staff?

I need a full complement of permanent staff and a team to clean the place from top to bottom.'

'If you want, I could make enquiries. I know someone who be looking for another position, for her mistress don't treat her right. She has a brother, who is outspoken, but honest, strong and willing. Good with horses, he is. And there's a hiring agency in Poole you could visit on your way through. As for cleaning the place, my wife would be only too happy to oversee that for you with some of the women from the estate village.'

Gazing round the spotless inn, Sorle smiled. 'Then I'll leave that to her. Miss Tibbetson has the key to the manor. I'll write her a letter before I leave and request that she obliges me by acting as my agent in this matter. Since she is familiar with the layout of the manor, I'll place her in overall charge and your wife will be answerable to her.'

The landlord gave a slight shrug. 'Mrs Batterby might object, My Lord. Miss Tibbetson is kept fully occupied about the house from morning to night, from what I hear.'

'Oh, I'm sure Mrs Batterby can be brought round,' he said with a slight smile. 'I understand Miss Tibbetson's uncle will be at the church before too long. I found him to be a decent gentleman. I'll put the proposition to him after my appearance has been attended to.' He ran a hand over his chin. 'Perhaps you would be good enough to send some hot water up to my servant.'

James Batterby was seated in the family pew, his head sunk into his hands, suffering pangs of remorse. Long ago, he'd slid into the habit of least resistance where his wife and children were concerned. The fact was, his head was always so steeped in the beauty of some composition of music, that it hardly had room inside it for anything else.

Not that he had much in the way of an instrument, except a rather overworked piano, at home, and a small church organ whose pipes needed cleaning and whose bellows were in desperate need of repair.

The exploits of his offspring had deeply embarrassed him. It was his own fault. He should have been stricter with them. He hadn't meant to cane poor Timothy quite so hard, and the wounded look in the child's eyes still remained with him.

A hand on his shoulder brought his head jerking up. 'I hope you are not berating yourself for the actions of your children, Reverend Batterby,' Lord Ashby said lightly.

'My Lord, I am deeply ashamed of my offspring, and cannot apologize enough.'

Smiling, Lord Ashby took a seat beside him. 'Were they my sons, I'd be proud of them. They're honest, and loyal to each other. I noticed they are very protective of your niece, too. Will you tell me about Miss Tibbetson, Reverend?'

'Such a charming child,' James mused. 'And a great help to Maudine about the house. I'm sorry the boys involved her in their exploits.'

'Indeed. I'm surprised you still think of her as a child. She's a young lady of singular beauty and intelligence, who appears to be past the age when most young ladies make their debut.'

James's eyes flew open in surprise. 'I'd never even considered . . .' He gave a defeated shrug. 'There never seems to be any money to spare for poor Geneva. She was left with such a small allowance, and no dowry, of course.'

'Ah,' said Lord Ashby. 'I wondered why she was so poorly dressed.'

James frowned. 'Is she? I hadn't noticed.'

The earl got to the point of his visit. 'Reverend Batterby, I am in desperate need of someone to interview staff on my behalf for the manor. Also, I'm desirous of someone to act as my social secretary. The person must know the district, live close by, have a neat hand and be capable of helping me to organize a ball.'

'I'm sure Maudine would be glad to oblige you.'

'I have no intention of taking your wife away from the execution of her domestic affairs, which must be considerable with eight fine sons to care for. With your permission, I should like Miss Tibbetson to have the position.'

Geneva was perfectly capable of such a task, but had Lord Ashby forgotten Geneva had entered his house illegally? 'But, My Lord—'

'I know what you're about to say, Reverend. Let me remind you that Miss Tibbetson has been visiting Welford Manor for seven years now. I'm satisfied that none of the contents are missing. I've left the key with her and she may visit any time she wishes – as long as you are happy with the arrangement.'

Lord Ashby drew a letter from his pocket. 'Here is a letter offering Miss Tibbetson the position, a list of the house servants I will require and the names of one or two people who have been recommended to me. I have left it unsealed so you, as her legal guardian, may peruse the contents if you so wish.'

He placed a purse on top. 'This is for Miss Tibbetson to pay for incidentals, such as the cleaning team. I would be obliged if you bought her a more suitable outfit to wear for her duties, for I do not like my staff to be shabbily dressed. Not uniform, sir, but something a young woman would be proud to wear at any occasion. She will need one outfit to change into whilst the other is being washed, for Miss Tibbetson must be a cut above if she's to command respect at the servant interviews.'

'I'm sure Geneva will be happy to be of assistance, Lord Ashby. She is a capable, intelligent young woman. I don't know what Maudine will say, for she relies on her help.'

'Surely it's of benefit to your household to place your ward in gainful employment, as it is the lot of most poor relations.'

'I was rather hoping Geneva would marry well. She's attracted attention over the past two years. Alas, she has no dowry, which has turned suitors away.'

Lord Ashby gave a small smile. 'Quite so, Now, as for a salary. I thought fifteen shillings per week might be suitable recompense.'

James gasped. 'It is too much, sir. My ward will be happy to offer her services without remuneration.'

'But why should she, sir? Do you offer your services for nothing? Do I? Not at all. Besides, it would put me under an obligation to her. And that will not do, for people might talk. We both have a reputation to preserve.'

'Ah, yes, how silly of me not to think of that.'

'Your niece will have great responsibility in my absence. There, it is settled, then.' Lord Ashby rose to his feet, his gaze on the church organ. 'Is that the instrument my grandfather donated to the church during his time as earl?'

'It is. Alas, it's in a bad state of repair now.'

Lord Ashby frowned. 'There's nothing as excruciating to the ear as good music played on an unworthy instrument. If you'd arrange to get the organ cleaned and repaired, you may present the account to me. Good day to you, Reverend Batterby.'

'Good day, My Lord.'

The man paused when he reached the door, and turned. 'There's a pretty outfit in the dressmaker's window. It looks to be Miss Tibbetson's size. Why don't you surprise her with it? She need not be embarrassed by knowing who provided it.'

James wondered what Maudine would say about the position offered to Geneva at the manor, for he was sure she'd say something at length.

But she might welcome the news, for, since Geneva had come to live with them, she'd complained constantly about the girl being underfoot, and the extra expense. It would be nice to have some peace.

He gazed at the organ and smiled, murmuring to himself, 'It's turned out to be a very good day indeed, Lord. Thank you.'

Three

Closing her eyes, Geneva held a gown of lavender checks against her body. It was so pretty with its tiny puff sleeves, pleated bodice and high waistline, and the tight under-sleeves could be removed for warm days. It came with a matching parasol, a frivolous affair, designed more for decoration than providing shade. From the box her uncle had given to her, she pulled out another gown, of pale blue muslin sprigged with tiny blue cornflowers. Tears of happiness pricked at her eyes.

'The gowns are a lovely surprise, Uncle.' Flinging her arms around the reverend, she hugged him tight, wrinkling her nose as she inhaled an odour of peppermints. 'Thank you, thank you, thank you! I really don't deserve them.'

If her uncle was embarrassed by this display of emotion, he didn't show it. He smiled as he hugged her back, coughed, and said in only a slightly gruffer manner than usual when he released her, 'My dear, of course you do. I've been remiss in my care of you. I should have noticed how shabbily dressed you were, not waited until the earl pointed it out.'

Her hands went to her face to still the rising flush of humiliation. 'My appearance is of no concern to Lord Ashby. When I see him again, I shall tell him so.'

Her uncle had a small, mysterious smile on his face. 'Ah, but he has made it his concern for a reason.'

She gazed down at the dainty leather pumps on her feet. 'What reason can he possibly have?'

'If the shoes don't fit you, they can be exchanged, you know.'

Geneva smiled and wriggled her toes. 'They're perfect.'

Maudine sniffed as she picked up a straw bonnet decorated with a posy of blue and lavender flowers. 'May I ask where the money for all this finery came from?'

'It hardly cost a fortune.'

'I'm the mother of eight sons. I'm intelligent enough to know when I'm being fobbed off. Answer me, James.'

James Batterby turned away from his wife's stern glance, a glint of annoyance in his eyes. She had become quite strident of late. 'Ah, then you must also be intelligent enough to realize I'm your husband, not your son. Therefore, I'm not answerable to you on this, or any other matter. Good day to you, Mrs Batterby. I wish to speak to my niece alone.'

Geneva had never heard her uncle talk so firmly to Maudine before. Obviously, neither had Maudine, for her mouth fell open a little and she flushed a dull red before she rallied enough to snap, 'What about, pray?'

'That, you will be informed of when I'm ready to tell you. Close the door behind you on your way out please, Maudine.'

Her aunt departed with an aggrieved sigh, an outraged rustle of skirts and a solid slam of the door. The draught formed in the wake of her departure caused papers to drift from the desk.

Stooping to retrieve them, Geneva set them back where they

belonged. Her uncle wore a slightly astonished expression, as if his authority, so firmly exercised, had surprised even himself. Giving a slightly bemused smile, he gathered himself together, then crossed to the window and drew it shut. 'There, now we shall not be overheard. Please sit down, Geneva.'

'What did you want to talk to me about, Uncle?' she asked, after she'd settled herself in the large, leather chair Sorle Ashby had used.

The reverend toyed with the paperknife on his desk for a few seconds, then gazed up at her. 'Lord Ashby has expressed a wish to hire your services. In the first instance, to supervise the hiring of staff for the manor. Then, when he is moved in, to act as his social secretary.'

Her eyes flew open. 'Me? But I have no experience at either.'

'As I pointed out to him. However, he dismissed such an idea. As for the first, he said that you're familiar with the lay-out of the manor and, since no damage has been done in the years since his uncle's death, he trusts you to act in his best interests.'

Geneva hung her head for a moment. He must have been mocking her when he'd said that.

'As for managing his social affairs, he intends to hold a ball at Christmas to acquaint himself with the people of the district. Since he knows only us, he'll rely on you to help him with invitations and arrangements.' The reverend smiled broadly. 'You start your duties on Monday, when a team of local women will arrive to clean the manor.' He placed a sheaf of paper and a purse on the desk. 'Here are his instructions and a purse from which to pay the cleaning staff. Make sure you keep a proper account, so there is no room for complaint.'

Butterflies appeared in Geneva's stomach. 'You've already accepted on my behalf? I'm not ready for such responsibility.'

'You most certainly are, Geneva. You're the most sensible girl I know, and have been keeping the church books perfectly for some time.' A blissful little smile hovered on his lips. 'Lord Ashby is going to pay for the repairs and cleaning of the church organ.'

Her eyes narrowed in on him as she thought: Ah, so the man had bribed her uncle into offering her services, how very underhand of him. She said, 'How exceedingly generous.'

'Yes, the repairs are long overdue. Perhaps I'll be able to resurrect the choir in time for the Christmas Eve service, now. After all, I already have eight choirboys to begin with. Lord Ashby has also insisted that you be awarded a salary of fifteen shillings per week.'

Geneva only just stopped her mouth from falling open. It was unimaginable riches! She could buy all the gowns she wanted with that, silks, satin . . . her imagination took her twirling in Sorle Ashby's arms around the ballroom in a whirl of different gowns, diamonds, pearls and feathers, as she spent an imaginary fortune on previously unimaginable fripperies. She fell to earth with a sudden thud. Hadn't Maudine said the earl had a wife and children?

Still, she could hardly breathe the words out. 'Fifteen shillings? That's a fortune. Are you sure you didn't misunderstand him?'

Doubt came into her uncle's eyes. 'I does seem rather generous, doesn't it? Perhaps he meant fifteen shillings every fortnight.'

Her sigh was a mixture of relief and disappointment. 'Yes, I should imagine he did. Still, that will help with my board, and I'll try and find time to help Aunt Maudine, as well.'

Her uncle came around the desk to gaze silently down at her for a few seconds. 'You're a good girl, Geneva. Your allowance adequately covers your board, so what you earn, you must keep. Save it for the future, if you can, it's always wise to have a little something to fall back on in times of need.' He took her hands, lifted her to her feet and kissed both of her cheeks. 'Your parents would have been proud of you, my dear. Ask Maudine to come in, if you would. She'll not be far away.'

Her uncle was right. Maudine was hovering outside the door, flicking a duster over a painting of a dead pheasant dangling from the jaws of a dog. No doubt she'd heard everything that had taken place, for her lips were pursed and her eyes had a mean look to them.

After Geneva passed on the message, a polishing cloth and a tin of beeswax were thrust into her hands. 'The dining-room furniture needs polishing.'

'I promised Timothy and Edward I'd take them over to the

farm so they could see Farmer Shapworth's new puppies.'

'Just make sure you don't bring one home. Timothy has been pestering his father for one, and I won't have it. Dirty, destructive things, dogs are. They harbour fleas. You'd best get on with the polishing then, else you won't have time.'

Aiming a sour look over her shoulder, Maudine sailed off through the study door, already complaining to her husband about what she'd overheard. 'I don't see why Lord Ashby didn't ask me to help him. I've had much more experience—'

'Do be quiet, Maudine.'

Tempted to eavesdrop further when the door closed, Geneva decided against it. It seemed as if the worm had turned. Dug from the comfortable hole he usually inhabited by the visit of the charismatic Sorle Ashby, Uncle James had demonstrated he was a force to be reckoned with where his wife was concerned.

Geneva had certainly not intended to purchase a dog, let alone a pair of them. What's more, she'd bought them with money taken from Sorle Ashby's purse.

The three of them sat on a fallen log in the sunshine to discuss the problem.

'Mother will be furious. I heard her tell Adam that Moth wasn't allowed to have a dog for his birthday.'

Moth's eyes mirrored his dismay. 'Leaping lizards! Wait till she hears that Gen has got one too. I wonder who's bought the little one. I liked him the best, didn't you? He looks as if he's wearing a mask.'

Geneva's spirits sank even further. 'Farmer Shapworth said the little one was going to a good home, and he was going to drown these two in the river. What else could I do but buy them from him?'

The practical Edward suggested, 'If you'd offered to drown them for him, you could have got them for nothing.'

Three pairs of eyes gazed at the pair of lively brown puppies chasing each other in the grass. Moth moodily kicked at a stone. 'It's not fair, drowning them, even if they are ugly varmints.'

Edward gazed at his brother. 'What does ugly varmints mean?'

'I dunno. The farmer's wife called them that.' Their eyes swivelled towards her like sunflowers to the sky.

It means nuisances, Geneva thought, stifling a grin as she decided interpretation wasn't in their best interests at the moment. 'It's a phrase young gentlemen wouldn't use, especially in front of their parents. You remember that, Moth. Don't be too pessimistic though, I'll talk to your mother.'

'It won't do any good. She'll make us take the pups back. They'll be drowned, and you'll have wasted your money,' Edward predicted gloomily. Taking an apple from a pocket, he sank his teeth into it. Juice dribbled down his chin.

'Your father, then.'

'I've already begged and begged. He said our mother wouldn't approve.' Moth eyed the apple. 'Where did you get that from?'

'Mrs Shapworth gave it to me. Wanna bite, you two?'

The three of them took turns to scrunch the apple as they watched the puppies and pondered on the problem they presented.

Edward's eyes brightened. 'I've got an idea,' he said, wiping his sticky hands on his front. 'You could take the pups to the manor, and we could visit them there.'

A worried frown crinkled Moth's brow. 'What would the earl say?'

'Lord Ashby won't be moving in for a few weeks. Geneva can tell him they're *his* dogs when he does. Then when he sees how much we like them, he'll give them to us. Mother wouldn't dare say no to him.'

For his age, Edward displayed a surprisingly devious nature at times. Technically, they *were* Lord Ashby's dogs, paid for from his own purse. Geneva grinned. An ingenious scheme if handled properly. Would Sorle Ashby prove to be so gullible, though?

It was a question she chose to ignore. 'Well done, Edward. We'll drop them off at the Welford stables and ask Tom to look after them for us until I start work on Monday.'

As it turned out, that couldn't come too soon for Geneva, for Maudine spent the whole weekend complaining, even though it was Moth's birthday.

The weather had a sultry feel to it. 'It looks as though we

might be in for a thunderstorm later,' her uncle remarked over the top of the paper his sermon was written on. 'We'd better have tea in the conservatory. I have a parishioner to call on after the service, so you may have to start without me.'

After the Sunday service, Geneva was about to follow her cousins when she overheard her aunt saying to a group of the district's leading ladies gathered in the church porch: 'Lord Ashby will regret asking for Miss Tibbetson's help. She is incompetent when it comes to household matters, let alone hiring staff. Were it not for the goodness of my husband's heart—'

Suddenly catching sight of her in the shadows, Maudine snapped, 'Why are you lingering there, Miss Tibbetson? Get along and see to your charges. You have Timothy's birthday tea to supervise.'

'My pardon, I had no choice since you were blocking my path. Excuse me, ladies.' Colour rising to her face, Geneva edged past them, aware of the variety of looks aimed her way, which ranged from disdain to pity.

'Bad blood . . .' Maudine said.

Chin held high, Geneva muttered under her breath, '*Toad*,' and felt instantly better. When Edward and Moth slipped their hands into hers, she felt better still. She'd love to have children of her own one day, she thought with a sigh, but such an event was remote, for governesses rarely married and had children of their own.

Maudine retired to her room as soon as they arrived back at Edgley House. 'This weather has given me a dreadful headache. I cannot face the thought of a noisy tea party.'

Geneva offered, 'I'll bring a cold compress. Would you like a cool drink as well?'

'I'd prefer a tray of tea and some fruit cake.' Maudine held out her arms. 'Timothy, my baby boy. Happy birthday. Here is sixpence for you to spend at the midsummer fair. Come here and give your poor mother a kiss first, then go and enjoy your birthday tea. Try not to make too much noise, and don't eat too much. You have a delicate stomach and will be sick.'

'No, Mama. Thank you, Mama.' A reluctant Moth, hugged tight against his mother's bosom, received upon his lips a perfunctory kiss. He scowled as he skipped off, the sixpence

34

clutched in one hand, surreptitiously wiping his mouth with the other.

Maudine's grey eyes were turned Geneva's way. 'Tomorrow, you can take the four youngest of my sons with you to the manor. You can set them some work and they can do their music practice there.'

'But, Aunt, I do not have the earl's permission. Besides, I'm to interview staff and oversee the cleaning of the place this week.'

'You didn't have Lord Ashby's permission to break into the manor either, but that didn't stop you from making fools of us all. Your uncle tells me the instrument is a Stein and has a Viennese action. He's a great admirer of it and, in fact, Lord Ashby's uncle purchased it on his advice at the time.'

'Does that make it special?'

'Goodness, how would I know? It was ordered as a gift for his wife, and it cost him a pretty penny. But it didn't arrive from abroad until a week after her death. I understand it has never been played, since the former earl couldn't bear to listen to anyone playing it.'

'Then it must be special, because it has sentimental value attached to it. Perhaps the boys shouldn't use it in case it's damaged.'

'How can it be damaged when they'll only be practising those dreadful scales over and over?' Placing her hand against her head, Maudine heaved a sigh. 'I can't bear all this argument. Cease it at once. I daresay I shall spend all day tomorrow in bed. If you cannot take the boys with you, then you must stay here and look after them, for clearly that's where your duty lies.'

Later, Geneva played charades with her cousins while they waited for the reverend to come home. They watched him go into the stables, then make a dash for the house as lightning sheeted across the sky and rain spattered about his shoulders. He just missed being soaked by a sudden, heavy deluge.

The reverend was beaming when he came into the conservatory, his hands clutched around a squirming bulge under his coat. 'Ah, Timothy, there you are. I do hope you've left me some cake to eat. Happy birthday, my boy.' Reaching under his coat, he produced a quivering bundle and placed it in Moth's arms.

'Lucifer's oath!'

'Holy Moses!'

'I'll be . . . *blessed!*' Geneva said more moderately.

Luckily, their simultaneously uttered words had been absorbed by a loud clap of thunder and the reverend didn't seem to notice. Still, the exclaimers glanced at each other with some consternation.

When Moth gazed at the masked puppy, a delirious grin spread across his face. 'Thank you, Papa. It's the puppy I wanted most of all. How did you know?'

His father chuckled. 'Oddly enough, a little voice kept reminding me of it. I'm pleased I thought to choose him in advance, though, because the other two have found homes.'

Holding the animal tightly against his body, Moth pulled on his desperate expression and said with agonizing intensity, 'Does Mama know?'

Everyone held their breath.

'I told your mother quite a while ago that you could have a dog when you turned seven.'

When the breath was collectively expelled, the reverend smiled. 'What will you call him?'

Moth gazed questioningly at his elder brothers.

'Bandit?' Gerald and Matthew suggested together.

So, Bandit the puppy became. Soon, it became obvious that James Batterby's 'quite a while ago' was too far back for Maudine to remember. She stormed down from her room when she heard the yelps and impaled the pup with a glare. Bandit hid behind the reverend's legs and gazed nervously out through his ankles when she demanded to know, 'What have we here?'

James gazed mildly at his wife. 'Why, I do believe it's a puppy, my dear.'

'I can see what it is. I told Timothy time and time again that he couldn't have one. How could you, James? As if I didn't have enough to do, there will be dog's hair everywhere, and worse.'

Bandit produced a small puddle to prove her words.

'I told you so,' Maudine snapped. 'Get rid of it, at once.'

The reverend's voice strengthened. 'We will not argue about

it. Bandit will stay. He can live in the stable. He's used to it.'

'Can I have a dog too?' Edward asked.

'You certainly cannot! See what you've done, James. The very idea!' Maudine stomped off in high dudgeon.

'You can share Bandit with me,' Moth offered.

'Thanks.'

Geneva gazed at the table, which was laden with good things to eat. Maudine was a fine cook, who enjoyed making pastries and cakes for her large family, even though her nature wouldn't allow her to enjoy the company of her children very often. 'Shall we eat?'

'Since it's Timothy's birthday, he can say grace today.'

One eye on a wobbling red jelly, Timothy managed grace in one rushed breath. 'Thank you, God, for my birthday tea and my dog Bandit, who's better than his brothers, the ugly varmints, begging your pardon, Lord, because I've remembered Geneva said it was rude to say that in front of my parents.' He sucked in a deep breath. 'Amen.'

The reverend's eyes flew open, but he obviously decided to overlook Moth's transgression. 'Very eloquent, Timothy. You may eat.'

'What are we going to do with the other two puppies?' Edward asked Geneva later that evening, when they were settling Bandit down in his bed of straw in the stall next to her uncle's horse. The Batterby mare gazed over the stall with interest at his new companion and snickered a greeting.

Bandit yelped.

'I'll think of something.' Geneva didn't know what, she only knew she wasn't going to give the pups back to the farmer to be drowned.

Geneva was faced with a different dilemma early the next morning.

'I'm asking you to let me have a job at the manor, Miss Tibbetson,' Sally said when Geneva entered the kitchen. 'I don't get paid enough for the work I do around here. You know what the missus is like. Do this, do that, and a clout across the ear to hurry you along if you don't do it quick enough. Since the second maid left, I have her work to do as well. If it wasn't for you, I'd be dead from overwork long ago.'

'But what will Mrs Batterby do without you, Sally?'

'I was thinking of leaving, anyway. The trouble is, I can never get time off to look for another job. Mrs Batterby will have to hire someone else.'

It would mean that more work would fall on her own shoulders. Still, Geneva couldn't deny Sally a chance to better herself. 'What position do you intend to apply for?'

'I dunno, miss.'

'Laundry, house or kitchen?' She gazed down the list. Nursery maid wasn't listed, and she wondered if it was an oversight. Though perhaps he would bring nursery staff from London with him. After all, children became used to their nurses and didn't like change.

'I do all of those things here.'

'Welford Manor is a bigger house and will carry a large staff, each with their own jobs to do.'

'What do you think I'm best suited to, miss?'

'You're very competent, and would be suited to any of those positions. The laundry maid's position pays seven shillings a week plus board. That's more than a housemaid, and the duties will be shared by two people. No doubt there will be fancy stuff to starch and iron. Can you manage it?'

'I used to do it before I came here, five years ago, and in London. The old admiral and his lady were very particular, too. They died within a month of each other and I was out of a job. I came down here to marry my sweetheart, but discovered he'd upped and joined the army, taking my savings with him. I haven't set eyes on him since. That's why I took this job. Though there was two of us doing the work then, and fewer people in the household.'

'How would you like to be the head laundry maid at the manor, then?'

'Head laundry maid?' Sally laughed with the sheer delight of it. 'I'd be answerable only to the housekeeper. I'd like it fine. Miss.'

'Then you'd better hand your notice in today, for, no doubt, you'll have to work your month out with Mrs Batterby.'

Sally nodded. 'Shall I tell her I'll be working for you, miss?'

'You won't be, Sally. You'll be working for Lord Ashby at the manor. Tell her that.'

A grin crossed the woman's face. 'There'll be ructions from her for both of us.'

'It can't be helped. We'll just have to put up with it. Now, let's hurry with breakfast for the boys, else I'll be late getting to the manor. Do you have any scraps?'

'Scraps? Whatever for?'

Geneva coloured. 'In case the boys get hungry.'

'I'll pack you a picnic basket. There's some pasties and cake left over from tea, and I'll give you a loaf straight from the oven, a pot of jam, some butter and fruit.'

The twins carried the picnic basket between them. Bandit yapped and yelped as he struggled to keep up with Edward and Moth, until he was picked up and carried too.

It was going to be a lovely day. The rain the night before had soaked the grass. The droplets shone and sparkled on the blades and hung like jewels from a lacework of spiderwebs. The harvest of moisture was gently gathered by the sun, to rise as mist into the infinite blue. Geneva wore boots and raised her skirts so her hems wouldn't dampen.

The manor appeared to stand in a field of waving red poppies, yellow buttercups and white daisies. She gathered some poppies and buttercups on the way, setting them in a pewter vase on the window sill of the little sitting room off the hall, where she'd chosen to conduct the interviews.

Bandit joined his siblings in the stables for a noisy reunion.

The piano was unveiled and dusted.

Adam gazed at Simon and a smile gleamed between them. It was an instrument of beauty. Its shining, black-panelled sides were inlaid with gold scrolls holding oval frames, inside one of which was a rustic scene of a woman on a swing. Adam ran an effortless hand over the keys and the smiles grew broader.

'No piano until the school work is finished. You're each to write an essay on a different subject. Moth, you can write about your birthday party. At least a page. Try and remember your punctuation.'

'I'd rather do arithmetic,' Edward said.

'That's for this afternoon.'

She'd no sooner got the boys settled down to their school work than the cleaning team arrived. 'Start with the servants' rooms, then they can move in as soon as possible.

Not long after the cleaning women started work, the candidates for the household positions arrived, driven in a long wagon for the occasion by the agency manager. As per Lord Ashby's instructions, the staff were the most experienced the man could find, which made Geneva's job much easier.

After lunch, Sally arrived, dragging her bag behind her. 'Mrs Batterby threw me out. She said she wasn't going to pay me another penny.'

'Good, you can help me then. I've hired Ellen Pickering as the head housekeeper. That's the woman in the grey gown sitting outside. I'll introduce you, then you and she can go and find where the various quarters are, and check on what the cleaners are up to.'

Mrs Pickering proved to be entirely competent. Soon, the sound of scrubbing brushes was redoubled as the efforts of the cleaning staff were properly dispersed and redirected.

Then she heard the sound of a sonata drifting through the house. How lovely it was, and how delightfully the twins played. She'd forgotten about the boys! Leaving the queue of applicants, she went in search of them. No need to check on Simon and Adam. Faces enraptured, they sat side by side on the piano stool. Simon was darker haired and longer of jaw than Adam, who was much shorter and resembled his father. Of Edward and Moth there was no sign. Four essays in various stages of completion were lined up on the table.

It was my birftday yesterday. I was sevun. Mamma baked me a cake and a red jelly and papa gave me a dog called Bandit. I ate it and was sic on the floor . . .

Geneva giggled and turned her feet in the direction of the stables, where she found the boys helping the stablehand eat his lunch of coarse thick bread, cheese and raw onion. A row of dogs sat gazing up at them. 'Why are you eating Tom's food, when we've brought our own?'

'We came to feed the pups, and swapped one of our pasties.'

'And right nice it were, too,' Tom said, smacking his lips. 'There's nothing like a swallow of hog's fat to grease a man's throat.'

Geneva didn't bother telling him it was mutton. 'It's time

to return to your studies, boys. Moth, you have spelling to correct and practise. There's arithmetic for you both, then piano practice. Adam and Simon can oversee that. I hope you've left something for me to eat.'

'Plenty. The innkeeper's wife gave us some of her pies.'

She really must get some supplies in. Sorle Ashby had opened accounts at certain shops for her to use. Making a list of basics, she gave it to the innkeeper's wife to hand to the grocer. 'Would you ask them to deliver it tomorrow? Perhaps you could bring some of your pies, as well. The boys loved them. Now, what else will the earl need, I wonder?'

'Lime wash for the stable walls and clean straw, like as not,' the woman said helpfully.

Then there were hens and ducks, a milking cow, laundry supplies and a couple of stable cats to keep the mice down. The list seemed never-ending. Beeswax, brooms, pot-pourri, mops and pails, soaps, and candles by the score. Geneva seemed to be spending a large amount of the earl's money.

By the end of the day the household was fully staffed. Some, including the housekeeping and gardening staff, were employed to start work almost immediately. The stable and kitchen hands would arrive a month later. Geneva was glad of Ellen Pickering's help, for the cleaning would take a week at least.

When the day was finally over, Geneva was dropping from tiredness.

'Watch out for the ghost,' Edward said to Sally when they left.

'If a ghost sets one foot inside my door, I'll scream so loudly you'll hear me all the way from Edgley House and come to my rescue. I reckon I'll lock the door and have them two puppy dogs with me for company, too. God knows what I'll have for my dinner though.'

'There's some food left in the picnic basket. Tomorrow, I'll bring some boiled eggs.'

'Ah, there you are,' Maudine said, grabbing Geneva by the shoulders and shaking her as soon as she walked through the sitting-room door. 'What do you mean by giving Sally a job at the manor, you spiteful, ungrateful girl?'

'She asked me if she could have a position, and—'

Geneva gasped and her head jerked as Maudine slapped her viciously across the face. 'Well, now you'll have to do her work as well. To start with, you can cook tonight's meal. Then you can wash the dishes and do the ironing. In the morning—'

Maudine spun round when the reverend's voice said from behind her, 'Geneva will go about her business. I've hired two maids from the agency and they will present themselves to you tomorrow.'

'You knew Sally was leaving?'

'Geneva sent me a note with the agency manager as he came back through, explaining that Sally was no longer employed by us and would not be serving out her notice.'

'I suppose the wretched creature told you I threw Sally out.'

'No, Geneva didn't mention that, but I suspected as much. The agent has two young sisters on his books who are in need of training. I've employed them.'

'*You* have employed them?'

'Yes, me, Maudine. And if I see you lay a hand on either of them, as you just did to my niece, I'll send you to live with your widowed sister. Is that understood?'

Maudine stared at her husband for a moment, her face a mixture of incredulity and fear. 'You wouldn't do such a thing.'

'Yes, I most certainly would, for I'm beginning to find your presence disagreeable in the extreme. Now, go and cook the dinner, as you usually do, for it's the one thing you are good at. Your husband and children are hungry and it's your duty as my wife to cook dinner for us.'

'And what will Miss Tibbetson be doing?'

'Resting. She's been working hard by all accounts, and must be tired. Come, Geneva, take a glass of sherry with me and tell me how your day went.'

As they walked towards his study, Maudine burst into noisy sobs.

The reverend remained unmoved.

Four

June was a delightful month for Geneva. Welford Manor had come alive. The interior panelling, liberated from years of neglect, shone with a warm patina. Chandeliers appeared from the dust to sparkle like stars, and the silver gleamed. Clocks ticked and chimed.

Feet pattered overhead. The maids sang softly at their work or hummed in time to the sound of the piano. There was an aroma of polish and pot-pourri, of bread baking in the kitchen.

Outside, the borders were being weeded, the hedges trimmed.

The stables were spotless, fresh straw bales were stacked in the coach house and the tack-room shelves cleared of old liniments. There were numerous stalls. Geneva didn't know how many horses Sorle Ashby possessed. Several, she supposed, since his wife was bound to ride. And there would be ponies for his children, and horses to pull the carriage.

She closed her eyes, imagining the stable filled up with horses, fretting, stamping and whinnying, their breath snorting from their nostrils in winter. She imagined Sorle astride his black horse, its mane and tail flying in the wind as he soared over a hedge. She imagined his wife, dark-haired and laughing, riding alongside him.

The excitement of the imaginary chase faded. 'We'll have to put the pups in the tack room when the horses arrive,' she said to Tom.

The pups seemed to have doubled in size over the previous two weeks. Unlike Bandit, who was still small, this pair had grown a set of long legs. Geneva gazed at them dubiously. One of them was growing a bit of a ruff, the other a hairy muzzle and tail. Their barks had deepened too, except when they wrestled and became excited. Now they huffed at her and whacked at her knees with their flailing tails.

'You're growing into such handsome creatures,' she told them as they leant against her legs having their ears fondled. 'The earl won't have the heart to turn you out.'

'I reckon the innkeeper's Irish wolfhound must've mounted the farmer's bitch to produce them two,' Tom said bluntly.

Pretending not to hear, Geneva turned away with a blush.

Soon, midsummer's day was upon them, bringing with it a blue, seamless sky. Excitement had been building for some time in the Batterby household, pocket money had been hoarded and assiduously counted.

Geneva and her cousins had left Edgley House earlier that morning. Led by Gerald and Matthew, Geneva brought up the rear. She felt confident in her cornflower-blue gown and straw hat, its ribbons fluttering in the breeze.

The staff at Welford Manor had been given permission to attend the fair too, even though there was still plenty of work to be done. After all, it was only once a year.

In a drawer, Geneva had discovered the last household inventory. Assisted by Ellen Pickering, she was about to embark on the momentous task of compiling another. This was necessary, not only to check that the contents of the house were still intact, but to isolate those items damaged by rodent or other pest infestation when the house had been standing empty.

The party left their picnic basket hidden in a shady spot by the bank of the stream, not far from the common. Gerald wedged the basket into the fork of the tree so it was hidden from sight. They arranged to meet at noon.

Moth jingled as he walked. He was smiling with delight, for his brothers' coins had added considerable weight to the cache in his pockets. 'I'm going to catch the pig,' he told them with great seriousness.

'More likely the pig will catch you, since it will be bigger than you and covered in grease,' Gerald joshed.

Moth looked hurt when his brothers fell about laughing. 'I don't care. I'm going to try, anyway.'

The fair was being held on the common on the outskirts of Edgley. It wasn't long before the sound of a band had the straggling crocodile of Batterby boys marching in step. Even

Geneva picked up the rhythm, her arms swinging and her stride lengthening to keep up with them.

Soon, the fluttering bunting and the marquees and tents came into sight. Already, people milled around the side stalls or strolled around the roped-off area where the main events of the day were to take place. The air held a mouth-watering aroma of fried onions and sausages.

Geneva stopped to buy herself a lemonade, whilst the boys went off together. The common wasn't big enough for them to get lost in, and indeed, she caught up with Edward and Moth, who were goggle-eyed as they watched a fire-eater swallow a flame, then blow it from his mouth a few moments later.

Grinning excitedly at her, they darted off into the crowd, their heads turning this way and that. And so it was for the rest of the morning, with the boys appearing every so often, relating tales of wonder. Edward's and Moth's faces and hands became grubbier and grubbier.

A stage had been set up in one of the marquees. A company of actors was to perform a one-act comedy. Geneva had never seen a play before.

'Ninepence for a seat, thruppence standing,' the woman at the entrance said. Gazing at the last sixpence in her hand, Geneva regretfully put it back in her pocket. She had other plans for it.

'Allow me,' Sorle said from behind her, dropping a florin into the outstretched hand. Before she could demure, his hand slid under her elbow and they passed into the marquee. They took up position on wooden benches at the front, where Sorle offered her a friendly smile as he extended his long, brown-booted legs and crossed them at the ankle. 'Do I find you well, Miss Tibbetson?'

She felt quite breathless under his solid scrutiny. 'I'm quite well, Lord Ashby. I've never been to a play before.'

'Have you not? Then this one will be an experience for you. As for the state of your health, you certainly look to be glowing, especially in that charming outfit.'

Recalling the remark he'd made to her uncle about her shabbiness, Geneva's face warmed. 'A gift from my uncle. I didn't expect to see you here today, My Lord.'

'How could you have, when I didn't think to inform you?'

Reminded of her place by what seemed to be a rebuke, she stiffened. 'My pardon. I was not inferring that you should have, of course.'

He seemed startled by her remark. 'Not for a moment did I imagine you were.' Now she hung her head in embarrassment. 'There, I seem to have unwittingly upset you. The reason for my presence here is simple.'

How mortifying. Desperately, she told him, 'It really is none of my business, My Lord.'

He gave a faint grin. 'Since I intend to make it your business, I'd be obliged if you'd listen without interruption.'

She opened her mouth, then shut it again when he gave her a stern look.

'I was attending a friend's nuptials in Hampshire yesterday and remembered it was the midsummer fair, so I decided to attend. I'll probably spend the night at the manor. I hope it won't inconvenience you.'

She felt a little huffed with him. 'Why should it inconvenience me? I think you'll be surprised by how ordered your house is now. Some of the staff will not be starting until early next month, but those already in residence can manage. After all, one man cannot be all that much trouble.'

'You don't think so?' he rumbled, to which question there was no time to answer, since the play started.

The farce proved to be hilarious, if sometimes slightly risqué. Geneva spent the time beset by laughter or suffused in blushes, sometimes both at once. Her uncle and aunt would probably be horrified if they found out she was here.

No reticence from Sorle Ashby though. He laughed often and without restraint. So did everyone else.

Then she saw Edward and Moth. The pair had levered their heads and shoulders under the bottom of the marquee and were watching the proceedings with rapt expressions.

When she gasped and was about to rise and go to them, Sorle placed a restraining hand on her arm. 'Leave them, they're not old enough to understand the comedy. I'll buy them a ticket for the children's pantomime afterwards and they'll forget anything they've heard here.

The warm air trapped in the marquee had become moist and ripe from the closely packed mass of humanity. When they escaped outside, the air felt fresh and cool in comparison. Geneva drew in a deep breath and pressed her hands against her warm cheeks. 'I hope nobody tells my uncle I was in there.'

His laughter mocked her. 'Did *The Rivals* shock your sensibilities, then, Miss Tibbetson?'

She flicked him a glance, said candidly, 'Is that what it was called? I confess, it did, but only a little, and I enjoyed being shocked, since I think that was the aim of the play. Thank you for escorting me in.'

'The pleasure was mine, for your reaction told me something about you.'

'Which is?'

'That you're not some prissy miss who would faint at the sight of a man's bared chest.'

'Why should I when I have eight cousins who have bared their chests in my presence often? A man is only a larger version of a boy, after all. Am I to take it you were laughing at me, then?'

'Only enjoying your amusement. The company presented excerpts and the actors were so excruciatingly bad the play became even more of a farce.'

She engaged his eyes. 'I swear the character called Lydia Languish winked at you.'

Sorle appeared slightly uncomfortable. 'Since Lydia Languish's role was performed by a male, it must have been you he winked at.'

Her eyes flew open. 'A male! How could you tell?'

Sorle gave a low chuckle.

Moth and Edward ranged either side of her to stare up at him. 'How do you do, Lord Ashby?'

'Very well indeed. It's Edward and Moth, isn't it?' He held out a hand to each of them in turn. 'Are you having a good time?'

Smiles beamed across both faces. 'Yes, sir,' they said together, then Edward gazed up at her, his face hollowing with imagined starvation. 'Is it time to eat yet, Gen?'

'There's an hour to go before our picnic. Lord Ashby has kindly offered to buy you a ticket to the pantomime. I'll be waiting outside the tent for you afterwards and we'll go and eat then.'

Sorle handed them a shilling apiece and indicated a stall. 'Buy yourself a pie and a glass of lemonade whilst I purchase your tickets. It will help fill the hungry bits.'

'They had a substantial breakfast and only imagine they're hungry,' she said after the boys had sprinted off.

'It's surprising how hungry young men can get when engaged in the pursuit of pleasure.'

'Moth plans to capture the greasy pig this afternoon.'

'Does he indeed? *That* I must see.' He nodded to someone he knew as they strolled through the crowds. 'Are the Reverend and Mrs Batterby not attending the fair?'

'Mrs Batterby's father had been taken ill, so the reverend has taken her to Dorchester to visit him. As her father is not expected to recover, my aunt may have to remain there for a while.'

'That's unfortunate,' he murmured.

'It is, indeed.' Especially for the afflicted, she thought, for she wouldn't care to die to the tune of Maudine's harping. She allowed herself a small grin at the surge of freedom her aunt's absence afforded her.

Sorle's glance was upon her, the slightly conspiratorial smile he wore made her laugh. He was a fine-looking gentleman who drew the glances of others as they strolled along. Men doffed their hats, whilst Maudine's friends offered him smiles and curtsies.

She realized she was being remiss in her manners. 'Would you care to be introduced to anyone, Lord Ashby?'

'Don't be tiresome, Gen,' he growled. 'I'm quite content with the company I already have.' He drew her towards a coconut shy. 'Here, I'll see if can win you a prize.' Taking off his coat, he handed it to her and rolled up his shirt sleeves. His first ball went wide of the mark, the second rocked the coconut. The third sent it flying from the cup.

'What's the prize?' he asked the stallholder.

'The coconut, sir.'

'How many strikes for the figurine?'

'Three in a row.'

It took several more goes before he scored all three, by which time a crowd had gathered to cheer him on. Laughter in his eyes and perspiration dampening his forehead, Sorle handed her the trophy, a dainty china shepherdess.

She looked up to see Gerald. 'Ah, there you are. Have you seen the others?'

Gerald looked slightly worried. 'Everyone is making their way to the copse to eat, but I can't find Edward and Moth.'

She handed Sorle his coat, thinking it a shame that his grey-striped waistcoat with its splendid silver buttons would be covered. 'They're at the pantomime. I was just about to collect them. You remember Lord Ashby, don't you, Gerald?'

'Yes, of course. Good day, My Lord. Will you be joining us for the picnic?'

'Only if you'll allow me to contribute to it, for I'm as hungry as a horse.' He consulted a gold watch on a chain. 'Perhaps I could purchase some pies, while Miss Tibbetson fetches your young brothers.' His glance came back to her. 'Though the pantomime doesn't finish for fifteen minutes so you'll have to wait a short time.'

'That's quite alright, since there's a stall I wish to visit next door to the marquee. Gerald, perhaps you'd accompany Lord Ashby, so he knows where we're situated.' She darted off into the crowd, clutching her figurine with one hand and fishing in her pocket for her sixpence with the other. Luckily, she didn't have to wait in a queue.

She handed over her sixpence and held her hand out for inspection. 'I only have ten minutes. Will it take long?'

The gypsy fortune teller had an orange scarf about her head, with gold coins sewn about the hem. The hand cupping hers was callused and dirty.

'What I see is many boy children in your life. The number ten comes into my mind.'

'My cousins, I expect,' she murmured, wondering if Maudine would have two more children, though she'd over-heard Maudine telling one of her friends that she'd reached a difficult stage in life, where further children were unlikely.

'Some have a different mother. A tall, dark-haired man has recently entered your life.'

Disappointment flooded through her. She'd heard that most fortune tellers said that to young women of marriageable age. The gypsy woman could easily have seen her with Sorle, and come to the wrong conclusion.

'Your life will take a different path to that which you imagine for yourself, miss.' The gypsy's fingers gently touched the lines at the side of her hand. 'Here are your sons. One . . . two.'

Geneva leaned forward to gaze at the tiny marks on her hand. 'There are three lines.'

'The third is a daughter.' A finger traced along a line. 'You're lucky, for the man who chooses you will set you above all others. See, here is your heart line. It reveals a sensual nature, one which will flout convention if you allow your heart to rule your head . . . and you will, missy, for this man will sense it in you and exploit it.'

Her heart began to beat a little faster, even though the woman's words made her slightly uneasy. 'Who shall love me?'

There was a noise across the way as children came jostling out of the pantomime, chattering and laughing. Geneva quickly withdrew her hand. 'Thank you, I must go and collect my cousins now, else I'll miss them.'

'I see the initials . . .'

But Geneva didn't wait to hear the rest, because she'd seen Moth and Edward, and hurried outside to meet them before they disappeared into the crowd.

They caught up with Sorle and Gerald on their way to the copse. Gerald carried a stone jar of lemonade and Sorle had a basket over his arm. His horse ambled along behind them like a faithful dog.

Soon they entered the copse, to discover Matthew up the tree. He was carefully lowering the picnic basket into the outstretched arms of Michael and Robert.

'Nice spot,' Sorle said, gazing at the glittering stream and the grassy banks dappled with sunlight and shade.

'Yes, we often come here to picnic.' She inspected the youngest boys before sending them off to wash their faces and hands in the stream. Spreading a cloth on the ground, she emptied the picnic basket of its contents – thick slices of ham, eggs boiled in their shells and piquant, crumbly cheese. Then there were two crusty loaves of bread, which Maudine had made the night before. They were already sliced, and there was a jar of gooseberry conserve to spread upon them. Sorle uncovered his contribution, a batch of pork pies made by the innkeeper's wife, placing them on top of the picnic basket.

'We'd better start before the ants discover us,' she said, politely offering their guest the only plate they'd brought. Sorle filled it with a morsel of this and that, then handed it back to her. Like the boys, he was content to use his hands as a plate, knife and fork.

Her cousins made short work of the food, washing it down with lemonade straight from the jar, though Sorle found a silver cup in his saddlebags for her to use.

Itching to get back to the fair, the boys ate quickly, then tallied their remaining funds. 'How much have you got left, Robert?'

'A shilling. I went to see the fire-eater twice, and the tumblers.'

'Adam?'

'One and sixpence.'

'I've only got thruppence left,' Robert said.

Gerald took several coins from his pocket. 'Perhaps we should pool our money and share it out equally.'

They handed over the contents of their pockets, including Moth, who stood to lose more than he'd gained from the Hares and Hounds game.

When Edward gazed at her, she shrugged. 'I only had a shilling to start with. I've spent it.'

'She went to see the fortune teller,' Edward told them. 'I saw her come out.'

Nine pairs of eyes swivelled towards her with interest. 'What did the gypsy tell you, Gen?'

'It's private.'

Simon grinned. 'I wager the gypsy told you you'd meet a tall, dark, handsome stranger who would fall in love with you. Adam hid behind her tent and listened, and she said that to all the girls, even Florence Potter, whose teeth stick out so she looks like a rabbit.'

Geneva tried not to blush as she lied. 'No, she didn't say anything like that.'

'Oh, go on, Gen!' they chorused.

'Go on, Gen,' Sorle said with a grin. 'Tell us.'

'I certainly will not.'

'Witches britches! I've suddenly remembered something.'
Moth looked tragically around him. 'There was a tall, dark
stranger in the pantomime. He had a big black beard and a
knife, and he eats children. I hope it's not him she's going to
meet.'

Geneva gasped. 'Where did you get that vulgar expression
from, Timothy Batterby?'

'From the pantomime,' Edward told her casually. 'Moth's
going to be an actor when he grows up.'

Sorle grinned and dropped a handful of coins on top of the
pile. 'There, that should see you boys through the afternoon.'

Amongst the chorus of thanks, Geneva's protest was a lost
sound as Edward quickly divided up the money and handed
it out.

'Don't forget, I'm going to catch the greasy pig, Gen. You
will come and watch, won't you?'

'Of course I will, Moth. I wouldn't miss it for the world.'

The boys grinned at each other, making it obvious that
neither would they. Eager to get back to the fun, they started
off, jostling against each other. But Gerald turned back. 'I'd
better stay with you, Gen.'

'Don't worry about your cousin, I'll look after her. We'll
catch you up before too long.'

A look of enquiry darted her way. 'Gen?'

She nodded. 'I've got to tidy away the picnic things, beside
which, Lord Ashby is my employer and probably has some
private business to discuss with me.'

'No business. It's too good a day to do anything else but
relax and enjoy it,' Sorle said when Gerald ambled off. Lying
on his back, his arms triangled under his head, her companion gazed up at the leafy canopy overhead whilst she repacked
the picnic basket. She shredded the leftover crumbs and scattered them.

Soon, Sorle's eyelids drifted shut. His lashes were a dark
sweep against his skin, the firm curve of his mouth softened
as she watched him sleep for a few minutes. His chest gently
rose and fell.

A speckled thrush came down to feed from the crumbs,
followed by another. The pair joined in joyous song before
hopping about the undergrowth.

She became aware of the gleam of his eyes under his lashes, then he lazily smiled. 'I've never heard a bird sing so well.'

'If you're quiet and keep still, we might hear them again.'

There was a blissful silence, broken when Sorle's horse took it into his head to pluck the hat from her head and toss it in the air. Tugged from its pins, her hair came tumbling down around her shoulders. Startled by her cry of dismay, the thrushes flew into the branches above them.

Sorle laughed, adroitly catching the hat as it fell to earth. 'Stop that, Rastus.' Dark eyes shining with laughter were turned her way. He gazed at her for a moment, then came to a sitting position, his smile fading. 'Your hair is exquisite, like moonlit silk.'

Geneva didn't know quite what to say. It would take time to arrange it as it was before. 'I shall have to braid it.'

He reached out to still her seeking hands. 'Allow me.'

She blushed. 'It wouldn't be seemly, My Lord.'

'It wouldn't, would it?' He smiled as he swept her observation aside. 'Since there's nobody here to observe us except for a speckled thrush or two, we'll behave in an unseemly fashion whilst I play lady's maid – and to hell with it.'

He moved to kneel behind her. When he began to weave her hair into a braid, tiny shivers gathered in her neck then raced across her shoulders and down her arms in pleasurable little waves, so her eyes half closed with the delight of it, and she purred inside like a cat being stroked.

'There, I've tied a ribbon from your hat around it,' he whispered against her ear.

Her surroundings came slowly back into focus, the murmur of the stream winding its way to the sea, the song pouring from the throat of a bird. Above her, the leaves on the trees sighed in the breeze, and the smell of honeysuckle was carried in the air. How perfect it all was.

Unaccountably happy, she turned her head to gaze at him. 'Sorle, I must go back to the fair, for my cousins are bound to get into mischief without me.'

'As all boys must, even big boys.' His eyes were dark as he murmured, 'My mind is contemplating such mischief now.'

Her breath came in a series of fits and starts, for her throat had suddenly tightened. 'There will be morris dancing to

53

watch, and the midsummer queen will be crowned. This year it is to be Miss Priscilla Hunter, whose father is the squire, My Lord.'

'Miss Priscilla Hunter will not hold a candle to you, and your lord likes it better when you call him by his name, as you did a few moments ago.' He gently set her hat on her head, tied the ribbons under her chin and gazed at her, a smile playing around his mouth. 'You look warm, my Gen.'

Her hands touched her glowing cheeks. 'It's a warm day. We mustn't forget that Moth intends to catch the greasy pig. And the reverend has entrusted me to look after his younger sons in his absence.'

There was laughter in his eyes as he gazed at her. 'Then we shall catch them up in no time at all.' He rose and pulled her to her feet. His hands spanning her waist, he lifted her sideways on to the saddle and, mounting behind her, set Rastus in motion. The gelding's head was turned towards the fair, and soon they caught up with her cousins.

She was laughing as Sorle swung her down, her bonnet all askew, so she missed the slight frown on Gerald's face.

The fair was great fun. They ran into Ellen Pickering in the company of Sally, so she was able to introduce master to servants. She left Sorle talking to them whilst she headed to the pig-catching area to join her cousins. The arena was now surrounded by straw bales. The greasy-pig chases were the last two events of the day.

Sorle joined her just as the adult pig was caught by the innkeeper. It would probably end up as a filling for his wife's pies.

'Do be careful,' she said when Moth lined up with the other lads to chase after the smaller pig, which was little more than an overgrown piglet. Moth looked so small when set against the sturdy farm labourers' boys.

But what Moth lacked in stature he made up for in speed, for he was over the start line in a flash and running after his quarry. Soon the pack caught him up and converged on the pig. Geneva's breath caught in her throat when Moth disappeared under the pack of lads.

The pig had a lively disposition and afforded them great sport. With a series of outraged squeals, the animal slid from under them and took off in a different direction. Moth did the same, whilst his brothers cheered him on and shouted themselves hoarse.

Beside her, Sorle began to laugh as the pig darted through Moth's legs, tipping him over before zig-zagging all over the common. But, as the herd of lads descended on it, whooping and hollering, it came back in his direction again. And so it went on, up and down the field for the next ten minutes or so.

Finally, Moth tackled the pig and caught it by its ears. Kneeling astride the protesting animal, Moth wore an ear-to-ear grin as he gazed triumphantly around.

His small stature had put the crowd on Moth's side. But just as they began to cheer, the pig wriggled out from under him and slipped from his grasp. The cheers became a groan. Losing his balance, Moth rolled over on his back and the pig ran straight into the arms of a farm labourer's lad, who snatched it up and held it tight.

His brothers groaned in unison.

The disappointment in Moth's face was hard to take as he staggered to his feet. Manfully, though, he congratulated the winner, before limping towards them, out of breath.

'Well done, young un!' someone shouted out to him, bringing the smile back to his face.

Edward held his nose as Moth neared them. 'Ugh . . . you stink like something gone rotten, Moth. Look at your clothes. Mamma would eat you alive if she was here.'

'Smelling like that, she wouldn't,' Gerald informed him.

'He can bathe at the manor if you wouldn't mind fetching him a clean set of clothes, Gerald. We can put my laundry maid to good use too. And since your parents are absent, I've told my housekeeper to inform the cook that you'll all be dining with me. I hope that meets with your approval, Miss Tibbetson. We will make it an informal occasion to suit the day.'

Geneva thought to defer to Gerald, who nodded.

It was a weary band who reached the manor. About to enter the stable yard, Geneva suddenly remembered the puppies.

'Excuse me, I'll just make sure the stables are clean,' she gabbled, and took off at a run, chased by the look of astonishment on Sorle's face.

The pups were asleep in one of the stalls. As she heard Rastus clip-clop across the cobbles, she hastily piled hay on top of the dogs and stood in front of them.

'You can use that stall,' she said, pointing to the empty space next to the one they were in.

'This one has straw in,' he pointed out.

Behind her, the straw began to rustle as the puppies woke with long, whining yawns to investigate the sound of human voices.

'There's something moving in the straw, Miss Tibbetson.'

Geneva felt a bit desperate. 'I can't see anything.'

'That's because it's behind you.'

There was a yelp, followed by another as the two pups emerged. She willed herself not to look at them.

'If you care to look behind you, you will see two puppies. To whom do these odd-looking creatures belong?'

The odd-looking creatures pressed one against each of her legs, and panted. Sorle grinned at her. 'They seem to know you well.'

So, he thought he had the better of the game, did he? She made her eyes round and innocent. 'Of course they know me. But they're *your* dogs. They're a gift . . . from me . . . but you have quite spoiled my surprise, Lord Ashby.'

'I doubt it, since you appear to relish mine. May I ask what breeding they have?'

'They're mostly Irish wolfhounds, I believe. They're so sweet. You do like them, don't you?' When Sorle gave a grumbling sigh of defeat, she smiled. 'There is one thing more, My Lord.'

One eyebrow lifted a fraction. 'Which is?'

She felt heat rise to her face. 'Since I had no money but your purse, I confess I borrowed two shillings from it to buy them with.'

'Two whole shillings?' Sorle clicked his fingers and the dogs went to press against his legs instead. They gazed up at him in quivering adoration as he fondled their ears. 'What gentleman would mind being robbed of a florin in light of such a delightful gift? These hounds would be a bargain at twice the price.'

She sucked in a breath. 'I did not say I *robbed* you of the money. It was simply a loan.'

'My pardon, Miss Tibbetson, and my heartfelt thanks for the gift. I'm overwhelmed by your generosity and I will overlook your transgression, an act which could have brought a prison term down on your head, had I not been a generous man.'

To a man, her cousins applauded.

Five

Gerald requested an audience with his father as soon as he returned home, presenting himself in the study early the next morning.

The Reverend Batterby welcomed his eldest son with a smile. Gerald had a strong sense of responsibility towards his siblings, and sometimes his confidences were illuminating. 'How can I be of service to you, my boy?'

'It's Lord Ashby,' Gerald said, coming straight to the point. 'I believe he's turning Geneva's head.'

James only just managed to hide his astonishment. 'What makes you suspect such a thing?'

'He's becoming awfully friendly with her, Father. Yesterday, he stayed behind to help her clean up the picnic. When they caught up with us, she was seated before him on his horse. Her hat was all awry, and her hair was untidy.'

'Ah, I see.' James hid his smile. 'There is probably a simple reason. Women wear elaborate hairstyles which can sometimes become loose, and her hat may have been dislodged by the breeze.'

A frown touched Gerald's forehead. 'Geneva blushes when he looks at her.'

'Young women of her age often blush when men address them, and Geneva is not used to socializing at such a level. Don't you like the earl, Gerald?'

'Enormously. We all do.' He shrugged. 'He teases Geneva.

When she chides him, he just laughs and teases her more instead of being annoyed.'

'And you're worried about it? It sounds as if they indulge in the same sort of behaviour you and your brothers enjoy with her. Up to now you've been blessed with her exclusive company. Now, an eligible young man is paying attention to her, and you might simply be reading more into this than you should.'

Gerald's frown became an expression of consternation. 'Are you suggesting that Lord Ashby is paying court to Gen?'

'I only wish he were, for she's a dear girl who deserves to be happy, and I'd like to see her well settled. However, we must not jump to conclusions, especially since the acquaintance is recent. You must remember, Geneva is the most trusted member of Lord Ashby's staff. His attitude towards her may well be more relaxed than is usual, since she's managing his affairs.'

'Surely Gen is far beneath the serious attention of the earl.'

'All things are possible,' he said gently. 'If he did happen to take a serious interest in her, her lack of fortune would probably be of no great consequence to him. If he has come here to settle down, he will seek a wife amongst those already living in the district, someone who is content to live here without hankering to be part of the London social set. Geneva is well placed, already being part of his household.'

Gerald frowned. 'I had not thought along those lines. Gen has never expressed a desire to leave us and marry. What would we do without her?'

James trod carefully, for his son didn't realize how telling his words were. 'It's natural for you to wish to protect your cousin, as you would a beloved sister. However, we cannot be selfish and keep her all to ourselves. Such a match, if an offer is forthcoming, is only to be encouraged. Geneva is a sensible young woman. I do not believe the earl's teasing will go to her head. You were right to bring it to my attention, though.'

'What if Lord Ashby's motives are not all they should be? I couldn't bear it if he broke Gen's heart.'

'It's early days yet. Geneva must learn to cope with her own emotions, for we cannot guard her from them. We must keep a good eye on her though, make sure she's adequately chaperoned. Would it set your mind at ease if I discreetly counselled your cousin on the matter? I would not break your trust or mention your concerns, of course. To know her behaviour had been closely scrutinized by her cousin would embarrass her.'

Although Gerald flushed at the gentle reprimand, his eyes brimmed with the relief he felt. 'Would you, Father?'

'Indeed, it would be my pleasure. I'll speak to her tonight. In the meantime you can seek out your brothers and tell them to present themselves for choir practice. Where are they?'

'They've gone to the manor with Gen. They wanted to bid the earl farewell, since they're very impressed by him.'

James's eyes shifted to the clock. 'They've had ample time to do that by now. We must go and fetch them, and I must apologize to Lord Ashby for the intrusion. Their home is here. I cannot have them cluttering up the manor uninvited.'

'Mother said they must practise there, since the constant noise gives her a headache.'

Colour flooded James's face. Maudine had gone too far in fobbing the children off on to his niece when Geneva was being paid to carry out her employer's tasks. James knew he must share the blame himself, because he'd turned a blind eye to what was going on.

'I think I'll start Edward and Timothy at the school in town next year, since Geneva cannot be expected to do two jobs at once. Oh dear, it seems as though I've been remiss in my parenting, allowing this to go on.'

'Don't be too hard on yourself, Pa. You were not to know. Besides, Geneva doesn't mind looking after them. She adores the boys and they adore her.'

'Which is exactly the point I'm making. Geneva is your cousin, not your mother. When I took her under my roof, it was so she could have an education, and a decent upbringing in a loving family, not with the intention of using her as an unpaid servant.'

Geneva and her nephews were breakfasting with Lord Ashby when Gerald and the reverend were ushered into the dining room.

Sorle flashed him a friendly smile when he was announced.

'Ah, Reverend Batterby, and Gerald. Have you come to join us for breakfast? It's rather late, I'm afraid, but I don't have to leave for another hour or so.'

Taking his watch from his pocket, James mustered up a frown as he gazed at it. 'Actually, I've come to remind my sons that they have a home of their own, and I expect them to turn up for choir practice in exactly one hour.'

A chorus of unmusical groans came from around the table.

'But you have time enough to stay a while with us, I hope. Draw up chairs, the pair of you, there is plenty of food to go around.' Their host nodded to the servant, who stepped forward to provide two more settings.

After swallowing a bowl of thin grey oatmeal for breakfast, the aroma of coddled eggs, bacon and other breakfast delights was far too tempting for James to refuse. His stomach beat Gerald's into giving an inelegant growl as he offered up a token resistance. 'I'm sure my sons were adequately fed before they left home. I cannot have them queuing up at your table every mealtime, like beggar boys.'

Protests came swiftly from around the table. 'Our new maids can't cook as well as Mama or Sally.'

The usually quiet Robert said, 'The porridge tasted like dog's bath water.'

Michael tried to outdo him. 'Mine tasted like boiled horse-shoes.'

'Ugh!' Moth's eyes rolled up in his head and he clutched at his throat with both hands. 'Remember that time—'

'Enough, gentlemen,' James said firmly, before some inappropriate and unpalatable horror rolled from Timothy's tongue. He allowed his glance to rove around the table as he and Gerald seated themselves. 'Have you said grace, boys?'

It was Michael who answered. 'Yes, Papa, at home, if you remember.'

'Ah yes, I do indeed remember, Michael.' He tried not to grin with the pleasure he felt as the servant slid some eggs, a solid slice of ham and a serving of mushrooms on to his plate. 'We are all witness to the power of your prayer. You requested a good breakfast and the Lord has kindly provided it for us. Well done.' He nodded to Lord Ashby. 'And thank *you*, My Lord. We're indebted to you.'

Everyone laughed as Lord Ashby gazed round at them all, a smile on his face. 'Rarely have I enjoyed such friendly and entertaining company for breakfast. You must be proud of having so many fine sons, Reverend Batterby.' His dark eyes came to rest and reflect on Geneva. 'And your niece is a credit to you.'

Indeed, James felt a glow of satisfaction just looking at them all.

A shy smile on her face, Geneva asked him, 'Do you have sons, My Lord?'

Lord Ashby gazed at her in astonishment. 'I'm unmarried, Miss Tibbetson.'

'Oh!' Geneva's fork dropped to the floor. Colour suffused her face as she scrambled to retrieve it. 'I do beg your pardon. Aunt Maudine said . . . I understood . . .'

Lord Ashby placed a restraining hand on her arm as she tried to fit her head under the table to look for the fork. 'Leave it to its fate. The servant will bring you another.' A crooked finger brought an instant result. 'Are you uncomfortable, Miss Tibbetson? You appear to be quite agitated.'

James saw his niece take a deep breath and gather herself together. 'I'm sorry. It was unforgivably rude of me to make personal enquiries.'

He chuckled. 'Not entirely unforgivable, Miss Tibbetson. Since you show interest in my single status, perhaps I'll allow you to marry me off. To that end, you may introduce me to all the eligible females in the district before the Christmas ball.'

Geneva threw Lord Ashby a rather challenging glance. 'I have no interest whatsoever in your status, and you're being deliberately provocative, My Lord. Please accept my apology with grace, then eat your breakfast before it cools. You have a long journey ahead of you.'

'Geneva!' James reproved her.

Lord Ashby laughed. 'Pray, do not chide my social secretary, Reverend. She deals with me as she would one of her cousins. I would not have it any other way. Apology accepted, Miss Tibbetson.'

James exchanged a significant glance with Gerald, who nodded as Geneva and their host exchanged a comfortable grin and the company settled down to finish their breakfast.

Gazing from one to the other, James thought with real regret, Gerald is worrying about nothing, for Lord Ashby treats Geneva like a sister.

Sorle was wondering just how long he could restrain himself and keep a brotherly distance from Miss Tibbetson as he followed her into the little sitting room she'd made her own. Somehow, she'd managed to creep under his skin, which tingled every time she came close to him.

Her mouth was a delectable morsel, the bottom lip full, soft and blushing, so he wanted to nip it gently between his teeth and run his tongue over it to taste of its ripeness.

He gazed around the room she'd made her domain – a small, feminine room with large windows opening on to the sunny garden. A jar of wild flowers in a battered pewter pot stood on the window sill, filling the room with perfume.

Sprawling on to a chair covered in needlepoint tapestry, he stretched his legs out, crossing them at the ankles. He gazed at her, a half smile on his face. 'What did you want to talk to me about, my Gen?'

Taking up position behind a table, she gazed intently at the blank page of an account book laid open on the desk. 'Money, Lord Ashby. I seem to be spending rather a lot of yours.'

'There is no limit to what you may spend to prepare the house for residency.' He sent her a smile. 'I thought we'd agreed that you'd call me by my first name when we were alone together.'

Her eyes came up to his, wide and innocent, and as blue as cornflowers. 'We agreed no such thing! You *decreed*, as I recall. To encourage such familiarity between us would be wrong.'

'Dammit, Gen, I thought we'd left such nonsense behind.'

'This is a small town, Lord Ashby. People have nothing better to do than talk. My position in my uncle's house is tenuous. Since I have nowhere else to go, I must not fall into the trap of allowing myself to be gossiped about.'

He rose to his feet and crossed to where she stood, annoyed by her reasoning. 'You can only be referring to my unmarried status, something of which you've just become aware.

Surely there would be more reason to gossip had I a wife and children, and we then used each other's names familiarly.'

'You'd be considered *safer* company.'

'Like a wise old uncle, you mean?' Sorle cracked a laugh as he recalled the conduct of some of his married colleagues. 'Good grief, how old-fashioned you are, girl. I'm not your uncle, and I'm not always wise. Right now, I'd like to kiss you, which would certainly be unwise. Having a wife would not change that urge, nor the ability to control it.'

'May I remind you that I'm employed by you.'

'What difference does that make?'

A tiny sliver of uncertainty entered her voice. 'You're a gentleman, you wouldn't take such a liberty.'

'I'm a man first – and, yes, not only would I kiss you, I intend to.' Leaning across the table, he kissed her gently on the mouth and felt it tremble beneath the caress. She didn't flinch from the pleasure he stole from her, didn't move away, just gave a sigh when it ended.

'Was that so very bad?' he asked.

'Sorle,' she whispered when he drew away, sounding so unsure of herself he knew she'd never been kissed before. 'You shouldn't have done that. Somebody might have seen us.'

He closed his eyes, the innocence of her filling him with guilt, because he knew he'd think nothing of ruining her reputation if his blood was sufficiently aroused and the opportunity presented itself.

Roughly, he said, 'My pardon. If having you relaxed in my company depends on me being married, you'd best get on with your work and find me a wife.' He drew a purse from his pocket and threw it on to the table. 'Thank you for reminding me of your position in my household. Here is your first month's salary, Miss Tibbetson. I intended to give it to the Reverend Batterby, but forgot.'

Her eyes became crushed cornflowers floating on a lake of tears as she whispered, 'It was not my intention to anger you so.'

What sort of lout was he to toy with the emotions of a sweet country maid like this? As suddenly as it had arrived, his temper deserted him. He managed a wry smile. 'It was entirely my fault. Will you forgive me?'

When she nodded, he took her chin between his finger and thumb and gently dabbed the tears from her eyes with his handkerchief. Her long lashes had clumped into spikes. 'My thanks. Tell the housekeeper to prepare a room for Mrs Ashby, who will be my guest for a while when I return.' He gave a faint grin as he released her. 'In case you hadn't realized, Mrs Ashby is my mother. Her name is Sarah.'

Geneva recovered quickly, her eyes glinting as she lifted her chin a fraction. 'Do you always have to command the last word?'

'Usually, but on this occasion I will humour you by allowing you to command it.'

She possessed a passionate nature, for her annoyance was hardly contained when she almost snapped, 'Damn you then, Sorle!'

He ran a finger down the perfect slope of her nose, smiled, then departed without another word.

As he rode away, Sorle sensed she was watching him. Twisting in his saddle, he gazed back at the sun-polished windows of the house. Although he couldn't see her beyond the glare, he waved, then put his horse to the canter to see if he could catch up with the Batterby family to say his farewells.

Geneva was at the window in her favourite bedchamber over the porch. When Sorle rode out of sight she gazed around it with a critical eye. Although it was her favourite chamber, one the previous lady of the house had called her own, this was not a room in which to place Sorle's mother, for every visitor to the place would be using the door underneath it, and there were bound to be guests coming and going.

There was a smaller, prettier, corner room at the back of the house, with a sitting room through an adjoining door, and a maid's room opposite. Fetching Ellen Pickering, they went upstairs together to inspect the room. The bed had narrow fluted posts, a carved wooden cornice and a soft down mattress. The commode was enclosed by a fine lacquered cabinet, and set behind a screen.

'We'll use this chamber for Lord Ashby's mother, but the mattress must be beaten and aired and the bed canopy and curtains will have to be replaced, so it's fresh and comfortable for her.' Head to one side, Geneva gazed into the distance and set her imagination to work. 'Lavender sprigs on white muslin would be pretty, with a lavender bedcover made of brocade. We'll have the panels of the screen re-covered in the same material, so it matches.'

'The new monogrammed bed linen you ordered arrives today, Miss Tibbetson. The decorators can take the old hangings down and use them as a pattern. I'll send them to your sitting room with fabric samples as soon as they arrive.'

'Tell them the hangings will be needed by the end of the month.' She threw open the door to the sitting room, wondering about Sorle's mother. Was she dark-eyed, like Sorle?

She smiled a little as her fingers grazed across her mouth. What a fine experience her first kiss on the mouth had been. His kiss had shocked her, though, not because it had happened, but mostly because she'd wished for it and her wish had come true. Such feelings it had evoked in her, for she was so very aware of him now.

Now she'd learned Sorle wasn't married, after all, she wanted to laugh aloud at the joy of it. Not that he'd consider her as a wife. Her hand closed around the purse in her apron pocket. It contained three pounds, a surprisingly generous salary, after all. She had never had so much money of her own before.

Tears pricked her eyes, so she had to blink them back before Ellen Pickering saw them. Despite her good fortune, Geneva relived the moment of humiliation she'd felt when he'd thrown it on to the desk. Whatever the title of her position in his household, with that one churlish action he'd made it plain she was his servant.

She stopped her uncomfortable musings to take a critical look around. It was a pretty room, one in surprisingly good condition. Three Chippendale sofas, upholstered in pale pink velvet, formed a cosy three-sided setting around a table with matching rosewood legs. Against the wall stood a dainty writing table inlaid with mother-of-pearl.

Figurines, and a clock with an enamelled face, topped by a silver cupid with bow and arrow, stood on the mantelpiece. She inserted the key and wound it. A few minutes after it started to tick, it chimed. She smiled, imagining Sorle's mother taking refreshment and exchanging gossip with other women here. Sorle was in attendance, his large frame perched uncomfortably on the small sofa, unable to extend his legs. He had a cup and saucer balanced on his large hands, and appeared slightly bored.

A cough from Ellen Pickering brought her from her pleasant musings. 'We must start the inventory, Mrs Pickering, for it must be completed as soon as possible. Everyone can help. Sally and her assistant can list the contents of the linen cupboards to start with. The cook can count the pots and pans and dining-room equipment. Take note of anything which is damaged, or needs replacing. We will inspect the best dinner service ourselves, since most of it is monogrammed and irreplaceable.'

Monogrammed calling and invitation cards, stationery and a social diary arrived from a local printer that day. It reminded Geneva that Sorle had practically ordered her to introduce him to all the eligible females in the district.

'I'll give you enough eligible females to sink a ship with,' she muttered, and drew a blank sheet of paper towards her. Priscilla Hunter, she wrote at the top, and grinned.

Later that evening Geneva handed her salary to her uncle. 'I'd like to buy some new hose, if I may.'

He pushed the purse back at her. 'My dear, the money is yours to do as you wish with, since you earned it. If you can take a morning off from your duties, we will go into Dorchester together. Would you like that?'

'Thank you, Uncle. I was going to ask you to take me there anyway. What about the boys, though?'

'I'll set those rascals to weeding the vegetable patch. That should keep them employed for an hour or two. The maids will keep an eye on them. The sisters might not be able to cook, but they're good with the boys.' A smile spread across his face. 'Hannah and Essie are good workers, despite their lack of kitchen skills. We are lucky to have them.'

The atmosphere in the house was less strained now Maudine was no longer in it. 'Has there been any word from Aunt Maudine?'

'Not so far.' Her uncle cleared his throat. 'How are you coping with your new occupation, my dear?'

'Fairly easily. There is a lot of work at present, with the inventory due to start. But the house is now habitable and the household is running smoothly. I am enjoying it.'

'Lord Ashby seems impressed by your efficiency. Does he treat you well?'

She felt the blood rising under her skin. 'I have no complaints about my employer.'

Her uncle's honest brown eyes rested on her face. Immediately, her mouth began to tingle, as if Sorle's wicked little kiss was a visible sin, laid there for her uncle to observe.

'I couldn't help but notice the free and easy manner you adopt in his presence,' he said. 'He seems to encourage it.'

'It means nothing.'

'If his familiarity overstepped the bounds of good behaviour, you would tell me, wouldn't you, Geneva?'

'Good gracious, Uncle James, you're embarrassing me,' she said, and placed her hands against her blush. 'Lord Ashby is a gentleman. He wouldn't be so crass. If he was, I would strike his face so soundly he wouldn't be able to smile for a week.'

His eyes became sad. 'I hope you wouldn't go that far, Geneva. Such behaviour is unbecoming in a woman. He is our neighbour, after all, and the man is unwed.'

Geneva wondered if he was remembering Maudine striking her. 'If you're suggesting a match might occur, please put it from your mind, at once. He shows no interest in me and has made it clear that he wishes to meet every eligible girl in the district.'

The way the lies tripped so easily from her lips astounded Geneva. She was fully aware that Sorle appreciated her as a woman, but that was something she must learn to handle by herself. After all, she'd had plenty of practice with managing the opposite sex. Though, at times, Geneva wished there was an older woman she could confide in or ask advice of.

Patting her hand, her uncle grimaced as the pitter-patter of feet came from upstairs, followed by a crash and a yelp. He rose to his feet. 'That sounds very much like Bandit.'

And it was Bandit. Chased by Hannah wielding a broom, the dog streaked down the stairs and shot out through the French windows.

'Don't you come sneaking in here again, you varmint, lest

you want the mistress to chop off your tail when she comes home. The very idea, making yourself comfortable on her bed!' Hannah muttered, closing the door behind the dog. When she caught sight of them, she bobbed a curtsy. 'Dinner will be late, sir. I forgot to stoke up the fire, and the oven has cooled.'

Geneva remembered the indigestible stew they'd eaten the night before. 'If you start preparing the vegetables, I'll come and give you a hand with the dinner in a moment.'

'Thank the Lord,' the reverend muttered, for he dreaded what the sisters would do with the fish he'd brought home from the market. Two days without Maudine's cooking had made him realize how very talented his wife was in the kitchen.

The following afternoon Geneva began the monumental task of doing the inventory. This was despite several interruptions from the boys, who had followed her over to the manor. She set her cousins to music practice. With Adam acting as choirmaster and Simon at the piano, they practised the hymns chosen by their father.

Their sweet young voices brought tears to Ellen Pickering's eyes, so she had to keep mopping them with her apron. 'Lord, what sweet angels those boys are.'

Hah! Geneva thought, imagining her cousins with wings and haloes, flying about the music room.

Finally, the house fell silent. Suspicious, she placed the last delicately gilded Worcester plate gently back on the table and smiled. 'Those are in perfect condition, and can be placed back into their cabinet.'

She went in search of her cousins, finding them in the kitchen with the cook. 'I thought I'd give the poor lads something to eat, since their mother is away and they have nobody to feed them properly,' the woman said.

How the pack of them managed to look like a nest of hungry magpies was beyond Geneva's comprehension. She wanted to laugh.

'I cannot allow them to constantly dine at Lord Ashby's expense. What would he say?'

'He told me before he left. "They be growing lads. Any time they want to eat, you feed them, Cook, so they grow up

68

straight and strong. If anyone has got anything to say about it, refer them to me." Now, you draw up a seat too, Miss Tibbetson. You need to keep your energy up. I have some pasties made from lamb and vegetables, and there are some almond tarts that have just cooled, to eat with your lemonade.'

'Lord Ashby is too generous, but I must admit I'm feeling hungry after all that counting. And it's only just started.' She seated herself between Edward and Matthew, who smiled winningly at her as they waited politely for her to pick up her knife and fork, then followed suit.

Two weeks later the inventory was finished, and the house and its contents were so familiar to her she could have laid her hands on anything at a moment's notice. She had grown to know every nook and cranny of the place, too.

The weekend brought some sad news, a message from Maudine saying her father had died. Geneva attended the funeral out of respect for her cousins. She'd only met the deceased on one occasion, and had found him to be very stern.

The day was fine and warm. The dark horses drawing the two hired carriages clip-clopped sedately through the countryside, which was a delight of greenery. Wheat undulated in the fields and the hedgerows blazed with flowers of every hue.

How sad to be lowered into the cool, dark arms of the earth on such a brilliant day, Geneva thought.

Maudine gave her children a perfunctory hug. Her lips pressed together when she set eyes on Geneva. 'Since you are not a relative, I am wondering why you bothered to come.'

'Somebody needed to look after the younger children in the carriage.'

Maudine and her sister were very much alike. They darted looks of dislike at each other across the grave. The reason became apparent after the will was read. The estate had been divided between the pair, on the strict understanding that the widowed sister could live in the house.

'It's not right,' Maudine complained loudly to her husband. 'I'll be liable for half the maintenance. I think Emma should pay rent for living in my half.'

Emma Mason put her hands on her hips. 'I won't be living

in your half, only in the rooms where I've always lived.'

'You have to bear in mind that Mrs Mason cared for your father whilst he was alive, my dear,' the reverend said, a little desperately.

'I've offered to buy her half of the house,' Mrs Mason said, obviously aggrieved.

Maudine was equally aggrieved. 'And I've offered to buy your half. This house is larger than the one Reverend Batterby provided for his family. We could be housed quite comfortably in it.'

Turning Geneva's way, her uncle nodded. 'Would you and the boys kindly wait for me outside. Tell the carriage drivers I'll be just a few minutes.'

The reverend kept to his schedule, appearing on time, minus Maudine. He said calmly to the boys. 'Your mama will be staying on until she and her sister have reached agreement.'

'Was our grandfather in that box?' Edward asked Geneva on the way home.

'Yes, he was.'

'But Papa said he'd gone to heaven.'

'Only his soul. The soul lives inside your body, and when the body dies, the soul simply leaves the body and flies up into heaven.'

'I saw grandfather's soul fly up a tree,' Moth said.

Edward's eyes widened. 'What did it look like?'

'It was black and glossy. It had wings, a pointed nose and staring eyes.'

Robert laughed. 'That was a raven, silly. They live in churchyards and catch souls for the devil. Perhaps it was there to collect grandfather's soul.'

'Whoo-whoo . . .' Michael wailed. 'His ghost might come to haunt you in your bed, Moth.'

Moth turned his face against Geneva's arm, and Edward pressed against her other side. She gave the two older boys a stern look. 'That's enough, you two. You're scaring them. Besides, your papa would expect you to show proper respect for your grandfather.'

Edward gazed up at her. 'Why doesn't Mama come home? Doesn't she love us any more?'

Geneva's arms came around him and she hugged him tight.

'Of course she does. You heard your father. Your mother has to sort out estate matters with Mrs Mason.'

'You'll never leave us, will you, Gen? I couldn't bear it.'

'Not unless I have to.'

'Gen might get married one day,' Robert said.

'You can marry me, then you'll never have to leave us,' Moth offered.

'Thank you, Moth. You're too young to be married, so I think it would be better if we just remained as we are for the present.'

Edward grinned as he whispered in her ear, 'Why don't you marry the earl?'

She pretended not to hear him.

Six

Geneva had positioned her cousins along the lane.

As soon as Gerald caught sight of the Ashby carriage, he shouted the news to Matthew, who called out to Adam, who called out to Simon, and so on down the line to Michael, Robert, Edward, then Moth, who raced in an erratic and ungainly motion across the meadow fronting the manor, scattering the rabbits who'd come out to gambol in the midday sun.

Scrambling up the steps and gasping for air, Moth staggered into Geneva's sitting room, threw himself on the settee and held his side. 'They're coming, and I've got a pain from running too fast.'

'Thanks, Moth. When you've recovered, go and tell Cook the news, and ask her to give you a lemonade.'

Running into the hall, she assembled the servants with a vigorous few peals of a hand bell. They began to appear, tugging nervously at their aprons. She lined them up outside, and was joined by Tom from the stable, unconcerned by the

71

fuss and chewing on a piece of straw. The dogs, tall and hairy now, shambled after him. Spotting the rabbits, they began to bark, and raced off in haphazard circles across the meadow, their ears flapping.

'Daft buggers,' Tom muttered. 'Where do you want me to stand then, Miss Tibby?'

'With the gardeners, Tom. Where are they?'

'They'll be in the potting shed, I reckon.'

Geneva prayed for patience. 'What are they doing in the potting shed?'

'Sharing a jar of ale. 'Tis Tully's birthday.'

She felt like tearing her hair out. 'Go and tell them to come – and at once.'

Tom grinned. 'Don't you worry, Miss Tibby. I'll fetch 'em for you.'

But he wouldn't be in time, she realized when Sorle and another man, astride their mounts, came into view. Two carriages followed behind them, the first displaying the family crest, and pulled by a pair of greys. The second, hauled by matching horses, carried a couple of servants and a large amount of luggage.

As Sorle dismounted, the broad smile he sent her way set her heart skittering and jerking like a squirrel up a tree, so she couldn't keep an unladylike smile from lighting up her face as she moved forward to greet him. 'We are not quite all here, My Lord. The gardeners are celebrating Tully's birthday in the potting shed, and Tom has gone to collect them.'

'I see you had your sentries posted. Would you like us to repeat the approach so we can await the pleasure of the presence of the gardeners?'

Her smile lost a little of its shine. 'Such a notion wouldn't have occurred to me. However . . . if it pleases you, My Lord.'

He ignored her irony, raising an eyebrow as he gazed over the row of servants. 'It was not necessary to go to so much trouble on my account, you know.'

'I assure you, it wasn't on your account, My Lord. I thought your mother might like to meet the household.'

Laughter trickled from inside the carriage as the driver jumped down from his seat to open the door and lower the step. A woman in her late forties was assisted from the carriage. She was petite, fair of face and form, with a generous mouth. Her eyes were pale-blue and large, her hair a riot of light-brown curls. 'She has you there, Sorle.'

'And, as usual, has trounced me for my arrogance.'

As the woman shook the creases from her skirts, Geneva saw the dogs heading for them at a run. They'd been in the stream, for droplets of mud and water flew from their saturated bodies.

'Quick, back into the carriage!' Geneva cried. Practically throwing the woman back into her seat, she scrambled in after her.

She'd hardly closed the door behind them when the dogs leapt upon Sorle with barks of welcome. His horse shied and took off as mud was slashed across everything within range of their flaying tails.

The servants dispersed in disarray. Tom chose that time to come round the corner, the smocks of the grinning gardeners clutched in each meaty fist. 'Bugger me!' he said loudly. 'What be they ugly varmints up to?'

Dropping the gardeners, he called the animals to him and captured them by the scruffs of their necks. 'Beggin' your pardon, My Lord. I reckon they needs their shaggy arses kicking. I'll take 'em back to the stable.'

As Sorle tried to wipe the mud from his clothing, he cursed succinctly, then, allowing his manservant to take over the cleaning task, he turned narrowed eyes her way and forced out darkly, 'I beg your pardon, ladies.'

Unable to stop grinning, Geneva gave a nervous giggle. 'Unfortunately, the welcome didn't go exactly as I planned.'

'One hopes not.'

Sorle's mother laughed out loud and engaged her eyes. 'Actually, I quite enjoyed it. I'm Sarah Ashby and I've heard a lot about you, Miss Tibbetson. I believe I'm going to like you.'

'Like her or not, mother, if this sort of thing carries on, I'm likely to put her over my knee and beat the bounce out of her before the day is over,' Sorle growled.

Just then her cousins turned up, leading Rastus, Sorle's big black horse. Moth came from the house to greet them. Swallowing the remains of a tart he'd collected on his detour to the kitchen, he paused on the step to wipe his hands on his trousers. His eyes rounded like saucers when his glance fell on Sorle. 'Muttering mud balls! You're a sorry looking sight, Lord Ashby!' he exclaimed.

'You have a talent for alliteration,' Sorle said drily, and his mouth twitched into a smile as he gazed at Moth. Then he turned his head and caught Geneva's eyes. As they exchanged a glance, she collapsed into giggles and Sorle began to roar with laughter.

'Your Miss Tibbetson is an efficient young lady, despite appearances to the contrary. Your household is up and running well. I find it extraordinary that she gave me the same chambers I used when your father and I visited your uncle, just before we married. Some of the furnishings have been replaced, so it looks feminine and fresh. She has also placed flowers on the tables, which was thoughtful of her, for it adds fragrance.'

'Miss Tibbetson is a tiresome creature who provokes me beyond measure,' Sorle grumbled, gazing through his glass. Sarah noticed he was smiling though.

'But you like her?'

'Geneva is interesting. She's the poor relation of the Reverend Batterby. Her aunt is a harpy and Gen seems to have sole charge of her eight cousins.'

In the space of a couple of breaths, Sorle had progressed from Miss Tibbetson down to the informal, Gen. Sarah raised an eyebrow and insisted, 'You *do* like her, don't you?'

His eyes slid towards her and he grinned. 'Yes, I like her, but don't read anything into it. She's hardly more than a child.'

'I cannot believe you've overlooked her charms.'

'I have overlooked nothing about her. She has no fortune, no breeding, and hardly any social skills. And if today's little drama was anything to go by, she is also insane.' He swallowed his drink and lumbered to his feet. 'I'm going to check on the horses. Henry said he thought Rastus was a bit lame.'

'And I'm going to retire. Goodnight, Sorle.'

He kissed her gently on the cheek. 'Goodnight, Mother. Sweet dreams.' He strolled off towards the door, looking more happy and relaxed than he had in a long time.

* * *

74

The groom was still in the stables. 'Is everything all right, Henry?'

'Yes, My Lord. Your mount has loosened a shoe. Tom will take him to the blacksmith in the morning.

Tom touched a finger to his cap. 'That I will, My Lord.'

The dogs came to lean against Sorle's legs. Absently, he scratched their ears. He'd never seen dogs quite like these gangly creatures, but at least they'd been washed and brushed. And they had amiable natures.

'Stunk to high heaven, they did.' Tom grinned. 'But I guessed you knowed that. A right carry on, that was. It amused Miss Tibby though. It doesn't take much to make her laugh.'

'What are the dogs' names?'

'Can't rightly say they have any. I call them ugly varmints.'

Sorle grinned at that, for it wasn't far from the truth. But he couldn't wait to see Geneva's face when she found out. 'They've got names now. We'll call one Florin and the other Shilling. And I must teach them some manners before they get completely out of hand.'

He walked off and the dogs followed him back to the house. 'Sit,' he said as they reached the door. They gazed up at him and wagged their tails. '*Sit.*' He pushed down on their haunches and they sat.

'Stay,' he said, walking into the house. He turned to find the dogs behind him. 'I thought I told you to stay?'

They sat and gazed up at him. Florin had one ear cocked upwards and his head to one side, as if awaiting instructions. Shilling had his tongue hanging out the side and seemed to be smiling. Sorle laughed. 'You're not entirely dumb, and that was not too bad for a first lesson. I shall soon make aristocrats out of you.'

Collecting the social diary from Geneva's sitting room, he carried it through to his study, poured himself another brandy and, with the dogs at his feet, opened it.

Shock filled him when he looked over his engagements.

'But I only carried out your instructions, My Lord,' Geneva said the next day, making her eyes all round and innocent. 'The invitations have been accepted, and all the mamas and their daughters are having fine gowns made for the occasion.'

He had taken care with his appearance, wearing a grey striped waistcoat under a blue cutaway jacket, and grey trousers braided at the side, tucked into short boots. His stock was immaculate. Yet she didn't even afford him a glance when he said, 'I didn't expect to separately entertain thirty-three spinsters and their mamas.'

'It's halfway through August. You will only have to entertain two eligible girls a week between here and the ball. I've made afternoon appointments, so you can arrange your other activities around them. By the time the Christmas ball comes, you'll have some idea of which of them you intend to wed.'

'Perhaps I'll not wed any of them,' he said, his voice as grave as his expression.

She gave him a quick, searching glance, then shuffled through the invitations. There are several dinner invitations and a request that you speak to the local Literary and Philosophical Society next week.'

'Speak about what?'

'Philosophy and literature, I suppose.'

'I know nothing about philosophy. Decline it.

'Your uncle started the society, I believe, and Reverend Batterby is a member. Not that I'm attempting to pressure you in any way, of course.'

'Of course. You would not do anything so utterly aggravating, Miss Tibbetson.' He gave a martyred sigh. 'There must be something in the library I can study on the subject. Accept, but suggest a later date so I have time to prepare.'

'The squire extends an invitation for you to join the hunt.'

'That, I will accept with more pleasure.'

She nodded. 'The Reverend Batterby has requested that you read the lesson in church next Sunday.'

'Can't he read it himself?'

'Attendances have been low lately. He thinks your presence might change that.'

Sorle chuckled. 'I'm not the second coming.'

'You are to him. Your appearance amongst us enabled the organ to be repaired. Apart from the church and his children, music is the great love of my uncle's life. Because of your generous gesture, he can resurrect the choir.' She looked troubled. 'I told him you'd probably decline.'

'That was rather presumptuous of you.' Was that a gleam of triumph in her eyes? He went to sit on the couch beside her, shoved the papers aside and took her hands in his. A fragrance of rose water lingered about her. 'You're trying to make a fool of me, Gen.'

Her eyes damned him. 'And you didn't intend to make a fool of me by calling the dogs Florin and Shilling?'

A grin flirted around his mouth. 'I've grown very fond of those animals. They'll be good companions once they're trained. 'Do *you* want me to read the lesson?'

'My uncle is a good man, with a kind heart. I don't want to see him disappointed.'

'Is it so hard to answer my question without diversion?'

She drew in a breath, trying not to giggle. 'No, it's not hard at all. You have a delightful rumbling voice, which commands attention. Truly, I would love to hear you read the lesson.'

A compliment? He grinned and tightened his hold on her hands. She must be warming to him. 'Then I'll do it for you. I appreciate what you've done here for me.'

Her hair shone, as if threaded with the sunlight coming through the window. Her eyes were blue and wide and, for a moment or two, her mouth was sensuous and wanton.

He thought: *You have no idea of the passion hidden inside you, Geneva Tibbetson. Happy the man you sacrifice your innocence to, for once he unlocks it he'll be your slave for the rest of his life.* Perhaps that man would be himself. All he had to do was lean forward and—

Adam said from the doorway. 'It it alright if Simon and I still use the music room to practise, Lord Ashby?'

Letting go of her hands, Sorle rose casually to his feet. 'I'm sure the piano will be all the better for the exercise, but it might prove convenient to set a certain time for this activity each day. Discuss it with Miss Tibbetson, who will then inform me.'

Now Sorle and his mother were in residence, her cousins would not have such freedom of access. For that, Geneva was pleased.

'I'm about to take my mother into Dorchester, Miss Tibbetson. She's waiting in the drawing room and has suggested you might like to accompany us. Since she's not been there before, perhaps you'd be kind enough to show her around whilst I conduct some business at the bank.'

'Thank you, I should love to. I have a florin in my purse, which should cover my purchases.

'A florin,' he said incredulously. 'What on earth can you buy with such a paltry sum?'

Her eyes sharpened and her smile had a mocking edge to it. 'Why ... two dogs, of course, sir. I'd be obliged if you'd transfer the first florin into your own pocket, as I have no wish to be indebted to you or have the possibility of a prison term hanging over my head. Excuse me while I fetch my hat and shawl.'

He'd had himself to blame for walking into that trap and could only grin as she walked away. 'You have mortally wounded me, Geneva.'

'Since I've always admired you for your invincible quality, I doubt it,' she flung over her shoulder – a remark which pleased him mightily for some reason.

Geneva enjoyed the ride into Dorchester. Sorle drove the phaeton at what seemed to be a fast pace, but then, she was more used to the middle-aged gait of her uncle's mare.

Sarah Ashby didn't seem perturbed by the speed at all, just hung on to the rail with one hand, and to her hat with the other. Geneva relaxed and did likewise as the countryside sped by, but since she was seated between them, she was obliged to take Sorle's arm instead. He turned his head for a moment, his smile causing the disturbing darkness of his eyes to lighten. She ignored the tiresome instinct to lay her face against his arm.

Just before they navigated the bridge and passed Saint George's Church on their left, Sorle slowed the rig to compensate for the increased traffic.

Dorchester bustled with people and animals, for it was market day. There was a country aroma of sheep and cattle in the air. Stallholders competed with each other to sell their wares, and members of the Dorset Yeomanry regiment shouldered through the crowds in their smart uniforms.

Sorle managed to find a place to leave the rig, and a lad willing to water his horse and guard it until their return. He assisted his mother to alight, then, when Geneva was about to clamber down, he took her by the waist and swung her to land lightly upon her feet.

They parted company, agreeing to meet in one hour outside the town hall.

Sarah took her arm as they strolled amongst the crowd.

'If I may say so, you hardly look old enough to be a mother to Lord Ashby,' Geneva ventured.

She smiled at that. 'I was only seventeen when Sorle was born, and barely married a year. He has his father's dark looks. The Ashbys are descended from a privateer who married his Spanish captive. That's where the fortune came from in the first place, I'm afraid. It was stolen from the Spanish.' She gave a tiny, breathless laugh. 'I understand you are Joseph Tibbetson's daughter.'

Geneva gazed with interest at her. 'Did you know him?'

'He and his wife dined with us on a couple of occasions. It was so sad when he died, for he was an interesting and well-read man, and well thought of in certain circles. I was sorry to hear your mother had passed on, too. You must miss her.'

'I can hardly remember her, for she was ill for a long time before she died. Most of my childhood was spent with my cousins.'

'A wasting disease is such a cruel way to die. I gather Mary was in such pain she was unable to care for you, which is why she handed you over to the Reverend Batterby. It must have been hard for her when she parted with you, knowing she'd never see you again. And to die in an impoverished state! Though she was not entirely alone, at least. I heard that your uncle hired a woman to see to her needs, and he and Mrs Batterby were with her at the end.'

Geneva gazed at her in shock. 'But I was told my mother . . . Are you sure it was a wasting disease?'

'Of course. Mary had an incurable growth inside her.' They drew to a halt and Sarah gazed at her. 'You're trembling. What is it, what have I said to upset you?'

'I understood that my mother died from drinking too much spirituous liquor.'

'My dear, that is simply not true.' Sarah's head slanted to

79

one side. 'It's possible she became addicted to the laudanum, since she took it in increasing doses to help ease the terrible pain she suffered. Somebody may have mistaken her state for one of drunkenness. You should ask your uncle about this.' Sarah took Geneva's hand in hers. 'Let's abandon this sad conversation and go into that shop over there. They have some interesting haberdashery in the window. Didn't you say you wanted to buy some ribbons for your hair?'

She hadn't, but Sarah had changed the subject so adroitly, Geneva was obliged to follow her into the shop. Once in there, she found herself fascinated by the many pretty adornments on display, whilst Sarah went off to inspect some gloves.

It was there Maudine came across her. She entered from the bright street into the dim interior of the shop panting slightly, as if she'd been hurrying. There was a determined look on her face. 'Ah, I thought it was you. You've come here to waste your money on frippery, no doubt. And who is looking after my sons, pray?'

'The reverend is, though Adam and Simon were at the manor practising their music when I left there.'

'So, you're taking advantage of my husband's kind nature to neglect my children. Lord Ashby must still be absent. I wonder what he'll say when he learns you're taking time off from your paid duties.'

'Hush, Aunt Maudine,' Geneva begged, desperately casting her gaze to where Sarah stood. But her back was turned towards them.

'You would tell your benefactor to hush?' Maudine said more loudly. 'You ungrateful creature. I warned my husband about the bad blood you inherited from your parents.'

Sarah turned. 'Pray, what bad blood might that be, madam?'

Clearly taken aback, Maudine stammered, 'I beg your pardon . . . and who are you to enquire into a private matter between myself and my husband's relative?'

'I'm Lord Ashby's mother, and, since you are uttering untruths about Miss Tibbetson's parents, who were dear friends of mine and are no longer here to defend their good name, I must insist that you apologize immediately.'

Maudine's mouth fell open and she twittered, 'I'm sorry . . . I had no idea Lord Ashby was taking up residence so soon.

I do beg your pardon, Mrs Ashby. I'm Maudine Batterby, the reverend's wife. Geneva, why didn't you introduce us right away? I was referring to the disease Mary died from, not casting aspersions upon her character.'

'I rather thought you were, since you stormed into the premises and attacked my companion in an unpleasant manner and without provocation.'

Maudine placed a hand against her throat and closed her eyes for a moment. 'The weather is sultry and has brought on one of my dreadful headaches.'

'Dreadful indeed, when one's afflictions are allowed to gain the upper hand.'

Geneva began to feel sorry for Maudine. 'I'm sure my aunt didn't mean it, Mrs Ashby. She was enquiring about her sons, and spoke hastily.'

'Her sons? Ah yes, I've met them. Such dear, well-mannered boys on the whole. They seem to take after their father.'

Maudine's face turned the colour of beetroot.

Having obtained the last word, a trait obviously inherited by her son, Sarah turned her back on Maudine and smiled. 'I'll be looking at those pretty hats, Miss Tibbetson. Do join me as soon as possible. Your advice would be greatly appreciated.'

Sarah Ashby was formidable when she was angered, Geneva thought in surprise.

Her bosom heaving with embarrassment, for the conversation had been overheard by Mrs Pringle, a member of the Edgley Church Ladies Committee, Maudine mumbled, 'Perhaps you'd ask Reverend Batterby to collect me from my father's house as soon as possible, for the estate matter with my sister has been settled.'

'Satisfactorily, I hope, Aunt?'

The smile Maudine gave her had a chagrined look to it, but since her aunt rarely smiled at her these days, it was an improvement. 'Ah yes, my dear. We've devised a solution which suits both parties. Good day, Mrs Ashby,' she called out. 'I look forward to meeting you on a more auspicious occasion, perhaps when my health has improved.'

Sarah, inspecting a hat, affected not to hear. Maudine left the shop followed by the titters of Mrs Pringle and her eldest daughter, Arabella.

81

Mrs Pringle advanced on them, a determined smile on her face, obliging Geneva to introduce them. Afterwards, the woman said, 'Perhaps you and Lord Ashby would grace us with your presence at a card evening tomorrow.'

'Unfortunately we've only just arrived, so are not accepting any invitations immediately. However, I believe you've been invited to take refreshment with myself and my son next week. Is that not so, Miss Tibbetson?'

'Yes, Mrs Ashby, on Friday afternoon.'

'Until then, Mrs Pringle. I shall look forward to meeting you and your delightful daughter again.' Paying for the few trinkets which had taken her fancy, Sarah nodded and swept from the shop, leaving Geneva to follow.

Sarah linked arms with her when they stood outside. Forthrightly, she said. 'Has your aunt always been so unpleasant to you?'

Geneva could remember a time when Maudine hadn't been quite so disagreeable, but as more and more children had arrived, her patience had deserted her. 'I'm grateful for the home she and my uncle provided for me. Mrs Batterby has not been well of late, which accounts for her irritability. Her headaches are sometimes quite severe. Even though I do my best to help her, with eight sons to rear it's only natural she should regard me as an extra responsibility and resent it.'

'You're a thoughtful girl, Geneva. She doesn't deserve you. I think I shall try to avoid her.'

'I beg you not to, Mrs Ashby,' Geneva said with some alarm. 'Mrs Batterby has a position to uphold in the community. To avoid her would embarrass her husband and sons and place them in the untenable position of having to take sides.'

'And you, my dear. How would you feel?'

'Saddened. After all, you have not properly met Mrs Batterby yet. Although she may prove to be a little tedious, she is as tolerable as the next person.'

Sarah nodded. 'You're right. For you, I'll reserve my judgement until we are better acquainted. Look, there's Sorle. Who is he talking too?'

'It's Squire Hunter. His wife and daughter Priscilla are first on the list of people Lord Ashby indicated he wished to meet before the Christmas ball.'

The gurgle of laughter Sarah gave was accompanied by a probing look. 'You were rather naughty there, my dear. Don't be surprised if Sorle turns the tables on you in some way.'

The look of innocence Geneva tried to assume dissolved into laughter. 'I don't know what you mean, Mrs Ashby.'

'You most certainly do. Entertaining young ladies of marriageable age irks Sorle no end. I've introduced him to every eligible woman I can think of, and to no avail. Which reminds me, we must send out the invitations to the ball, since some people will be coming from neighbouring counties, and some from as far away as London. We'll have to cater for overnight guests, too.'

'Welford has plenty of rooms and linen enough for the beds. We'll have to hire some temporary staff for the occasion though.'

'Our household staff will come down from London. They're used to catering for large parties. We might have difficulty finding an orchestra for the dancing hereabouts, though.'

'Mrs Batterby told me the squire hires a fine orchestra to entertain his guests on occasion.'

'Then I'll ask his wife about it on Tuesday.'

Just then Sorle looked their way. Exchanging a handshake with the squire, he dodged between the horses and carts to get across the road to them. He gazed from one to the other, smiling. 'Would you like to come to the horse sales before we go to the tea room for refreshment? There's a mare I'm interested in and the bidding starts in ten minutes.'

'Take Geneva with you,' Sarah said. 'I have very little interest in horses and intend to investigate the dressmaker's establishment. We passed the tea rooms a little while ago. I'll meet you there.'

'Well, Miss Tibbetson?' Sorle said, as his mother walked off into the crowd, and extended his arm. 'Will you join me at the auction? It's but a short stroll.'

Shyly, she placed her hand on his arm, trying to hide the darns in her glove as they made their way towards the auction ring. The stench of massed horses ripened the air in the warm sunshine and her nose wrinkled.

Handing her his handkerchief, Sorle grinned. 'Use this if it becomes too much.'

'Which one is your horse?'

'She's standing next to the grey in that stall.'

Geneva saw a dark bay with a dirty, tangled tail and her ribs pressing against her coat. She slid Sorle a glance. 'Are you sure you know what you're doing? She looks as if a good meal wouldn't go amiss.'

'Several good meals, in fact. But she's young and comes from good bloodstock. I should pick her up cheaply.'

There were no other bidders, so, as predicted, Sorle paid very little for her.

The horse-trader told him, 'She's a nice-looking mare, and was abandoned and left to starve with her dam. There's not much call for fancy stock around here, but she should suit the lady once she's in condition.'

'That she should,' Sorle said. 'You mentioned the dam. Where is she?'

'Waiting for a bid from the knacker. She's in a worse condition.'

'Will you sell her to me?'

The horse-trader shrugged. 'It's your money. I'll fetch her out and put them together. I'd be obliged if you'd collect them before two, for I'll be moving on then.'

Geneva didn't want to move away when she saw the mother, a painfully thin black horse with her backbone ridging through the flesh. When the pair were reunited, they huddled together for comfort, making whickering noises as Sorle talked to the horse-trader. Money changed hands and he came to where she stood.

Tears came to her eyes. 'Can we find the poor beasts something to eat?'

'Not until we get them back to the Welford stables, since it might cause them distress. My head groom will know what to do.'

'Why would you want to buy a horse in such feeble condition, Sorle?'

He grinned, but whether it was because she'd slipped up and called him by his first name, or because he was about to astonish himself as well as her, she couldn't tell. 'If she survives, I intend to enter her in the Dorsetshire Gold Cup next July, that's why.'

There was a short silence, then she said, 'It's a four-mile race. If she recovers, can she win it?'

'Against the stallions? It's a long shot, but I wouldn't contemplate it if I didn't think so.'

'And what makes you think so?'

'I've seen her run.'

Seven

September was a busy month, as the last of the corn crop was harvested and stacked on stone staddles to prevent it from rotting. The weather had remained fair into autumn. The sheep were penned and being fattened on the lush grasses growing where the meadow lands had been flooded.

Maudine Batterby had returned to her husband's house. The parting from her children had brought benefits to both parties. Her ever-hungry chicks welcomed her back with open arms and rumbling stomachs and eagerly awaited each meal. Maudine, basking in a sense of being needed, expressed pity for her sister, who had no children of her own.

'Emma is lonely,' Maudine told her husband. 'We've agreed. When she dies, her estate will be willed to me, or to my children.' She didn't tell him of the other matter, regarding Geneva, for the approach must be made from her sister directly to her husband.

Her relationship with Geneva became one of toleration. Maudine had realized that the girl was held in great affection by her family. Although she couldn't bring herself to praise Geneva, she admitted to herself that the girl never did anything wrong. But even so, she intended to break the hold Geneva had over her sons if she could.

The presence of two hardworking maids who pandered to Maudine's needs made life a little easier for her. She made the older one her ally. Hannah, her manipulative nature recognizing the need to insinuate herself into her mistress's good books, reported back to her anything they overheard.

It helped too, that Geneva spent every day at Welford, usually with one or two of her cousins in attendance. Had she been at home, she would have noticed Maudine's interest every time a letter arrived, and her sense of waiting, and would have wondered about it.

At Welford Manor, Miss Priscilla Hunter and her mother were the first to enjoy Sorle's hospitality.

Priscilla was acknowledged to be the beauty of the district, with her grey eyes and dark hair. Her figure was well proportioned, her complexion flawless. The gown and shawl she wore were blue. Frills decorated her embroidered apron, the hem of her gown, her sleeves, her shawl and her parasol. Her little straw hat was adorned with stuffed bluebirds, which nodded as she walked. Her imagination substituting a couple of chickens, Geneva found it hard not to laugh when Priscilla twittered. 'I'm so happy to make your acquaintance, Lord Ashby.'

Sorle's glance wandered assessingly over Priscilla before he turned to her mother. 'Welcome to my home, Mrs Hunter. Miss Hunter. Shall we go into the drawing room and wait for my mother to join us?'

Mrs Hunter's assortment of clucks passed as an affirmative, and caused Sorle's eyes to slide Geneva's way.

Geneva smiled artlessly at him. 'I'll send the housekeeper in with some refreshments, My Lord.'

'Mrs Pickering is busy. Bring them to the drawing room yourself, Miss Tibbetson.'

'But I have some arrangements to—'

He placed a finger across her lips and his expression had something of the predator about it. 'I'd prefer it if you didn't argue with me all the time, Miss Tibbetson. My guests can't be expected to serve themselves, so your other tasks can wait.'

She expelled her breath against his finger in a hiss. It gave him cause to withdraw it rapidly, as if he'd expected her to bite it, something she'd considered.

Priscilla offered Sorle her sweetest smile. Ignoring Geneva completely, she, along with her frills and bluebirds, swept regally into the drawing room after her mother.

Geneva had the feeling the tea party was going to be an ordeal – and it was. It was not that she minded waiting on Mrs Hunter and Priscilla, for she'd done so on occasion when they'd visited Mrs Batterby.

But now they knew she was employed, it was different, and Priscilla made sure Geneva was aware that her status had changed when Geneva asked her, 'Would you like a slice of cake, Priscilla?'

'Perhaps you could inform your staff to address me correctly,' Priscilla said to Sorle with excruciating sweetness.

And to think Priscilla had cheated at school by copying her answers.

Sorle sent a grave glance her way. 'You're aware of how to address a guest in my home, are you not, Miss Tibbetson?'

Arrogant Lord! So that was how it was going to be. A warm glow centred in her cheeks. 'Since Miss Hunter and I attended school together, up until now we have habitually addressed each other by our first names. However, since you request it, My Lord . . .' Geneva bobbed a curtsy. 'I most humbly beg your pardon, Miss Hunter.'

Priscilla's bluebirds bobbed as she nodded her head in regal fashion. After she finished serving the women, Geneva took a seat by the wall until they needed something more.

That was often, and they soon had her dashing back and forth.

The two women prattled incessantly. Priscilla seemed to have swallowed a bowl full of affectations. Her eyelids fluttered, her hands described limp arcs in the air and her laughter was as shrill as a frisky mare exercising its voice in the morning.

Sorle's smile began to freeze into position, his eyes glazed over a little as Priscilla took the floor once again, and he gazed desperately at the door as if wishing his mama would arrive to rescue him. Geneva grinned to herself as she gazed at the clock. And, of course, Sarah would arrive in exactly five minutes.

'I saw Arabella Pringle yesterday. She'd just come back from her music lesson. She sings dreadfully out of tune. Such a shame when one has no accomplishments.'

'You should sing for Lord Ashby,' Geneva suggested, gazing

87

at the harpsichord standing in the corner. 'I'd be quite happy to accompany you.'

'Oh, what a good idea,' Mrs Hunter said in a jolly voice, as if it hadn't occurred to them before.

Priscilla's nose went up in the air. 'My mother is capable of accompanying me, Geneva.'

'Servants are usually addressed by their last names, so you may call me Tibbetson if that's more comfortable for you,' she told Priscilla gently.

A strangled sound came from Sorle, but he covered it with a cough as the two women stood. Priscilla's daintily floating hand hit a cup, sending tea spilling across the table.

Hand against her heart, she gazed with helpless feminine entreaty at Sorle. 'Oh, I'm so exceedingly clumsy, My Lord.'

Sorle was boringly and predictably gallant. 'Not at all. Tibbetson will clean it up, won't you, Tibbetson?'

'Certainly, My Lord. Would you like me to polish your shoes as well?'

His frown was a classic. 'Polish my shoes?'

'Yes, My Lord. Some of the tea is dripping on them.'

His lips twitched. 'You needn't bother, I can manage for myself.' Taking out his handkerchief, as he bent over to deal with it, he whispered. 'Go and see what the devil's keeping my mother.'

Sarah had timed it to perfection, for she chose that moment to sweep in. Her glance went around the room and she smiled. 'Geneva, my dear, I wondered where you were. Ah, Mrs Hunter. How lovely to see you again. And your charming daughter. Were you about to entertain us? How wonderful. Please go ahead, we can talk afterwards.'

When Mrs Hunter opened the harpsichord, a mouse scurried out, leapt to the floor and dashed across the carpet to disappear into a hole in the wainscotting. Mrs Hunter gave a terrified scream. Priscilla took a hasty step backwards and tripped over a stool. Drawn by the noise, Florin and Shilling came dashing through the open door to investigate. The smell of food took precedence over their hunting instincts, and their tongues swept over the plates to scoop cake into their mouths, whilst their tails lashed the china, scattering everything across the floor.

All was pandemonium for a while, and the two guests were almost in hysterics until Sarah managed to calm them down. Grabbing the dogs, Sorle dragged them from the room and shut the door on them while Geneva cleaned up the mess. Sarah continued to placate the guests.

Afterwards, Geneva dared not look at Sorle when she enquired, 'Will you be needing me again, My Lord?'

'I rather think not, Tibbetson. You've done enough for one day.'

Sorle was still apologizing to his guests when Geneva left the room carrying the heavy tray. She handed it directly to a hovering maid to convey back to the kitchen, and turned back to press her ear against the door panel, her shoulders shaking with repressed laughter.

'A unfortunate set of circumstances, ladies. I cannot apologize enough. A drop of brandy for medicinal purposes, then, when you're recovered, I'll ask your coachman to convey you home.'

But the matron of the duo had different ideas. 'Thank you, but neither of us imbibes spirituous liquor, My Lord. In fact, my daughter and I are recovered enough to enjoy your hospitality a little longer. We did promise you some music, didn't we, Priscilla?'

'Yes, Mama.'

The harpsichord behaved valiantly except for a couple of clunking notes, but, although Priscilla sang in tune and with great enthusiasm, her voice was decidedly shrill.

Offering each other a glance, the dogs aimed their snouts at the ceiling and set up a mournful howl. The music suddenly stopped. Grabbing the animals, Geneva dragged them away into her sitting room, where they escaped through the windows into the garden and began to wrestle with each other. She collapsed on to a chair and began to laugh uncontrollably, especially when the music started all over again and Priscilla managed a false start.

Sorle sought her out an hour later. He gazed suspiciously at her. 'You didn't put that mouse in the harpsichord on purpose, did you?'

The dogs, now lying at her feet, opened their eyes at the sound of his voice and flapped a languid tail apiece.

She turned to him, her eyes widening. 'Are you about to blame that debacle on me?'

Dropping into a chair, a brandy held in his hand, he sighed. 'I suppose imagining you trained the Welford mice to frighten local matrons is a little far-fetched.'

'I didn't let the dogs in,' she pointed out, as the pair casually rose, stretched, then went through some canine ritual of turning round three times before depositing themselves at their master's feet.

'No, you didn't.' He grinned as his eyes met hers, and fondled the pair's heads. 'They were in fine voice, weren't they?'

'Oh, was it them singing? I imagined it was you who was performing a duet with Priscilla.'

'I admit it, the dogs and I do have similar voices.' He chuckled. 'I am now in the position of having to write Mrs Hunter a letter of abject apology.' He stood and strolled to the window to look out at the lengthening shadows. The evening still held some warmth and the air was filled with flying insects. 'The leaves are turning. It's been a good summer.'

'Yes. The harvest has been an exceptionally good one. Do you think you'll be happy living here, Sorle?'

'Eventually.' He turned to gaze at her, a half smile on his face. 'You know, Gen, I don't think this idea of yours to find me a wife is a good one.'

'As I recall, it was your idea, and you were quite adamant about it.'

'You know very well you goaded me into it.'

'As certain as I am that you'd never allow me to goad you into doing anything.'

That made him chuckle. 'You'd be surprised how easily you're able to goad me. You have a knack of out-thinking me, knowing exactly how I'm going to react. I blame that on your upbringing. Your cousins' influence is very apparent, in that you lack female artifice.'

Geneva didn't know whether she liked his assessment. 'Are you saying that I am unfeminine?'

He grinned. 'How can you be when you look like an angel, behave like the devil's handmaiden and don't give a fig for what anyone thinks of you? I'm saying you don't know how to use your femininity to your own ends.'

'Ah.' Lifting her hand she waved it limply under his nose and fluttered her eyelashes at him. 'Like this, you mean.'

He took her hand and kissed her knuckles before she was able to snatch it away. 'Something a little more subtle, perhaps. You should encourage a man, flirt with him, let him know you like him a little.'

'Then how would you get rid of him if you met another man you liked better?'

'In society, men expect to be rejected. Love is a game.'

'You consider it a game to encourage a man's most tender feelings then cruelly reject him?'

'A man's most tender feelings are not always in his heart, Gen.'

She felt her colour rise. 'Ah, but now you are not talking of love. Isn't it best not to encourage a man at all when his intentions may be different to what he leads a woman to expect? And when that man is clearly above her in status, what hope may she then have but to be brought so low that every man – or woman come to that – will turn aside from her?'

'An interesting point. You've been well warned against the vices, I see. Perhaps too much Bible study in your youth.'

'It's a conversation I have no desire to pursue.' Picking up her shawl, she said more formally, 'Farewell, Lord Ashby. When I see you in church on Sunday I shall hope the lesson you have chosen is one that has given you occasion to reflect on your sins.'

'Reflecting on sin gives me much pleasure, since sinning is one of my favourite pastimes. When I look at you, I cannot see your pious little soul. When you laugh, I feel the warmth you show in your eyes. When you chide me, I want to lay my head against your hand to be comforted. When you look upon me with pleasure in your eyes, I want to reward you, and when you challenge me, I want to prove to you that I'm your master.'

'But you're not my master and, since I see no wisdom in encouraging you in such thinking, I shall no longer laugh, chide you, nor look upon you with pleasure.'

'But you'll continue to challenge me, will you not?'

'Alas, challenging people is one of my worst faults. I cannot promise to eliminate that, for it's something that's part of me

91

in a life where I'm dependent on others. I will not allow you to master me under any circumstances.'

'Thank God, for you'd then be as well trained as a man's hound, and as bland as a bowl of oatmeal.'

'May I remind you that your hounds will be a legend in Edgley by nightfall and, to the needy, a bowl of oatmeal is a banquet.'

'My hounds are too young to have gained sense, so cannot be blamed. You have a barb for a tongue, Tibbetson,' he grumbled, and, taking the shawl from her hands, he draped it about her, holding her by its ends. 'Allow me to kiss the nonsense from your lips.'

She was laughing as she gazed into the enigma of darkness his eyes held for her. 'I will allow you no such liberty.'

'Ah, Gen, then I must steal it, since, for all your protests, you're plainly a woman who needs to be conquered. Haven't your instincts led me to the point of doing so, quite knowingly?'

'Sorle Ashby, not only do you twist my words to suit your purpose, you arrogantly overrate your attraction. Release me, this minute, sir.'

A chuckle tore from his throat. 'You're not struggling, my Gen, and your eyes are so full of laughter you know you have me at your mercy. I believe you want to be kissed.'

He believed right. She only had to take one step forward and she would be enfolded in his arms. She stopped the tiny involuntary movement that would make her take that step. More kisses would follow until her good sense was drowned in them, until her passions were so inflamed he would take advantage of her fevered state.

She could feel them inside her skin, furtive little prickles and scurries that sensitized her breasts so they thrust, full of want, against her bodice. And she felt it in her groin, making her moist, so she wanted to press herself against him and accept the hardness of him into her. Geneva knew what the act of love consisted of. The desiring of it made her feel gloriously alive so she knew no fear, just the excitement of savouring the unknown.

No other man was so attractive to her, and she longed to give him all of herself. He was right, she did want him to conquer her. She closed her eyes and, giving in to the pressure of the shawl against her back, swayed forward, feeling as if her heart was about to leap from her chest.

Their mouths were hardly a heartbeat apart when there came the pattering sound of footsteps across the hall. 'Damn it!' Sorle dropped the edges of her shawl and took a step back as the door swung open and Sarah came in.

She gazed from one to the other. 'Ah, so here you are, Sorle. Geneva, you're looking quite flushed, my dear. I do hope Sorle hasn't been chastising you for that little scene this afternoon. Who would have thought a tiny mouse could cause such mischief.'

'Of course I haven't chastised Geneva. I've been trying to talk her out of this silly idea of finding me a wife. We have been debating the issue ever since, which has afforded me much entertainment, since she's quite determined that being wed will save me from myself.'

'It most certainly will, and if Geneva succeeds where I have failed, I will be eternally grateful to her.'

'Hmmm, it may be that I'll allow her to succeed. I was just about to walk the dogs and escort her home at the same time. Did you want me for anything in particular, Mother, apart from aiding Geneva in her plan for my downfall?'

'I intend to visit Mrs Hunter tomorrow morning to personally apologize for what happened, and you must send them a small token apiece, a posy perhaps. I saw an establishment in Edgley which sells floral arrangements. I intend to issue an invitation to the squire and his family to dine with us in the evening.'

'Won't a written apology suffice?'

'Certainly not. You may personally sign the card to present with the flowers, and the apology will be taken as offered. The incident may have amused us all, but it embarrassed them both dreadfully. And you must make sure those dogs are secured out of earshot when they're here.'

'They were just being dogs.'

Florin and Shilling gave twin yawns, feigning indifference as they looked up at Sorle and huffed impatiently. 'Alright, we're going. After you, Miss Tibbetson. I hope we can resume our interesting conversation on the way to your home.'

Something her expression told him she wasn't exactly enamoured of.

But Sorle was thwarted in that too, when Gerald was discovered waiting outside.

'I've come to escort my cousin home, Lord Ashby.'

Sorle swore under his breath. 'I'll walk part of the way with you if you don't mind, Gerald.' And he did, talking pleasantly of general topics such as his dogs or his horses, and being kept at a safe distance by Gerald, who, whether by accident or design, walked between them.

Sorle offered her a wry grin as they parted at the stile. 'Good day, Miss Tibbetson. Gerald. Please give my regards to your parents.' He turned and strode away, the dogs at his heels.

Stimulated by his earlier encounter, Sorle smiled to himself as he headed back to Welford. Geneva was no fool. As soon as he advanced a step, she managed to retreat one, though, if his mother hadn't come along at that very moment, she would have allowed him the liberty of a kiss, he was sure.

Priscilla Hunter came into his mind and he frowned as he remembered the way she'd snubbed Geneva. Miss Hunter was fair of face, with a form bordering on perfection. That was a plus. As a minus, she had plenty of airs but hardly any graces and was shrill and self-aware. Put to the test, he thought he might be able to enjoy her body, but he couldn't imagine facing her over the breakfast table every morning for the rest of his life.

'Miss Hunter has no sense of humour,' he said to the dogs. 'Geneva would have made light of such a mishap, not suffered the vapours.' In fact, she'd laughed as soon as she'd thought she was out of earshot. When he'd gone out to rescue the dogs from the excruciating tone of Priscilla's singing, he'd pressed an ear against the panel of the door to her sitting room and she'd been laughing uncontrollably.

He grinned, until he remembered there were over thirty of her hand-picked candidates waiting to be entertained. 'Thirty!' His grin departed as he thought of the ordeals ahead. He must think of something to extricate himself.

Stopping off at the stables, he gazed at his latest acquisitions. Was it his imagination, or were the beasts acquiring a little gloss and brightness of eye? He stroked the older mare's nose. She'd once been owned by William Sedgewick. Sedgewick had fled the country to avoid debtors' prison, and his horses had been turned out into a field by the departing groom to fend for themselves. Sedgewick had died intestate and his estate had been seized by the Crown to pay his debts.

'She be looking a bit livelier, I reckon,' Tom said, coming up behind him. 'It'll take time to put some flesh on her bones, though. And damn me if those carriage horses of yours haven't taken a liking to her, too. A right pair of princesses they be, tossing their heads, snorting and demanding attention all the time.' He chuckled. 'The groom acts like a lady's maid to them. He won't let me lay a finger on them, on account that he thinks I'm a bit mazed.'

'What tasks do you do then, Tom?'

'Shovel shit mostly, someone has to. But when the groom is gone, I come in here and I talk to the nags, for they be good company.' He looked down at the dogs. 'I hear Florin and Shilling cut up a bit of a rowdy when you was courtin' the squire's daughter this afternoon.'

'I was not courting her, Tom. Miss Hunter was visiting with her mother.'

'That's all to the good then, My Lord. She be a handsome wench, I grant you, but she has the nature of a terrier. Take my advice, don't let her get a grip on your balls.'

Sorle tried not to grin, for it wouldn't do to allow Tom to become too familiar. 'I'll bear that in mind, Tom, but I'd rather you kept your opinion of my guests to yourself.'

'Yes, My Lord. I reckon you would, but I've heard you'll be taking a wife from these parts and thought to do you a favour. Miss Tibby is as nesh as a wood nymph in spring, for all that she's as poor as a church mouse. A trim little thing though. A man might get it into his head to take advantage of her.'

Sorle frowned. 'I'm well aware of the virtues of Miss Tibbetson, and I find the conversation offensive.'

'No offence offered, My Lord.' He changed the subject and caressed the mare between the eyes. 'The man who put her in this condition should be flogged with a horsewhip.'

95

Sorle wasn't such a fool that he didn't know what Tom was getting at. He terminated the conversation by walking away.

Sorle survived the ordeal of entertaining the Hunter family at dinner, but he had the foresight to remove the harpsichord from the drawing room in case Priscilla was tempted to sing again. She was inclined to simper, but her glance was calculating as her eyes absorbed the contents of the room.

'I believe you have a house in London, Lord Ashby.'

'I inherited the family home, which is also my mother's residence, of course.'

Sarah's smile was pure steel as she stated her prior claim to it. 'It's a home my husband provided for us, and is mine to use for life.'

'I've always thought it might be rather lonely to live in a large house by oneself.'

'Not at all, and it's not all that large when compared to Welford Manor. I have many friends and a rather busy social life in London. My daughter lives a short distance away with her husband and children, and my son comes and goes as he pleases. Life is neither lonely nor dull for me.'

'I'd love to live in London. I have an aunt there. She's promised me a season when her daughter comes out, which is next year.' Priscilla's eyes slid archly towards him. 'Unless I get settled before the New Year, of course.'

Her mother nodded. 'We're expecting several offers if she goes to London. Priscilla has a large dowry, for she inherited her uncle's property and fortune, and stands to inherit all her father owns. A good match shouldn't be too hard to arrange.'

Priscilla couldn't hide the smugness of her smile. 'I'm so looking forward to receiving the invitation to your Christmas ball, Lord Ashby.'

Sorle couldn't help aiming just a tiny barb her way. 'You haven't received one? I understood they'd been sent out.'

When Priscilla's eyes filled with alarm, Sarah slid him a frown and rescued her. 'I believe Miss Tibbetson is still addressing them.'

'Such a nuisance when one's staff are incompetent,' Priscilla said.

His mother bridled at that. 'Yes, I suppose it would be.

However, planning a ball is a daunting task, and Miss Tibbetson, although inexperienced, is certainly not incompetent. There are over one hundred and fifty invitations to be sent out. The more distant ones were placed on the mail coach a day or so ago. The local ones have yet to be despatched. They're of lesser urgency, of course, since, if there is an overflow, we'll have to arrange accommodation for some of our London guests.'

'My house is at your disposal, of course,' Squire Hunter offered.

'That's very kind of you, Squire. I'll let Miss Tibbetson know.' Sorle's mind sifted through the unattached males of his acquaintance to find one who might overlook Priscilla's flaws in favour of her fortune. No doubt the girl would prefer a titled gentleman. He smiled. Viscount Ainsley, of course. Impoverished and nearing forty, Tobias had just about given up on finding a wife to bear him children as well as keep him in luxury. He'd certainly attempt to take advantage of Priscilla's charms, since he had a healthy appetite for the carnal, and a way with women. He hoped Priscilla proved to be susceptible.

Which reminded Sorle, he must warn Tobias to keep away from Geneva.

'Sorle,' his mother said in a low voice, bringing him from his reverie. It seemed his guests were about to depart. He rose to his feet, helped Mrs Hunter arrange her shawl, bowed over her hand and brushed his lips over Priscilla's glove.

She staged a small gasp, held her hand against her chest and tried to engage his eyes in a soulful exchange afterwards.

As their carriage rolled away, Sorle released a huge sigh of relief, making his mother laugh as she laced her arm through his. 'It was a pleasant evening on the whole. I think we redeemed ourselves, and there wasn't a mouse in sight.'

'That's because Geneva forgot to tell the rodents that Priscilla was visiting. I was thinking perhaps that Tobias Ainsley would be a good match for her.'

His mother jumped, as if alarmed by the thought. 'Viscount Ainsley! Oh no, Sorle. Although he is charming in his ways, he is tremendously shallow. He is all wrong for Geneva. I won't hear of it.'

He glowered at her. 'Of course he's all wrong for Geneva. I'd run him through before I'd allow him to get within a yard of her. My mind was running more along the lines of Priscilla and Tobias.'

She smiled at him then. 'Ah yes, how silly of me, Sorle. Tobias Ainsley would be perfect for Priscilla, for she desires position and he needs a fortune. You're showing quite a flair for matchmaking.'

Sorle hunched into his shoulders, grumbling, 'Matchmaking seems to be everyone's favourite pastime around here. Geneva and Tobias Ainsley. Hah! The very idea.'

The very idea, indeed, Sarah thought.

Eight

Sorle was not looking forward to his Friday appointment with Arabella Pringle. The ritual of looking over candidates, with an eye to breeding infants to inherit title and estate, left him with an unpleasant taste in his mouth. He felt more like a victim in the marriage game, for most of the women on offer were only too willing to exchange their bodies and cash for the dubious honour of writing Countess before their name.

However, he found Arabella to be a definite improvement on Priscilla Hunter. She had a sweet face. Her creamy skin was tinted delicately with rose, and her mouth was small, but gently curved. Her eyes were an innocent, pale blue. She appeared to be a child in development rather than someone verging on womanhood. In her pink gown trimmed with lace, Arabella reminded Sorle of the dainty figurine on the mantelpiece.

A shame to offer her up to the altar of marriage at such a young age, but, as he was soon informed by her mother, the girl had several younger sisters coming on.

Her eyes lowered modestly to her lap, Arabella spoke only when directly addressed, and then in a desperate, whispery voice. Even his mother couldn't draw her out. Mrs Pringle monopolized the conversation, nerves making her prattle. She managed to bring up the fact that she was distantly related to an earl, and ploughed through a lot of ancestral details, as though presenting Arabella's pedigree.

Sorle felt sorry for Arabella after they left. 'She can't be more than sixteen years of age, but she's very sweet and shy,' he said to his mother.

Sarah looked thoughtful. 'Hmmm, appearances can be deceptive, since the girl was not quite so shy when I was introduced to her in Dorchester. In fact, she acted quite unpleasantly when I was obliged to put Maudine Batterby in her place. She followed her mother's lead in smirking unpleasantly, as though she'd enjoyed the spectacle. I remember thinking that when Arabella is older and her character is set, the girl will be quite unpleasant.'

'I formed no such opinion, but then, she hardly spoke.'

'I can only think the sight of you must have intimidated her so much she was rendered speechless.'

'As the sight of me would do to most young women,' Sorle said, laughing at the thought. 'Except Priscilla Hunter. I have the feeling that nothing would render her speechless, except for a sore throat.'

'And we mustn't forget Geneva, of course. She feels no awe whatsoever in your presence and gives you as good as she gets. Better sometimes.' Sarah chuckled. 'Oh, I like Geneva Tibbetson so well that I'm thinking of inviting her back to London with me.'

He raised an eyebrow at that. 'How did Geneva take the snub you dealt her aunt?'

'She was distressed, so I felt quite in the wrong when she begged me not to snub her aunt again. Although Maudine Batterby treats her abominably, Geneva is accepting of her situation and will not talk badly against her. The girl has a kind heart and is loyal, and I'm of the opinion she doesn't wish to estrange herself from her family, no matter how badly her aunt treats her. She's intelligent, too.'

'As if one could overlook it. However, I've not yet discovered the key to rendering *her* speechless. She has altogether too much to say for herself on occasion.'

Nevertheless, Sorle made all haste to Geneva's sitting room to inform her of his progress. He'd decided earlier that having Geneva present at his meeting with Arabella might prompt him into making a bigger fool of her than he had of Priscilla. Not that the mouse had been Geneva's fault, of course, and neither had she encouraged the dogs to join in the singing. But he'd noticed that, when they were together, Geneva seemed to attract trouble.

Gerald had been keeping Geneva company, and he stood up politely when Sorle entered. 'Good afternoon, Lord Ashby.'

'Gerald.' He smiled at the lad and turned to Geneva. 'What were you thinking of?'

She shrugged, knowing exactly what he was talking about. 'Her mama cornered me and was quite determined she should be presented. A pity she's so painfully shy. You did like her, didn't you?'

'How can you not like her? She's a kitten.' He grinned. 'You know, this farce will have to be brought to an end, Gen. I can't marry a child such as Arabella.'

'But the eligibles have all accepted their invitations. Besides, not all of them are so young. Miss Jane Whitmore is next on the list. She's quite mature, at least twenty-six.'

Sorle winced. 'Twenty-six is not *that* old.'

Gerald gave a yelp of laughter. 'Miss Whitmore sniffs a lot and her nose goes red in the winter.'

'She can't help that, Gerald.' Geneva turned her eyes back his way and sighed. 'Why are you being so difficult when you asked me to arrange these meetings? Miss Whitmore has a good seat on a horse and rides with the hunt. Her father is a magistrate and heads the Literary and Philosophical Society, so you cannot insult him by cancelling the engagement with his wife and daughter at such short notice, and without cause.'

Sorle could, but he decided it might be judicious to allow Geneva a small victory. 'I'll entertain her, if I must. You must cancel the other ladies though. My mother might wish to arrange a soirée some time with the mothers and daughters of the district. I can always put in an appearance then, so their maidenly hearts will not feel insulted.'

Her steady gaze was designed to make him feel guilty, and it worked.

'Now, Gen, don't look at me like that. It can't be helped.' He managed to dredge up an excuse. 'I've decided to go to London. I need to make arrangements with my staff for the Christmas ball.'

'When are you leaving?'

'I haven't made up my mind yet.'

Her eyes narrowed. 'Couldn't you convey your instructions in a letter?'

'I have business to deal with as well. I might stay in the capital longer and act as escort to my sister and her children when they come down for Christmas.'

'You're as slippery as an eel, Lord Ashby, and I don't believe a word of your explanation.'

He was startled by her bluntness. 'Are you calling me a liar?'

'I wouldn't go so far as to call you that, Lord Ashby. But I believe you plucked that excuse out of thin air.' She picked up her hat and gloves, clearly put out. 'However, since you feel you need to go to such lengths, with your permission I'll start out now to cancel the engagements personally.'

Immediately, the hovering guilt engulfed him, so he felt unaccountably humble and needed to redeem himself in her regard. 'I'll take you in the phaeton.'

Gerald stepped forward. 'No need to waste your valuable time, Lord Ashby. I can easily escort Geneva myself.'

The devil he could! These cousins of Geneva's were being ridiculously vigilant, Sorle thought, slightly annoyed.

Geneva actually looked relieved, as if the attention he'd bestowed upon her in the past had proved to be irksome to her. She should have regarded it as a compliment, as most women would, for he was not without looks or social prestige. After all, who was she to turn her pert little nose up at an earl? But then, what would a country mouse know of such things?

As if she'd read his mind, she offered him a small smile before saying to her cousin, 'I accept, Gerald. That's good of you, since it will take up less of my time. People are bound to want to pass the time of day with the earl, and he's made

101

it perfectly clear he regards the necessity to entertain strangers as tedious. Afterwards, you can deliver me home before you bring the rig back.'

Her words were cruel little barbs in Sorle's soul. Imagination momentarily laid her across his lap, crying out for mercy whilst he meted out a dose of richly deserved punishment with the palm of his hand. He came back to the present, smiling as he rang for a servant to order the rig be brought round. He said to Gerald. 'I take it you'll be escorting your cousin here again tomorrow.'

'No, sir. My father needs me to help decorate the church for the harvest service.'

Sorle's heart leapt at the thought of having Geneva to himself. If the weather was still warm he'd pick her up when she was on the way over here and surprise her with a picnic at her favourite spot. But what was this Gerald was saying . . . ?

'You've forgotten that Geneva doesn't work at the weekends, and, starting on Monday, it's Matthew's turn to chaperone her.'

Giving an aggrieved grumble of a sigh, Sorle looked over to where Geneva stood, only to discover her eyes brimming with laughter. She offered him a slightly quirky grin and bobbed a graceful curtsy. 'Your servant, My Lord.'

For one innocent in the ways of love, she played the game instinctively well, and, Lord, how she provoked him! 'Like hell you are,' he growled, and slouched off. It would serve her right if he married this Jane Witless she was about to serve him up with.

The church, decorated with wheat sheaves, apple boughs and baskets of produce to be distributed after the service to the poor, was packed to capacity. Reverend James Batterby smiled benevolently over the congregation, for the choir had sung sweetly, nobody had fallen asleep during his sermon, and Lord Ashby was just about to read the lesson.

Geneva was squashed into the end of the second pew, with Maudine and the weight of several other people pressing against her from the other end. The front right of the aisle was reserved for Squire Hunter's family, the left side for Lord

Ashby's. Their pew had been polished to a soft glow which revealed the grain of the wood. Intruders were kept out by a blue velvet rope supported by brass poles at each end.

Sorle was dressed in black, his buttoned cutaway coat revealing a double-breasted waistcoat of silver and pale green stripes, secured by silver buttons. He looked quite relaxed as he took the lectern and gazed down at the paper in his hand before looking at the congregation. His dark eyes swept slowly over the heads of the people and he smiled.

A sigh issued in unison from the throats of the females present, and his dark eyes settled on Geneva, crushed as she was against the end of the pew. He raised his eyebrow a mere fraction, so she wanted to giggle. An irritable elbow in the ribs from Maudine as the woman tried to expand into the too-small space allotted to her caused Geneva to wince instead.

'You look extremely cramped to me, Miss Tibbetson. Perhaps you would be more comfortable sitting next to my mother?' Sorle rumbled from amidst the apple boughs decorating the lectern. 'There's plenty of room in our pew.'

'Yes, please do.' Pushing the barrier aside, Sarah smiled and beckoned to her.

All eyes swivelled Geneva's way, and there were murmurs as she rose to her feet, some of them slightly scandalized at the favour being shown her, since the church was packed to the rafters and most of the congregation was cramped and uncomfortable. Geneva sighed, not daring to look at anyone now Sorle had drawn attention to her. She was pink-faced as she settled herself beside Sarah.

Sorle gazed directly at her whilst he informed the congregation. 'Somebody told me to examine my sins before reading the lesson. However, I am all too human and my sins are too numerous to count, so I can only say to that person. Let he or *she* who is without sin, cast the first stone.'

'Hah!' Geneva said under her breath, and her blush progressed from pink to red, so she felt as if her cheeks were on fire. Beside her, Sarah laughed softly.

'The lesson, Lord Ashby,' the reverend whispered frantically.

Sorle smiled benevolently at everyone. 'Ah yes, Reverend. Ecclesiastes. "To everything there is a season, and a time to every purpose under the heaven. A time to be born, and a time to die; a time to plant, and a time to pluck up that which is planted . . ."'

Geneva closed her eyes, listening to his voice, which was clear, dark and warm, despite the rumble of thunder in it. There was a moment of reverential silence when he finished. Not a cough, a scraping foot or an errant indrawn breath did she hear. Then she heard his tread on the flagged floor and opened her eyes as he slid in beside her.

'And still in Ecclesiastes, a thank you to celebrate the harvest,' the reverend murmured, nodding to the choir, which consisted mostly of his sons, who looked surprisingly angelic in their white robes.

'"Now thank we all our God . . ."'

As they stood and the choir began to lead them into the hymn, Sorle sang softly to the second line, '*Especially read for you, Gen.*'

'*Who wondrous things have done.*'

'*Thank you, sir, I loved it,*' she sang back.

'*Who from our mo-u-ther's arms.*'

'*I'll treasure your comp-li-ment.*'

Geneva, on glancing up to confront the acute gaze of her uncle, sang hastily, '*With countless gifts of love.*'

'*And still is ours today,*' they finished together, then smiled at each other.

People were inclined to linger after the church services, exchanging gossip. Today was no exception, except there were more people, and all were pressing around the earl. Squire Hunter introduced him to the several worthy businessmen trying to be noticed, who in their turn introduced their wives. Then they all stood there chatting.

Sarah took Geneva's arm. 'He will stay there long enough to be polite, so now might be a good time for you to present me to your aunt.'

Maudine, looking all forlorn, was standing in the porch with Bandit as a companion, the dog having followed them to church. Her usual crowd of acquaintances had abandoned her to crowd around Mrs Hunter, who smiled as they approached. 'Ah, Mrs Ashby. I was just discussing with the parish ladies how well Lord Ashby reads. We were quite enthralled.'

'Quite so, Mrs Hunter. Would you excuse us? Geneva has promised to introduced me to her aunt, Mrs Batterby.'

Maudine looked quite relieved when they joined her. 'There you are, Geneva. I wondered where you were. There was such a terrible crush in church today. It made me feel quite faint.'

Her aunt did look rather pale. 'Are you feeling any better now, Aunt? I could fetch you some water from the stone jug in the church, if you'd like.'

Maudine's eyes slid towards Sarah, slightly accusing. 'The fresh air has revived me a little.'

'Then may I present to you Mrs Sarah Ashby, since she has expressed a wish to be introduced. Mrs Ashby, this is my aunt, Maudine Batterby.'

Sarah smiled at Maudine, saying right away, 'I feel we got off on the wrong foot when we last met. Perhaps you'd allow me to apologize. I was too hasty.'

After her initial surprise, an expression of shame filled Maudine's eyes. 'Indeed, that is most gracious of you, Mrs Ashby. It is I who should offer apologies.'

'Then, with your permission, we will both take them as offered and accepted, and put it behind us. I would like to compliment you on your sons. They're delightful boys who are a credit to you and your husband.'

'Why, thank you, Mrs Ashby. It's hard raising boys, especially so many.'

'Male offspring can certainly be annoying creatures. Although they may grow into men and sometimes go on to do great and important things, I do believe they're always boys at heart.'

'I cannot imagine Lord Ashby being annoying. He seems so self-assured.'

'Sorle has always been a law unto himself. I was wondering, Mrs Ashby, your sons sing so delightfully; at the Christmas ball, would you allow them to entertain our guests during supper with some Christmas carols?'

'I'll consult with my husband, of course, but I do not see why not.'

'Perhaps you'd like to sing for us too, Geneva. I noticed in church that you have such a lovely voice.'

Geneva's heart sank a little. 'I'm not confident enough.'

'You would not be the only lady to sing. Miss Hunter will be taking a turn.'

'Miss Hunter sings with gusto,' Maudine said, quite unexpectedly. 'But Geneva's voice is much better. My husband says she controls it well and she sings with feeling.'

Sarah patted Geneva's hand. 'I shall ask Sorle to persuade you.'

'Ask me to persuade her to do what?' he said, coming up behind them.

'Sing for her supper at the Christmas ball.'

'Of course she shall. I insist on it.'

Did he then? Geneva thought. 'As you well know, Lord Ashby, insisting makes no impression on me at all.'

A scandalized expression appeared on Maudine's face, as if her tenuous acquaintance with the Ashbys was suddenly being eroded. 'You should speak to Lord Ashby with more respect.'

Sorle merely laughed. 'She should, but Miss Tibbetson has such a quixotic nature. Although she tries my patience no end. I haven't got the wit to keep up with her. Come, what will it take to persuade you to sing for me, Miss Tibbetson?'

Head slanted to one side, Geneva gazed at him. 'I must think about it, since I'm unused to singing in public.'

Slowly, Sorle drew in a deep breath and contemplated her. Then his eyes darkened and a smile slowly inched across his mouth as he purred, 'Then you must sing for me in private.'

'In private?'

'Not entirely, of course, for that would not be proper. But I have invited Reverend Batterby to bring his entire family to dine with us tomorrow. Will you sing for us then, when you're safely amongst family and friends?'

Maudine looked delighted at being invited to dinner. 'Of course she will.'

Sarah squeezed Maudine's hand and turned to smile at Geneva. 'Do say you will, Geneva. It's a long time since we've had an evening of entertainment. I will sing too, and Sorle can recite something if he puts his mind to it.'

'I'm sure I can apply myself to that. A Shakespearean speech perhaps.'

Sarah turned to Maudine. 'What about you, Mrs Batterby?'

Maudine turned pink. 'I'm not very musical.'

'You used to tell the older boys wonderful stories when they were small,' Geneva said, but slightly wistfully, for the only way she'd heard them was if she'd listened at the keyhole. Perhaps you could tell us a story. Gerald said they were always full of mythical creatures.'

Maudine's expression softened, as if she'd remembered a time when mothering was a pleasure instead of a chore. 'Perhaps I could, but they were children's stories and we are adults. Besides, it seems such a long time ago now.'

'Well, I for one would like to hear a story for children, especially if it contains dragons,' Sorle declared.

'There, then it is settled, Mrs Batterby. Didn't I tell you that men are always boys at heart?' Sarah and Maudine exchanged an indulgent smile as Maudine's sons came to join them.

After they'd greeted the earl, Edward said to Geneva. 'Don't forget you promised to take Moth and me to the beach.'

'Can I come?' Robert asked, a request which was followed by a chorus of: 'And me!'

Geneva cast an assessing glance at the grey clouds scudding across the sky. 'We'd best hurry then, for it looks as though it might rain later on.'

Soon, they started off up the road, Moth and Edward holding her hands, Bandit following after, his short legs trotting him along at a fast pace.

'Such a delightful girl. You'll miss her when she weds,' Sarah said to nobody in particular.

At the thought of Geneva marrying, Maudine looked alarmed.

Sorle growled something unintelligible.

Sarah merely smiled.

The wind coming off the sea was fresh, and smelt of rain.

Geneva and her cousins built a huge castle, covering the ramparts with shells. A moat was filled by a trench open to the incoming waves. Geneva had a job keeping her hat on her head in the breeze. Giving up the battle, she loosened the ribbons, allowing it to fall to the sand, where she weighed it down by filling it with sand. Soon her hair came loose from its pins too, and streamed untidily about her in the wind.

She didn't care. She loved these times with her cousins,

free of the restrictions imposed on her at home. She had to admit, though, Maudine had been kinder to her of late.

'Let's race around the rock and back,' Robert shouted, pointing to the landmark a couple of hundred yards along the sandy beach.

'Staggered start.' Gerald drew graduated marks in the sand. Slipping off her shoes and stockings, Geneva hitched up her skirts with her hands and lined up with them, as she'd always done.

'Ready, steady—'

'Go!' shouted Moth and took off as fast as his legs would carry him.

Astride his horse at the top of the cliff, Sorle laughed as he watched them pound across the sand, a line of straggling lads, their arms pumping and their legs labouring as their feet sank with each step into the soft, yielding surface. Bandit followed after, kicking up sand and barking.

Geneva soon fell behind and, clearly winded, bent double. Her skirt ballooned in the breeze, affording Sorle a glimpse of shapely ankles and calves before she sank to her knees. The older boys waved to her as they dashed past on the way back. Edward and Moth, who'd run out of puff at the rock, tramped dolefully back along the beach. As they passed her, she caught them both by the ankle and brought them down. Then she tickled their ribs until they rolled about screaming with laughter. Their legs and arms went everywhere as they tried to escape her clutches.

Florin and Shilling caught up with Sorle as he made his way down the cliff path. Both dogs bayed loudly and the Batterby family stopped their activity to turn and see what the fuss was about. Bandit did a little dance in the sand, kicking it out from his scuffling feet as his siblings came down to tower over him. The trio went racing up the beach together as Sorle made his way towards the family group.

Geneva immediately brushed sand from her skirt and, grabbing up her hat, shook the sand from it before attempting to stuff her errant hair into the crown. She glowed from her efforts and her eyes were full of laughter. Tendrils of flaxen hair escaped to curl about her face. He closed his eyes for a second, thinking, *You'll look like this after I've made love to you.*

108

She made no further effort to tidy herself, just gazed at him as he dismounted, the laughter in her eyes slowly being replaced by awareness, as if she were changing from girl to woman before his eyes – as if she'd read his thoughts and knew the inevitability of it.

'My Lord,' she said, her voice husky from her laughter. The hair at the nape of his neck prickled in warning at the sound of it, and his groin tightened against his linens. A woman had not affected him in such a way for a long time.

'I have come to invite you and your cousins to take refreshment with my mother and myself.'

He could almost hear the collective growl of her cousins' stomachs at the thought of food. They scrambled to pull on their hose and shoes, except for Geneva, who merely slid her shoes on to her feet and kept her folded stockings concealed in her hands.

When he raised an eyebrow, she shrugged. 'I'm afraid we're not in a fit state to be guests.'

'My mother's maid will tidy you, and my man will see to it that the boys are made presentable.'

A few drops of rain were borne on the wind. Geneva gazed at the darkening sky as thunder rumbled in the distance. 'I should take the boys home. My aunt and uncle will worry if there's a storm.'

'I'll send a servant with a message to say you're all safe. If need be, you can stay the night. There's plenty of room.'

When the news was greeted by a chorus of whoops, she smiled. 'We're beginning to take your hospitality for granted, Lord Ashby.'

'A thought which affords me great pleasure.'

'You are gallant, My Lord.'

'Coming from your delectable mouth, that's a compliment as sweet as honey. I will treasure it.'

Trying not to imagine exactly how her lips would taste, Sorle placed the four youngest boys astride Rastus, handing the reins to Gerald to lead them. The wind increased as they reached the cliff top. Light rain hurled itself in desultory fashion against their backs. Gradually, the cousins hurried on towards the manor, the younger ones clinging to the horse and each other, and the dogs sniffing at their heels.

When the boys entered the stand of trees which shielded the manor from the worst of the sea winds, Sorle stopped to removed his coat. He placed it around her shoulders and gazed down at her. He felt unaccountably warm toward her, protective and loving. There was more though, much more. He'd never felt like this about any woman before. He examined the churning ferment of his feelings with regard to her, coming to a startling conclusion. Lord Ashby was probably in love with Miss Geneva Tibbetson, an impoverished and orphaned country maid.

'Good grief!' he said out loud.

'What is it, Sorle?'

Should he tell her? Hell, no! His feelings were too new and he didn't know if he could trust them. So he smiled inanely at her and mumbled something. Then he drew her towards him and instinctively kissed her. When she struggled against the kiss, which was altogether too intimate and intrusive for a maid of her innocence, he kissed her harder.

He tasted the salt of her tears against his tongue before he released her. 'I apologize,' he growled, nudging at a tuft of grass with the toe of his boot, and not feeling in the least apologetic.

Her anger was entirely unexpected. Her eyes blazing, despite tears enough to quench a forest fire, she spat at him, '*You cur! You wolf in sheep's clothing!* I am not your plaything to be handled so. How dare you demand such liberties from me?' Even more unexpected was the stinging slap she gave him, which flattened against his cheek with a crack and dented his pride in a way nothing else could have.

Clearly taken aback by her own action, her voice dropped to a whisper. 'Why did you make me despise you enough to do that, Sorle? I may be poor, but I'm not one of your London lightskirts to be treated so. Do my feelings count for nought?'

Innocent she might be, but she was obviously aware of what went on in the world. 'What *are* your feelings towards me, Geneva?' he said, resisting the urge to soothe his abused cheek, and hoping to hear his feelings were reciprocated.

'They are nothing . . . nothing, d'you hear . . . I have none. I cannot have feelings, since you employ me. I'm one of your servants, remember? You must treat me like one, for if you

110

cannot respect me, I shall be forced to leave your employ.'

'Will you break my heart, then?'

A pulse throbbed against her throat and he wanted to place a caress against it.

'You indicated that a man does not always love with his heart, and I believe that to be true in your case. Your heart cannot possibly be involved, for you're an earl and I am a nobody. If your finer feelings are involved, then you must tell me now. Then I will go away and never set foot in your home again.'

Something he couldn't risk. 'No, my heart isn't involved,' he lied, for his innermost feelings were evolving still, and were too tender to reveal themselves in their entirety to himself, let alone to her. He only knew that if she left him, it would kill him.

She flinched as if it was he who had struck her this time. Her voice thick with tears, she whispered. 'My apologies to your mother, and I beg your pardon for my behaviour in striking you. Unfortunately, I've developed a headache. Perhaps you would send the boys home in your carriage later.' Shrugging the coat from her shoulders, she let it fall to the ground, then turned and headed off towards Edgley House at a run. Her hat fell from her head into the grass, but she didn't seem to notice.

Sorle watched her go, his heart in a tumult, for he longed to call her back. When she reached the stile, the sky opened and she was engulfed in a torrent of rain. Within seconds, her clothes were plastered to her body, her hair tumbled in water-slicked spirals to her waist.

You damned fool, he accused himself as he went to retrieve her hat. *Now look at what you've done.*

Monday morning. Geneva woke heavy-eyed, her throat aflame and her body fevered and shivering.

On being informed, Sorle didn't believe it one little bit. It was a ruse to avoid him. He rode to Reverend Batterby's house, in a mood to put paid to such nonsense, arriving just as the doctor was leaving.

Taken aback, Sorle asked him. 'How is Miss Tibbetson? Is her condition serious?'

'If she is careful, and rests, Miss Tibbetson will recover within two weeks.'

Relief sizzled inside him. 'Thank God for that. I was worried. May I see her?'

'That's entirely up to her uncle and aunt, My Lord. I wouldn't recommend it though, unless you wish to risk infection yourself. Good day to you, sir.'

Sorle found the reverend in his study. 'How is Miss Tibbetson?'

'She's suffering from a fever and sore throat, which was brought on by getting soaked in the rain yesterday. I can't understand why she didn't arrive home in the carriage with the boys.

He wondered what Geneva had told her uncle, and decided to be as truthful as possible. 'We had an argument. Quite rightly, Miss Tibbetson decided to end it by returning home rather than tolerate my company any longer by staying for refreshment with your sons.'

'Geneva can be headstrong at times,' the reverend observed.

'The argument was entirely my fault. May I see her, to apologize?'

Shaking his head, the reverend smiled at him. 'I'm afraid not, Lord Ashby. Geneva is resting. Besides, a bedchamber is not the proper place for a young lady to receive male visitors. I will present your apology to her myself.'

At least the man hadn't pried as to what their argument was about. 'Of course . . . you are quite right to refuse me admittance. I'm sorry. I don't know what I was thinking of.' Collecting his wits, Sorle rose to his feet. 'Perhaps you'd convey to her my best wishes and a wish that her recovery will be swift.'

'I most certainly will.' James stood up to see his unexpected guest out. 'We will see you later this evening for dinner, Lord Ashby. Maudine is so looking forward to it.'

'And so was I, Reverend, but I'm afraid we must postpone the date until your niece is fully recovered, for a social dinner without her presence is unthinkable. You *will* let me know if she needs anything, won't you?'

The reverend's spectacles glinted in the light. 'Quite so.'

'Good day to you then, sir.'

As Sorle was about to mount his horse, he heard a sneeze, and looked up to see Geneva gazing at him through a gap in the lace curtain. Her cheeks were flushed, her glorious hair hung about her shoulders and she looked sorry for herself as she managed a wan smile.

When he smiled in return, the curtain fell back into place, but he could see her shadow behind it. Pressing his hand to his mouth, he blew her a kiss, then mounted and rode away.

Nine

It would be unthinkable to hare off to London while Geneva was ill, Sorle convinced himself, giving a bemused smile at how easily that conclusion had come to him. He found himself at a loose end, for not having her there to consult was an inconvenience.

On the other hand, she had his household running like clockwork, even in her absence. And if he left for London before Geneva recovered completely, when he arrived home again everything would be back to normal.

He stared at himself in the mirror as he brushed the dust from his riding suit, wondering if his unruly hair needed a trim. He'd enjoyed his exercise, and so had Rastus, as they'd headed inland through the leafy lanes and up into the hills to explore. He thought he might enquire if Geneva owned a riding dress, so she could accompany him from time to time. But since she didn't seem to own a horse, perhaps she couldn't ride.

He thought he heard some geese honking, but the noise stopped as soon as it started.

About to go and change, he remembered the horses in his stable, a pair of lathered, but muscular, chestnuts. Since the ladies had ridden over, he decided his appearance would probably suffice for Geneva's latest candidate.

The woman and her mother had been waiting on his return from his ride. They were in the drawing room being entertained by his own mother, or so Sorle had been informed by Mrs Pickering.

Florin and Shilling pressed their noses into his palms, making little huffing noises. He remembered the fuss they'd caused Priscilla Hunter and smiled benevolently down at them. He decided to draw on Geneva's ingenuity, for he still had suspicions that she'd somehow arranged the mouse and dog fiasco to suit. 'Perhaps you'd like to take tea with us today.'

The pair wagged all over at the honour he'd bestowed on them, as they followed him to the drawing room, where he paused to press his ear against the panel of the door. 'My son should not be long now, for I thought I heard his horse,' his mother said.

'Damned men,' somebody honked. 'You can never rely on them to be on time for anything.'

He stepped back in some alarm as another person honked louder and longer, thinking, *Ye Gods!* Surely that was not the sound of laughter? He was about to sneak away when the dogs looked up at him and whined.

'Ah . . . that sounds like the earl now,' his mother said loudly before he could escape.

'Traitors,' he hissed and, throwing open the door, he smiled expansively at everyone, and lied. 'I'm so sorry I'm late. My horse threw a shoe.' Nodding to the older woman, he then turned to the younger, desperately trying to remember her name. Ah, he thought, as it suddenly came to him. 'Mrs Whitless . . . Miss Whitless. How lovely to meet you both.'

'Not the dogs,' his mother said faintly, pressing her palms together in an unconscious attitude of prayer.

There was a short silence, in which Miss Whitless patted the space on the sofa next to her. Surely she didn't expect him to . . . ? But no, thank God, it was the animals' close attention she required.

Sensing something to their advantage, the dogs left him and arranged themselves obediently either side of her. Laying their traitorous heads in her lap, with their tongues hanging out of their mouths, they simpered at her while she fed them titbits from her plate.

'Pathetic fellows, aren't you?' she said, fondling their ears as they drooled on her riding skirt.

Miss Whitless and her mother had certainly dressed casually for the occasion, as if, from experience, they were not expecting anything to come of it. Jane was certainly good with dogs, was a thought that strayed into Sorle's mind.

Jane looked at him directly then, as if she'd read that thought and wanted to rout it. 'I'm surprised Geneva gave you such an ill-bred pair. The farmer was about to drown these two. The girl's too gullible, of course. Two shillings she paid the farmer for them. Still, it gave everyone in the district a laugh. The squire's hound would have sired these. They look just like him – wouldn't you say so, Mother?'

'That Irish breed of his is always sniffing around the local bitches. Damned males, they all need castrating.'

Feeling the need for protection, Sorle seated himself, crossed one knee over the other and prayed for a bolt of lightning to come through the window and strike these two harpies dead.

His mother had given a small gasp at their vulgarity, which went almost unnoticed in the scornful laughter of Miss Jane Whitless. He exchanged a rueful smile with her.

'My dear Sorle,' his mother said, in a feeble attempt to rescue him from his dilemma by changing the subject. 'Perhaps I should point out that you pronounced our guests' name wrongly. Miss Tibbetson must have misspelled the name in your social diary. This is Miss Whit*more* and her mother, Mrs Benedict Whit*more*.'

Laughter bubbled up inside him. 'My humble apologies, ladies. I will check my social diary more thoroughly in future. If Miss Tibbetson is at fault – which she very rarely is, I might add – I shall take her sternly to task when she recovers from her illness.'

In fact, he would reward her by kissing her senseless if he got the chance. Reflectively, he rubbed his face where her slap had landed the last time he'd tried. Had it been worth it? He grinned. Most definitely!

'No need to apologize, My Lord. It happens all the time. Do you hunt?'

'On occasion.' He was hunting now, but not for a long-necked goose with beady eyes and a red beak.

'I saw the mares as I came in. I looked over the pair at the market, and thought the dam was only fit for the knackery. The youngster is off to a bad start. Although she's gained a bit of flesh, she'll never be anything but a lady's riding horse. I've got no use for a nag that can't hunt. What are you going to do with the dam – use her for dog meat?'

Sorle winced. 'I bought them as company for one another. I work on the theory that if the pair are kept together, it will help the older mare to survive. Their condition has improved considerably and they're sweet-tempered beasts. Actually, I'd thought to run the mare in the Gold Cup next July, if my groom can get her up to condition.'

His two guests looked at each other and began to laugh loudly. Jane Whitmore's lips rolled back to show a set of pink gums, in which her large teeth gleamed. 'Against the stallions? Oh, how utterly droll you are, My Lord ... wait till I tell father. He's one of the course stewards, and he does so like a man with a sense of humour.' She fed a cake to each dog. 'There you are, you scrounging mongrels. You have some charm but I wouldn't give either of you house room.'

'No pedigree,' her mother said loudly. 'I wouldn't have a male of any type who didn't have papers to his name. They breed low types.'

'Quite right, mother. I must say, that Tibbetson girl was a damned fool parting with her money. It's not as if she has much, though, if her appearance is anything to go by.'

Sorle exchanged a glance with his mother, and, despite her warning glance, leaned forward, stung by the criticism of Geneva. Through gritted teeth, he said, 'I'd prefer it if you didn't refer to Miss Tibbetson in that manner. She happens to be a valued employee, and her intelligence is above reproach. Her personal situation is not something she can be faulted for.'

'Quite so, My Lord. It's just words, nothing to take umbrage at, you know, since the girl knows her place. I daresay you London dandies aren't used to a straightforward country woman. Give me a man of the land any day, I say. You know where you are with them.'

He raised an eyebrow at that. 'And where exactly are you with them, *Miss* Whitmore?'

Although she gave him a grey, intimidating stare, her cheeks took on a ruddy tinge. Abruptly pushing the dogs away, she rose and brushed the crumbs from her skirt to the floor. 'Come on, mother. It's time we left if we're to go over to see the squire's new hunter. I daresay I'll see you at the next meet, My Lord. I'll give you a run for your money, for I'll pit my hunter against anything in the district.' The snort she gave doubled as a laugh, and she slowly shook her head. 'The Gold Cup . . . what an absolute whinny of an idea. Squire Hunter will fall over when I tell him.'

His smile almost a scimitar, Sorle rose from his chair. He felt like taking Jane Whitmore's stupid tongue between his thumb and forefinger and pulling, just see how far it would stretch before it came out by the roots. To hell with her!

He was startled when Jane suddenly bared her teeth at him. 'I must say I'm looking forward to your ball, Lord Ashby. It's not often us country fillies get a chance to show our mettle.' She added wryly, so he experienced a fleeting moment of liking for her, 'We'll do you proud, just you wait and see – like a string of show ponies trotted out for inspection.'

Sorle wondered what Geneva would be wearing, as the pair strode off, laughing. Could she afford a ball gown? He doubted it.

His grin disappeared as soon as the Whitmore women cantered off like a couple of Valkyries into battle. He turned to his mother, shaking his head. 'I would rather be eaten alive by lizards than venture into matrimony with that one. What on earth was Geneva thinking of?'

'Geneva cannot afford to slight anyone by leaving them out. I felt sorry for Miss Whitmore. She knows she's unattractive and compensates for it by acting as if she doesn't care. You were rude to her, Sorle.'

'Dammit, mother. When they think they have the right to criticize Geneva, it annoys me. She has more intelligence, and is more fun, than any woman I've ever met. But at least I will not be afflicted by any more of her candidates, since I've instructed her to cancel them all.'

'You're altogether too touchy about her, Sorle. Is there something between you? It would please me if there was.'

Eyes hooded, Sorle contemplated his mother. It was not the time to tell her, for he needed to savour what he felt for Geneva.

His deep affection for the girl was mellowing delightfully, like a fine brandy. He would enjoy it even more when it had proved itself and matured.

Only a fool rushed into marriage, especially with one such as Geneva, who was impoverished. No matter how sincere his own feelings were – and he still wasn't completely convinced by them, for they were too tumultuous and strange – he needed to know that those feelings were not some passing fancy, but something of lasting value.

So far, Geneva had shown more than a passing interest in his charms, but very little interest in his finances, except to express gratitude over the meagre salary he paid her.

His glance lit on Florin and Shilling. Moreover, she had no taste in dogs, as the cumbersome Jane Whitmore had ably proved. 'A breed would have growled, not grovelled at her feet for a mouthful of cake,' he told them.

They grinned, then came to lay their shaggy heads against his legs and pant hotly into his riding boots. He fondled them, thinking: *Without Geneva's soft heart they'd both be dead.* Sorle was pleased that his mother liked Geneva, but he had no intention of allowing her opinion to sway him. 'You wouldn't want me to wed somebody just to please you, would you, mother?'

'Of course not. Besides, I know you wouldn't, else you'd have been married off long ago and given me some grandchildren by now. I just want you to be happy with the woman you choose. As for what Geneva has got lined up for you in the immediate future, I don't know. I can't find her social diary.'

'Then I must go over and ask her where she's hidden it. Though, so far, Reverend Batterby hasn't allowed me near her.'

'The reverend is taking precautions, since the girl is his niece and he feels the need to protect her.'

He raised a quizzical eyebrow. 'From me?'

'Especially from you, I should imagine, Sorle. There's nothing that would pique your interest more than resistance. The reverend is no fool.'

'It's not as if I'm about to pluck her from her bed and run off with her . . . at least, not while she's ill.' He gave a faint smile at the thought. 'Am I such a menace, then?'

'As much a menace as a fox in a hen house, but you'll never really understand that until you have daughters of your own.' She gave a light laugh. 'You have a reputation for breaking hearts, Sorle. As well you know.'

He thought about the statement for a moment, acknowledging that it was probably true. But it wasn't his fault that women lost their hearts to him on occasion. He didn't deliberately encourage them. And he'd never seduced a woman who wasn't willing to be seduced, or one scarcely out of childhood and innocent of the ways of the world.

He grinned. He'd seduce Geneva Tibbetson without a moment's remorse though. His mother was right, her very resistance had become irresistible to him. She had not dealt much with men, and the mixture of naivety, confusion and the need to taste of life, was endearing to him. He would have her before too long, he knew it.

Sarah struck him on the arm and laughed. 'I know that look, your father had one exactly like it. You're hatching some mischief.'

He kissed her cheek and chuckled. 'And look what a bargain my father ended up with. Perhaps I shall do the same.'

'Speaking as your mother, I think you'll make a wonderful husband and father ... once you meet the right girl. I just want you to be happy.'

'And so I shall be, I promise, for I'll not wed until I'm very sure I'll be content to live with and love just one woman for the rest of my life.'

Geneva's throat was still raw, her nose was a painful rub of red, her voice hardly more than a croak. When she coughed, the hacking spasms now arrived at longer intervals. She felt only a pinch better, but that was progress.

'How are you today?' her uncle asked, gazing over his glasses at her.

'A little better, I think.'

'Good ... good.' He unfolded a piece of paper, obviously a letter, then refolded it and placed it in his waistcoat pocket. 'Mrs Batterby's sister has requested that you be allowed to spend every weekend in Dorchester with her. I have considered it carefully, and after talking it over with your aunt, we've decided that perhaps it will be a good idea, for it will make a change for you. If you suit her, she will consider taking you on as her companion.'

'But what about my position with Lord Ashby?'

'Ah yes . . . you must be aware that it has given rise to certain speculation. After the ball, when he has chosen a bride for himself, it's probable that the position will no longer exist, for the earl's future wife will want to manage their social engagements herself.'

A tear rolled miserably down Geneva's cheek. She held Sorle Ashby close to her heart and didn't want to leave him. The thought frightened her somewhat and she found a more acceptable reason to substitute. 'I love my cousins, I don't want to leave them.'

'I know you do, my dear, and they love you. But you're grown up now, and they're not really your responsibility, even though there's a strong attachment between you.' Gently, he cleared his throat. 'Maudine says she is able to cope with the boys alone now she has the two maids, especially when Timothy and Edward start school. At first, you will only need to attend Emma Mason at weekends. The parting will be gradual, allowing you all to grow used to it.'

She nodded, then turned her face away from him, distressed beyond measure. She had not thought that her uncle would bow to pressure from Mrs Batterby to get rid of her, but she couldn't bring herself to disappoint him by making a fuss. 'I'm grateful for your goodness towards me all this time, and will do as you instruct, but, Uncle James, I'll miss you all so much.'

He took her hand in his. 'Dearest Geneva. All things must change, and although sometimes they seem to change for the worse, it's often for the better. Besides, we'll not be far away if you should need us.' He handed her his handkerchief. 'Dry your eyes, my dear. The earl has ridden over to see you again.'

Blood rushed to her cheeks. 'Oh . . . what did he say?'

Her uncle sighed. 'The same thing as he says every morning, in that he wishes you a speedy recovery. He enquired about his engagement diary too, suggesting he was unable to find it. He requested a meeting with you on that account.'

Alarm filled her. 'He can't be allowed to see me, not while I look so horrid.'

120

'I assure you, Geneva, my dear, you're not as ugly as you imagine. Being ill has given you an air of frailty, it's true, but that in itself is appealing. The Lord has created you more than passing fair, for which we should be grateful. But the fact remains, it would be unseemly for the earl to be admitted to your bedchamber. He'll have to wait until you're completely recovered before you can meet again. I have told him so.'

'Would you inform Lord Ashby that the diary is in its usual place in the bureau drawer. I have no idea why he cannot find it.'

The reverend smiled then. 'None at all? Perhaps he mislaid it on purpose, so he'd have an excuse to come and see you. Despite my constant reassurance, he seems unduly worried about your state of health.'

She shrugged as she croaked, 'Truly, uncle, sometimes the earl can't see past the end of his nose.'

He smiled at that. 'A particular type of short-sightedness which afflicts us all from time to time. I think the Lord arranges this, so as to delight and surprise us when he clears our vision and allows us to see more clearly.' He stooped to kiss her fore-head. 'Now, Geneva, my dear, do stop talking and give your throat a rest.'

She managed a small smile at that, for he'd been the one doing all the talking. 'Would you thank the earl for his good wishes on my behalf.' Then, as her uncle was about to depart, she added wistfully, 'I do so enjoy working for Lord Ashby. Perhaps you'd tell him not to worry on my account, since I'm feeling a little better and will soon be myself again. Also, I'd be obliged if you would inform him that arrangements for his Christmas ball are well in hand. He will find the details in the blue ledger, on the first page of which I have written, *Lord Ashby's Ball, Christmas 1800*. His mother knows where it is kept.'

Her uncle bestowed a smile of great warmth on her. 'I'm sure Mrs Ashby can manage to complete the task. I've permit-ted Lord Ashby to write you a note, and will bring it to you in a little while. Meanwhile, the earl is staying to take refresh-ment with me, as he and I have some church matters to discuss.'

Her uncle's study was below her bedchamber. In a little

while she heard the exchange of muffled voices, but she couldn't catch a word. Sorle's voice was a slow rumble, his laughter deep and delightful, like a salve to her soul.

She closed her eyes and lay back on her pillows, smiling to herself when Sorle laughed, and weaving pleasant daydreams about him, in which she centred in his life. The room was pleasantly warm, the shadows shifted and danced to the crackle of the fire in the grate.

She wondered if her uncle had told him that she was being banished. If so, Sorle didn't sound in the least bit perturbed about it, for there was a companionable male rhythm to the rise and fall of the conversation. There was something she thought she ought to tell Sorle, but she couldn't quite recall what it was as she drifted off.

After a while she woke and the voices had stopped. Somebody began to play the introduction to a Christmas carol, and she recognized her uncle's delicate touch on the piano keys. He would be seated there, his eyes faraway and with an absorbed smile on his face. Everything else but the music would be forgotten – including the note Sorle had written to her.

Then the boys began to voice, '*Hark the Herald angels sing* ...' A tear rolled down her cheek, then another. She didn't want to go and stay with Emma Mason, she'd miss her cousins too much.

Of late, Maudine had felt much improved in health. This was due to one of the new maids massaging her neck and shoulders every night before she went to bed, which was so relaxing it provided relief from her headaches.

She was coping better with Geneva too, now the girl was gainfully employed and out from under her feet for most of the day. Maudine conceded that Geneva tried her best to please them all, though, personally, she felt tolerated, rather than liked, by the girl. Once Geneva moved out, Maudine hoped her boys would pay her the respect that was due to her as their mother.

Maudine had expected to experience relief when the letter from Emma Mason arrived. Oddly, she did not, even though it meant Geneva would be absent at weekends. Her elder sister had always been a tyrant by nature, and had resented having to return to the family home after she'd been widowed and left impoverished.

James had hinted that he hoped to settle a match on Geneva. To whom, Maudine couldn't imagine. Who would take her off their hands, when there were girls going begging who were less strong-minded, wealthier, and with impeccable family connections?

Of course, it could be that farmer from over Wakeham way. His wife had recently died, leaving his ten children motherless. Or there was the Reverend Blunt from the next parish, a rather squat-looking creature with beady eyes.

James had not allowed himself to be drawn. In fact, he'd seemed annoyed with her. 'All I said was that a man had admired her many good qualities. It might come to nothing, so I should be obliged if you didn't tell anyone,' was all he would say.

She felt a small twinge of guilt about letting the girl go to Emma, though. As her husband had pointed out, she could have treated Geneva more kindly over the years. Emma would not treat Geneva kindly, either, for there was no compassion for the less fortunate inside her sister. But Maudine hadn't told her husband that.

James had been put quite out of countenance over her past behaviour. He'd said quite sternly, 'The Lord judges us by our actions, Maudine, and you must find it in your heart to be more charitable towards Geneva. I've been remiss in allowing it to go on for so long.'

'It's not me, James. The women of the district are of the opinion that she is too close to the earl, who allows her too much authority over his affairs. There are whispers about her conduct.'

'The earl is at liberty to allow her as much authority as he deems appropriate. It's a compliment to our family that he places so much trust in her. So why should the women of the district resent that authority? I suspect they have taken their lead from you, and are being unjust in their assessment of her.'

Maudine's promise to reform had fallen on deaf ears.

'On Sunday, I shall preach my sermon accordingly.'

And he had, his voice impassioned as he'd pointed out the evils of gossip and innuendo, so Maudine halfway expected tongues of fire to issue from his mouth and burn the congregation to cinders. She'd been quite stirred by his oratory, and had resolved, there and then, never to utter another mean word about Geneva.

After the sermon there was a resentful silence, until Lord Ashby said clearly and loudly, 'Well preached, Reverend Batterby,' and the other men followed suit.

But the women had exchanged glances and knowing nods, and had worn tight little smiles on their faces as they'd gathered together in small groups to gossip about the situation all the more viciously. Their daughters stood like a bunch of spring flowers. Pinch-faced, they shivered in the cold wind, their smiles too wide, their voices over-animated in the need to be noticed.

Maudine joined Sarah Ashby as she waited for her son in the porch. There was a hollowness inside her, so the people who had always mattered to her appeared to be strangers with nothing to admire in them.

'Silly creatures, they will catch their deaths,' she said of the daughters.

Sarah turned to gaze at her, a faint smile on her face. 'I did the same thing myself once. I fell in love with John Ashby at first sight and would have crawled the length of England on my knees, just to see him smile. Whenever we met, he was always surrounded by admiring women, so little did I know that he would have done exactly the same for me. What about you, Mrs Batterby?'

Maudine experienced astonishment, because nobody had ever been interested enough to ask her such a detail before. 'Me?'

'Did you fall in love with Reverend Batterby?'

'Yes, I suppose I did, though the marriage was arranged.' A smile drifted across her face. 'My husband has such a kind nature, and his childlike quality is endearing. He is a creature of habit who enjoys peace and quiet, but when he is roused by injustice he surprises me with his fire and eloquence.'

'The reverend's sermon today was particularly stirring. It seems to have evoked some passion among the congregation.'

'Ah yes. There has been some mischievous talk about his niece. James intends to put a stop to it.'

'You cannot blame the women for regarding her as a threat to the future of their daughters.'

'Geneva . . . a threat . . . that's ridiculous. What harm could she do them?'

'They think she's setting her cap at my son, perhaps,' Sarah said lightly. 'But you forgot to mention they were *both* being gossiped about.'

'I'm sure the earl's behaviour is above reproach.'

'Lord Ashby is a man, Maudine. Men are rarely above reproach.' She smiled and pulled her shawl more closely around her. 'Geneva is a fine-looking girl with a good mind and a sense of humour, albeit a rather odd one . . . and she arranges the earl's social affairs, which means the local women have to consult with a young woman they consider their inferior. My son has come to rely on Geneva, so is it any wonder that she's resented?'

Regarding the comment as a warning, Maudine flushed to the roots of her hair. 'Pray, be reassured on that count. Geneva will be leaving Edgley before too long to act as a weekend companion to my sister. Besides, the girl has been made fully aware of her position in life. Becoming a countess has not been considered as part of her future. Geneva knows her place, we have made sure of that. She would not dare to set her aim so high.'

The laugh Mrs Ashby gave was a little peeved. For all her airs and graces, Sarah Ashby was not of high birth herself, and even her son had inherited his title from his uncle. 'In all confidence, James has told me he's hopeful of settling a match on Geneva soon.'

Sarah's eyes widened. 'A match. With whom?'

'Oh, I'm not sure, but I believe two gentlemen are interested. One is a farmer who needs a mother for his children, the other a church official who requires a wife conversant with the needs of a parish.'

'We must arrange our dinner together before she leaves us then. Shall we say Thursday week. Geneva should be well by then, should she not?'

Maudine graciously inclined her head.

Ten

'You cannot marry Geneva off to some farmer with ten children to support,' Sorle informed the Reverend Batterby.

James Batterby offered him a slightly bemused look, along with a glass of sherry. 'I can't?'

'She's too young for such responsibility. Before the year is out she'll be worn down by hard work and will end up in an early grave.'

'Dear me, not a fate I'd wish on my ward, though the Lord would value her skills, no doubt.'

Sorle set the sherry aside and glowered at him. 'The Lord has no need for a social secretary. He employs clerics to look after his holy affairs. And talking about church matters, Geneva cannot be allowed to wed an elderly vicar who suffers from gout, either.'

'Gout . . . ah yes, a painful condition, I would imagine. Are you referring to Reverend Blunt by any chance?'

'I believe I am.'

'I cannot recall him ever asking for Geneva's hand in marriage, though he might have taken it into his head that he'd need a wife to look after him in his dotage. I must ask her if she's been approached. How did you come by this piece of information, pray?'

Sorle slumped into a chair and placed the parcel he was carrying in his lap. There was something wrong with this conversation he was having. 'My mother told me. She heard it from your own wife, I believe. Though I've since heard it from others. The affair is being talked about publicly.'

'Is it?' Slowly the reverend shook his head, then he smiled. 'I thought my sermon of last Sunday was sufficient to put a stop to idle talk in the district. Now I discover that my wife

126

appears to be the instigator of it. Oh dear.' He rang the bell for the maid, and said, when she arrived, wiping her hands on her apron, 'Ask Miss Tibbetson to attend me in my study please, Hannah.'

Sorle tidied his already immaculate cravat, then rose to his feet when he heard the patter of her feet coming across the hall. His heart behaved most erratically, making his legs want to leap and dance. He made sure he was solidly attached to the floor.

A delicate blush tinted her cheeks when he smiled at her. 'I didn't know you were here, My Lord. Where is your horse?'

'My horse?' What the devil did she want with Rastus? He made a show of patting his pockets. 'Odd, but I seem to have mislaid him. Ah. I know, I left him in the stable chatting with your uncle's mount.'

She laughed, her voice displaying a delightful huskiness brought about by the illness she'd suffered. It was wonderful to see her after all this time.

He offered her the chair he'd just vacated. His eyes drank her in, taking note of the frailty in her pale face, the slight redness to her nose. She filled him with delight. He seated himself on the stool next to her and, on impulse, took her hand between his. 'I've been anxious about you, Miss Tibbetson. I'm pleased to see you're recovering. Let me know if there's anything I can do to assist you in that.'

An alarmed glance was sent towards her uncle, who was polishing his spectacles, so luckily noticed nothing of the little intimacy. Her hand was hastily withdrawn and folded against the other in her lap, like two little white doves resting there.

'Best you sit a little further away, Lord Ashby, lest you catch my ailment. I'm not quite over it.'

'Oh, I'm never ill.' He placed the parcel on her lap. 'I've brought you a gift.'

Her glance went past him to her uncle. 'May I?'

'It's a shawl to keep you warm. I chose it myself, with my mother's help, of course.' Noting her uncle's slight frown, he hastily added, 'It's a gift from both of us . . . mostly from my mother. Actually, it was all her idea. I only paid for it . . . though she has promised to reimburse me.'

Sorle was thinking that God might strike him speechless

for uttering such falsehoods, when the reverend helped him out. 'Then the shawl is really a gift from your mother?'

'Exactly.'

'Ah, you should have said so in the first place. Under the circumstances, of course you may accept it, Geneva.'

The shawl was fashioned from soft blue velvet, the fringed edges were decorated with white silk rosebuds and pearls. Her eyes filled with tears as he placed it around her shoulders. 'I've never had anything quite so pretty. Thank you.'

Had her uncle not been there, Sorle would have taken her in his arms and kissed the tears away. Instead, he removed himself to the other side of the room. Although at a safer distance there, he watched her fingers delicately stroke the fabric and his skin tingled, craving the same treatment.

'My dear,' her uncle said. 'The earl has arrived with some preposterous tale about Reverend Blunt having asked for your hand in marriage. Is there any truth in it?'

She gazed at her uncle in shock, her eyes widening so they were filled with infinite blueness, like the sky in summer. Then she turned his way and laughter lightened them, her obvious amusement making him feel foolish. 'How very odd. You really shouldn't listen to gossip, My Lord.'

A growl gathered inside him as he pressed. 'But is it true?'

Unhurriedly she got to her feet and her voice was full of laughter. 'Any proposals I may have received would remain confidential. Why are you concerned about it?'

He hunched into his shoulders and muttered, 'I'm not concerned,' then, in the same breath, 'Damn it, Gen, just give me a straight answer, can't you? I've heard that the man is old enough to be your grandfather.' As her eyes met his, again he felt a rush of blood in his ears.

'I consider my answer to have been clear. May I point out that your position as Lord of the Manor does not give you jurisdiction over my private affairs. However, to satisfy your curiosity, no, the Reverend Blunt has not proposed marriage to me. Given the choice, I'd sooner wed the farmer with his ten children.'

The growl gathered momentum inside him and escaped. Although disguised as a cough, it didn't fool her, for the smile she gave him was creamy with the delight of trouncing him.

'I do hope you're not catching my cough. Excuse me now, Uncle, I must go and write a thank-you note to Mrs Ashby for this lovely shawl. If I leave the note on the hall table, perhaps you'd deliver it to your mother for me, My Lord.'

When she left, the room seemed empty. He turned to stare at the reverend, frustrated. 'Is Miss Tibbetson always so provocative?'

'Only when she's put in a position where she's obliged to defend herself. She attacks rather than retreats. In fact, she plays a rather good game of chess for a female.'

'Does she, by God?' Sorle said, then, to pass on from taking His name in vain, 'She's not really thinking of marrying the farmer with ten children, is she?'

The reverend heaved a heavy sigh, as though he was dealing with an idiot.

By the time the dinner engagement with Sorle and his mother came round, Geneva was feeling much more like her old self.

The boys were word perfect with regard to their songs, and good use had been made of the piano, of late. Maudine shook out her best gown, a grey silk creation with a lace collar, which was only slightly out of fashion. With it she wore a matching turban, the feather trim held in place by a silver brooch.

With only two gowns to choose from, Geneva picked the prettiest of the two, the high-waisted cornflower-sprigged muslin. Both were becoming a little grubby around the hem. She threaded some blue ribbons through her hair to match her sash. She'd have liked to have worn the blue pendant Sorle had given her all those years ago, but didn't dare, for her aunt was bound to kick up a fuss about being kept in ignorance about it, even though they were getting along better now. Her uncle would most likely make her hand it back.

Lifting the stone to her eye, she gazed through it, admiring the afternoon light, now tinted a pretty deep blue. When she'd been a child, she'd thought the pendant to be a cheap trinket. Now she knew the value of the gold mounting and chain. The stone was probably an amethyst, though she'd never seen one of such a deep blue. She shoved it into its hiding place under her mattress when she heard her aunt's heavy tread on the landing.

'There isn't enough room for all of us in the carriage,' Maudine told her, 'and it's too muddy underfoot to walk over. Gerald will come back for you and the four younger boys.' Maudine's glance darted over her, looking for something to criticize, for old habits died hard with her. She sighed. 'You still look sickly, Geneva. Pinch your cheeks to bring some colour to them before you leave. And you're slouching, do straighten up.'

'Yes, Aunt Maudine.' Geneva's fractional shrug of the shoulders seemed to satisfy her aunt.

'Make sure the boys keep the rugs over their laps. It's cold out and I don't want them to take a chill.' Her aunt gave her a meaningful look. 'It's inconvenient having to run back and forth after an invalid, when using good sense can prevent the illness from taking a hold in the first place. And impress on them the need to be on their best behaviour.'

'I think the earl likes them just as they are.'

'From what I observe, Lord Ashby is no judge of how boys should behave. Boys need a strong hand. When the earl is wed and has sons of his own, if he allows them their heads in the same way as he does mine, they will grow up to be wilful.'

Her aunt was mistaken. Sorle would adore his children, for there was no cruelty in him. In their turn, they would grow up secure in his love, and would do their best to please him, Geneva thought, as she followed Maudine downstairs to be with the boys.

Their faces all scrubbed clean, hair neatly brushed, the younger Batterby boys, all dressed in their Sunday best, were seated stiffly in a row on the sofa like a quartet of stuffed monkeys.

Geneva stifled a smile when Maudine instructed them, 'Don't you dare move until the carriage comes back for you.'

'We won't, Mama.'

As soon as the door closed behind the first party, the leftovers slumped against one another in an exaggerated, untidy heap, making faces and rude noises at each other. She smiled, knowing it was best to let their energy expend itself before they went to the manor. 'Let's go into the drawing room and dance while we're waiting.'

Their exercise was interrupted by Hannah, who put her head

around the door to gaze sourly at her. 'The carriage is coming back, and the missus said them boys should sit still. Your mother will give you the strap when she finds out.'

'If you don't tell her, she won't find out,' Robert said. 'And if you do, we'll put spiders in your bed. You just want to get Gen into trouble.'

Hannah gave him a long look, which Robert didn't quite manage to out-stare. 'Miss Tibbetson doesn't need me to get her into trouble. Why do you think she's being sent away to live with your aunt? Because of all the talk about her.'

Her cousins stared at her, then Moth put his arms around Geneva's waist and hugged her tight. 'I won't let them send you away. I hate them.'

Edward's bottom lip stuck out. 'So do I.'

'Don't start blubbering,' Michael said. 'Gen's only going for weekends. I overheard Papa saying so.'

'We shall still see each other during the week.' Gathering them all together, Geneva made sure they were tidy. 'I'm sorry you've found out like this, since I'd planned to tell you tomorrow. You'll soon get used to the arrangement, and you'll all be in school after Christmas. You'll enjoy that, Edward and Moth.'

'I doubt it. Miss Lilliput uses a cane when you misbehave,' Michael told them with great relish.

'Hell's bells!' Moth whispered, his palms pressing protectively against his behind.

'Stop teasing them, Michael.' But having been on the stinging end of Miss Lilliput's cane herself, Geneva resolved, as they fitted themselves as best as they could into the confined space of the carriage, to break the weapon in two if the woman dared use it on either of her young cousins.

Soon they were at the manor. Sarah kissed both her cheeks. 'My dear, I'm so glad you are better. I've missed your company so very much.'

When Sorle kissed her hand, his smile sent a quiver of anticipation through her. 'So have I,' he murmured, so only she could hear.

Lights twinkled along the table. Sarah wore a gown of cream silk, and, although Sorle was dressed in his usual black, his waistcoat was of pale blue brocade with buttons that glittered in the light.

The soup was served in porcelain plates. It was creamy and delicately flavoured with mushrooms.

Geneva tried not to stare at Sorle – tried not to notice the way his hair curled behind his ears, or his long fingers toying delicately with his cuffs. Tall and powerful, he dominated the room and suited the manor. Moreover, instead of taking position at the head of the table, he had ushered her uncle to the place of honour instead, with Maudine at the other end. Seating himself among the four older boys, he was directly opposite where she and Sarah divided the four younger boys.

Now, as the plates were being removed, his smile embraced her in warmth. 'You're a woman who looks comfortable amongst children, Miss Tibbetson.'

'I've always felt comfortable with my cousins. They've been good companions over the years and we've had some fine times together.' Eight grins rewarded her for those fine times as she gazed round at them all.

Sorle chuckled. 'Including hares and hounds.'

She blushed. 'How can I forget, when you bruised me so.'

'A hundred apologies. No . . . a thousand.'

She drew in a deep breath, hoping he wasn't going to goad her all evening. 'A thousand acceptances then, My Lord. Can we now allow the matter to rest?'

'We can, though it was you who raised it, I believe.'

'Remember when I nearly won the greasy pig at the midsummer fare?' Moth said.

'We were all so proud of you.'

'You stank something ripe, after,' Adam muttered.

Maudine gazed severely at her sons. 'Greasy pigs are not a suitable topic for the dinner table.'

Just then the main course arrived. It happened to be a suckling pig, its skin glistening and brown. There was an apple clenched between its teeth. Around it were roast chestnuts, turnips and onions emitting a cloud of fragrant steam.

'Holy hogsbodies!' Moth exclaimed, and when the room went silent, there came a muttered, 'Sorry, Papa.'

Heads down, the other boys exchanged glances across and along the table, grinning amongst themselves.

Trying to stifle a giggle, Geneva lifted her eyes to Sorle, who promptly winked at her, encouraging it to escape. He dissolved into laughter when it did. Soon they were all laughing, including Maudine, whose bosom heaved at the beginning of each spasm as she took in a breath. Geneva, who had never seen her aunt quite so unrestrained before, enjoyed the sight.

The reverend gazed from one to the other and, seeming to reach the conclusion that by reprimanding his family he'd also be reprimanding his host, he gave a resigned sort of sigh, then relaxed and joined in.

And that set the tone of the evening. Geneva had never enjoyed herself so much, as they all entered into the spirit of the gathering.

The boys sang like angels, Adam and Simon played Bach to perfection and basked in the delight of everyone. Sarah sang a lullaby she used to sing to Sorle and his sister when they were babies.

Watching her, and watching Sorle gazing at her, a faint smile on his face, Geneva wished she could remember her own early childhood. Had her mother ever sung lullabies to her so sweetly?

She could imagine Sorle as a child, sturdy-limbed, with dark, mischievous eyes and hair, his head a mass of bobbing dark curls. He had distinctive looks that his own children would favour – infants any woman would be proud to carry within her. But she would think no more on that. It was dangerous territory.

Then his eyes left his mother and flicked almost lazily towards her. His gaze brushed over her, slightly intimate, making her skin rise and tingle deliciously where it touched. Where he couldn't see; her skin became heated and moist, so parts of her seemed sugar-coated, and the rest a melt of syrup. His smile took on an ironic twist, as if he was aware of the effect he had on her, and she knew that her desire for him lay naked upon her face.

Then it became Geneva's turn to sing. Her uncle had suggested a ballad, one easy to sing. Since her throat hadn't been well enough to rehearse to any great length, she was glad of its simplicity.

Her voice still slightly husky, she followed in perfectly on her uncle's introduction. '*Come with me and be my love, and we will all the pleasures prove . . .*'

It was a charming love ballad. Her face warmed and she avoided Sorle's eyes when she saw the faint smile on his face. How embarrassing; in his conceit, he would think she was singing it especially for him. She didn't know how she got to the end of the song without forgetting the words, but Sorle joined in the last few lines, his voice low and intimate, so as not to dominate hers.

'*If these delights thy mind may move, then live with me and be my love.*' Sorle led the applause. 'Well done, Miss Tibbetson. A thoroughly enjoyable rendition, and sung with great tenderness. Wouldn't you say so, Reverend?'

'As always, beauty lies in the eye of the beholder – or in this case, the listener.'

'Both,' Sorle avowed as she moved past him to resume her seat on the sofa.

'I've heard Geneva sing the ballad better, but her recent illness has affected her voice a little, so I'll not be too hard in my judgement of her performance.'

Edward said staunchly. 'I liked it, all except for the love bits.'

'Me as well,' said Moth. 'I liked the love bits, as well.'

'Yes, yes gentlemen,' the reverend broke in hastily. 'You need not jump to Geneva's defence like an army of toy soldiers.'

Pouring a glass of lemonade, Sorle came to where she sat, and handed it to her. 'Perhaps this will help soothe your throat.'

'It's no longer sore, but thank you. I am a little thirsty.'

'May I?' He took the seat beside her without waiting for an answer, but since it was his sofa, Geneva could hardly push him to the floor. She'd have liked to, for he was a little too close for comfort and she was too aware of him.

'Perhaps Mrs Batterby would like to tell us her story now, after which I shall take my turn to conclude the entertainment. Then we shall have some supper.'

While Maudine was preparing to take her turn, Sorle whispered from the side of his mouth, 'Did you get my note?'

She shook her head slightly. 'My uncle forgot to give it to me. 'Was there anything of importance in it?'

He draped his arm casually along the back of the sofa. 'It was to say that I miss you, and to hurry up and come back to me . . . *to the manor.*'

'Now I am back. Tomorrow, though, I'm to be packed off to Dorchester to spend the weekend with Mrs Batterby's sister.'

'A pity, since I'm off to London on Monday to help escort my sister and her children here.'

A stab of dismay ran through her. 'Oh, will you be gone for long?'

'Two weeks.'

Two weeks without seeing Sorle suddenly seemed like a lifetime.

'Is there anything I can obtain for you there? My sister is a woman of fashion and knows where to purchase the best ball gowns and the fripperies that women need to go with it.'

He'd forgotten her poverty, and goodness, she had no idea of what to wear to his ball. She supposed she could make a lace overskirt for the gown she was wearing tonight. And she could trim the neck with lace and afford some new gloves.

'Thank you, but London fashions are not very practicable for country women to wear, and I don't often go to balls.' She'd never been invited to any ball before, not even the local one held by Squire Hunter at the start of the hunting season. Excitement suddenly filled her to the brim. 'I'm so looking forward to it.'

Maudine gently coughed, drawing their attention to the fact that she was about to begin her story. 'Long ago in the land of Carfael, there lived a band of thieves who terrorized the good citizens of the town . . .'

Sorle's finger found a curl at the nape of her neck and wound it gently around his finger. Goosebumps escaped down her spine.

'While boys who'd been naughty shivered with fear in their beds . . .'

Creeping to where they sat, and wriggling in between them, Moth snuggled against her side. She put her arm around the boy, smiling at Sorle when he was forced to move.

Sorle had performed the act-three speech from Hamlet he'd learned by heart at school, though Shakespeare would have rolled in his grave at his delivery of it. Still, the Batterby boys had enjoyed it, and Geneva had seemed entranced.

How sweet she was, he thought, but still, *'To be, or not to be . . .'* still remained an unanswered question in his mind.

He'd hoped to run into her over the weekend, but she'd been whisked off to be of service to the Dorchester relative on the Friday evening.

Now it was Saturday morning and he was off for a ride. He'd take the dogs for a run along the beach, he thought, then he might go and visit the widowed farmer and his ten orphaned children to satisfy himself they were being looked after.

The stable was warm and ripe. The coach horses were being exercised and schooled and Tom was mucking out their stalls. Sorle took his saddle down and fitted it on to his gelding's back. 'Is everything all right, Tom?'

'Yes, sir. 'Tis a grand morning for a ride. Your boy be right mettlesome. 'Tis the mare, sir. She be in season, and the gelding has the memory of the scent in him, if not the urge. Thank God there be no stallions, since they'd kick the stable down to get at her.'

'I intend to breed from her when she's up to condition.'

'Squire Hunter has a good stallion to cover her, with bloodlines as long as your arm. Nimrod, he be called, and he's as black as satan. I wouldn't mind his life myself. It would beat shovelling dirty straw into a pile.'

'You should find yourself a wife, Tom.'

'Ah, who would want me, when I've got a head that's a nail short of a plank?'

'But you're a well-set-up sort of fellow. I saw that girl giving you the eye last Sunday after church.'

'That'll be Betty Crump. She gives everybody the eye, because one of them do look to the left and the other do look to the right.'

Sorle grinned. 'You wouldn't see that in the dark.'

''Tis true, right enough.' Tom adjusted his crotch. 'And Betty has got comfortable parts a man could get a grip on. She lives with her ma in a cottage that needs a bit of fixing, too. A man could be right comfortable with two women seeing to his needs if they didn't nag him too much.'

Tom threw his shovel aside. 'I'll be callin' on Miss Betty Crump tonight to ask her to be my sweetheart then, if you do think she be a right un for me.' He grinned. 'Likely Betty'll give me a bit of ease at the same time for the honour. Nobody else would have me, I reckon, for I'm a stupid great lump and that's a fact.'

'You sell yourself short, Tom. And best you go to the pump and wash the dung off yourself before you go a-courting,' Sorle said, trying not to laugh as he mounted.

Horse and rider moved out. The dogs ran this way and that, noses to the ground and tails waving high as they darted after the trail of each scent they came across.

It was a fine, cold day, the thick-bladed winter grass crunched with frost under the hooves of his horse, and steam spurted from its nostrils. When Rastus's muscles had warmed a little, they made their way down the cliff to the beach, and Sorle gave Rastus his head. The horse surged powerfully forward along the waterline, kicking up sand. Steaming breath spurted from his mouth.

It reminded Sorle of the dragon in the story Maudine Batterby had told. She'd been nervous to start with, but it soon became obvious she was a born storyteller. Moth had fallen asleep cuddled against Geneva's side, and he'd watched her tenderly kiss the top of the boy's head.

That small action had filled him with envy, and now the thought that he wouldn't see her before he returned from London made his heart ache. Perhaps he should give the farmer a miss. Instead, he could go to Dorchester, then drop in on Mrs Batterby's relative and make sure Geneva hadn't suffered a relapse.

He turned his horse around and headed back to the house. Leaving the dogs with Tom, he headed in the direction of Dorchester. Two hours later he entered the town and looked around him. The streets were sparsely populated, the tall chimneys smoked greyly against the pale winter sky.

'Damned fool!' he muttered, mentally kicking himself, for he'd just realized that he didn't even know the woman's name, let alone where she lived. He sucked in a deep breath, as if the very action would bring Geneva out of hiding.

Feeling thwarted, his stomach rumbling from the exercise, he crossed to the Antelope Hotel, where he consumed a venison pie rich with gravy and topped with a high-suet pastry crust. He washed it down with ale, then set off back.

Leaving his horse to cool down with the groom, he strode

to the house, the half a dozen carriages in front of the house barely registering. He supposed his mother must be entertaining, in which case he must put in an appearance. She expected it, and it would take his mind off his disappointment at not being able to enquire after Geneva.

His man soon had him suited and his hair tidied. Sliding down the bannister rail, he leapt into the hall, pulled a smile to his face, threw open the drawing-room doors and sailed inside.

Scent filled his nostrils, making them contract slightly. His eyes were assailed with a multitude of colours, his ears with a multitude of feminine voices.

Then the voices stopped, Several pairs of eyes swivelled his way, bosoms heaved and there was a combined sigh from the throats of the several women present.

God save me! he thought in horror. Was there going to be no end to Geneva's torture? She had combined the eligibles into one social event without telling him.

His mother came forward, her eyes full of laughter, enjoying his shock. 'You're late, Sorle. Had you forgotten we were entertaining today?'

'I'm so sorry, my social diary is missing.'

How many times would he have to use such an excuse? He would kill Geneva the next time he saw her. He would take her slim white throat between his hands, squeeze the breath from her body and laugh while she begged and pleaded for release. After that he'd kiss her senseless to add to the punishment. He found it hard not to smile at the thought of such sweet retribution.

His mother placed her hand on his arm. 'The housekeeper was in possession of the diary. Luckily, she'd catered for the event, as per Miss Tibbetson's instructions. Allow me to introduce you to the ladies.'

As if he had any choice now. 'Must you?' he whispered.

'I must,' she whispered back, 'and don't you dare call those disgraceful dogs in to help you out this time. I won't have it.'

His mother threaded her arm through his in a tight grip and drew him towards the solid mass of females, who had formed a line. They stopped at the first.

'This is Mrs Merryweather and her eldest daughter, Antoinette.'

'Miss Merryweather,' he murmured, picking up the lace handkerchief she dropped at his feet, and handing it back.

Behind him, the door closed, trapping him inside.

Eleven

It soon became evident that Emma Mason had been born with no sense of humour at all. Sour and demanding, even if Maudine's sister had been paying a wage, she would have been the worst mistress a maid could ever have suffered.

But her ageing servant had been dismissed the month before in anticipation of the free labour Geneva would provide Emma with. It was obvious that she was going to take advantage of it right from the beginning.

The house was large and draughty and smelled of mould. Only two rooms were warmed by a fire, the smaller of the two sitting rooms and the kitchen, the stove of which was kept damped down until used for heating water. Still, Geneva had no time to become chilled as, brush in hand, she scrubbed several months of ground-in dirt from the cold grey flagstones of the kitchen floor. Even when that was done, her tasks didn't stop.

'My sister's half of the house needs to be kept clean, whether the rooms are used or not. You can gradually clean the whole house from top to bottom. Once you've done that, you can start all over again. Then there are the insides of the windows, the mirrors and the furniture to polish. After that, I'm sure I can find some mending that needs to be done to keep you fully occupied.'

'I am not your maid, Mrs Mason,' Geneva gently pointed out. 'I'm here to keep you company.'

The woman fixed her with an icy stare and pinched her arm cruelly. The unexpectedness of the action made Geneva give a little scream and move away from her.

'Be very careful I don't take a rod to your back, Miss Tibbetson. The reason you're here is because my sister doesn't want you back. She told me so when she was staying here after our father died. We have an arrangement. You will stay here with me. In return for your board, you will do any work I consider necessary. You will rise at five a.m., when you will clean the grate and stove, light the fire and bring in the coal. You'll retire at midnight, but only if the work you were allocated has been carried out to my satisfaction.'

'And where will I sleep, in the cellar?' Geneva thought to ask.

'You may keep your sarcastic tongue to yourself, young lady. Fortunately for you, there is no cellar, else I'd be sorely tempted to put you there.'

The bedroom Geneva was given was the one Emma's late father had died in. It had a stuffy aroma of old man, tobacco, dust and perspiration. The dead man's clothes were still in the wardrobe, sad old things, dangling empty, like hanged corpses.

She shivered and, pulling a quilt around herself, curled up in a chair. She refused to sleep in the bed where Emma Mason's father had breathed his last. As a result, she slept hardly a wink.

Food was sparse compared to the amount and variety served at the Batterbys' house. A pot of mutton broth and a loaf of bread was made on Mondays by Mrs Mason. Precise portions were dolled out and eaten every day of the week, sometimes with the addition of cabbage or potato. By the weekend, when Geneva needed to eat, it consisted mostly of thin gravy, and was practically unpalatable.

The water pump was at the bottom of a long, overgrown garden. Taking many trips back and forth with a bucket, Geneva's gowns soon became bedraggled and muddy, her shoes ruined.

Gerald and Matthew came to collect her on Sunday evening. Exhausted, she climbed into the rig, glad to get away from the place and the harping Mrs Mason. By comparison, her aunt Maudine was an angel.

'Thank goodness you're back. The boys have been surly and unmanageable,' she complained. 'I don't know what's the matter with them, they won't sit still for five minutes.'

Making conversation was hard work that evening. Geneva daren't complain to her uncle lest she be sent away permanently before she had time to think what could be done. Hadn't her uncle made it perfectly clear that earning a living was to be her lot in life?

Better that she was Sorle's servant than Mrs Mason's, she thought. If she put her predicament before him, he would probably accommodate her in his servants' quarters. She would ask him when he returned from London.

But she daren't. Now she'd been made aware of the speculation in the district about her, that could prove to be a mistake. Sorle's manner towards her was already too familiar, and her feelings towards him too warm for her own good. Her worries roiled inside her like butter in a churn, so she was almost sick from the motion of it.

Wishing she had someone she could talk her problems over with, that night Geneva cried herself to sleep. She woke late, and when she arrived at the manor it was to discover that Sorle had already left for London.

Geneva looked tired, Sarah thought, as she gently took her to task over the weekend arrangements.

'My dear, Sorle and I found ourselves unprepared to entertain the afternoon party you arranged. Why didn't you warn us of it?'

To Sarah's surprise, tears filled Geneva's eyes. 'I'm so sorry. I was taken ill before I could, and forgot. It was in the diary, and I'd consulted with Mrs Pickering over catering arrangements. Were the refreshments unsatisfactory, then?'

'The refreshments were fine, but the earl was displeased to be involved with so many gathered here at once. For a man in his position, to be forced to entertain so many young ladies with their minds set on marriage was an uncomfortable experience.'

The girl looked crushed at being reprimanded. 'But the suggestion was Lord Ashby's in the first place. When he asked me to cancel the single appointments, he remarked that he'd rather see them all at once.'

'A casual remark, no doubt, and as such, one that need not have been taken at face value. I'm sure you knew that, Geneva. I know how aggravating Sorle can be and, no doubt, you thought he deserved to be taught a lesson in humility, hmmm?'

She hung her head. 'I'm sorry. It was stupid of me, when you've always been so kind. I'll apologize to the earl as soon as he returns, and hope that you'll forgive me too.'

Goodness, Geneva seemed quite distressed. Sarah inserted her hand under her chin and lifted it. There were dark shadows under her eyes. 'You look tired. I hope that woman isn't working you too hard after your illness.'

Geneva avoided her eyes, which was unusual. 'I didn't sleep at all well last night.'

Sarah subjected her to a thorough scrutiny before she released her. It was obvious that the girl had something on her mind. 'I've left you a list of extra guests to write out ball invitations for. Sorle thought it might be a good idea to invite some officers from Dorchester as partners for the ladies. Soldiers always add a bit of dash in their uniforms, and there is a sense of danger about them. I'll expect you in my rooms when you've finished, we'll take refreshment together.'

But Geneva didn't turn up. When Sarah went looking for her, she discovered the girl sound asleep on the sofa. Geneva lay on her side, tear tracks drying on her cheeks and her hand dangling to the floor. Sarah's annoyance fled. How ill-used the girl looked. Apart from her tiredness, her exposed palm was blistered and red. The hem of her gown was torn and bedraggled, her shoes and hose ruined. Placing a rug over the girl, as Sarah stooped to lift her arm under it, she saw some discolouration. Carefully she peeled back her sleeve, to reveal a dark bruise.

Sorely tempted to go and see Reverend Batterby, Sarah decided to allow Sorle to handle it when he returned from London. A little hardship wouldn't hurt Geneva, and she was sure Sorle was up to rescuing a maiden in distress, especially when the distressed maiden was Geneva Tibbetson.

But the following Saturday something occurred which made Sarah wonder if her judgement wasn't at fault.

Earlier that day she'd remembered a pair of diamond and ruby earrings which had belonged to the late countess – earrings she thought might look pretty with the gown she intended to wear to the ball.

The jewellery was not in the strongbox where Sorle kept

his valuables. Puzzled, she returned the key to its hiding place and went to Geneva's sitting room to fetch the inventory. Her eyes moved slowly down the pages of neat writing and figures and she smiled, thinking how thorough Geneva had been in her housekeeping. However, there was no mention of the jewellery collection.

A search of the room the late countess had once occupied revealed nothing. The room had been meticulously cleaned. She sent a maid to fetch the housekeeper. 'What happened to the personal items in this room, Mrs Pickering?'

'They were packed in trunks and stored in the attic. Miss Tibbetson and I did it between us. She was most particular that the garments be folded correctly, with layers of muslin between each item. We put pomanders in to keep the moths at bay, though they'd already been at some of the garments. I thought Miss Tibbetson was making too much fuss about the garments, since they were old.

'Best we give them to the poor, who can use the fabric to make clothes for their children, I said, but she wouldn't have it. "It's not my property to give away, but I will bring the matter up with the earl and he can decide that for himself," says she.'

'Which was the correct thing to do, of course. I do hope you were not questioning Miss Tibbetson's authority, Mrs Pickering.'

Ellen Pickering looked mortified. 'Indeed not, Mrs Ashby. Miss Tibbetson is a very capable young lady for whom I have a great deal of respect. Indeed, all the staff think very highly of her.

'That's good news indeed. Did you see any jewellery when the trunk was packed?'

'No, Mrs Ashby.'

Dismissing the housekeeper, Sarah thought about the problem. Sorle had been careless in leaving the house unattended for all that time, when access to it had turned out to be child's play. Perhaps Geneva had hidden the jewellery somewhere. It was possible Maudine Batterby knew where that hiding place was. Indeed, Geneva might have taken it to the rectory and given it to the reverend for safe keeping.

Ordering the carriage to be brought round, she drew a warm wrap around herself and paid the rectory a visit.

Taking an apron from about her waist, Maudine hurried forward, a smile on her face. 'Mrs Ashby . . . Sarah. How unexpected. Do come into my sitting room. It's warm there.' She turned to her maid. 'Fetch us some coffee, Hannah, and some of those almond tarts I made yesterday. Use the best china.'

As soon as she was seated on a chair by the fire, Sarah said, 'I cannot find the Ashby jewellery, Maudine. I wondered if Geneva had brought it here for safe keeping, and thought that perhaps your husband may be able to throw some light on the matter.'

'Indeed, Geneva has never mentioned any jewellery to me, and if she'd given it to her uncle for safe keeping I'm sure he would have told me. Unfortunately, the reverend and our sons are at the church, so I cannot ask him.'

The tea was brought. Hannah hovered as Maudine said, a note of uncertainty in her voice. 'I'm sure there's a simple explanation for the jewellery being missing from the manor. Geneva has been raised up to be honest. If she brought the jewellery to my home, it would be to protect it from thieves and felons.'

'I would be loath to consider any other explanation, Maudine. In fact, I'm not even suggesting anything to the contrary.'

'Would you like me to look in Geneva's room then? She may have put them in one of the dresser drawers.'

'I think I'd prefer to wait until she's home, so I can ask her myself.'

Maudine's voice took on a slightly frosty tone. 'I won't hear of you waiting that long.' She turned to the maid. 'Go and look in Miss Tibbetson's room to see if you can find some jewellery. What exactly is it that you're looking for?'

Sarah began to wish she hadn't come. 'I can't itemize it. It's the whole Ashby collection which is mislaid. Much of it I'd recognize, since the late countess showed it to me when I was first married. Diamond necklaces, ruby earrings . . .'

Maudine tittered. 'A collection of diamonds and rubies, you say. I'm sure I'd have seen all those glittering jewels, had they been brought into my home.'

Sighing, for Maudine looked affronted, as if she'd been

144

accused of stealing them herself, Sarah gazed at her, wondering now if Geneva could possibly have been tempted. After all, she was impoverished. But no, she must not jump to such conclusions.

'Not for one moment have I considered that a member of your family might have stolen them, Maudine.'

It was the wrong thing to say. 'A-hah!' Maudine cried out with great passion. 'Now it is coming out, you consider my entire family to be nothing but a pack of thieves.'

Just then Hannah came back, her face twisted into a triumphant smile. 'I found this hidden under the mattress, Mrs Batterby.' Dangling from her finger was a blue pendant on a gold chain.

'I remember that,' Sarah said, her disappointment causing her heart to fall. 'It's a sapphire, the only one in the collection and quite rare, because of its size. But where's the rest of the jewellery?'

'There's nothing else, Mrs Batterby, 'ceptin' this,' and Hannah dropped a jingling purse into her lap. 'I reckon she's got them jewels hid and is selling them one by one, for where else would the money have come from? The same thing happened in a house I worked in afore. The maid got caught and was transported for life, but not before her mistress gave her a well-deserved thrashing.'

Maudine gave a tormented cry. 'Oh, the deceitful girl! How could she, after all I've done for her? I am so ashamed of her. Hannah, make all haste to the church and fetch the reverend. Tell him to alert the constable. We shall have her arrested and they will soon get to the bottom of it.'

'You'll do no such thing!' Sarah snapped. 'We will wait until my son comes back and I will place the facts before him. There might be a simple explanation as to how the pendant came to be in Miss Tibbetson's possession. She can then tell us what has happened to the rest of the jewellery.'

'My husband must be informed.'

'Of course he must. The earl can then decide what is to be done with her. He may wish to investigate the affair himself and, if the jewellery is recovered, he may well wish to drop the matter altogether.'

'Whatever happens. She shall not come back to my home

145

and be a bad influence on my sons,' Maudine vowed.

Hannah began to massage Maudine's shoulders. 'Best to keep your husband's poor relation in the dark about this, Mrs Batterby, lest she take it into her head to run away. I could deliver a note to your sister's house in Dorchester on my half day off tomorrow – ask Mrs Mason to keep Miss Tibbetson there until she's sent for.'

Maudine patted her hand. 'Yes, Hannah, perhaps we will do that.'

'And perhaps you should not. In fact, I would advise you to think for yourself, not allow some maidservant, who obviously holds a grudge against Miss Tibbetson, dictate to you.'

The maid gave her a bold look as Maudine whispered, 'I don't know how I'd manage without Hannah.'

'Then more fool you.' Unwilling to take refreshment in a household where one of the servants seemed to rule the mistress, Sarah stood. 'If I hear any gossip about this affair before my son has had time to investigate it thoroughly, you will regret it, I think, Mrs Batterby.'

'Oh, don't worry,' Maudine said bitterly, 'having a thief in the house is not something I intend to shout about.'

'You lay blame on the girl too easily. It has not been proved that Geneva is a thief, and she must be given the chance to clear her name before it is slandered in public.'

'Clear it or not, I rue the day I took the Tibbetson girl into my home, indeed I do.' Holding out the pendant, she added, 'Pray, take this with you. I'm mortified by the thought that I've harboured a criminal under my roof, and I feel one of my headaches coming on. I'll never be able to show my face in public again.' Maudine burst into hysterical sobs.

Sarah didn't stop to comfort her. Not only did Maudine Batterby act before she thought, she jumped to conclusions too readily and was only concerned about what people thought of *her*. Sarah's fist tightened around the sapphire and she prayed that Geneva had a plausible explanation for being in possession of this valuable piece.

Geneva was cleaning the inside of the landing window when she saw Hannah marching down the street, a smirk on her face.

Afterwards, she couldn't say what it was about Hannah that

made her heart instantly sink, except she knew that the maid didn't like her. Hannah was the more dominant of the Batterby maids. Essie, the younger one, was quieter and more pleasant, but less intelligent.

Geneva remembered interviewing the pair for the manor household, and although she would have hired Essie, Hannah's overbearing and familiar manner had not worked in her favour. And since Essie wouldn't stay without Hannah, neither of them had been employed.

She heard the murmur of voices and was tempted to creep downstairs and listen to what was going on. But the stairs creaked badly. Then the sitting-room door opened. Footsteps crossed the hall and the door shut firmly behind Hannah.

Two hours passed, time which produced an atmosphere of tension in the house, so her ears were tautly strained by the silence. Then came a shout. 'Miss Tibbetson. Come here at once.'

Geneva ran, for to be slow earned her a pinch, and she was already covered in small bruises. 'Is everything alright, Mrs Mason?'

'The woman stared her up and down, her lips thinning. 'Why shouldn't things be alright? I'm advised by my sister that you're to stay here until further notice.'

'But why?'

'Because I've told you so.' Emma handed her a piece of paper. 'I have worked out your duties and you will carry them out to the letter.'

Geneva gazed at the list of tasks to be done and rebellion roiled in her. 'But, Mrs Mason, this is too much.'

Emma Mason stood. She was larger than her sister, stronger. One meaty arm was held across her waist, the other hung at her side. 'Do you have complaints about your treatment then, Miss Tibbetson?'

'I'm just saying it is too much work to expect one person to do in one day.'

She had not seen the cane in Emma Mason's hand until the woman lifted her arm from her skirt. Blows began to rain down on her, one after the other. Shielding her face, Geneva cowered away from her, shocked by the violence and groaning with each blow.

Suddenly, the woman ran out of breath and the blows ceased. 'You will do what is written on that list and you'll not receive any food until it's finished. Do you understand?'

Tears trickling down her cheeks, Geneva nodded, resolving to run away as soon as darkness fell. But it started to rain heavily, and the temperature plummeted. She would have no protection against the elements.

As soon as her work was finished, she was allowed to eat her bowl of broth then marched to her room. The key turned in the lock with a solid thunk.

'Where's Gen this week?' Moth said to Edward.

'She had to stay with Aunt Emma.' Edward lowered his voice. 'Everybody's whispering, so I think something is going on that they don't want us to know about.'

Moth gazed at him, eyes wide and tragic. 'Gen hasn't been murdered, has she?'

'Of course not.' Edward's voice cracked as he considered it. 'At least, I don't think so. Let's go and ask Gerald.'

They found their six elder brothers already gathered in Gerald and Matthew's room. 'What do you two want?' Adam said.

Edward stared hard at him. 'We want to know what's going on, and if you don't let us stay, I'll flatten you.'

'So will I,' said Moth.

That settled, the pair seated themselves cross-legged on the circular rug with Bandit, who'd been sneaked in earlier, sitting between them. Moth got down to the business at hand straight away. 'Has Gen been murdered?'

'Don't be such an idiot, of course she hasn't, but I heard Hannah telling Essie that Geneva might go to prison.'

Moth's mouth dropped open and stayed there. Then he gave a disbelieving cry. Grabbing him by the neck, Matthew clamped a hand over his mouth. 'Quiet, Moth. You don't want anyone to hear, do you?'

'I don't want her to go to prison and be hanged by the neck until dead. Has she killed mean old Aunt Emma, then?'

The Batterby siblings expressed appropriate noises of support when Robert said gloomily, 'I wish she had. But it's something worse, much worse. Geneva stole precious jewels from the manor.'

'You mean she's become a robber? What did she do with the jewels?'

'She hid them somewhere! Mama's in a foul mood and Papa is breathing fire and brimstone in his study.'

'Creaking gates! Fancy Gen doing something like that. Can't they find them?'

'All they can find is one piece, a gold and sapphire pendant. Hannah found it under Gen's mattress.'

'But that's Gen's magic stone, remember!' Moth cried out. 'She's always had that. It used to belong to an Egyptian princess. If you look through it when the moon's full and it turns everything a purple colour, the wish you make will come true.'

After a totally irrelevant discussion on the authenticity of the stone's powers, they all looked at one another. Gerald got to his feet. 'I'm going down to tell Papa.'

'But we agreed to keep this meeting a secret.'

'Sometimes secrets can't be kept. You don't want her to end up in prison, do you?'

'No. But don't mention the stone's magic powers. I heard Papa telling the devil off, this morning, so mention of magic stones might set the cat among the pigeons.'

Bandit came alert and managed a small yelp at the word cat, before Edward's hand closed gently around his nose to shush him.

'We all ought to go and see Papa. He always listens better when we're together.'

Moth said gloomily, 'Last time we did that he tanned my hide with a cane.'

'He won't this time, since you haven't done anything wrong,' Robert predicted.

James Batterby was not really in the mood to counsel his sons, but his duty forbade him from turning them away.

'What is it, gentlemen?' he said shortly.

They looked uneasily from one to another.

'Gerald, you're usually the one to present the petition. Don't waste my time by standing there.'

'It's about Geneva.'

James heaved a sigh as heavy as his heart. 'I thought it might

149

be. If you're here to request her immediate return to the fold, the answer is no. Until the earl returns and this matter is resolved it would be better if she remained isolated from the family.'

'It's about the blue pendant,' Moth cut in. 'She couldn't have stolen it, because she's had it for ever. It belonged to an Egyptian princess and is—ouch!'

Edward had kicked him.

James leaned forward. 'Go and stand in the corner, Edward, I'll deal with you afterwards. 'Now, finish what you were about to say, Timothy.'

'The stone has magical powers. You can make a wish on it and it'll come true.'

'I'm not in the mood to listen to such rubbish. A belief in magic is the work of the devil on idle minds. You will write the line "I do not believe in magic" one hundred times and present it to me at precisely four p.m. Thank you. Is there anything more you wish to tell me?'

'We don't believe our cousin would steal anything,' Gerald said with some fierceness.

'Neither did I, but you're overlooking one pertinent question. Notwithstanding how long it has been in her possession, where did Geneva get the pendant from in the first place?'

'She's had it since I was about Moth's age.'

'About eight years then. Wasn't that about the time you invented that game where you broke into the manor?'

The boys looked guiltily at one another.

James's voice softened. 'All I can promise is that Geneva will get a fair hearing. You may go . . . no, not you, Edward. I will not have you kicking your brother when he's trying to tell me something. Hold out your hand.'

'It didn't hurt,' Moth told him, stepping forward, 'and I kicked Edward yesterday.'

Picking up his cane, James came around the desk. 'I see, then both of you may hold out your hands.'

Two strokes each were dished out, but James had been lenient and had put no strength into the strokes. He was worried sick about the situation with Geneva, and the thought that he'd failed to raise her successfully weighed heavily on him.

'Did we do our best for her?' he said wearily to his wife a little later in the day.

Unexpectedly, she answered, 'I could have been more forgiving towards her, perhaps. I resented her presence in my household and was envious of the love our children offered her. James, I tried to prepare Geneva for a life outside our household by denying any expectations she may have harboured. Now I'm sorry I couldn't bring myself to love her more, for I believe my indifference towards her became a habit over the years.'

'Should we tell the girl what lies ahead of her, Maudine?'

'No, we must wait until the earl returns, which will not be very long. I have promised Sarah not to think the worst of Geneva, and you mustn't either. Not until she's proven guilty. My sister will keep her counsel and Geneva will be safe there. Perhaps the earl might not press charges. He has always thought highly of her, you know. I had hopes in that direction.'

'As does every mama in the district. When the earl finds out about this, any esteem he holds Geneva in will evaporate swiftly, for the Ashby jewellery collection is worth a fortune.'

'Then it was downright stupid to leave temptation lying around for eight years,' she snapped. 'Anybody could have got inside the manor and stolen it. In fact, somebody else probably did. There were some gypsies living on the land two summers ago, so how dare they blame Geneva?'

'She has the pendant in her possession.'

'Ah, yes. I'd forgotten.'

The pair of them fell silent.

Twelve

B ecause constant rain had turned the highways to mud, the earl's party had been forced to break their journey just past Southampton, where they became guests of family friends for a few days.

Elizabeth Chambers and her two young daughters had declared themselves pleased to take a break from the swaying carriage. Although grateful for the chance to warm himself, as the weather had been inclement, Sorle was eager to return to Welford Manor, for this grander Hampshire home, with its echoing corridors, lofty rooms and cold marble floors, was not the most comfortable of places.

But servants had been sent out by his host, and as soon as the roads were declared passable, Sorle announced his intention to depart. He supervised the loading of the carriage himself, grumbling good-naturedly about the amount of luggage he was required to lift for his sister.

'Some of it belongs to Richard,' Elizabeth said, referring to her husband, who'd been detained by business but who intended to travel down on horseback the following week. 'Besides, you have plenty of luggage yourself. What's in those fancy boxes?'

'Oh . . . some formal garments I bought to be worn at the ball,' he said vaguely.

When Elizabeth smiled and raised her eyebrow, she reminded Sorle of his mother. 'From De'dargan and Paige? That's a most exclusive ladies' establishment. I can't believe you intend to wear a gown yourself. Who's the lady?'

He shrugged. 'The gown is for Miss Tibbetson . . . my social secretary.'

'Your secretary is going to the ball and can afford to buy a gown from De'dargan and Paige? You must pay her a fortune, since their clients are usually from the ton. Has she a title, then?'

'No, but I knew the title I inherited might turn out to be useful one day, and it was,' he mocked. 'It gave me a licence to buy a frilly gown for a young lady who deserves one.'

'You paid for the gown yourself, didn't you?'

He nodded. 'You'll find that the country is much less formal than London. Her whole family is invited, so I could hardly leave her out. She's the poor relative, and cannot afford a ball gown on her own.'

'I would have thought something less expensive would have been more suitable. Something already made, from a dressmaker, not an exclusive design.'

'Miss Tibbetson will not realize its exclusivity unless you tell her. Besides, it was already made. The Countess of Farnmouth had ordered the gown and accessories for her daughter's coming-out ball, but the girl disgraced herself by taking off for Scotland with an officer of the King's Regiment. The gown will suit Geneva admirably, I think. Now, stop spoiling my fun.'

Geneva? Elizabeth's eyes narrowed as she gazed at her brother. 'You're incorrigible, Sorle. Take my word for it, you will give her the wrong idea altogether if you call her by her first name.'

'I do hope so. I prefer women who have wrong ideas. Now, stop looking at me like a hound on the scent, I get enough of that from our mother.' He grinned cheerfully at her. 'Climb into the carriage with your brats, Lizzie, else I'll leave you behind. I want to be home before dark.' His eyes went to his nieces. 'Behave yourselves, you two. Please don't squash those boxes, else I'll make you walk the rest of the way. And don't allow your mother to satisfy her curiosity by opening them.'

Madeleine and Barbara, two russet-haired beauties with glistening hazel eyes and merry smiles, giggled. At aged eight and nine they were already heartbreakers, he thought.

There was a mass waving of hands and shouts of goodbye as they took leave of their hosts, then the coachman's whip cracked and they were off.

Geneva couldn't understand why she was being locked in her room.

Cold and unhappy, she'd done her best to please the woman she now seemed to work for. Every time Emma Mason went out, Geneva found herself locked inside her room until she came back.

'Why am I being locked in?' she demanded to know one day, and the woman backhanded her across the cheek with such force that Geneva fell backwards on to the floor.

Emma gazed down at her, her eyes venomous. 'I cannot take the risk of you absconding with the contents of my house, missy, that's why.'

'Don't be so ridiculous, I could hardly carry your household goods away on my back,' she retorted. It was a remark which earned her a savage pinch. Tears in her eyes, Geneva muttered. 'My uncle will not be pleased when he discovers I've been treated so brutally.'

'Brutally!' Bringing her face down close to Geneva's, the woman spat out, 'Wait until you see the inside of a prison, my girl. No doubt you'll discover what brutality is then.'

'Prison? Why should I go to prison when I've done nothing wrong. I demand to see my uncle.'

Emma Mason's voice became strident. 'Demand all you will, hussy. You've disappointed your uncle, and he doesn't want to see you. I told them years ago that taking you in was a mistake. Now I've been proved right.'

'How sad it is that you take comfort from such meaness of spirit, Mrs Mason.' Springing to her feet, Geneva tried to push past the woman, but to no avail. Two palms in Geneva's stomach stopped her forward motion before she was shoved backwards on to the bed. The bedroom door slammed shut, the key turned in the lock before she could get up. Emma Mason's footsteps thudded off down the stairs and, in a little while, Geneva heard the front door slam behind her.

She gathered herself together and sprang towards the door, bent to inspect the keyhole. Her adversary had taken the key with her. Geneva kicked the door in frustration, cursing when she hurt her foot. She had more than enough bruises as it was.

Pulling open the drawers in the dresser, Geneva tipped them out, scattering the contents around the room as she searched for something she could use to force the door open.

There was a pistol. She picked it up and gazed at it. Had she known, she could have used it on Emma Mason to demand the key. Her mood lightened and she laughed. Pulling on a ferocious expression, she aimed the weapon at her reflection in the wardrobe mirror and pulled the trigger.

The result was unexpectedly dramatic, for she hadn't expected the pistol to be loaded. The explosion propelled her backwards. Crying out in terror as the glass shattered at her feet, she dropped the weapon to the floor. Thank goodness she *hadn't* aimed it at Emma Mason, she thought, waiting for the ringing noise in her ears to subside and the thump of her heart to calm. However much she disliked the woman, she wouldn't have wanted her death on her conscience.

Coughing as the smoke from the gunpowder dissipated, Geneva picked up the glass and placed it carefully on the dresser. She began to wonder what else she'd damaged. A cursory glance inside the fusty interior of the wardrobe revealed that the bullet had passed through a coat and exited through the back of the cupboard, leaving a neat hole.

Grunting with the effort, she gradually slid the heavy piece of mahogany furniture forward a few inches, then she placed her face against the wall and peered into the cobwebby shadows behind it.

Rejoicing filled her heart. There was a door to the adjoining room! But, push and pull as she might, Geneva couldn't move the wardrobe another inch forward. Then she saw the rusty key in the keyhole. She managed to get the length of her arm along the back of the wardrobe, then cried out with frustration. Although her fingers could touch the lock, they were not long enough to close around the key.

'Damnation!' She pounded her fists on the side of the wardrobe.

A bamboo cane rolled off the top of the wardrobe and hit her on the head before bouncing on to the floor. *Had the devil heard her plea?* she wondered uneasily, as she poked the cane through the hole in the key. At first the key was stubborn, but some vigourous wriggling loosened it from its hiding place. Tipping the cane upwards, Geneva smiled as the key slid gently downwards into her palm.

'Thank you, Lord,' she whispered, just in case He'd been offended. She rushed over to the other door and gave herself instructions.

'It fits! Now ... gently ... gently, Geneva Tibbetson, you don't want to go to all this trouble for nothing.' Holding her breath, she manipulated the key in the lock, and heard a satisfying clunk. The door gave a long-drawn-out creak as she opened it. She slid the key into her boot in case she needed it again, then picked up a pair of scissors and inserted them into the key hole. If she was caught, Mrs Mason could make what she liked of that.

The atmosphere in the house outside the room seemed to seethe with menace. Holding her breath, Geneva crept down the stairs, the wooden risers complaining with each tread, no matter how lightly she stepped. She jumped a mile in the air when something snapped at the back of the house, and hoped the ghost of Emma and Maudine's father didn't haunt the place.

'Oh, for goodness sake,' she told herself crossly, and had just lifted her wrap from the peg on the hallstand when she heard Emma Mason in the porch. She'd have to go out through the back and climb over the wall.

Hurrying through the house, she unlocked the back door just as Emma was unlocking the front to let herself in. As Geneva ran out into the overgrown back garden, someone caught her by the upper arm and swung her round. Her yell of fright was cut off when she found herself in the grip of Emma Mason's next-door neighbour, the magistrate, Mr Bowers.

He stared down at her. 'I heard a shot. What have you done, girl?'

'Nothing . . .'

'We'll see about that.' He propelled her before him and through the door.

Waiting with a cat-like smile on her face, Emma took her by the earlobe and twisted it. 'And where do you think you were off to?'

'She's holding me a prisoner,' Geneva told Mr Bowers.

'I fail to see any bonds.' The man cocked his head to gaze at Emma, and said mockingly, 'My dear Mrs Mason. Can this tale be true of a respectable woman like you?'

'Certainly not, Mr Bowers. As you know, I'm forced to lock her in her room when I go out. Since you're kind enough to listen to my deepest confidences, and are good enough to advise me on them, then you're aware of the reason why I cannot trust the girl, with her dishonest nature. As you can see, her intention is to abscond before her sins catch up with her.'

'And her uncle?'

'They cannot keep her at the rectory, because they're worried she'll be an influence on their boys. Bad blood in her family, you see.'

'That's not true,' Geneva protested. 'I'm not dishonest, and I would never harm my cousins in any way. My uncle will vouch for that.'

She received a stern look from Mr Bowers. 'Hold your tongue, girl. Count yourself lucky I'm not about to incarcerate you in the lock-up, for that's where thieves usually end up. We'll see what the earl has to say about being stolen from by one of his servants, once he arrives home.'

'Lord Ashby?' Her heart lifted at the mention of his name, then it sank like a stone as the reason for her being kept here suddenly became clear. 'What have I been accused of stealing?'

Reaching up, Emma took down the long-handled iron spoon from its hook on the wall, the one she usually stirred the broth with. 'Perhaps you'd like to think about that while I punish you for trying to escape from my custody. Rest assured, if you've damaged any of the locks in the process, you will pay for them.'

'You're not going to hit me with that, are you?' she said, backing nervously away from her.

Mr Bowers's fingers closed around her wrist. 'Perhaps you'd allow me to hold the young woman down across the table while you mete out a suitable punishment, Mrs Mason,' he said

It was almost dark when they arrived at Welford Manor, and the air was chill.

After a rapturous welcome from their mother, Elizabeth and her offspring had been taken off to their quarters by the housekeeper to unpack.

Sorle had been cornered by his mother, who, now Elizabeth was out of earshot, seemed agitated and edgy as she told him of the situation that had cropped up.

He couldn't believe what he was hearing. 'Geneva a thief? I've never heard anything so utterly ridiculous!' Patting his dogs, who were nearly turning themselves inside out in the effort to greet him, Sorle began to laugh heartily. Florin and Shilling joined in with deep baying howls and huffs.

His mother's voice rose above the din. 'For goodness' sake, do stop that noise, you silly creatures. Sorle, pay heed to what I'm saying, please. This is serious.'

Her sharp tone sobered him. 'What is it Geneva's supposed to have stolen?'

'The Ashby jewellery collection. It's not on the inventory and it cannot be found anywhere.'

He started at that. 'I'd never even considered there might be a jewellery collection here. Geneva's probably hidden it somewhere. Have you asked her?'

His mother looked slightly ashamed. 'I didn't get the chance. Her uncle and aunt have left her with Mrs Batterby's relative in Dorchester, though I asked them to wait until you returned, so the matter could be investigated properly.'

Sorle heaved a sigh. 'So, Geneva has already been condemned as a thief. You'd better tell me the events leading up to this, right from the beginning.'

'It was all my fault, Sorle. You see, I was looking for a pair of earrings to wear with my ball gown and . . .'

Listening to his mother's account, Sorle could imagine how this had happened. The people who lived in the district jumped to such conclusions too readily. 'Even if the jewellery is missing, there's no proof that Geneva took it. For goodness' sake, mother. Surely you can see that.'

'Of course I can. But, Sorle . . .' She took the blue pendant from her pocket. 'This was found concealed under her mattress, and I recognized it at once as part of the Ashby collection. Moth and Edward concocted some story about Geneva having been in possession of it since they could remember. She must have stolen it years ago, when she was a child. Not that it excuses her, of course, but she would have been unaware of its value then.'

His heart falling, Sorle took the pendant and gazed at it. Then a memory of his uncle's funeral came into his mind, of a thin, blue-eyed child, fevered and husky with cold. She'd been miserable, her aunt unsympathetic. He'd given her a peppermint lozenge and had received in return a smile of genuine warmth and great beauty.

He smiled himself at the very thought of it, for it had brought a gleam of sunlight into what had been a sad occasion. 'I gave Geneva this bauble a few days after my uncle's funeral. I felt sorry for her, and I thought it would match her eyes.'

'You gave a child something as valuable as this?'

'To be quite honest, I saw it lying on the dressing table and slipped it into my pocket. I didn't give its monetary value much thought, but I was paid in full by her smile. She was a pretty little thing.'

His mother tut-tutted. 'You've always had a soft heart where children are concerned, Sorle. Tell me, this is not some tale you've just concocted to get the girl out of trouble, is it?'

'It's not. I spun some story to Geneva about the stone being magic, and swore her to secrecy.' His smile widened as he remembered the Egyptian princess. 'Geneva placed her hand against her heart and swore she would never break the sacred trust between us. She was so solemn about it that I was hard put not to laugh. I'm surprised she didn't tell those concerned that I'd given the pendant to her.'

'Geneva has been kept in ignorance of what's taken place. She hasn't been charged with stealing anything, as yet. At least she is not locked up.'

Sorle frowned at the thought. 'Nevertheless, she will be gossiped about without being given the chance to clear her name. He didn't believe Maudine Batterby would overlook the opportunity to malign Geneva, for she lacked generosity of spirit, and only just tolerated having her in the house.

His gaze dropped to his mother's as he slipped the pendant into his pocket. 'So, Geneva kept our secret for all these years. What a true and loyal girl she is. I must go and see her uncle and set him straight about the matter.'

'Sorle . . . what about the rest of the jewellery?' she said, as he walked away.

'What about it?' He turned, his feelings deeply wounded on Geneva's behalf. 'I'll bring the matter up with her, but, be warned, I'll take this place apart brick by brick with my bare hands before I'll believe Geneva Tibbetson would steal from me. Then I'd have to hear it from her own lips.'

Picking his way through the cold, dark night, and guided only by the faint glow coming from the Batterby household, it was nearly eight when Sorle arrived at the rectory.

He found Reverend Batterby in his study. The man looked grey with worry. 'I've just been made aware of the unpleasant matter which arose in my absence, and which involved your niece,' Sorle said. 'May I invite Mrs Batterby and your sons to this meeting, since I have something to say to all of you?'

Soon they were all gathered together. Maudine Batterby looked as worried as her husband, and Sorle wondered if he mightn't have misjudged her. The boys looked downright glum.

He smiled reassuringly at them as he took the pendant from his pocket. 'Let me clear this matter up straight away. This pendant was not stolen. It was a gift I made to Miss Tibbetson eight years ago, after my uncle's funeral. I swore her to secrecy about it, which is probably why you were unaware of its existence, and have now all jumped to the wrong conclusion.'

A long sigh of relief came from the reverend, the older boys nudged each other and smiled, the younger ones whooped. Maudine Batterby gazed everywhere but at him. When the family had settled down again, Sorle fixed his gaze on Maudine. 'As for the rest of the Ashby jewellery, I do not believe Miss Tibbetson has taken it, any more than I would believe you or your husband had stolen it, Mrs Batterby . . . or any of your sons, come to that.'

Maudine indignantly opened her mouth, then thought better of it and shut it again when he held up a hand. 'I intend to go and speak to Miss Tibbetson about the matter, and would be grateful if you'd furnish me with her address.'

'Geneva has been kept in ignorance of the charges pending against her,' Maudine told him. 'Only my sister, who lives in Dorchester, knows of what's taken place.'

'Which, may I remind you, is nothing untoward. But how long do you think it will be before the story is abroad and twisted? Miss Tibbetson's name will be slandered in public. What will she think of you, her family, when she has to tolerate the accusations, the whispers and taunts of the good citizens of Edgley?' When Maudine burst into tears, his voice softened. 'Miss Tibbetson must be offered the courtesy of being advised by people she knows, and before word leaks out – for if it hasn't already, then it soon will.'

The reverend stood. 'It's late, Lord Ashby. We will leave it until morning, and you must allow me to accompany you, for it's my duty to tell Geneva of what has occurred, and to apologize for my lack of faith in her.'

'Take the carriage and bring her back home,' Maudine sobbed into her handkerchief. 'I shouldn't have allowed that wretched maid, Hannah, to influence me.'

Sorle's lip curled as he wondered if Maudine Batterby would ever accept responsibility for her own actions. As his glance shifted to the reverend, he could have sworn that the same thought was mirrored on his face. Suddenly, he felt sorry for him.

Geneva ached all over from the beating. In the broken shards of glass from the mirror, she examined what she could of her body. She was covered in welts and bruises, and in some places the skin had been broken.

Emma Mason and the magistrate had been so enthusiastic in their beating of her that now she suspected that the pair of them had enjoyed it. She was hungry too, after being sent to her room without the meagre portion of food she usually had for supper.

But she'd done with crying and had stopped feeling sorry for herself. She'd learned early in life that self-pity would get her nowhere. Her hand closed around the key. She now had the means to leave, and she had no intention of staying here to be subjected to further abuse. She would go to her uncle, tell him what had happened and throw herself on his mercy.

After her aunt had gone to bed and the house had settled, she waited until the clock struck midnight. Using the chimes to cover the noise, she unlocked her bedroom door and swiftly made her way downstairs. She paused at the bottom, but needn't have worried, for Emma Mason's loud snores could be heard all over the house.

Geneva let herself out through the kitchen into the garden, carefully pulling the door behind her so it latched with a gentle click. The sense of freedom in her was euphoric as she swiftly made her way along the side of the house.

It was colder outside than she had imagined it would be, and she pulled her wrap tightly around her. The darkness was dense as she set off towards Edgley. Warmth leached from her body with every breath she exhaled. She'd been tempted to borrow the blanket from the bed, but knew Emma Mason would have used the slightest excuse to have her hunted down and arrested. She seemed to be in enough trouble already, but she couldn't think why. What was missing from the manor? It would have to be something worth a lot of money for Sarah to accuse her of stealing it, and for her uncle to believe it.

That was what hurt the most, the lack of trust in her. She felt like crying again, but fought it off. After a while the excitement of her flight wore off. Her sore body responded badly to the constant walking. Muscles began to ache. Her stamina – which had been weakened by her recent illness and further eroded by the heavy workload she'd been subjected to – ran out. But she plodded on, her feet numbed by the cold and thinking about nothing in particular.

By the time Geneva reached the church, there was a streak of silver dawn low on the horizon. She badly needed to rest, and was so exhausted she could hardly place one step in front of the other as she made her way up the path.

In the small back room her uncle used for an office, she found the rug he usually placed over his knees for warmth. Teeth chattering, she wrapped herself in it, then went through to the church. There, she laid down to rest on a choir stall.

Music woke her, played gloriously on the restored organ. It was the first cantata of Bach's *Christmas Oratorio.*

It was either Simon or Adam, for the twins were equally talented. Then she thought she heard Gerald's voice. When she tried to sit up, her body was too stiff to move, so she groaned with the pain of trying.

'What was that?' Matthew said.

'Ghosts.'

Robert shushed him with, 'Shut up, Michael. You'll scare Edward and Moth.'

The back of Moth's head came into her vision. 'I'm not scared of ghosts. Pa said there's no such thing.'

Edward laughed. 'We're in the church. It might be the holy ghost Pa talks about at the end of prayers.'

The playing stopped. 'How do you expect us to practise when you keep talking.'

Geneva tried to move and groaned again. Moth whipped round, his eyes like saucers. Then he relaxed and shouted loudly, 'Holy headstones, it's Gen!'

'It can't be, she's staying in Dorchester with Aunt Emma. Pa and the earl have gone to fetch her home.'

'It is her. What ails you, Gen? Has the holy ghost struck you down because you're a sinner?'

Moth was elbowed aside by Matthew, who peered down at her. 'Don't be so daft, Moth.' He turned his head and shouted out. 'It is Gen, and she looks ill.'

'I'm very cold and stiff, that's all,' she croaked. 'I walked all the way from Dorchester last night.'

There came a clatter of feet, then gradually all the boys came to peer down at her. They didn't seem to know what to do, but she managed to hold out her arm to Gerald. 'Help me sit up, would you, but slowly.'

Moth had been sniffing. Now he gave a huge sob and tears trickled down his face. She touched his hand. 'Don't cry, Moth. Once I'm on my feet and moving, I'll be fine. The house isn't far and I don't think your father will turn me away.'

With their help, she made it a quarter of the distance along the lane, then could go no further.

'We'll have to carry you.' Matthew and Gerald formed a chair with their joined hands and they progressed towards the house in a slow-moving, wobbling crocodile.

The carriage was driven up behind them at a fast pace, the horse snorting with the effort. They moved to one side and, as the vehicle came to a halt, Sorle leaped down from the driver's seat. He looked set to explode and uttered a succinct curse, one which put Geneva to blush and made Moth's eyes shine. It was the warmest she'd felt in hours.

'Why the hell did you run away? Emma Mason is having hysterics and your uncle is half out of his mind with worry.'

It serves them right, she thought.

Without ceremony he plucked her from her cousins' arms. For a brief moment she experienced the bliss of being in his, her head cuddled against his heart.

The euphoria didn't last long. 'You damned fool,' he said, gazing down at her with anger and frustration in his eyes. 'We've been looking for you everywhere, and you're frozen half to death. What on earth possessed you to run away in the dead of night?'

Her eyes gazed into his. Crushed by his anger, she couldn't tell him the reason, especially in front of her cousins. It would be too embarrassing, and it would only upset her cousins.

Sorle sighed when her mouth tightened. He grumbled, 'You've caused me trouble since the moment I set eyes on you, Geneva Tibbetson. I should take a horsewhip to you.'

Rebellion roiled in her. 'Ha—ah!' she whispered, 'You would—n't,' which didn't sound at all effective when forced out through chattering teeth.

His mouth twitched. 'Wouldn't I, then?' He handed her on to the seat, then climbed up beside her. His eyes suddenly softened. Removing his topcoat, he wrapped it around her. 'Let's get you home. Gerald, take the reins, would you? The rest of you climb on if you can find the room.'

'I'm going back to the church,' Matthew said. 'I don't want to be at home when Mama finds out about Gen running away. Adam and Simon, you're supposed to be practising, so you can come with me.'

'Steam will spurt out of Mama's ears and she'll do a fine dance,' Edward predicted.

Moth's eyes widened. 'I should like to see that.'

'All of you stay with Matthew,' Gerald ordered, climbing into the driver's seat and taking up the reins. 'Geneva needs to rest. I'll be back shortly.'

'What crime is it that I've been accused of committing?' she said wearily to Sorle.

'No crime. It was merely a misunderstanding.'

A misunderstanding she'd been beaten half to death for! She was so furious with him she wanted to scream, but she couldn't find the energy inside her. Instead, she managed a small, strangled growl.

'You're angry, aren't you?' he said, an understatement which made her grit her teeth. 'I don't blame you.'

Sorle supported her against his side as Gerald set the carriage in motion. He smiled faintly when her head fell against his sleeve and, bringing his free arm across the front, tenderly cupped the side of her face.

He held her there for the rest of the ride, soothing her as he would a fractious horse, with a palm that smelled deliciously of leather.

164

Thirteen

Maudine surprised Geneva. She allowed Sorle to carry her up to her room, then shooed the earl, and Gerald, out of the house.

Sorle had already stated his intention to return to Dorchester to find her uncle, while Gerald asked to be dropped at the church.

Geneva didn't spare Maudine by attempting to hide her injuries as Maudine helped her undress.

Without a word being said, a bowl of warm water was brought up by the maid.

'Is there anything I can do to help, Mrs Batterby?' Hannah asked, her glance going this way and that, trying to penetrate the shield of Maudine's body.

'You've done enough, I think, Hannah.' Her aunt brusquely banished Hannah from the room. 'Bring up a glass of warmed milk and leave it on the table outside the door. The kitchen floor needs scrubbing. Get on with that afterwards. I'll call you if your services are needed.'

Taking up a soft flannel and a ball of lavender-scented soap, Maudine gently washed her all over. Geneva couldn't help whimpering as Maudine tended her bruises with witch hazel, then brushed the tangles from her hair.

Maudine's mouth was a thin, mean line when she'd finished her ministrations. 'Emma Mason will regret this if I have any say in the matter.' The eyes that met hers held curiosity. 'I'm surprised you allowed her to beat you so badly, since you have never taken to authority kindly.'

'I had no choice. The neighbour, Mr Bowers, aided her. He held me down across the table.'

Maudine gave a small cry of distress. 'Oh . . . the wicked, wicked man! How dare he punish you when you haven't been

165

convicted of any crime. I shall ask your uncle to consult with a lawyer and seek recompense from both of them.'

Alarmed, Geneva placed a hand on her aunt's arm. 'No,' she begged, 'for then everyone will know what has happened to me, and your sister will only say I deserved it. It will sit badly upon my uncle's shoulders, and I wouldn't deliberately have his name blackened – yours either.'

'There's that . . . I won't deny that you can be trying, at times, but not to the extent of this beating. Perhaps it would be better if sleeping dogs were left sleeping, after all. Tell me, what did you do to deserve such a beating from my sister?'

'I escaped from my room, where she'd locked me in for no good reason.'

'Locked you in?'

A shred of sympathy in Maudine's voice brought words tumbling from her. 'I thought I was to be a companion, yet I worked from dawn to midnight . . . I had one bowl of broth and a slice of bread every day.' Her voice began to wobble. 'All my life I've tried to be good, and be of service to those I love. I had never expected to be accused of dishonesty, nor to be punished so severely. I don't even know what I did to deserve this.'

Even more surprising, Geneva was drawn against Maudine's bosom in a hug. 'Hush, Geneva, you're safely home with your family now, and here you will stay. Oh, my dear, we have so badly misjudged you. I'll fetch your glass of warm milk, it will help you sleep. When you wake, your uncle will have returned. Between us, we'll clear the matter up, and it will never be mentioned again. I'm sure your uncle feels the need to apologize, and the earl wishes to talk to you, too.'

The unexpected tenderness with which Maudine kissed her caused tears to flow from Geneva's eyes. When the glass of milk was placed into her hand, she obediently swallowed it, then, fatigue overtaking her, she sank back on to the pillows. Geneva barely heard the door close behind Maudine when she left, and she fell into a deep sleep.

Sorle was seething, but he refused to allow it to show.

He had not been allowed to see Geneva alone. Not only was the entire Batterby family there, even his mother had insisted on being present. He'd managed to keep Elizabeth at bay, though she'd insisted on knowing the whole story.

'I'm looking forward to meeting this secretary of yours, since she seems to be so special to you,' she'd said afterwards, and she'd grinned widely and kissed him on the cheek.

His bland gaze around the rectory sitting room hid his true intention, which was to glare ferociously and scatter them all to the four corners of the house. Why couldn't they leave Geneva and himself to converse alone? It wasn't as though he was about to molest her ... A tempting notion though. His mood lightened. Yes, he most probably would molest her in some way, if given the chance ... right now he'd like to eat her, though he'd be compelled to spit out the thorns.

Geneva lay on the daybed, propped against some pillows, and covered completely by a patchwork blanket, except for a creamy column of throat emerging from the well-darned collar of her nightgown. He imagined placing a tender little kiss on the spot. That glorious hair of hers was tied back with a white ribbon, but it tumbled about her shoulders in shining ripples. Her eyes, hauntingly blue and bewildered, were so wounded he would have died a thousand deaths to go into battle for her, had she so commanded.

She hadn't. Instead, she was instinctively using her position as victim to her own advantage.

Her voice had a tiny trembling catch in it. 'Ah, so that was it ... you thought I was guilty – that I stole the Ashby jewellery.'

There came a chorus of family denials, followed by a rush of excuses. When they were all done, her eyes gazed into his.

'And you, My Lord? Did you really think I would steal from you?'

Her voice was like a knife blade that had just been honed. He must be careful. The slightest touch would slip easily under his skin and peel it, inch by inch, from the flesh. It set the hair on the nape of his neck on end. Geneva was out to wound someone. She'd chosen him, and unfairly.

'Never for one moment did I think that.' Nevertheless, he found himself making his own excuse. 'This all happened whilst I was away.'

'But you now feel it necessary to ask the whereabouts of

the Ashby jewellery – jewellery which had been left lying about the manor for several years without you giving it a thought.'

'Only because my mother couldn't find it. She wants to wear some earrings to the ball, and couldn't find the jewellery on the inventory.'

Her eyes flicked to Sarah, then back to him. They sharpened. 'The jewellery is in the library. It's in a velvet bag on the left-hand side of the room, top shelf, seven books from the end. It's hidden behind a brown leather volume called, *Tall Tales from the Egyptian Bazaars*. The sniff she gave was every bit as effective as one of her *hahs*. 'You can't miss the book, Lord Ashby, because it protrudes from the shelf.'

He wanted to laugh at that, for the tale of the princess he'd spun her had come from the same book. His hand closed around the pendant. He brought it from his pocket and held it out to her, a peace offering. 'Yours, I think, Miss Tibbetson.'

'No, it's yours, Lord Ashby. Had I known its worth in the first place, I would never have accepted it. Of late, I've been wondering how to return the gift without causing you offence. Under the circumstances, that no longer seems to matter. Now, I cannot accept it.'

So, she would dash his magnificent gift in his face? A crippling blow below the belt, for his face most certainly felt as if it had dropped that far from the shock of her rejection. 'Damn it, Gen . . . *Miss Tibbetson*. You're just being contrary.'

'My intention was not so calculated as to cause you affront, My Lord.'

Like hell it wasn't, he thought, feeling affronted all over at the glint in her eye. If he'd been alone with her he would have found some way to persuade her, he knew. As it was, with all her family looking on, he couldn't continue to make a fool of himself.

He slipped the pendant back in his pocket and rose to his feet, ready to retreat with as much dignity as possible. She would get over her megrims in a day or two, he imagined. 'As you wish. When can I expect you to return to your position at the manor?'

'I haven't decided whether I *will* return.'

'I'd prefer that you remained in my employment until after the ball, as arranged.'

Flags of colour appeared in her cheeks, as they always did when he mentioned her position in his household. This time, he had *her* on the run. But she threw it back at him.

'In that case, I'll make sure I give you full value for your recompense. I wouldn't want you to be out of pocket.'

The ends of Sorle's ears seemed to blister and his eyes narrowed in on her. Geneva Tibbetson most certainly would give him value, he thought, and in more ways than one.

She seemed suddenly to remember her manners, for she gave him a smile of singular sweetness. 'Of course I'll come back to work for you, since I enjoy the company of your mother so.' The two women shared a mutual smile. 'Thank you for helping me, Lord Ashby. It was kind of you and I'm most grateful.'

He basked in her approval for a moment, then he bowed. 'I make a habit of rescuing ladies in distress, so the pleasure was all mine.'

'Ah . . . a pity you made no mention of that earlier then, since I formed a distinct impression that you regarded me as a nuisance, at the time.'

He chuckled. Geneva was rapidly becoming her old self again. 'A nuisance? On the contrary, I've never met anyone who could offer me so many hours of amusement. Till we meet again then, Miss Tibbetson.'

Geneva opened her mouth, then must have thought better of what she'd been about to say, for she shut it again.

'No doubt that will be the day after tomorrow, at church,' the reverend said drily.

'I'll look forward to the event.' Giving a slight bow, Sorle left.

He remembered his mother when he got to the front door. Snatching her wrap from the hallstand and feeling like a fool, Sorle gently knocked, then opened the sitting-room door again. 'Mother, I've brought you your wrap.'

Sarah said lightly, 'Ah, I wondered why you'd left the room so suddenly without me. I thought I'd been forgotten.'

Geneva giggled.

The next day, James Batterby and his wife announced their intention to go out.

He gazed at his sons. 'Gentlemen, we may be some time, so I expect you to behave yourselves and find something productive to occupy yourselves with.

His glance fell benevolently upon Geneva. 'My dear, we would prefer it if you'd confine yourself to the house and garden today. Your clothes are unsightly and, as your aunt assures me they're past repair, we intend to purchase something suitable for you to wear.'

'Thank you, Uncle.' She remembered her savings. I'll be able to reimburse you.'

'That will not be necessary,' Maudine said, nodding her head in a most determined manner. If I have my way – and I certainly intend to – it will not be necessary at all.'

And, on that mysterious note, they left.

So did the boys, informing her that the earl was going to start training the horses he'd bought at the market, and they'd been invited to take breakfast with him, then watch.

She watched them go from the window, lining up in the garden, then running to hurdle the low hedge instead of using the gate. When Moth fell flat on his face, Gerald picked him up, dusted him off and hoisted him up on his back. Bandit rushed back and forth barking frantically, until he found a small hole to push his way through and follow after them.

It was quiet without them. Her cousins were such nice-natured boys that she hoped she had some just like them if she married. Not quite so many perhaps. What had the gypsy predicted for her . . . ? That she'd have two sons and a daughter. They would look like Sorle, of course . . . dark-haired and dark-eyed.

Her smile faded as she thought wryly, *Stop those foolish imaginings*. Of course they wouldn't look like Sorle. They would look like her husband, if she married. Her heart sank then. Rumours had obviously got back to the widowed farmer. The last time she'd seen him he'd given her a speculative glance, as though she was a sow he was thinking of buying.

She shuddered and put him from her mind. She had better things to do than concentrate on the merits of various husbands, and would probably not marry at all.

Geneva's attempt to clean the drawing room was met with resistance from a strangely subdued Hannah. 'Mrs Batterby said we mustn't allow you to work, Miss Tibbetson. You can go to the sitting room and rest. Essie has lit the fire.'

Idle for the first time in her life, Geneva didn't appreciate the gift of having time on her hands. She practised her scales, read some poetry, darned a hole in her glove, then sat at the window and stared out at the frosty morning.

She was pleased when the Ashby carriage pulled up. Sarah descended, followed by a younger woman and two little girls.

'How nice to see you,' Geneva said, rising to her feet when they were announced. 'I was so bored sitting here by myself and doing nothing.'

Sarah kissed her cheek. 'I've brought my daughter Elizabeth to meet you. And here are my two granddaughters, Madeleine and Barbara.'

The younger woman had the dark colouring of Sorle about her, but she had Sarah's bone structure and smile. The girls were a merry-looking pair who greatly resembled Sarah. They smiled, then dropped a charming curtsy and sat side by side on the piano stool.

'You don't have to curtsy to me, you know.'

Looking at each other, the pair giggled. 'Uncle Sorle said you were a magic princess and if we didn't curtsy you'd turn us into clucking hens.'

Geneva laughed. 'Your uncle makes up fairy stories, I'm afraid.'

'See, I knew she wasn't a princess when we came in. Her dress is too shabby.'

Elizabeth said firmly, 'That's a rude thing to say, Madeleine. You will apologize, at once.'

The girl went red in the face and mumbled something.

'It's all right, Madeleine. I know I look shabby, but I met with an accident and my gown got torn and dirty. My aunt has gone to buy me a new one to wear.'

'Uncle Sorle said you were kept prisoner by a wicked witch, and he rescued you.'

'Did he now?' Meeting Sarah's eyes, Geneva choked back a laugh. 'Ah . . . yes, your uncle was very heroic indeed. There's no doubt about that at all. He made it clear what he thought of the witch, and she went up in a puff of smoke.'

171

The girls eyes grew as round as saucers, so Geneva changed the subject. 'Did you meet my eight cousins?'

'Those boys!' Barbara said indignantly. 'The one called Michael said our hair was the same colour as foxes' tails.'

'My cousins are well-meaning boys. I expect Michael meant it as a compliment. Have you ever seen a fox? They have very pretty tails.'

The girls seemed mollified by that. Geneva rang to order some refreshment. When she turned, she found Elizabeth examining her. The woman smiled. 'You have a way with children. My girls are not usually so outgoing.'

'With such a recommendation from Lord Ashby, how could I fail to invite interest from them?'

Sarah chuckled. 'Well, what do you think, Elizabeth?'

'I like her.'

Looking from one to the other, Geneva smiled when Essie came in. 'I'm glad that's settled then. Would you prefer tea to coffee?'

'Tea, thank you.' When Essie had gone, Sarah opened her reticule. 'Now, I have something to ask you, and I do hope you won't take this amiss, for you embarrassed my poor son yesterday.'

Geneva raised an eyebrow at that.

'Oh, don't get on your high horse, Geneva, I know he deserved it, but still . . . he gave you this in good heart, and it wasn't his fault you were accused of stealing it. Sorle sprang to your defence the moment he arrived home. He said he'd never believe anything dishonest of you, unless he heard it from your own lips.'

'I'm honoured by his trust in me. The pendant was always a treasured possession, but had my uncle known about it then, he would have made me return it. I'm not the same child he gave the pendant to, and I know my uncle wouldn't allow me to accept such a gift now. Besides, the pendant is part of the Ashby jewellery collection. You have no idea how much shame I felt over the incident – shame I now wish to forget. Accepting the pendant would only remind me of it.'

Elizabeth and Sarah exchanged a glance. 'In this eventuality, Sorle has requested that you take the pendant on loan, and oblige him by wearing it to the ball.'

The ball was only three weeks away now. Geneva gazed at the skirt of her gown, a garment which was now past redemption. All the lace and frills in the world wouldn't hide its disgrace.

She doubted that Maudine would buy her something as pretty, since she'd look for something serviceable. It would be nice to wear the pendant though, because it would look pretty. If it was only on loan, she could hand it back straight afterwards.

'Yes, I should like to borrow it . . . with my uncle's permission, of course.'

'Then I'll leave it with you. Here is a note for your uncle. It's from the earl, requesting that permission be given.'

As her palm closed around the blue stone, Geneva thought, for all his endearing vagueness, Sorle had been ingenious in getting his own way.

Her aunt and uncle returned later that afternoon. Maudine had a triumphant look in her eyes as the reverend carried their purchases into the house.

'Your uncle had words with Mr Bowers about the attack on you. James was quite wonderful. He told them he was thinking of having them both charged with assault. They soon came round, of course. A sum of money was offered as damages, and negotiations are taking place. A pity that word has got out though. My sister swore she wouldn't tell anyone.'

Horrified, Geneva placed her hands against her face and whispered, 'I'm ashamed that this is being talked about. I don't want damages, I just want it to go away.'

Her uncle took her hands in his. 'It's not going to go away, Geneva. You'll just have to be strong and keep your dignity. As a family, we will defend and support you through your trials.'

'Thank you, Uncle. I'm grateful for that support.'

A kiss was placed against her cheek. 'Since we were responsible for sending you away in the first place, your attitude is laudable. If the situation were reversed, I doubt if your aunt or myself would harbour such charitable feelings.'

Maudine coloured, and fussed about, removing her bonnet

and gloves and saying brightly, 'Yes . . . well, I must go and supervise dinner. I'll send Essie to take those packages to Geneva's room.'

Geneva waited until Maudine had disappeared in the direction of the kitchen. 'May I talk to you for a moment, Uncle?'

'Of course.'

'Mrs Ashby, her daughter and granddaughters visited me today. Through his mother, Lord Ashby has offered me the pendant on loan. He thought I'd like to wear it to the ball.'

James gazed at her. 'Would you like to wear it to the ball, my dear?'

She nodded. 'Lord Ashby has left a note for you, seeking your permission.'

'What exactly did it say?'

'I didn't open it, but have placed it on your desk. Don't forget to read it.'

'Thank you, Geneva.' A smile touched his face. 'Would you prefer me to drop the petition for damages?'

Relief soared through her like a flight of singing birds and she gave him a heartfelt hug. 'Oh yes . . . Thank you, Uncle James. It would be unpleasant for all concerned if word of my beating was bandied about.'

He patted her on the shoulder. 'I'm pleased you have the goodness to turn the other cheek. Your aunt won't like it, of course. But, no doubt, the Lord in his heaven will find some way to punish that pair for their cruelty.'

Meanwhile, the earthly lord of the manor was gazing up at the highest shelf in his library with some perplexity. 'How the devil did Geneva manage to get up there?'

'There must be a ladder somewhere.'

'Look, can't this wait until morning, mother?'

'Certainly not. I asked you to fetch the jewellery down *this* morning.'

'I forgot,' he grumbled. 'Couldn't you have asked a man-servant?'

'It's not always wise to reveal how much jewellery is in the house to servants. They talk to outsiders.'

'Can you see a ladder anywhere?'

'No.'

'Then in God's name, how do you expect me to reach up there? I'm not a fly who can hang upside down from the ceiling.'

'Well, then, it will have to be in the morning. By the way, Sorle, Geneva accepted the pendant on loan, but how do you expect to persuade her to accept that expensive gown to go with it?'

He slid her a grin. 'I'll leave that up to you. Tell her it's one of yours that you've grown too fat to fit into, if you like.'

'I don't like.' He grinned when his mother gazed with some alarm at her arm, pinched it, then said, 'Am I growing stout, then?'

'You're amazingly beautiful and look much too young to be my mother. As for Geneva, I'm quite determined that she shall be the belle of the ball, you know.'

'I hadn't realized I'd raised a son so full of intrigue. What if she refuses the gown?'

'Then I shall strip her naked and dress her myself.'

'Sorle!' she gasped. 'If you make remarks like that about her, no wonder Geneva is being talked about.'

His face darkened. 'Believe me, to the best of my ability I shall make every one of them eat their odious remarks.'

'How?' she said.

He gazed at her then, his eyes bland, her only answer the faint grin he gave.

The following morning Sorle was up early.

He patted the mare and her offspring, both of them filling out nicely now. They were well-behaved creatures.

Tom was sleeping on a bale of straw and Sorle nudged him with his foot. He nodded when Tom scrambled to his feet. 'How's your courtship going?'

'Betty Crump be saying yes, My Lord.' A wide grin lit his face. 'She can't get enough of it, though her ma won't have a bar of me till the vows be said. 'Tis a long way back to the stables, so I'm tramping half the night, and a man gets tired.'

'You'd better marry her before you get her with child, then you can move into her bed. I'm not paying you to sleep all day.'

Tom whipped his battered old cap from his head. 'Yes, sir. I don't rightly know how you go about marrying.'

'You and Betty had better talk to the Reverend Batterby after church on Sunday. I'll tell him to expect you. I'll buy you a new Sunday suit and stand up for you at the wedding, if you'd like. And I'll arrange for an extra shilling a week to be paid to you once you and Betty are wed.'

'I'd be right proud, My Lord.'

Sorle was grinning to himself as he rode off. He almost envied the man having a woman to share his bed, since the only woman he wanted in his was chaperoned so well he could hardly get within touching distance. One of these days she would drop her guard though, and things would work in his favour. He was certain of it.

His ride set him up for the day. Later on he was going to school the younger mare with Elizabeth on her back. The youngster was strong, despite her daintiness. He was going to give her to Geneva for a Christmas gift.

Without giving direction much thought he wound up at the reverend's house. He dismounted, thinking it would do no harm to visit her, and anyway, he could do with a cup of hot coffee to warm his insides.

The door was answered by Geneva, who wore a rather odd-looking gown of brown and green stripes. They zig-zagged busily about her, so the eyes automatically followed.

'Sorle.' Looking flustered, she patted her hair, which sprouted charming tendrils to curve about her delicious face and to escape from her braid.

'Are you feeling better, my Geneva?' he said, his glance following the stripes about her person.

'Yes, thank you.'

'Good Lord!' he whispered, frowning a little. 'That's the most dire pattern I've ever set eyes on.'

Her lips became a wry twist. 'It is, isn't it? But I have to wear something.'

Apart from keeping the cold at bay, Sorle didn't see why, for he was sure she'd look at her most delectable naked. He grinned as he stepped inside the hall, causing her to step back.

'Have you come to visit my uncle?'

'No, I came to visit you.'

He would have cupped her face in his hands and kissed her if Maudine Batterby hadn't come bustling down the stairs. The woman must possess a nose for visitors and she was in a mood to gush.

'Ah, Lord Ashby. How lovely to see you. I'll inform my husband of your presence.'

'There's no need,' he said. 'It was Miss Tibbetson I came to see. I'm here to enquire after her welfare.'

'Perhaps you'd like to join us for refreshment in the sitting room.'

'I'd be grateful for a cup of coffee.'

'Geneva, take the earl in. I'll go and tell the maid to prepare a tray before I join you.'

He followed her in, spun her round and quickly stole a kiss from her mouth. As a clatter of feet came down the stairs, he let her go and moved towards the window, smiling as Michael and Robert came dashing in to greet him.

'Hello, Lord Ashby, we thought we heard you. It's our turn to look after Gen this week, so we thought we'd better come downstairs.'

'As you can see, Geneva has come to no harm.'

Looking rather pink now, Geneva rearranged some ornaments on the table, then moved them back to their usual position. She took a seat on the sofa, her gown clashing horribly with the dark blue velvet. When she found the courage to meet his eyes she unconsciously touched her mouth with her fingertips. When he smiled at the gesture, so did she, but she quickly lowered her eyes.

Ah . . . charm of my heart, he thought, I could look upon you with adoration all day, even in that mess of stripes.

He lingered for an hour, not really tasting the coffee or the cake he was served, just looking at Geneva and making small talk between Mrs Batterby's chattering about nothing.

Finally, the reverend poked his head around the door. 'Ah, there you are, boys. It's time to go to the church and practise.' His glance travelled on. 'Lord Ashby, I wasn't expecting you to call.'

Maudine shook crumbs from her skirt. 'The earl came to see Geneva.'

'Oh, is it something to do with her duties at the manor?'

'I just wondered where the library ladder was kept.'

'It's in the library.'

'Thank you. I'll look for it there, then.' He stood, placing his cup gently on the saucer. 'Thank you for your hospitality, Mrs Batterby.'

Geneva rose. 'I'll see you out.'

'I'll see you at church tomorrow,' Sorle said as she handed him his hat in the hall. 'Try to look forward to it.'

Her strangled laugh contained more desperation than mirth. 'I expect there will be talk.'

'I won't listen, I promise.'

Sorle returned home and found the ladder leaning in a dark corner, but in plain view. He couldn't imagine how he'd missed it the evening before.

Placing it against the shelves, he scaled the thing. Seven books from the left, she'd said. He pulled out a brown leather book about Egypt and groped in the dusty space behind it.

The bag of jewellery was not there.

Fourteen

Geneva had dithered over whether to wear the striped gown, or the other creation, a plain grey taffeta which did nothing for her fair colouring, and which would be more suited to an older woman. She decided she might be able to trim it with some silk roses for the ball, so she hung it back in the wardrobe.

A critical glance in the mirror had then informed her that the striped gown clashed horribly with the blue velvet wrap Sarah had bought her. Sending her cousins on ahead, so they wouldn't be late for the service, she quickly changed into the grey.

It started to drizzle when she was halfway down the lane, so she was forced to lift the hem of her skirt so it didn't drag in the puddles. Then the feather in her bonnet began to droop miserably over her left eye. It bobbed back and forth, spraying her face with water. Irritably, she snatched the feather from the band and threw it into the hedge, muttering, 'Stupid goose!'

The congregation had their heads bowed in prayer when she edged into the church and gently closed the door behind her. After the amen sounded, she started off down the aisle to join her aunt. But soon, it became apparent to her that her aunt's pew was full.

Arabella Pringle's family had managed to seat themselves behind the Ashby pew, she noticed. There was a space. As she headed for it, Mrs Pringle saw her coming and moved along to fill it.

Silence had followed her progression down the aisle, then a woman hissed loudly from the back of the church where the servants stood, 'Thief!' As the word dropped into the hostile silence, ripples of gasps and titters spread outwards.

Geneva had nowhere to go. When all heads turned to stare at her, she hesitated, tempted to run. The silence seethed with ill intent. It hurt her deeply. These were people she'd known all her life, girls she had gone to school with. They'd become monsters in their need to capture a husband of note. Poor Sorle. He was just as much a victim in this as she was.

The earl rose to his feet and held out his hand to her, standing to one side to guide her into his pew. Sarah's smile had gathered a strained edge to it. Elizabeth gave her a sympathetic nod. Her two girls, oblivious that anything untoward was happening, offered her a pair of merry smiles.

In the choir stall her cousins gazed at her, their expressions mirroring her suffering. Edward looked downright mutinous, so she smiled and blew him a kiss. She could feel the love coming from her cousins like a warm wave as she seated herself next to the person she was supposed to have robbed. Tears pricked the corners of her eyes.

Sorle took her hand in his and gently squeezed it. 'Have courage, Gen,' he whispered from the corner of his mouth, and handed her his handkerchief. His public display of support astounded her.

So she blinked away the tears, stiffened her spine and smiled as if she didn't care what people thought of her. But she *did* care. The gossip hurt her. It made her despise them, when she didn't want to think badly of anyone – and that negative emotion made her feel less worthy to herself.

The service seemed interminable. Her uncle's sermon was lost in a sea of whispers and coughs, as though people had lost respect for him as well. He was a kindly man who didn't deserve such treatment.

Then it was over. As the people filed out, Sorle spoke briefly to her uncle, then came back to her. 'You can go home in my carriage with my mother and sister.'

Too dejected to argue, she simply said, 'Thank you.'

Apart from a curt nod here and there, Sorle ignored the people waiting outside the church.

Squire Hunter hurried forward, placed a detaining hand on the earl's arm. Sorle stared down at it until it was removed, then gazed at the man, a question in his eyes.

'Mrs Hunter wondered if your party would like to join us for dinner tonight.'

Geneva nearly gasped out loud when Sorle smiled at her. 'Would you care to join the Hunters tonight for dinner, Miss Tibbetson?'

The squire hummed and hawed a little, then cleared his throat. 'The invitation is extended only to your family, of course.'

'My regrets then, Squire. I'm otherwise engaged!'

'Tomorrow then,' Priscilla said, making her eyes so large, round and fluttering that Geneva, indulging in a moment of unexpected jealousy, wanted to poke her fingers into them and blind her.

'I'm afraid my social calendar is full until after the ball. Isn't that so, Miss Tibbetson?'

Just as unexpected as the jealousy had been to Geneva, so was this moment of pleasure at being offered a small moment of revenge. 'Yes, My Lord, I'm afraid it is.'

Sorle gave the Hunter family a small bow then turned his back on them and walked her towards the carriage. Assisted inside, she was greeted by his mother, who said, 'My dear, how pale you look. You handled that dreadful display inside the church with the indifference it deserved, don't you think so, Elizabeth?'

She wanted to howl like a baby at the display of kindness. 'I was far from indifferent. The local people are not usually so . . . so . . .'

'Malicious and ill-mannered?' Elizabeth suggested. 'I'm afraid I would not be as charitable as you are. You handled the situation with dignity, I thought.'

Sarah gave a small shrug. 'One has to. It was most unfortunate that they chose to believe in the lie rather than the truth. I feel ashamed of myself, because my input into the matter started it. Oh, Geneva, my dear, I do hope you can forgive me.'

The sympathy in Sarah's voice seemed to release the emotion damned up in Geneva. Burying her face in Sorle's handkerchief she began to weep quietly, saying incoherently, 'No, you mustn't blame yourself, Sarah. I . . . don't know how . . . I would have managed . . . not without your help.'

Madeleine and Barbara patted her gently on the knees and tried to soothe her with gentle shushing noises. Sarah placed her arm around her shoulder.

Sorle said. 'Look after her mother. I'll tell the coachman to take you to the rectory first.'

'You're not coming home with us?'

'I promised to talk to the reverend on Tom's behalf.'

'Then I'll send the carriage back for you?'

'No, I'll walk home. I badly need the air.' A tap of his cane and the carriage lurched forward.

'Well, Reverend Batterby,' Sorle said, when their business was over and done with and they were walking along the lane together. 'What are we to do about Miss Tibbetson?'

The reverend gazed at him, sorrow in his eyes. 'No doubt my niece will live her life as the good Lord intends. This situation will blow over when the truth gets out. Geneva is strong and will weather the storm – as we all will.'

'I do hope so. The guilty parties will be charged with their assault on her, will they not? And compensation for her injuries obtained.'

'No, Lord Ashby. To take a widowed female relative to the magistrate's court would not sit easy with any of us, especially Geneva, who would find the responsibility of it a heavy burden. My niece is not a vindictive girl. Her wish is that the matter be dropped. Compensation has already been offered and accepted for her clothing.'

Sorle grimaced as he thought of the outlandish striped gown. And the grey one she'd worn today had made her look faded and lifeless, like an ageing spinster. 'And Bowers?'

'To charge him would be to invite more gossip. His peers would not find it easy to bring down a guilty verdict on him. Sides would be taken, the talk would change from malicious to speculative and vicious, then Geneva's pain would be prolonged.'

Sorle heaved an aggrieved sigh. 'May I ask what Miss Tibbetson's reasoning is?'

'My niece is hurting, but she's coping, Lord Ashby. 'She doesn't wish to be reminded of the incident. If you'd been held down and beaten with an iron ladle, would you want that to become public knowledge?'

'They were that vicious?' Sorle's eyes narrowed and he muttered, 'The perpetrators of the crime against her will pay in some way, I promise.'

The surface of the reverend's spectacles were impenetrable, reflecting only the grey, cloudy sky as he turned. 'You have forgotten, perhaps, that both of our families are culpable as regards the source of this incident?'

Had Sorle been home at the time, the problem would never have arisen. 'Then the least we can do is seek proper compensation for her. I would be willing to negotiate privately on her behalf with Bowers.'

'May I remind you of something you also seem to have forgotten, Lord Ashby, and my pardon for speaking so bluntly. Miss Tibbetson is my responsibility, not yours. Although we're grateful for your interest and support at this time, if you seek revenge on her behalf, it will only cause more speculation.'

'You're asking me to mind my own business, then?'

'Exactly,' the reverend said drily. 'I will go further, with no intention to offend, you understand, and offer my opinion that the reminder is long overdue.'

'I admit, nobody has advised me thus of late. Not since I was about Gerald's age, in fact.' Sorle grinned widely and nodded. 'Thank you for being so honest. I hope you'll allow Miss Tibbetson to continue in my employ.'

'She may work out her salary. After the ball, I must seriously question the arrangement and look to her future, you understand.'

'Perfectly,' Sorle murmured.

'You're welcome to come in for refreshment, My Lord,' the reverend invited him when they stopped at the rectory gate.

'Thank you, but no. I'd be honoured if you and your family would join me for dinner this evening, though. I so enjoyed the last occasion, and I'd like to properly acquaint you with my sister and my two charming nieces.'

'So did I enjoy it, for you have a fine cook and the company was pleasant. However, a colleague is calling on me later, and we have important business to discuss. Also, I do think it unwise to ask my niece to socialize tonight, after what took place today. She's clearly upset and I've noticed that your presence has an unsettling effect on her. I'd prefer her to spend a quiet day and evening with her family before she resumes her duties on the morrow.'

'Perhaps you'll give her my regards then, and my fervent wish for her speedy recovery.'

The reverend heaved a sigh. 'By all means.'

When he reached home, Sorle went to the library and scaled the ladder again. A sweep of his arm along the top shelf sent several books thudding to the floor in a cloud of dust. A house spider went galloping off across the floor with Florin and Shilling in pursuit.

Gradually, Sorle moved the ladder along the shelf, his arm sweeping the books away, the dogs barking and dodging each one that fell. When the shelf was empty he frowned into the dark recesses of the space he'd created. He could have sworn Geneva had said this was the shelf.

Perhaps she'd meant the shelf below. Using the same method, he swept the shelf underneath clean, ending up with the same result. There was no jewellery to be found. Though tempted to uncover every shelf in the room, the great heap of books already accumulating on the floor warned him not to. Surely they hadn't all come from just two shelves?

'What on earth is all this thumping about? It echoes all over the house,' his mother said, advancing into the room. She pulled up short at the sight of the books, then gazed up at

183

him, her head to one side. 'I hadn't thought you were serious about pulling the house apart brick by brick to prove a point, Sorle.'

He shrugged. 'The jewellery is not where Geneva indicated.'

'That's obvious from the mess you've made.' She clicked her tongue in the same annoyed way she'd used when he'd been a boy, and tut-tutted. 'Just look at that dust on your coat.'

Her expression brought a grin to his face. 'It will brush off.'

Her eyes came up to his. 'You do realize that we must ask Geneva about the jewellery tomorrow?'

'Geneva will feel uncomfortable if we do. She might think she's a suspect again.'

'Be that as it may, Sorle, a valuable collection of jewellery has gone missing. You can't ignore that fact in favour of the sensibilities of one person, especially when we are to have a house full of guests who might stumble across them. Not everybody is honest, even those considered to be our closest associates. A thorough search of the house must be made, and we can't do that without Geneva knowing. She must first be given the chance, though, to point the hiding place out to you.'

Recognizing that he must bow to the inevitable, Sorle and his dogs retired to his study, where he subsided into his favourite chair in front of a roaring fire, to ruminate over the problem and console himself with a cup of coffee containing a medicinal amount of brandy.

The maid who'd served him had a fresh bruise on her cheek.

'How did you come by the injury, Maisie?'

The girl had difficulty hiding her grin. 'Someone threw a stone at me. We didn't start the fight, though.'

'We?'

'Sally, the head laundry maid, and me. Sally used to work for the Reverend Batterby, so she's known Miss Tibby since she was little. She didn't take kindly to what that flibberti-gibbet, loud-mouth servant said, and made no bones about telling her so.'

We gave the pair of 'em a good clouting, and Sally sent the mouthy one back to the squire with a fat lip for her trouble.'

'Ah, I see.' Sorle managed to keep his grin under control. 'I hope you and Sally are not going to make a habit of beating up the squire's servants after church on Sunday – I don't want a war on my hands.'

Maisie dropped a curtsy. 'No, My Lord.'

He grinned as she left, thinking he might tell his clerk to slip a bonus shilling into the maids' wages this month.

'I don't know what's come over Sorle, he walks around in a daydream half the time,' Sarah said to her daughter after the children had been tucked in their beds.

Elizabeth chuckled. 'I wonder if he realizes how often he mentions Geneva Tibbetson.'

'Sorle was never one to rush into a situation, but I think he has finally met someone he could happily spend the rest of his life with. He just has to make up his mind to it.'

'How do you feel about Miss Tibbetson, Mama?'

Sarah couldn't stop a smile coming to her face. 'Geneva has captured my heart. She is spirited, and has a wonderful sense of humour. I knew her parents slightly, and although they died in tragic circumstances, they were from decent stock.

'Geneva would be a perfect wife for Sorle, I'm convinced of it. If he decides she doesn't suit him, I'm going to invite her back to London with me, where I'll do my damnedest to make a brilliant match for her. *Then* he'll be sorry.'

'And *then* it will be too late for both of them. No, Mama. Somehow, we must make him realize that she'll be good for him. Besides, Geneva strikes me as being a country girl at heart. She may not want to go to London.'

'Geneva adores Sorle. It's written all over her face every time she looks at him. If Sorle breaks her heart, she won't want to stay in the district.'

'I heard whispers in the church that there were suitors who were considering her.'

'Oh, the farmer, you mean.' Laughter tripped lightly from Sarah's mouth. 'He has ten children by all accounts, and since she has practically raised her eight cousins single-handed, I shouldn't imagine she'd want to become stepmother to ten more.'

'But you said Geneva loves children, and they adore her. Ten orphaned chicks would surely appeal to her mothering instincts.'

Slightly alarmed now, Sarah gazed at her daughter. 'Do you think so?'

Elizabeth chuckled. 'Of course not, mother. The whole idea is ridiculous, as is the notion of her marrying the arthritic clergyman from the next parish. She needs a husband who will adore her, and give her children of her own.'

When the door suddenly opened and Sorle came in, they looked at each other and burst into laughter.

A pained expression on his face, Sorle glanced from one female to the other. 'I know the sound of a conspiracy when I hear it. Have the pair of you been plotting something?'

'We've been speculating about Miss Tibbetson's suitors,' Elizabeth told him. 'I thought I saw the farmer in church. A handsome gentleman, if one likes earthy types. He was gazing at her with a rather speculative expression on his face, I thought.'

Sorle gazed from one to the other, his expression bland. 'Everybody was gazing at her with speculation today. I don't know how she managed to bear it.'

'She wouldn't have without your intervention, Sorle.'

'It was the least I could do, since I know she's innocent of any wrongdoing.'

Sarah slid a glance Elizabeth's way. 'Geneva was very brave, I thought. Unfortunately, mud sticks. With these rumours circulating, she'll be lucky to get an offer of any sort – even from the farmer.'

'I don't know why you insist on bringing the farmer into the conversation, Mother,' Sorle purred. 'I have it on good authority that he is wooing a widow from Wareham who has some property to her name.'

'Whose authority?'

'The farmer himself.' Sorle looked rather smug and pleased with himself. 'He told me when I dropped in to enquire about his children's welfare, just before I left for London. In the meantime, he has a female relative living there to help look after his children.'

Sarah and Elizabeth looked at each other, then Sarah brightened, and said, 'Well, there's always the Reverend Blunt, I suppose. I thought Mrs Batterby said he was dining with them tonight.'

'The devil he is! When the Reverend Batterby said a colleague was visiting, I didn't—' Sorle prevented himself from saying anything more of the matter, and rose casually to his feet. 'I haven't met the old gentleman yet. I might drop in and introduce myself.'

After Sorle had stormed off, Elizabeth's shoulders began to shake with laughter. 'You're incorrigible, mother. You're tying my brother up in knots.'

'Nonsense. I'm just helping him to make up his mind. Sorle can be very stubborn. Geneva Tibbetson is the first woman he's ever shown more than a passing interest in. He's always been adept at sliding away when affairs of the heart begin to look as though they're getting serious, and this time he's not going to escape.'

'Affairs of the heart? Since when have Sorle's affairs included the heart?'

'There's a first time for everything – and this time it's different. I'm sure Sorle loves Geneva. We just have to get him to convince himself of that fact, and the rest will naturally follow.'

Sorle wanted a good look at his rival, so he left his horse eating the hedge and crept around the house to where a beam of light shone through the reverend's study window.

Ah, he thought, peering through a crack in the curtain, where he observed a dark head bent over a chess board. Of all the damnable luck, the fellow had his back to him. But then the stranger stood up and moved to the dresser to pour himself and his host a glass of brandy. Sorle's heart dropped. The man was not as old as he'd expected. He was of average height with a muscular build, nearing forty. His face was reasonably handsome, if a little stern.

James Batterby was facing Sorle. His glasses reflected the candlelight, so it seemed as if his eye sockets were empty except for a fire burning inside his skull. Sorle's skin prickled, for those fiery sockets seemed to be staring right at him. Then the reverend smiled like a cat with a mouse, and he pounced.

Sorle smiled as his glance skimmed over the board. Mentally, he upturned the Reverend Blunt's king. The mild-mannered James Batterby played a killer game of chess.

Just then a menacing growl came from somewhere near

187

Sorle's ankle. Bandit! He retreated quietly from the window, hoping he wouldn't tread on the animal. Immediately a set of teeth closed around his ankle. Throwing his leg out sideways he managed to toss the dog off, but Bandit came back, his jaws working as he worried and snapped at his boot top.

Managing to get around the side of the house without mishap, Sorle stooped to get a grip on the dog's body and whispered loudly, 'Let go, you stupid mongrel.'

Beyond the hedge, his horse whinnied loudly. Sorle cursed. He should have left him tied up down the lane somewhere.

Light flooded from the window when the curtain was pulled to one side. Geneva stared out into the darkness, then she opened the window and put her head out. Sorle was so close he could have leaned forward and kissed her.

'Is that you, Moth?' she said. 'You're supposed to be putting Bandit in the stable for the night.'

'It's not me,' Moth said from behind him in a quavering voice. 'It's a murderer, I think. I'm going to shout for Pa.'

Sorle managed to catch Moth by the slack of his coat before he took off, and clapped a hand over his mouth in case he yelled. Bandit redoubled his efforts to savage him. Moth kicked his foot back and his heel caught him a crippling blow on the shin.

'It's me!' Sorle hissed. 'Call the bloody dog to heel before it bites off my leg!'

'Lucifer's oath! It's the earl!' Moth cried out when his mouth was released. 'Drop him, Bandit!'

Detached from Sorle's boot, Bandit posted himself a mere yard away and displayed a snarling set of teeth. He was a game little bugger.

Geneva giggled and opened the window to its full extent. 'Take Bandit away and lock him in the stable, Moth.'

She waited until Moth had gone before she whispered, 'My Lord, why are you floundering around in the shrubbery? You should have asked the maid to announce you.'

'Nobody answered my knock,' he lied.

'There will be ructions if anyone sees you loitering in the grounds. Truthfully, what are you about?'

Loitering! He raised an eyebrow and thought: Yes, he supposed he was loitering. But he was loitering with *intent*, which would probably earn him a longer sentence if anyone thought to haul him in front of a magistrate.

What was your intention, Lord Ashby?

To steal a kiss from Miss Tibbetson, M'Lud.

And was that intention carried out?

Sorle smiled winningly at his intended victim. *Not yet . . . but it will be.* 'Isn't it obvious why I'm here. I came to see you.' He ruffled Moth's hair. 'Stand around the corner and warn me if anyone comes.'

'Papa will have a fit and foam at the mouth like a rabid dog if he finds out.'

'I just want to tell Gen something. I'll be gone in a few moments.'

Geneva leaned further out of the window. 'What is it that can't wait until tomorrow?'

He spanned her waist with his hands and lifted her out through the window, setting her on her feet in front of him. 'This can't.' He kissed the soft curves of her mouth until he felt her body surrender to him in a little yearning surge. He was doing himself no favours, he thought.

'Lord Ashby, you must have been drinking,' she said faintly when he allowed her to speak. 'Go home before you're caught, else I'll get into trouble.'

'You most certainly will.' He ran a finger lightly down her nose and feathered her mouth with another kiss.

'Tongues of fire!' Moth said accusingly from the corner. 'You were kissing my cousin when I wasn't looking.'

'I would not presume to take such liberties with your cousin, especially when you were not looking. I was merely removing something from her eye.'

'Liar,' she breathed, and he could hear the laughter bubbling in her voice.

'Timothy!' Mrs Batterby called out from inside the house. 'Where are you?'

'We've just been settling the dog in the stable, Aunt Maudine,' Geneva called back. 'We'll be in directly.'

Moth gazed at Sorle. 'Do you want this visit kept a secret, Lord Ashby?'

There was a moment of understanding between them. 'It would be in everybody's best interests, I think.' Sorle fished in his pocket and came out with a shilling, dropping it into Moth's outstretched palm.

'That's bribery,' Geneva said.

'Nonsense, Moth is an enterprising young man who has just discovered the art of making a gentleman's agreement.'

'Did you say art, or craft?'

'Who left a window open and allowed the warmth to escape from the room?' Maudine grumbled just a few inches away from them, and it was forcefully shut.

Sorle suddenly remembered what he'd come here for. 'If that cleric proposes marriage, you won't accept, will you? He's not half good enough for you.'

'Which cleric?'

'The one playing chess with your uncle.'

'I certainly wouldn't accept any marriage proposal from him, Sorle. Since the bishop is already happily married, I rather doubt if he'd consider indulging in bigamous liaison, anyway.'

He saw her shoulders shaking with laughter as she walked away, towing Moth behind her.

She had him there. Feeling like a fool, Sorle made his escape while luck was on his side. His horse ambled up to him, whickering softly. Leading the animal quietly away from the house, he mounted and headed back towards the manor at an amble, a smile on his face after the encounter.

It was a clear night. Cold silver stars cascaded across a black sky, and a crescent moon rode high above him. How pretty the night was, he thought, and wondered why he'd never noticed that before as he returned the moon's smile. He calculated that it would be full on the night of the ball, and he hoped the weather would remain clear.

He could hear the sigh of the waves in the quietness of the landscape, as if the sea was a lover embracing the shore. He could almost feel the first caress of frost upon the ground.

He wondered what Geneva was doing now, this moment. Was she reliving his kiss upon her mouth and the pleasurable effect it had had on her body? He had no doubt that she'd found it pleasurable, for her reaction had given her away. She would not be an unwilling partner in bed.

The pleasures of courtship far outweighed the dangers. After all, what was the worst that could happen if they were caught together? Absolutely nothing, for he was a man of a certain status in the district. It would be Geneva Tibbetson who would bear the shame of it.

A girl in her position, the possessor of such charm, wit and innocence, would be fair game to the bloods in London. She was a fresh flower to be plucked from the bough, to be enjoyed until she lost her freshness and was then discarded.

It was very different here. The hunters were of a different ilk. Already the people of the district speculated on their relationship. The men would wonder about the carnal nature of it compared to their own wives, and taste of it themselves if they could. The women would condemn it, reading what they would into it – spite without reason, except the uncertain threat of her presence to their own well-being.

They would bring her down if they could, but turn a blind eye to his own part in her downfall. In her place they would offer him some simpering miss hardly out of the cradle, whose dreams of romance would be cruelly shattered on their wedding night.

Ah . . . if only they knew of the warmth of the friendship existing between Geneva and himself. It was something he'd never thought to experience with a woman.

'Guard her well, Reverend Batterby,' Sorle whispered, 'for this is a man intent on seducing her, and she knows it. All I need now is the opportunity.'

Fifteen

Sorle had been watching from the window of his bedchamber. His vigilance was rewarded when Edward climbed over the stile, then held out his hand to assist Geneva. Moth came over after, leaping from the top rung to land on his hands and knees.

He could almost hear Geneva admonishing the smallest of her bodyguards as she stooped to brush the dirt from his knees and hands. Moth received a kiss on top of his head to compensate.

Geneva was wearing her striped dress, which blended well into the copse behind her if one was looking to compliment it, he had to admit.

There came a bark or two from the direction of the stables. Florin and Shilling streaked across the ground to greet the visitors, their long coats streaming out behind them, their tails slightly curved, to keep them off the ground. After them came the rugged-up mare and her offspring. They must have escaped from the stable yard, for they travelled at a fast amble, covering the ground quickly.

The animals converged on Geneva. There was a general melee, where the horses and dogs were hugged and patted. Pockets were searched and treats were handed over. That done, the animals followed after Geneva and the boys in a line towards the house.

Barbara and Madeleine went running from the door beneath him, followed more sedately by his mother. Standing on the edge of the meadow, the pair of them waved furiously at Geneva and the boys. He could just hear the high-pitched voices of his nieces as they shouted greetings to her.

Then the girls detached themselves from their grandmother and went skipping across the grass. Geneva scooped them both into her arms and hugged them. Ousting the two boys from their positions, the girls claimed a hand either side of her.

Sorle had a strong sense that Geneva was coming home. His own face wore a smile like a schoolboy. He lost it when he heard footsteps behind him. He chuckled and muttered to himself, 'Welcome home, Gen.'

'That's quite a sight,' Elizabeth's voice said from behind him.

'Yes . . . I must go down before the horses follow her into the house.'

'There's no need, Sorle. Here comes your stable hand.'

They watched Tom capture the mare with a rope bridle. The pair had a conversation, Geneva smiled and nodded. Then Tom touched his forehead and headed back to the stables, the younger horse following after her mother.

'Miss Tibbetson appears to have no side to her,' Elizabeth said.

'She's never been in the position to acquire any, thank God.' Sorle watched Geneva exchange a hug with his mother, then the party disappeared from his view. He sighed.

Elizabeth threaded her arm through his and kissed him on the cheek. 'You seem contented here, Sorle. Are you happy?'

Was he contented? He lacked for very little in life and liked his environment. He glanced at his sister. Elizabeth had made a good match with the architect Richard Chambers, who, although not wealthy, was comfortably off. But there was more to her marriage than that – it was obvious that the couple adored each other, something he'd always wanted for himself.

'I'm happier than I've ever been in my life, though sometimes I feel restless.'

'It's because you're alone. You need a purpose in life, brother.'

'You're right,' he said lightly. 'I must involve myself with estate matters more, I think. I'm going down to breakfast, are you coming?'

'I was on my way. The country air has made me hungry, and the girls will need my supervision.'

They went down the stairs, their arms about each other's waists. Parting at the bottom, he said casually, 'I'll just go and consult with Miss Tibbetson.'

Geneva had hardly settled herself. The boys were at the other table. Edward was doing some simple mathematical calculations, and Moth was writing an essay.

Before her on the table was a book containing room plans she'd drawn of the house, divided between several pages. Each room was numbered. Beside it was a list of guests who'd already accepted their ball invitations.

The fire had been lit early and the room was pleasantly warm. Although Geneva's bruises had deepened, she didn't ache too badly, since Aunt Maudine had treated them with arnica that morning.

She didn't hear Sorle come in until he said to the boys,

'Breakfast is being served in the dining room if you're hungry. You can look after the ladies until I get there.'

'When are they not hungry?' she said as, abandoning their work in a trice, the boys headed off.

'What about you?' he said, coming to where she stood, and his mouth had a wryness to it, as if he was remembering their clandestine meeting from the night before.

Her own smile was a tentative creature that came and went, then came again because being with him was fun. Although she wanted to laugh with the sheer joy of seeing him again, she really shouldn't encourage his nonsense. 'I've already eaten, and I've got too much work to do. Your guests' bed-chambers need allocating.'

He gazed down at the book and smiled. 'It can wait another hour and you can eat another breakfast. You've lost weight over the last two weeks and you need to regain it, otherwise you'll have no energy for dancing at the ball.'

'Who will want to stand up with me?'

'Every man there, I should imagine.'

'A rather daunting prospect. You're distracting me Sorle. Go away.'

His eyes pulled her into their darkness. 'Am I, Gen?'

'You know you are.' She pulled his social engagement diary towards her, fussing with it. 'You have an appointment with Sir Andrew Thorpe at the Antelope Hotel in Dorchester later in the morning.'

'I do? What's the meeting about?'

'Sir Andrew will probably be seeking a donation to provide Christmas fare for the orphanage.' Her eyes slid away from his as she casually said, 'It's possible he'll invite you on to the board too, since one of the board members has been taken ill, and is unlikely to return to the position.'

'What's wrong with him?'

'Old age. He took your uncle's place after he died. The late earl was well respected in the district for his philanthropic work. It's only natural Sir Andrew should want you on the board of directors.'

'Hmmm, you seem to know a devil of a lot about what's being planned for me. I'll consider it on the way in.'

'It's a good cause, Sorle. The orphanage is the only home

these children have. Some of them are quite alone in the world. Others have relatives who turn their backs on them, rather than assume responsibility. The children have very little hope for the future without generous people like Sir Andrew helping to provide for them.'

'Are you advising me to sit on this board?'

Geneva knew she could quite easily have ended up in an orphanage herself if the Batterby family hadn't taken her in. She was grateful to them for that. 'It would please me if you did, for my uncle is on the board, too.'

'And he's discussed the matter with you?'

The ghost of a smile appeared on her face, then she turned a delicate shade of pink. 'Certainly not. I ... *overheard*. I think the position would suit your nature, since you seem to like children ... other people's children, I mean, of course, not just your own.'

She became quite flustered as she remembered the gypsy's portent as to the extent of her own family, and her dreams of who would father them. She sucked in a deep breath and explained unnecessarily, 'Not that you have any of your own.'

'That's true,' he said gravely, 'But I hope to have an infant or two before too long. Which reminds me, I need to speak to Squire Hunter on a private matter. I'll drop in on him on the way home.'

A space opened up in her midriff at his words, but she must remember she was his employee ... and that Priscilla Hunter had impeccable breeding and a fortune to back it up with. No doubt she'd provide him with fine children.

'But when you do have children ... if you fell on hard times and died, wouldn't you be happy to know that there are people who'd care for your children?'

'Miss Tibby, I'm not as soft a touch as you think, so you may desist from practising the art of emotional manipulation,' he rumbled, a pained expression appearing on his face.

When she gazed into his dark eyes she couldn't help but laugh at the amusement in them. 'Indeed you *are* a soft touch, Sorle. I can tell from your eyes that you've already decided to accept the position when it's offered to you.'

'On this occasion I'll do whatever pleases you, and accept it with honour.' He took her hand in his, gently turning it over to place a kiss in her palm. 'In return, allow me the pleasure of your company for a little while. Come and breakfast with the family, for it will provide an agreeable start to our day. I promise to leave you alone for the rest of it.'

So, Geneva allowed herself to be led to the dining room, where Edward and Moth were either struck dumb, or practising their best behaviour, while the two young ladies offered them flirtatious sidelong glances from time to time and giggled.

Both looked relieved to see her. When Edward sprang from his seat to hold the chair out for her, the action had a bit of dash to it.

'Thank you, Edward,' she said. 'Have you finished your breakfast? If so, you can go back to the sitting room and finish the work I set for you.'

Edward slid back into his seat and toyed with his cutlery. 'Do I have to, Gen?'

'Edward? I thought you liked doing arithmetic.'

'He's gone all soppy over those girls,' Moth said in disgust.

The reply sent Moth's way was as heated as Edward's face. 'I have not. I promised them I'd play hide and seek, that's all.'

'Well, perhaps your cousin will allow you to play hide and seek first,' Sorle said comfortably. When everyone looked at her, Geneva had no choice but to agree.

'The children went off together, the boys laughing at the unexpected reprive. 'You can be the seeker first, Moth.'

'I want to hide.'

'You can all hide. I'll come and find you after I've eaten my breakfast,' Sorle called after them. 'But stay in the house.'

The children scattered in all directions.

After he'd eaten, Sorle called Florin and Shilling to his side. 'You two can smell the aroma of bacon cooking for miles. Let's see if you can sniff out the children. Excuse me, ladies.'

Over the next fifteen minutes, a certain amount of shuffling and stomping went on, with lots of giggling, screams of laughter, and high-pitched shouts of, 'You can't find me, Uncle Sorle. Shoo dog! You're giving my hiding place away.'

This was followed by Sorle's rumbling voice, 'Oh yes I can. You're in the cupboard.'

'No, I'm not. Moth is in the cupboard, I'm behind the door.'

Sarah and her daughter exchanged a glance and slowly shook their heads. Geneva giggled. 'I'd better get back to work, I think.'

A little later Sorle poked his head around the sitting-room door. 'I've got to go. I've told the boys to report to you when they've finish the next game. Elizabeth said the girls have some piano practice to do.'

'Thanks, Sorle.' She gazed at her list and chased after him into the hall. 'I'm going to have to use that bedchamber just up past yours, even though it's small.'

'I'll be honoured to have you sleeping there.'

She tried not to grin at his retort. 'Do you have any preferences as to the occupier?'

His eyebrow raised a fraction and he grinned. 'I'd like somebody small and pert with blue eyes and hair like cream silk . . . but alas, I think Viscount Ainsley must be accommodated there instead.' With that he was gone, striding out of the front door, but leaving the dogs trapped inside.

Florin and Shilling looked at each other then sped into her room, there to spread themselves out in front of the fire. Their tails thumped languidly on the floor when she followed them in.

It was a little while before Geneva remembered the boys. The piano practice had been going on for some time though, scales and beginner pieces the girls had not yet mastered. She went in search of her cousins when the practice stopped, and said to Barbara, 'Do you know where the boys went?'

'They were going to the library to look for a picture of a dragon,' Barbara said.

Heading for the library, she found her cousins sitting amongst a pile of books. 'Why are the books on the floor? You didn't do it, did you?'

Moth gazed up at her. 'Lord Ashby did. Madeleine said he was looking for the missing jewels.'

Thumping him on the shoulder, Edward shouted, 'Shut up, Moth! Madeleine said we mustn't mention it, because it's a secret.'

'But Gen didn't steal them, so why shouldn't she know?'

'Because she might think she's suspected and get upset

197

again.' Edward turned to gaze at her. 'You won't, will you, Gen?'

'Of course not, since the earl obviously looked in the wrong place.' The thought that they'd kept the information from her bothered her, though. She went upstairs to confront Sarah, saying straight away, 'Am I to understand that Lord Ashby couldn't find the jewellery?'

'I do believe Sorle said something about that being the case,' she said vaguely.

'But why didn't he tell me? Does he still doubt my honesty over the matter? Do you, Sarah?'

Rising, Sarah came to where she stood and took her hands. 'This is exactly the reaction Sorle thought you'd have, which is probably why he hasn't mentioned it to you yet. The simple fact of the matter is, he was unable to find the collection where you told him you'd hidden it. He intends to instigate a thorough search when he has the time.'

Geneva couldn't help but feel a little miffed. 'There's really no need to instigate anything. Lord Ashby simply looked in the wrong place. I told him it was on the left side, top shelf, seven books from the end. I meant the left-hand side going into the room, of course, not coming out of the room.'

'Oh, good. Perhaps you'll show him where they are when he comes back from Dorchester, dear.' Sarah eyed her striped gown nervously. 'Have you decided what you're wearing to the ball?'

'I thought I might wear my new grey gown and sew some silk flowers on the bodice. Though I've enough money saved to buy a new gown, I don't need one at the moment.'

'A woman can never have too many gowns, my dear.'

'I suppose that's true . . . in London, where balls go on all the time.'

'So, you do not have a ball gown?'

'I have no use for one.'

'But the earl will hold other balls. He likes to entertain on occasion, and when he weds, his wife will want to entertain too.'

Geneva didn't want to think about Sorle taking a wife. But since his mother had brought up the subject, her curiosity began to get the better of her. If he confided in anyone, it would be her. Geneva said, rather tentatively, 'Has Lord Ashby found someone to his liking then? Priscilla Hunter, perhaps?'

'Sorle has indicated that he's found someone local whose temperament and disposition suit him. He won't name the person until the matter is settled with her family, and his proposal is accepted. But enough of that, since the business of choosing a suitable spouse is all too tedious. Now, what do you think of my ball gown? Is it too bright for a woman of my age?'

The fine fabric of Sarah's red gown drifted, its bodice was delicately embroidered with gold beads and there was a gold headband fashioned like a snake. It was very dramatic.

'It's a wonderful gown,' Geneva said wistfully, wishing she could afford something half as pretty. But now she knew that Sorle had made up his mind to wed, the ball held no allure for her. Perhaps she wouldn't go, after all.

'You must come to me on the day of the ball, bringing your gown with you. We will see if it can be improved upon. And I'll ask my maid to fashion your hair.'

'My aunt might need me on the day.'

'As far as I'm concerned, that horrible Hannah creature can help your aunt with her fastenings. I have decided to keep you for myself that day. I intend to ask permission of your uncle first, and I know the dear man won't refuse me. Now, let's send for some refreshments.'

'I still have work to do, Sarah,' she pointed out.

'Since I know most of the people coming from London, I will help you with it afterwards.'

And she did, relating little snippets of information as she went, which caused Geneva to smile, and sometimes to laugh outright.

'Ah, the Anstruthers. They need a chamber with a strong bed. Truly, Henry's stomach is gargantuan. Now, who have we here? Harold and Fanny Pepper. He's tall and thin, with a protruding nose. I believe he's a palaeontologist . . . or is it an archaeologist? Anyway, he digs up fossils. Harold resembles a stork. His wife is the opposite, she's as round as an egg and clucks like a hen . . .'

And so it went on, until somebody knocked on the door. A few moments later, Ellen Pickering came in. 'Mr Chambers has arrived, Mrs Ashby. Shall I inform Mrs Chambers?'

There was no need, for the next moment came shouts of, 'Papa! Papa!' and the girls came flying down the stairs and hurled themselves into his arms. Edward and Moth came down more warily, to stand on the bottom step and eye this tall stranger who'd suddenly appeared in their midst.

'Hello, who are these two handsome fellows standing behind you?' the girls' father said. 'Surely you're not considering marriage already, my sweethearts.'

'Leaping lizards!' Moth said in some alarm.

Edward elbowed him. 'Don't be so bog-brained, Moth. He's joking!'

The girls giggled, then, prompted by a shove from Madeleine, Barbara said, 'These two boys are Edward and Timothy Batterby from the rectory, Papa, only we call Timothy Moth. They sing in the choir and Moth nearly caught the greasy pig at the midsummer fair last year.'

Moth swelled up when Madeleine added. 'He's going to catch the pig this year, and we're coming from London to watch him do it.'

'You two have obviously inherited your mother's talent for ferreting out a fellow's business. A greasy pig, eh! Well done, Moth. I've never, ever *nearly* caught a greasy pig in my whole life. I used to sing in a choir when I was your age, though, so my commiserations, gentlemen. Now, I'd better introduce myself. I'm Richard Chambers, the father of these two butterflies.'

'How do you do, sir?' the boys both said, holding out their hands together.

Richard Chambers shook them. 'I'm doing very nicely indeed.'

He looked past them. 'Sarah,' he said, a huge smile on his face. 'I hope you're not stirring up trouble. Where's that wonderful daughter of yours?'

'I'm here, Richard, and I was expecting you yesterday.' Elizabeth tripped down the stairs and was swept up in his arms. He swung her round, kissed her soundly then set her on her feet, all pink and flustered.

The boys moved to Geneva's side, Edward saying. 'Sir, this is our cousin, Miss Geneva Tibbetson.'

Astute grey eyes took her in. 'Ah yes, she appears to be

every bit as delightful as Sorle told me she was. It's nice to make your acquaintance, Miss Tibbetson.'

'Thank you, Mr Chambers. I'll look forward to building on it tomorrow, perhaps, since it's time for me to go home now.'

'Surely not,' Sarah protested. 'You needn't go on Richard's account, you know.'

Much as Geneva appreciated the hand of friendship she was constantly being offered in this house, she knew she couldn't stay. 'It's nearly four o'clock and it's getting dark. It's best for the boys to be inside early on these cold nights.'

Richard Chambers gazed around him. 'Where's the master of the manor?'

Sarah and Elizabeth looked towards Geneva, an enquiry in their eyes.

'Lord Ashby has gone into Dorchester. He had a business meeting to attend with Sir Andrew Thorpe just after midday, then he intended to drop in on the squire.' Fetching her wrap from the hallstand, she made sure the boys were wrapped warmly in their coats and scarves, then kissed Sarah on the cheek. 'I'll see you tomorrow.'

As the door closed behind them Geneva felt cut off. Sarah's family were a closely knit group, and there was a strong bond of affection between them. She wondered how different her own life would have been if her parents had survived . . . if she'd had siblings of her own, perhaps.

Then she smiled as she gazed at her small escorts. Her cousins had always compensated her for the loss she'd suffered. But they were growing up, and she couldn't help wonder what the future held for her as the three of them hurried into the gathering dusk.

One thing she knew – the biggest hurt was yet to come, and that would be watching the man she adored marry another woman.

Geneva wondered if that accounted for Sorle's urgent business with Squire Hunter. Did he intend to request Priscilla's hand in marriage? An agony of jealous darts ripped through her insides. Of all the eligibles Geneva had introduced him to, although Priscilla was the most suitable in looks, wealth and breeding, her disposition was the meanest.

* * *

Not long after Geneva and the boys reached the rectory, it began to rain.

Caught on the open road, Sorle pulled his collar up around his ears and hunched himself into it. Even so, a trickle of icy water found a way inside and rapidly cooled a little warm spot as it dripped into a hollow at the junction of his neck and shoulder.

On Geneva's advice he'd accepted the offered seat on the orphanage board, and had pledged a yearly sum from the estate towards the upkeep of the institution. A brief tour had revealed the orphanage building to be cramped. The plight of the inmates had touched him greatly, too. Children of all ages were crowded together, with nobody they could call their own.

His privileged position forcefully revealed to him by their poverty, Sorle had resolved to find some further way of assisting them. There was room for an extension to the premises, something he intended to consult with Richard Chambers over, while he was visiting. If Sorle could raise the money from his London contacts, he would then put the plan before his fellow board members.

His visit to the squire had been encouraging. The squire's stud stallion, Nimrod, had turned out to be a powerful black beast with an excellent bloodline.

'Nimrod's as gentle as a lamb. He knows his job, so you don't have to worry about nasty habits like kicking or biting,' Hunter had told him. 'He covers the mares easily and has sired several champions. Bring your mare over if she's in season. It shouldn't take long.'

'Not this time. I want to build up some muscle on her first.'

'Is that Sedgewick's broken-down mare we're talking about? I was surprised anyone purchased her, the state she was in, and I'm even more surprised to hear she's survived. I saw her run once. She won by a head. Come on well, has she?'

Sorle smiled. 'She's a different horse.'

'I nearly bought her myself, but I thought her wind had gone. The filly didn't have much potential. A pretty creature though.'

'She'll make a nice little riding horse.'

'Suit your mother, eh!'

They'd settled on a stud fee.

Sorle had hoped to escape without having to socialize, but he hadn't managed it, since the squire insisted that he mustn't disappoint the ladies.

There was a moment of empathy with Nimrod.

Priscilla was singing as they went inside the house, Mrs Hunter was accompanying her. He tried not to wince as the girl missed a high note. The music stopped and both women turned when they entered the drawing room, their hands fluttering against their hearts. He could almost swear they'd adopted a pose.

Priscilla looked lovely in a pink silk gown, her velvet wrap trimmed with white fur. Her mother's purple silk fought for dominance with it.

They looked flushed, as if they'd been dashing around, readying themselves for his visit. Priscilla's eyelashes dipped several times. 'Ah, it's you, Lord Ashby. What a wonderful surprise.'

He was manoeuvred on to the couch next to her, where he spent an hour being subjected to nonsensical prattle. He was further detained when she decided to sing again, a dirge about a scorned lover who hanged himself from the bough of a tree. Such an act might be a viable alternative to her singing, he thought.

He declined an effusive invitation to dinner afterwards. 'I'm expecting a guest to arrive, and need to be home in time to welcome him.'

'Did you get that nasty business cleared up?' the squire asked him when he rose to his feet.

The prattle immediately stopped, and there was a sensation of held breaths as he became the sole focus of their attention.

He was cautious. 'Which nasty business was that, Squire Hunter?'

'I heard that one of your servants had stolen some jewellery.'

'There were some malicious and libellous rumours about a gift I made to Miss Tibbetson when she was a child. Actually, I'd be obliged if you'd supply me with the names of the people who are spreading rumours about her. I'll certainly encourage her to sue for damages, since she is totally innocent of any wrongdoing.'

'I was at school with Geneva Tibbetson. I'd personally vouch for her honesty,' Priscilla said swiftly, taking his arm. 'Do allow me to see you out, Lord Ashby.' She escorted him to the hall, sighed and engaged his eyes. 'I'm so looking forward to your ball. We are lacking in entertainment here.'

'Then I hope I can provide you with some diversion from time to time, Miss Hunter.'

'I'm sure you can, My Lord.' With an arch smile, she held her hand up to be kissed. When he gave it a perfunctory peck, she said. 'I will reserve several dances for you.'

'It will be my pleasure if you reserve only one for now, Miss Hunter. There will be several London gentlemen present who will be queuing up for your favours, and I don't want to disappoint them.'

He pulled on his coat, took his hat from the servant and escaped from her clutches as fast as he could.

Despite the dusk, Sorle encouraged his gelding to adopt a more lively gait and, before too long, Welford Manor came into view.

Richard had arrived during his absence, for his mount was in the end stall. He left his gelding with Tom, then strode towards the house with some anticipation.

Sixteen

'*Tall Tales from the Egyptian Bazaars*,' Sorle muttered, gazing at the piece of paper in his hand. Left-hand side. Top shelf, seven books from the end.

But although the book was protruding from the shelf, the jewellery was not where Geneva had said she'd put it.

Sorle went to see her. Her eyes widened when he spread his hands and said, 'I'm unable to find the jewellery.'

'That's impossible. It must be there. She hurried before him into the library and gazed up at the shelf, a worried expression on her face. 'I'm sure I put it there. I couldn't quite reach the back of the shelf, so I pushed the bag there with the book.'

'Did anyone see you?'

'No. I'm sure they didn't, since I made sure that the door was shut. Besides, the house wasn't occupied then, so I was here by myself.' She gazed around her at the shelves lining the walls, her eyes uncertain now. 'It was a long time ago . . . I suppose I could have made a mistake. Perhaps if we examined every shelf one by one . . . ?'

'I don't want to involve the staff in a search unless I have to. It will just cause more speculation. I might ask Richard to give me a hand.'

'I'm so sorry I'm putting you to so much trouble.' Those cornflower eyes came up to his, and the desperation in them touched his heart. 'You do believe I put them there, don't you?'

He brushed a finger down the side of her face. 'Nobody suspects you of stealing them, Geneva.'

'Except most of the district, which is why they must be found soon, so my name can be cleared.' She stared up at the shelf again. 'I can't believe my memory failed me so badly. They just *have* to be there.'

'I'll look again, I promise. I'll take the room apart if I have to.'

She smiled at the thought. 'Some of the jewellery is so pretty. When I was a child I used to sneak into your aunt's room to play with the things in her dressing table. It was so peaceful there by myself. I used to pretend I was the lady of the manor and wear the jewels. The stones used to sparkle so in the sunlight.'

The wistfulness in her voice made him feel like hugging her close, but before he could, Richard came in. He gazed from one to the other, an eyebrow raised. 'Ah, here you are, Sorle. Miss Tibbetson . . .' A grin on his face, he gazed from one to the other. 'I'm not disturbing you both, am I?'

Geneva blushed a little and, realizing he was standing too close to her, Sorle took a step back. 'I was just going to look for you, Richard. Miss Tibbetson hid a bag containing the family jewel collection on that shelf there. We're now unable

205

to find it. I thought we might empty the shelves in the library one by one.'

Richard laughed disbelievingly as he gazed at the many shelves. 'Did you now? That's an action which would take us a month of Sundays. How bulky was the bag of jewellery, Miss Tibbetson?'

Geneva shrugged. 'It was fairly heavy and bulky, but I don't really remember.'

He gazed at her with approval in his eyes. 'Let me take a look at the shelf in question first.'

They watched as he took a measured glance at the shelves along that wall, then strolled to the end and eyed that. Climbing the ladder, he thumped against the back of the shelf.

He was grinning widely when he came back down. 'Problem solved, I think. The shelves were an addition to the house. There's a space between them and the wall all the way down, to take account of the skirting board at the bottom. The back of the top shelf is loose—'

'And when Geneva shoved the book back on the shelf, the bag was pushed through and fell into the cavity,' Sorle said, smiling at her. 'I knew it would be something simple.'

Richard nodded. 'It is simple if you know something about buildings. The bag could be stuck anywhere between the top and the bottom of that cavity, depending on where the battens fixing the shelves to the wall are. I've got a feeling they'll be lodged near the top, but we'll sound the back of the shelves one by one to locate them. I'll need a lever to take the side panel off.'

It didn't take long. The missing jewellery was lodged beneath the third shelf down. Carefully levering the side of the shelf off, Richard climbed the ladder again. Inserting his arm, he brought it out covered in dust, and with a velvet bag dangling on the end. He threw the bag down to Sorle, grinning triumphantly. 'I knew my architectural qualification would be of use.'

Peering into the depths of the bag, Sorle inserted his fingers and fished out a tiara, glittering with small diamonds. He set it on Geneva's head. 'There, my Gen . . . now you can be the lady of the manor again.'

Colour came and went in her face. Her smile began to slip

and her eyes became teary. 'Don't mock me,' she muttered. Snatching the tiara from her head, she pushed it into his hands and hurried away.

'Geneva . . . ?' he said in puzzlement. But she didn't answer, just sped across the room, slipped quietly through the door and was gone.

'Hold the panel in place, would you,' Richard called down to him. 'I'll see if I can tap it back into position.' Which put paid to Sorle's intention to run after Geneva.

'I would have thought she'd have been happy that the jewels were discovered. What did I say to upset her?' he asked Richard in some bewilderment.

'You don't know?' Richard's eyes searched his face, and the grin he gave wasn't exactly encouraging. 'Obviously not. Take my advice, Sorle. Don't even try to understand women. Who else can weep at weddings and wear a brave face at funerals? There's no logic to them.'

Now the jewellery had been found, the atmosphere in the house seemed to lighten. Geneva felt as though a large burden had been lifted from her shoulders – but it had been replaced by a heavier one, the imminent announcement of Sorle's intention to wed Priscilla Hunter.

The ball began to come together rapidly. Merchants' wagons arrived at the manor, to unload all types of goods. She and Ellen Pickering checked endless lists, endless inventories, and they made seemingly endless, and exhausting, tours of the house.

Sarah and Elizabeth made helpful suggestions, and were always ready with their advice if she needed it, but otherwise they didn't interfere.

One thing that pleased her, the local people relaxed in their manner towards her, especially the merchant families, who were hoping to secure the patronage of the earl.

But the gossip had done its damage and the friendly smiles she'd enjoyed from the women before Sorle's arrival were a thing of the past. The earl's need for a wife had stirred up the pot of the pecking order. While the eligibles were practising their airs and graces, Geneva was learning from them that her position on the ladder was a lowly one indeed.

She put up with it because she had to, gritting her teeth on the Sunday, when Priscilla Hunter, with an air of condescension, handed her a gown to wear to the ball, and within the hearing of a large number of women, said, 'This is for the poor, of course. You might even like to wear it to the ball yourself. It will need a few repairs, but I daresay you won't mind that.'

'Thank you, Miss Hunter, you're most kind,' Geneva gushed, taking the garment from her, even then knowing she'd tear it into shreds and dance in her chemise rather than wear it. But she had another use in mind for the gown as she collected the smaller of her cousins and headed off up the lane with it hanging over her arm.

Mrs Hunter muttered to Mrs Pringle as she walked away, 'The girl didn't sound in the least bit grateful for the favour Priscilla bestowed on her. She should count herself lucky she's received an invitation to the ball. It might be the last chance to secure a husband for her.'

'My cousin Frederick was considering her, but in view of the reputation she's acquired of late, I've advised him against it. I've heard her services will no longer be required after the ball, even though the jewellery has turned up. And I notice the earl didn't invite her to sit in his pew today.'

There was a bit of snorting as Jane Whitmore loudly joined in. 'It was rather presumptuous of her to try and queen it over the rest of us in the first place. No breeding, and all the looks in the world won't make up for the lack of it. Yes, she's definitely out of favour with him now.'

The earl came into the porch and stood talking to the reverend and his brother-in-law as he pulled on his gloves. He gazed towards them, frowning slightly when Priscilla smiled at him.

Jane hadn't seen him. 'An odd business, the jewellery suddenly showing up. Rather convenient really, as if the thief thought better of it and returned it.'

'We mustn't talk ill of the less fortunate,' Priscilla twittered, slanting Sorle a sly glance from the corner of her eye, which made him shudder. Sucking in her stomach to expand her bosom, she allowed her shawl to slip from one shoulder. 'Lord Ashby has such a gracious nature. He's attending his stable hand's marriage next Saturday, and has supplied him with a suit, I hear. I'm thinking of attending the wedding myself. It sets a good example to the poor, don't you think, mother?'

'Without a doubt.'

The earl was joined by his mother, sister and nieces, and together they proceeded towards the carriage, murmuring polite greetings as they passed by.

The two men strolled off after the carriage when it left, deep in conversation.

The gown Priscilla had given Geneva was fashioned from fawn muslin and had garlands of pink roses patterned on it. It was pretty, decorated with lace and ribbons around the bodice, but the seams of both sleeves had come apart, and the front was stained and the hem frayed.

Geneva repaired it, turning the hem up an inch to hide the frayed ends. Then she rubbed soap into the stains and soaked the garment overnight. Once it was clean, she sewed some pink bows on the bodice.

'How pretty that gown is,' Maudine said. 'It was generous of Miss Hunter to give it to you. You'll be able to wear it as a day gown after the ball.'

'Be sure, I will put it to good use,' Geneva told Maudine with a smile.

Her uncle looked sharply over his glasses at her. She offered him the most angelic of her smiles, which didn't seem to fool him a bit, for he chuckled. 'I'm glad to see you're getting your spirit back, my dear.'

'I'm relieved that the jewellery has turned up. It's as if a weight's been lifted from my shoulders. Anything else is a mild annoyance.'

'Only a fool would have imagined you'd stolen it,' Maudine said in an aggrieved manner, and her uncle's eyebrow lifted slightly before he went back to his book.

The day of Tom and Betty's wedding dawned bright and cold. Geneva donned her grey gown and her blue velvet wrap, then joined her uncle downstairs. Adam and Simon came clattering down the stairs after her, for they were going to play the organ for the event.

'I always enjoy conducting a wedding, even a small one

like this,' her uncle said, rubbing his hands against the cold and giving her a broad smile before he preceded his sons to the door.

No doubt her uncle would enjoy conducting the earl's wedding even more, which would be well attended. She closed her eyes for a few delicious moments of imagining herself exchanging marriage vows with Sorle, of the moment when he gazed into her eyes, smiling as he slid the ring on to . . . *Priscilla Hunter's finger!*

'Hah!' she said, suddenly brought back to earth with a jarring thud.

Her uncle looked slightly bemused as he gazed back over his shoulder at her. 'Hurry along, Geneva. We can't keep the bride and groom waiting.'

'Wait for me,' her aunt said, puffing as she came down the stairs. 'I've decided to come with you.'

Geneva had visited Betty Crump the day before and had handed over her gift. She was looking forward to the wedding, if only to see Sorle for longer than a few minutes.

Of late, except when they'd passed each other in the hall, he'd spent his time squiring Richard Chambers about, showing him around the district and visiting the locals. He'd also been training his new mare, which was proving to have an impressive turn of speed.

Her cousins were often recruited into the training, and both Michael and Robert were turning out to be adept horsemen. Geneva had been coaxed into mounting the younger mare, and had been led around the meadow on a leading rein – not caring that she was showing a little too much ankle. Eventually, she'd gathered enough confidence to ride by herself.

'Good,' Sorle had said, his praise bringing a smile to her face, and he'd placed a hand each side of her waist to assist her down. 'You make a pretty pair. We'll have to buy you a riding dress so you can exercise her.'

There would be precious little of that when he was married, so she didn't see the point of him wasting his money.

The two younger boys had become firm friends with the girls.

'I love having them here,' Elizabeth said, when Geneva enquired whether the smaller boys were a nuisance. 'They're good company for Madeleine and Barbara.'

Geneva was glad of the diversion, because there was not much time left to attend to last-minute details for the ball, which was to take place in three days time.

Tomorrow, the gardeners would place the Chinese lanterns in the trees outside and the halls would be decorated with holly and ivy. Some half-dozen of the earl's key London staff had already arrived, with boxes of china, glassware, bedlinen, cutlery. They wore airs of superior efficiency about them which annoyed the manor staff, so lots of sniffing went on.

That Sorle had seen fit to place his whole household under her command was an awesome responsibility which tested her skills to the limit sometimes. But everything seemed to run smoothly for most of the time, even though he'd thrown her into the deep end right from the beginning.

When they reached the church, her aunt looked pleased when Sorle invited them both to sit with him. No sooner had they seated themselves than the women of the district came flocking in on a wave of perfumed silk and settled all around them.

When Sorle cursed under his breath, Geneva giggled softly.

'You're going to have to find some way to rescue me from all these females, you know, Gen,' he whispered in her ear.

Tom came in, looking self-conscious in a suit. He stood there red-faced and sweating despite the coolness of the day. He tugged at the cravat at his throat, until Sorle collected him and brought him down to the front. As they stood there chatting, Tom visibly relaxed.

The Welford servants had been given a couple of hours off for the wedding, and had filed into the back of the church.

Then Betty came in with her mother. An uncle who was to give her away trailed behind them, looking overwhelmed and terrified by the splendour of the congregation. They stood and looked at one another.

'How dare she do this to me!' Priscilla whispered.

There was a gasp from somewhere behind Geneva, and a loud exclamation was emitted from Mrs Hunter. 'Well I never!'

Beside her, Aunt Maudine gave a snort, then subjected her to a disbelieving stare.

Unrepentant, Geneva gave a faint grin and lifted her chin a trifle. The reaction was better than she'd thought it would be.

She raised her eyes to the crucifix. Thank you for small triumphs, Lord.

Betty gazed around her, a happy smile shining on her face. Dressed in Priscilla Hunter's cast-off gown and Geneva's straw hat, which Geneva had decorated with the pink silk ribbons and roses she'd bought to adorn her own ball gown with, Betty was glowing with pride, even though a pair of scuffed brown boots stuck out from beneath the hem.

When Geneva beckoned to them, Adam began to play softly on the organ. As the bride, her mother and uncle walked self-consciously down the aisle, several women held handkerchiefs to their noses.

'You look right fancy in that gown, our Betty, just like one of the gentry,' Tom said reverently when his bride reached him.

'Miss Tibbetson gave me it to wear. She said I'd be the prettiest bride in the district. And you look as handsome as a Lord in that suit, I reckon, Tom – beggin' your pardon of course, Lord Ashby, for I meant no disrespect.'

'No offence taken, Betty.' Sorle beckoned Betty's mother into a place of honour at the end of the Ashby pew, where she'd be able to watch her daughter plight her troth in comfort.

The bridal pair grinned in a slightly embarrassed way at each other when the music came to an end, then Betty said to James Batterby, 'Let's get it over and done with before Tom changes his mind then, Vicar.'

James Batterby's eyes lit on his niece for a moment, and his smile was one of complete and utter approval.

He then said, '*Dearly beloved, we are gathered here in the sight of God, and in the face of this congregation, to join together this man and this woman in holy matrimony . . .*'

Sorle added a moment of irreverence to the proceedings by taking Geneva's hand in his and tickling her palm.

'It was a well-executed put-down,' Sorle was to later tell his mother. 'The bride came down the aisle in the gown Priscilla gave Geneva to wear to the ball. And when Priscilla took Geneva to task over it afterwards, Geneva gently reminded her that she'd donated it to the poor, and that Betty hadn't got anything to wear for her wedding, except for an old skirt and bodice. The expression on her face was so saintly and angelic that I was hard put not to laugh.'

Sarah nodded. 'I can imagine how Geneva felt about being patronized in public. Priscilla deserved such a put-down.'

'Miss Hunter was certainly affronted by it. Her nose was stuck so high in the air that it resembled a church steeple, and I thought a crow might alight on the end. Her mother cornered me afterwards and she carped about it for at least fifteen minutes. I felt like strangling her.'

Sarah struck him on the arm and laughed. 'Stop being so dreadfully wicked, Sorle.'

He grinned at that. 'That wasn't the end of it. I thought Geneva was upset and contrite after her telling off, because she went off round the side of the church. I followed her to offer her comfort. She was seated on a tombstone with her head in her hands and her shoulders shaking. I thought she was crying, but she was laughing and couldn't stop. I ended up doing the same.'

'I wish I'd been there.'

'You would have thought it most disgraceful behaviour. Every time I catch her eye now, we'll share that memory and laugh.'

'My relationship with your father was like that. We never stopped laughing together.'

'Until he died, then you never seemed to stop crying.'

Her face assumed a wistful expression. 'You know, Sorle, I wanted to go with him for a while, but you and Elizabeth held me back. I'm so glad I had that short time of happiness with him to remember, though. I loved him so very much.' She gently touched his face. 'John Ashby is alive in you. Sometimes I see him looking through your eyes, and I know he'd be proud of the man you've become. If you ever have a son of your own, I'd be pleased if you would name him after your father.'

'It would be my honour to do so.' He gave his mother a hug. 'Have you ever thought of marrying again? What about the ever-faithful Sir Peter Falk? I'd thought he might offer you marriage.'

'Oh, he did, on many occasions . . . and still does. I considered his proposals, but I know he'd never be able to compare with your father.'

Sorle held her at arm's length and smiled. 'It's not wise to turn a dead man into a saint. I imagine my father would have wanted you to be happy, and Sir Peter wants the same thing. You're not being fair to him. Can't you accept that the two are different people, and Sir Peter has many admirable qualities of his own?'

'You're right, of course.' His mother turned pink and couldn't quite meet his eye. 'Peter does have many admirable qualities. Perhaps I'll accept him one of these days, for he's certainly good company.'

Good Lord, Sorle thought, slightly shocked, surely his mother and Peter Falk . . . ? But then, why shouldn't she. After all, she was an attractive woman, and as human as the rest of them.

'Now, enough of my private life . . .' she said, '. . . about Geneva Tibbetson.'

He turned eyes of blandness towards her. 'Ah, you'd rather talk about my private life would you? What of her, then?'

'I've been thinking . . . I might ask her to return to London with me after the ball. Geneva is such a dear girl, who has become just like one of our family. I thought I might take her under my wing, introduce her to people and give her an altogether different life than the one she has now. What do you think of the idea?'

Sorle nearly fell for it. For one who'd campaigned long and hard to marry him off, the feigned innocence in his mother's expression was totally overdone. He appeared to think for a moment or two, then shrugged, saying casually as he moved towards the door, 'Geneva hasn't got the temperament to be a lady's companion. She'd be better off married to the Reverend Blunt.'

He grinned when his mother snorted in exasperation.

The Batterby boys were crowded into Gerald and Matthew's bedchamber, relived that they'd done their final rehearsal before the ball.

'Where did you get the shilling piece from, Moth?' Robert asked, catching it in a mid-air spin.

'I'm not telling you. Give it back. It's mine.'

'You can't have it back until you tell me where you got it from.'

'Lord Ashby gave it to me.' Moth held out his hand. 'May I have it please, Robert?'

'Only if you tell us what he gave it to you for.'

'I'm not allowed to tell, it was a gentleman's agreement. A secret.'

'You're not old enough to be a gentleman, so it doesn't count. Besides, we're your brothers and you're not allowed to keep secrets from us.' Michael gazed at his brothers. 'That's right, isn't it?'

There were mutters of assent all round.

Moth gazed desperately towards Gerald for help. Gerald just grinned, which wasn't very encouraging. It was hard being the youngest, sometimes. He gazed at his brothers with all the disgust he could muster. 'Can't a fellow have a secret of his own sometimes? All right, I'll tell you. But you'll have to pay a penny each for it.'

'A farthing,' they all said, which was better than nothing, so Moth agreed with a nod of his head.

'It had better be a good secret.'

'It is. The best. Something you'll never guess in a hundred years. Where are your farthings, first.'

'I've already spent my allowance,' said Edward, an announcement which was followed by messages of similar hardship.

'All right, you can owe it to me.' Moth pocketed his shilling and gazed with some self-importance at his brothers. 'I saw Lord Ashby kissing Gen. He said he was getting some dust out of her eye, but he gave me the shilling and told me to keep quiet about it.'

His revelation was followed by a stunned silence, they had frozen into the position they were in. Seven pairs of brown eyes widened. The grin Moth had on his face expanded, for his brothers suddenly reminded him of seven mud crabs, their eyes on stalks, waiting to pinch him. He giggled nervously.

'That's not funny, Moth. You're lying,' Matthew said.

'No, I'm not,' he said, hot in defence of himself. 'It was in the garden. Lord Ashby lifted her out through the window and told me to keep watch. Then he kissed her on the mouth, like this.' Moth put his hands either side of Edward's face and puckered his lips.

Jerking away, Edward made a noise in his throat. 'That's disgusting! Did Gen cry?'

'She just laughed. Then Lord Ashby left and we went indoors.'

'Perhaps we ought to tell Papa,' Gerald said.

Fear came into Moth's eyes. 'We mustn't. They'll send Gen away from us again. Anyway, the earl would deny it and they'd all believe him and not us. And then the earl will forbid us from having breakfast there any more, because I'd have broken his gentleman's agreement.' Putting his head in his hands, Moth gazed morosely from one to the other, a worried look in his eyes. 'Not only that, Gen will never speak to any of us again.'

'Perhaps we should tell the earl he's got to marry Geneva,' Matthew suggested. 'It would save her from ruination.'

'But he's going to marry Priscilla Hunter, isn't he?'

'Oh, do shut up, Edward. Percy Pringle said he's going to marry his sister, Arabella. He overheard his parents talking about it.'

'You mean he's going to marry both of them?' Moth stared at Matthew. 'What does ruination mean?'

'It's as bad as going to hell, only you're still alive.'

'Holy hellfire! Poor Gen,' Moth whispered, and his face paled. 'I think I feel sick.'

Matthew passed him the chamber pot with a complete lack of sympathy. 'Do it in that, if you've got to.'

Gerald smiled at him. 'Is it possible you made a mistake, Moth, and Lord Ashby really *was* taking something from her eye?'

Moth couldn't bear the thought of Geneva going to ruination. Miserably, he admitted, 'It was dark where I was standing, and I couldn't see much.'

'The earl is a gentleman. He wouldn't do something so dreadful to Gen, would he?' Adam contributed to the debate.

'Of course not. The earl likes her. If he didn't, he wouldn't have given the magic pendant back to her.'

'And he'd only kiss Priscilla Hunter and Arabella Pringle if he was going to marry them, but even then he'd have to wait until after they were married.'

216

'So, Gen won't go to ruination, after all,' Moth said, feeling mightily relieved.

'Not if we don't tell the parents,' Gerald advised them all. 'And we might have to look after her a lot better in future.'

There was a combined heave of relief as the position of their cousin and the earl was suddenly reversed.

Nevertheless, Moth was going to ask Gen if he could look through the magic stone and make a wish.

He was going to wish that Lord Ashby married Geneva before the earl thought to ask the other two girls – then they could still have breakfast at the manor.

Seventeen

The work had been done and the overnight guests were beginning to arrive.

The affairs of the house were in the hands of Mrs Pickering, and the ball had been taken over by the head butler from Sorle's London house. Mr Duncomb wore an air of command, and had infinitely more knowledge of the way affairs were run for the ton than Geneva.

Mr Duncomb had relieved her of her lists. Casting his eyes over them, he looked down his superior nose and picked out the couple of things she'd forgotten.

'Very well planned, Miss Tibbetson, but you have forgotten the wines. And you will need to appoint a major domo for the ball. Someone who has experience of social events would be a best choice. Naturally, I'd be pleased to accept the position were it offered, since I have conducted such affairs for the earl in the past, so I'm aware of his likes and dislikes.'

His scant praise brought a genuine smile to Geneva's face. But little white lies dripped from her tongue, as if they'd been rehearsed rather than newly born, for there was an air of affront about Mr Duncomb, as if he was annoyed to think that a country wench such as herself had arranged an event such as this so almost right.

'The very person I'd intended to ask. Thank you so much. Actually, Mr Duncomb, I thought I'd wait and consult you about the wines too, since the earl informed me you were an expert in that field. There's a well-stocked cellar, and if anything else is needed we can send someone to the wine merchant in Dorchester.

Mr Duncomb hurrumphed a little bit. 'I do have a certain expertise in that area, though you have left it a little late. We'll need the ingredients for a punch and some cordials, because the dancing will make the ladies thirsty. No spirits, of course. If you would trust me with the key to the cellar, I'll be pleased to act in this matter on your behalf.'

'Thank you, Mr Duncomb.' Geneva found the key in her desk and handed it to him. 'Just let me know if there's anything else you need.'

Sarah chose that moment to come tripping down the stairs. 'He certainly will not. Mr Duncomb is quite capable of organizing everyone and everything with his eyes closed. Aren't you, Mr Duncomb?'

The head butler managed a sparse smile for Sarah. 'I have certain skills I can draw on if need be, Mrs Ashby.'

'I'm certain you have.' Sarah took Geneva by the arm. 'My dear, you will now leave everything to the staff and you'll come upstairs with me. I insist that you rest after all the work you've done, else you'll be too tired to enjoy the ball. Did you sleep last night?'

'Not very well, I kept thinking there was something important I'd forgotten . . . and there was, for Mr Duncomb accidentally reminded me of it.'

Mr Duncomb awarded himself a self-congratulatory smile, then he bowed slightly and took his leave of them.

Geneva was then borne off to Sarah's rooms, where she was tucked under the covers of Sarah's bed. The curtains were pulled across, for the weather was fine and the light was a bright distraction through the window.

'Now, sleep, my dear. When you wake we'll eat, then we'll begin our preparations for the ball, for those will take two or three hours at least.'

'But don't you need to have a rest, Sarah?'

'I shall rest in my chair with my feet on a stool. I'm quite comfortable there.'

Geneva didn't think she'd sleep, even though she was weary. She gave a small smile at the thought of needing all that time for preparation, when all she really needed to do was pull on her grey gown and re-braid her hair.

When Geneva woke she felt decidedly creased. The sun had moved and the day had a feel of late afternoon to it. There was the sound of voices in the other room; her heart lifted when she heard the rumble of Sorle's voice.

'She's resting and I'm not going to disturb her. You can see her at the ball and not a moment before. Go and be pleasant to your guests. I saw Tobias arriving earlier, no doubt you will want to greet him and catch up on the London gossip.'

Another rumble, then the door opened and shut.

Sarah began giving instructions to her maid. 'It's such a nuisance when the men can't think of what to do with themselves and look for the distraction of female company. Don't they realize we need time before social events, so we can delight their eyes with our splendid appearances.'

'Yes, Mrs Ashby. Time's getting on. Shall I wake Miss Tibbetson?'

'I'd rather she woke naturally. The poor girl was quite worn out. If she's not awake by four, we'll wake her then. You can start on her while we wait for refreshments to be brought up.'

Wearing a velvet robe, Sarah glanced up when Geneva came through the door. 'Ah, you're awake, dear. How rumpled you look, but that sleep will stand you in good stead. Go behind the screen and slip into that robe, so Jessie can start on you.'

Starting on her consisted of intimacies that Geneva never knew existed, so afterwards she felt smooth and naked. Scented oil was then massaged into her skin. When Jessie finished the ritual, Geneva felt relaxed.

Sarah smiled at her when she came out from behind the screen. 'You can soak in that oil for a while. It will work its way into the skin and make it feel soft and smell fragrant.

219

They ate a meal of boiled eggs, a slice of ham and some cheese and crusty bread, served on trays and washed down with tea. Geneva hadn't realized how hungry she was.

Sarah smiled at her. 'We won't be fed again until supper time.'

Both of them were dressed in Sarah's robes when a knock came at the door. An army of maids with buckets of water filled the tub. It was the first time Geneva had experienced the joys of a bathtub, usually having to make do with a bowl of cold water and a flannel.

The experience of soaking in warm water was extremely pleasant and relaxing. She laid back in it, her eyes closed, wishing she could stay there for ever. But she couldn't, for her hair had to be washed and rinsed.

Wrapped in her borrowed robe, she now sat before the fire to dry her hair. When the room gradually darkened, the maid lit several candles.

Sarah went behind the screen to dress, coming out a little while later looking like an Egyptian princess in a drifting red silk gown with gold edging. On her head a gold snake curved, keeping in place a drift of red silk with gold tasselled ends. The Ashby ruby earrings glittered in her ears.

'Now it's your turn. Bring her gown, Jessie.'

Geneva gasped and opened her mouth when she saw it. 'But—'

Sarah placed a finger under her chin and closed her mouth. 'Not one word, Geneva Tibbetson – not until you've listened to what I have to say to you.'

Geneva nodded.

'This gown is a gift from the earl – a reward for your hard work. He worried that you might be too proud to accept it, and he begged me to employ subterfuge to engage your consent. You're a grown woman, so I've decided it will not do to insult your intelligence. My son offers you this gift with all humility. I'd not like to see his feelings hurt over such a trite matter because of misplaced pride. So, Geneva, my dear, can you accept the gift with the grace it deserves? It will give all of us pleasure if you will.'

Geneva couldn't believe this was happening to her, and she couldn't wait to try it on. She nodded. A smile spread across her face. 'Truly . . . it's a wonderful gift . . . I'm so touched . . . I feel like crying.'

'And make your eyes turn all red and puffy? Good gracious, you'd better control that urge immediately. Dress her then, Jessie. We shall make Miss Tibbetson the sensation of the ball.'

Sorle had not worn evening dress for quite a while. His blue breeches were buttoned and tied above the rise of his calf, his darker cutaway coat was worn over his favourite pearl-grey waistcoat, and sat comfortably on his shoulders. His neckcloth felt a little irritating, but his man had trimmed his hair so it curled less abundantly, and his side-whiskers barely brushed the high points of his collar.

Sorle intercepted the Batterby family in the hall, and took the reverend aside for a moment of private conversation. 'There's something of importance that I wish to discuss with you, a formality to be observed. We cannot talk now, but may I call on you? The day after tomorrow, perhaps.'

The reverend gave him an astute glance. 'You may, My Lord. Will eleven o'clock in my study suit you?'

'Perfectly,' he said, before the man moved off to join his wife, who looked rather handsome tonight, in lavender and lace.

He glanced up the staircase, watching as Elizabeth came down with her children, and smiling at the profusion of white tulle and ribbons his nieces wore. He said to their mother, 'Who are these pretty creatures with you? Do I know them?'

'It's us, Uncle Sorle. Madeleine and Barbara.' They dropped him a curtsy and giggled. 'You can kiss us if you want to.'

'A most unseemly pastime. I wouldn't dream of it.'

'But Edward and Moth said you kissed their cousin Gen.'

'Edward and Moth need their tongues pulled out by the roots. The pair are over there, perhaps they'll favour you with a kiss instead.'

The girls looked at each other and screwed up their faces.

'Don't make ugly faces, it will turn you all wrinkly,' and he scooped one up in each arm and kissed their downy cheeks. He turned to Elizabeth as the girls scampered off. Her wide smile and cocked head invited an explanation from him. 'They

221

were mistaken, of course,' he lied. 'I was merely removing some dust from her eye.'

'Of course they were, Sorle. You wouldn't dream of kissing Geneva Tibbetson, would you?'

'I dream of it all the time.' He grinned. 'Where is our mother?'

'Still in her sitting room.'

'And Miss Tibbetson? All the guests are here, so where is she?'

'She's still dressing, I believe. In the meantime, there are a dozen young ladies giving you languishing looks.'

'I haven't been announced yet, and I've decided my first dance will be with Miss Tibbetson anyway. She's never been to a ball before and I thought it would help her relax.'

'Yes, well –' Elizabeth gave a faint smile – 'being led on to the floor by an earl in the first dance is bound to be a relaxing experience for any country girl.'

His eyes rested on her for a moment, trying to find a hidden meaning. He couldn't 'You think so?'

Elizabeth smiled and kissed his cheek. 'You look handsome tonight, brother Sorle, like a man with his mind on seduction.'

His mind was definitely on seduction, and Elizabeth was being too curious. Luckily she was distracted.

'Oh look, here comes Sir Peter. How distinguished-looking he is.' Elizabeth took the baron's hands and received a kiss on her cheek. 'Mother said she'll be down in a few moments.'

'Then I'll wait here for her.' He joined Sorle at the bottom of the stairs, silver-haired and upright.

'I believe you've proposed marriage to my mother,' Sorle said gruffly to him.

Sir Peter raised an eyebrow. 'On many an occasion. Sarah has told you?'

He nodded. 'You should try again. If it counts for anything, you have my approval.'

'Thank you, Lord Ashby. I might take your advice.' His eyes lit up as he gazed up the stairs.

Sorle's mother was alone. Her fashionable gown would keep the local ladies gossiping for months, and he complimented her on her appearance. Even so, he frowned slightly. 'Where is Geneva?'

'She lacks the courage to come down. I've come to ask the reverend to talk some sense into her.'

Sighing, he muttered, 'She'll put in an appearance even if I have to throw her over my shoulder and carry her down. We can't keep the guests waiting all night.'

'Be gentle with her, Sorle.'

But he was in no mood to be trifled with. Taking the stairs two at a time, he threw open the door to his mother's rooms, and strode inside. Geneva turned, her eyes wide and filled with fright, stopping him dead in his tracks. Her hand fluttered against her chest. 'Sorle . . . I'm scared to go down.'

'You look . . . quite exquisite.' And she did. The gauzy over-skirt of her hyacinth-blue gown was frosted with crystals, the little puffs of sleeves sparkled with them. Dressed in Grecian style, her hair was secured by a clip of blue silk flowers set in a spray of crystal leaves. Between the twin rise of creamy breasts the sapphire pendant glowed.

Sorle's anger dispersed. Behind her in the window was the shape of a full moon rising. The light touched on the frost, sparkling across the land. It had a magical quality to it.

He crossed to where she stood and turned her round to face it. 'When I gave you the pendant you're wearing, I told you it had magical qualities. I said that if you looked through it when the moon was full, and the landscape turned the colour of amaranth, anything you wished for would come true.'

She was reflected in the mirror, as lovely and as fey as a nymph. The fragrance rising from her body was exotic, making him want to kiss the part of her neck where the tiny pale ringlets curled against her hairline. He would allow his mind to go no further than that small action at the moment.

'Look through it now, if you would. Perhaps you could wish for some courage.' His fingers touched against her breast as he lifted the jewel, the slight action making her shiver. His eyes narrowed in on her reflection as he thought: *Oh yes, my lady, you're ready for me.*

Geneva gave a small exclamation of delight as she held the jewel to her eye. The entire landscape had taken on a delicate purple hue. Then her vision shortened and she saw the reflection of Sorle in the window, tall and imposing behind her.

223

'Make a wish,' he whispered against her ear. 'Then we'll go downstairs – together, for it's as much your ball as it is mine.'

She could feel his heart beating against her back as she closed her eyes and wished for the only thing in this world that would truly make her happy – something that was way beyond her reach.

She'd hardly finished wishing when she was turned in his arms. She gazed into his eyes, hardly daring to breathe, her hands pressed against his chest. A smile touched his mouth. He placed a kiss against her forehead. It was as delicate as a butterfly alighting, when she would have welcomed his mouth taking hers with a demanding force. It was obvious at that moment that his feelings towards her were of a more paternal nature.

Voice tender, he murmured, 'Are you ready now, my Gen?'

She nodded, finding her voice, though her mouth was dry from disappointment. 'Thank you for the gift, Sorle. It's a beautiful gown, but I don't know what my uncle will say when he sees it.'

'He'll say nothing, for he'd never deliberately spoil your happiness.' Sorle took a step back and proffered his arm, a resting place for her silk-gloved hand as they made their way to the top of the staircase.

Beneath them in the deserted hallway, Mr Duncomb stood, resplendent in his livery. Sorle nodded to him. They descended the staircase together, following Mr Duncomb towards the drawing room.

'Ladies and gentlemen, your hosts, Lord Ashby and Miss Geneva Tibbetson,' he bellowed.

Sarah's eyes widened.

There was instant silence as they went inside, as Duncomb's introduction sunk in. Then, clearly, Moth's voice rang out. 'Gen, you look like a princess. I'm struck speechless!'

'One can only pray,' his father said drily, when people began to laugh.

Then everyone began to talk at once. Sorle escorted her around the guests, introducing her to those people she didn't know. She bore the hostile glances and glares from Priscilla Hunter, Arabella Pringle and their mothers stoically, and enjoyed the bewildered expression on Aunt Maudine's face. Her aunt's hiss of 'Where did you get that gown from?' was left unanswered. Her uncle kissed her hand and told her to save him a dance.

Outside in the hall, the music struck up. Sorle bowed slightly. 'You promised me the honour of partnering me in the first dance, I think, Miss Tibbetson.'

The guests spilled into the hall after them, chattering and laughing. Sarah, Elizabeth, their partners and Geneva's aunt and uncle joined them, and they had an eightsome. Geneva had never seen Maudine dance, and was surprised how light on her feet she was.

When the music stopped there was a spattering of applause and the rest of the guests crowded on to the floor. Viscount Ainsley tapped Sorle on the shoulder. 'My turn I think, Ashby. I can't let this exquisite creature escape my grasp.'

'I'm reluctant to turn her over to you, my friend. Just remember, Miss Tibbetson is off limits. If you as much as step on her toe, you will incur my wrath.'

Tobias Ainsley was an outrageous flirt, but enormous fun. His charm was enhanced by a glib tongue and a ready wit. Soon he had her almost helpless with laughter. Geneva warmed to the viscount, but found him a little on the shallow side, and not to be taken seriously.

Other people then claimed her attention, she danced with her uncle, her elder cousins, several young men from London, as well as the squire and a couple of officers from the Dorset Regiment.

The next time she saw the viscount he was sitting on the stairs wearing a languid air, and with several young ladies crowded around him. He was laughing as he regaled them with tales of life in London. Priscilla was amongst them, and she seemed enthralled by him.

The music stopped and Geneva's cousins sang the selection of Christmas carols they'd been rehearsing. There wasn't a sound from the audience as their voices rose and fell in perfect harmony.

During the applause, Geneva sensed, rather than saw, the earl come up behind her. The nerves in her neck prickled when he said quietly into her ear. 'May I escort you in to supper afterwards?'

225

She nodded and, feeling eyes on them, looked across the room to meet Jane Whitmore's pensive glance. As Geneva's eyes met hers, Jane gave a faintly regretful smile and transferred her attention to the soldier standing next to her, a rather plump major with a paunch.

The younger children were sent to bed after supper, while her cousins were sent back to the rectory in the Ashby carriage. The dancing began again. With a little too much wine in him, Tobias Ainsley whirled Geneva under the stairs, then tried to snatch a kiss. Pushing him backwards, she escaped his clutches and ran straight into Sorle.

'I'm sorry,' she gasped.

Sorle inspected her flushed face. 'Has Tobias been misbehaving?'

Geneva hoped there wouldn't be a scene. 'Only slightly. He's had too much wine, that's all.'

'Ah, yes, this delicious angel is off limits as I remember,' Tobias said, placing his finger to his lips as he emerged from his hiding place. 'My apologies, it seems the earl has a prior claim to you.'

Sorle was claimed by Arabella Pringle's mother for a dance.

The viscount looked around him. 'Ah . . . there's the delicious Miss Hunter, all alone. She's a maid who'd welcome a bite from the big bad wolf, I'll be bound. Miss Hunter, my sweet girl,' he cooed. 'Come and keep me company. Shall we sit on the top of the stairs with a glass of wine and watch the dancers? You can tell me all about yourself.'

Priscilla's smile was smug at being singled out.

A card table had been set up for the men, attracting the older of them, for, as their energy for dancing was sapped, their appetite for whist increased. Their wives sat in groups, chatting, watching their menfolk, and keeping an eye on the dancers.

Too soon, the ball was over. Cloaks were fetched and people began to depart.

'Have you seen Priscilla anywhere?' The squire asked Geneva.

'She was on the stairs earlier with –' her faced paled – 'with, 'um, Miss Pringle and some of the other young ladies.'

226

She caught Sorle's eye for a moment and he picked up her silent message. 'She may be resting in my mother's rooms. I'll go and look for her.'

'But before he was halfway up the staircase, Priscilla came running down, her gown and hair in disarray, and with Tobias in hot pursuit. She giggled when he grabbed her, and kissed him full on the lips.

'What's the meaning of this, Priscilla?' the squire thundered, knowing all the while what the meaning was.

Priscilla blushed, hung her head and said nothing.

Luckily, there were very few people in the hall, and Sorle managed to herd the Hunter family towards Geneva's sitting room without any more fuss.

'Tobias, would you care to join us and explain your behaviour to the squire?' the earl said calmly.

The miscreant gazed owlishly around him. 'Seems as though I have no choice, eh?'

'The devil you don't,' the squire replied. 'I could shoot you out of hand instead, you blackguard.'

'I'll never forgive you if you do,' Priscilla said with a sob, as the door closed behind them.

It was a while before they came out. The squire and his wife were tight-lipped. Priscilla was smiling. Nose in the air, she swept past without a word. The Hunter family departed.

Tobias Ainsley had a defeated expression on his face as he emerged with Sorle. A smile spread across his face when he saw her. 'A pity you didn't allow me to kiss you properly, sweet one,' he said, 'because damn me if you don't have the most delicious lips.'

Sorle's mouth tightened. 'I'll see you to your room,' he told his guest, and the pair started up the staircase together.

Geneva's uncle and aunt came into the hall. 'We're leaving now, Geneva. Go and fetch your wrap.'

Geneva had left it in Sarah's rooms. Placing it around her shoulders, she was wondering whether to go in search of Sorle to bid him farewell, when she heard him say to the viscount. 'You've insulted my guests enough for one night. You know what this means, don't you?'

'Pistols at dawn?' Tobias gave a short bark of laughter. 'You know I'm a crack shot, Ashby. Exquisite flower though she is, are you sure you'd want to die for her?'

'I adore her, Tobias. My future will be worth nothing if I cannot have her . . .'

Face pale, Geneva fled.

The rectory had settled down to its familiar quietness when Geneva rose from the chair. It was three o'clock in the morning, and she was wearing Gerald's cast-off breeches. Shoes in hand, she crept downstairs, freezing to the spot when one of the risers squeaked loudly.

As soon as her wildly beating heart settled down, she continued on her way, closing the door quietly behind her and heading in the direction of the manor. She'd rather have Sorle married to Priscilla, who she now knew he loved, than see him killed in a duel with Tobias Ainsley.

'No wonder Priscilla was smiling,' she muttered. 'She'd enjoy having two peers of the realm fighting for her hand in marriage.'

Pulling her wrap around her, she shivered, for it was bitterly cold. The moon rode high in a clear sky. It was surrounded by a ring of brilliant clarity, as if it was floating in a circle of crystals. The earth had an eerie light to it. Still wearing the pendant, she lifted it to her eye. How pretty the earth and sky was. She sighed, wishing that Sorle had fallen in love with *her*, not with Priscilla.

She gained entrance to the house through the front door, cautious in case people were about. Not that the servants would question her presence. They were too used to seeing her here.

There was a candle burning in a glass holder in the hall. She left it where it was, for she could navigate the house in the dark. As she gained the upper reaches, she felt as though she was being watched.

Her eyes were drawn to the portrait of Sorle's uncle, and she grinned at his stern countenance. 'No haunting tonight, please,' she whispered.

Creeping past Sorle's room to the one occupied by Viscount Ainsley, Geneva pressed her ear against the panel. He was snoring loudly. She took a door key from her pocket, carefully turned it in the lock, then heaved a sigh of relief.

Suddenly, an arm came around her from behind and a hand was pressed over her mouth. Dragged backwards into Sorle's chamber, she was thrown on to a bed. Before she could move, he sat on her middle and pinned her arms above her head.

'State your business in the viscount's room at this time of night, Geneva.'

With his hand still pressed over her mouth, she could only mumble something rude against his palm while she struggled furiously to shift his weight.

He loosened the hand and stared down at her, laughing. In the moonlight, his face looked slightly devilish. 'Have you got nothing to say for yourself?' he whispered.

'I'll scream and wake the whole household if you don't let me go,' she threatened. Not that she had any breath left inside her to scream with – and, in fact, she felt like giggling.

'Go ahead. I've got nothing to lose.' He bent his head and kissed her. His mouth coaxed with sweetness and fire. He melted everything her body consisted of, and she enjoyed this suspension of her will to the more tacit delights of the body, something she'd like to explore with him at her leisure, and to the limits of her endurance.

'Oh dear,' she sighed. 'You're making me think and behave like a hussy.'

He gave a rueful chuckle. 'Which is nothing compared to the effect you're having on me, I'd imagine.'

And indeed, the effect on him was rather . . . *pressing*. She grinned. 'Perhaps you should move. It would be more comfortable for both of us, I should imagine.'

He removed himself, propped himself on his elbow next to her and said silkily, 'Explain Tobias Ainsley.'

'I overheard you challenge him to a duel over Priscilla.' She touched his face, whispering, 'He said he was a crack shot. I couldn't bear it if you were killed, Sorle. I came back to lock his door so he couldn't get out.'

'You came to save my life then?'

She realized he was nearly naked under his banyan robe, when his thigh slid sinuously from under it. His fingers toyed with her braid, removing the ribbon to unravel it and spread her hair. He pressed a small kiss against the hollow of her throat and murmured, 'There, that's better.'

Her mouth went dry and she said huskily, 'I think I ought to go home, don't you?'

'No.' When his fingers trailed over her breasts, goosebumps raced over her and she knew she would rather stay. 'It would be better for me if you stopped thinking in negatives just at this moment. I like having you in my bed and hope to enjoy your company a little longer.'

'I have . . . *tender* feelings towards you,' she said desperately. 'You mustn't take advantage of that, Sorle.'

He chuckled. 'Mustn't I? If you think an appeal to my better nature will prevent my seduction of you, think again, for I'm acting on my own feelings. Do you realize how often I've imagined you in my bed? Now, here you are. And here am I.'

His second kiss was a devastating and deliberate attack on her senses, and her body yielded to the sweet torture of his touch. Her curiosity about the act of loving was about to be revealed to her, and her body told her she was willing to experience every sweet intimacy of her ravishment. After that, she would go to him every time he wanted her.

When his mouth sought her breasts, they thrust up to meet his tongue. He loosened the flaps on the breeches she wore, slid them down over her hips. She opened to his touch like a flower to the sun, accepted the moist caress of his tongue with increasing abandonment, and took the length of him into her hands to explore the silken sheath with delight.

Then came a new intensity in him as he cast her playfulness aside. He gazed into her eyes, watching her face, listening to her reactions to his increased attention. He placed a hand over her mouth when she would have cried out with the intensity of her pleasure.

He straddled her, nudged gently against her.

'My love for you is so intense that this feeling cannot possibly be a sin,' she whispered. 'And even though you love another, I will treasure this moment always.'

His eyes glittered in the firelight as her gaze clung to his. 'We should stop now, before it's too late for you,' he said gently.

But her hands smoothed over his buttocks and she pulled him into her in the most natural and giving manner, so he went on willingly and definitely. When he felt her give, she gave a small sigh, and her muscles embraced his length.

230

It was agony to pull himself away from her, unsatisfied. He rolled to one side, said in a harsh whisper, 'Dress yourself. I'll make sure you get home safely.'

'Sorle,' she whispered, feeling the disappointment of unfulfilled love descending on her, for what she'd experienced couldn't possibly be all there was to the act of loving. 'Let me stay longer and learn.'

'No,' he said, almost harshly. 'You're new to the ways of love. You came to my home tonight with the purest of motives in your mind. I cannot take advantage of that by using your innocence for my own base needs. And I find myself unable to break the trust your uncle placed in me.'

Water splashed into a bowl and she heard him draw in a swift breath at the coldness of it. While he dressed, she scrambled into her clothes, shamed by her own brazenness. What would he think of her now?

Neither of them spoke as Sorle led her through the cold night back to the rectory.

'No light is burning, so your absence hasn't been discovered yet,' he murmured. 'Go this moment, Geneva. We will forget tonight.' And he gave her a little shove towards the house.

From behind the curtain, Gerald heaved a sigh of relief as he watched Geneva come towards the house. If she'd had a secret assignation with Lord Ashby, it hadn't lasted long.

The earl had worn the look of a man resolute in his actions, he thought, one whose intentions were sincere and honourable. Yet he'd blown a kiss towards the house as the door had quietly closed behind Geneva.

The stair creaked as Geneva crept up to her room. He heard her settle herself in bed. Then came the sound of a muffled sob or two, followed by some soft weeping before sleep claimed her.

Gerald was not such a fool that he hadn't noticed that Geneva was attracted to the earl. And he was not such a child that he wasn't aware of the urges that beset males when faced with an attractive woman.

To be truthful, his cousin had shocked them all tonight. The exquisite woman who'd turned the men's heads at the ball was not the Geneva he and his brothers had always known. She'd become an adult, a woman who now stood apart from them. Their familial relationship had somehow changed.

He wished now that he'd roused his father, for he didn't know how to approach her. He certainly didn't like to hear Geneva cry, and it was obvious that the earl had upset her in some way.

Tomorrow . . . he intended to talk to the man.

Eighteen

Most of the good citizens of Edgley must still be in bed, Geneva thought, noticing with some relief that the Ashby pew was empty. Even her aunt had stayed in bed.

She'd been dreading the meeting with Sorle this morning – and now decided to call on a headache as an excuse to miss the evening service, and the earl along with it. It wouldn't be a falsehood, since lack of sleep had made her feel decidedly out of sorts.

She suspected that her state was more to do with her behaviour the night before. Her face began to burn and she placed her hands against her cheeks. The enchantment of moonlit nights and the mixture of Sorle's kisses and caresses were too potent to be borne in the cold light of day.

She and Sorle had been naked together. She'd touched him, explored the most secret part of his body – not with shame, but with enjoyment. In return, his intimacy with her had been an experience of learning, mostly showing her what a hussy she was capable of being!

Thank goodness he'd had enough restraint to stave off what had seemed an inevitable conclusion to the romp – though the rejection had been a sobering reminder of her own lack of moral fortitude.

With some dismay, she realized that she was no longer a

virgin. Then the irreverent thought crept into her mind that losing it had been more pleasurable than painful, and there was something funny about the concept of virginity now. Laughter bubbled up in her.

Stop that. You're in church!

Damn him! Why was she blaming herself? He was unethical for leading her on. It had been Sorle who'd dragged her into his bed, who'd undressed her, who'd kissed her until her brain had ceased to function. How dare he uncover such dangerous desires in her, then throw her out without fulfilment of them – as if she was lacking in feminine attraction?

When a delicate little shiver ran up her thighs, her muscles clenched it into the moist centre of her. How addictive such sweetness was – already she craved for more, right here in the house of the Lord, where her mind should be on prayer, not sin.

How could she have been so forward? How could she ever look Sorle in the eye again?

What was worse, her grey gown had been left at the manor and she'd had to wear the striped abomination to attend church in.

The richness of the gown the earl had given her had left her dissatisfied with her life. From the very moment she'd walked into Sarah Ashby's rooms, her day had become one of sensory delights. Nothing would be the same again.

There would never be an occasion when the gown could be worn again. It would hang in the closet for the rest of her life, for she'd never be able to part with it. The crystals, which had seemed so bright in their promise of pleasure, would become dull. Empty, apart from her imprint, the gown would dance by itself in the draughts every time she opened the wardrobe door – a sad reminder of what once had been, and of a time she'd believed she could wish for the unattainable on an amaranth moon.

She might try it on from time to time and whirl around the room, imagining she was on Sorle's arm.

The almost empty church echoed as footsteps thudded on the flagstones leading down the aisle. It was Sorle's walk. Why hadn't he stayed in bed? Cringing a little, she fell to her knees and muttered a prayer. 'I know my actions need to be punished, Lord, but did you have to send the earl along to do it, when he was equally to blame?'

Her adversary sat in the pew in front of her and whispered from the side of his mouth, 'Is your conscience troubling you, my Gen?'

'Certainly not, since I've just convinced the Lord that my lapse of judgement was your fault. However, I will admit to feeling extremely embarrassed and ashamed of myself. Please, don't dare to tease me, Sorle, for I'll probably become aggressive and smite you from behind with my Bible.'

He chuckled. 'I'm already smitten by you. Come and sit next to me. We can hold hands.'

'Hah!' she said, turning pink and thinking that if she leaned forward she could place a kiss on his jaw, just in front of his ear. 'I certainly will not. Go and sit in the Ashby pew.'

Her uncle cleared his throat and gazed severely down at him. 'We are here for the service. Are any more of your household attending, My Lord?'

'I passed a few of my servants on the way. Most of my guests are readying themselves to leave, and Viscount Ainsley is still asleep. He'll be at the evening service though. My mother and sister have asked me to proffer their apologies for their non-attendance. We'd be pleased if you and your family would spend Christmas with us at the manor, Reverend. The squire, his wife and Miss Hunter will also be guests.'

'Indeed, we would be delighted. That's most kind of you,' her uncle said, forgetting his previous instruction in his pleasure at the invitation. When the reverend beamed a smile at Sorle, Geneva hardly stifled a giggle.

James Batterby turned towards the choir stall and murmured something. The choir then filed down to join the congregation, just as Sorle's servants began to wander in. Geneva found herself surrounded by her cousins. She smiled when Moth took her hand and grinned up at her. One of his front teeth was missing.

'I wiggled it and it came out, and the other one is loose,' he said proudly.

'You look as fierce as an otter without it.'

'I am fierce. Lord Ashby said he'd teach me sword fighting when I grow bigger.'

'Lord Ashby should find something less dangerous to occupy himself with,' she said, just loudly enough for him to overhear.

'Perhaps you could suggest something more suitable, Miss Tibbetson,' he purred. 'Wrestling perhaps?'

Her blush came like a raging fire. 'Oh . . . you!'

Gerald whispered something she couldn't quite hear to the earl, who gazed at him in surprise for a moment. Then Sorle nodded.

'Let us pray,' the reverend said, after they'd settled themselves.

A clatter of feet signified a late arrival.

Irritation evident in his face, Reverend Batterby raised an eyebrow at Hannah and Essie, who slid into the nearest pew. The pair lowered their heads and gazed at each other with a grin.

With the choir strengthening the voices of the congregation, the service went ahead. Geneva shivered in the bitter cold and was glad when it was over.

Afterwards, the boys hung around awkwardly. After greeting Sorle's horse, who whiffled gently into her palm in case she had a treat hidden there, Geneva gazed at Gerald in puzzlement. 'Aren't you coming home?'

'I want to talk to Lord Ashby before he goes to call on the squire,' Gerald muttered, gazing intently at the toe of his shoe before kicking at a stone.

She felt rooted to the spot. 'He's going to call on the squire?'

If her heart had sunk a little before, it now fell to the ground with a thud, and shattered into several pieces when Matthew added, 'It's something to do with a marriage settlement.'

The two maids, Hannah and Essie, had gone on ahead. Gathering up the rest of the boys, they ambled after them. Geneva's head was bowed against the wind, which she blamed for the tears trickling down her face. She felt wretched, would have preferred her own company today.

A robin was perched on the hedge up ahead. It watched them approach, its head cocked to one side, then flew off with an alarmed cry and a flash of red.

The boys raced on ahead while she dawdled, giving each other piggy-back races. Their energy was boundless.

Winter had its own charm, she decided, jumping as a fox ran across the lane in front of her. There was the taste and aroma of Aunt Maudine's deliciously thick oxtail stew, with suet dumplings floating on it, the glitter of frost on the hedges, the ice crystals on the window panes in the morning, and the rain beating against them when you were snug and warm in your bed.

Then there were the fiery holly berries, as hot and red as the throes of love. They contrasted oddly with their rich green leaves – so lovely, yet so cruel with their spikes.

Her uncle was bringing home a Christmas tree in a day or two, and she and the boys would decorate it. She could afford gifts this year, if she didn't buy herself a new gown. But if she bought an inexpensive length of fabric, perhaps she could learn to stitch one for herself. She could unpicked the seams of the one she was wearing and use it as a pattern.

They were going to the manor for Christmas, where she'd have to smile at everyone and feign happiness for the happy couple. How cruel life was sometimes. All this yearning inside her, and nobody to share it with.

She wondered then if Priscilla Hunter felt the same way about Sorle that she did. She scowled. That would be even worse!

Irrationally, she thought: Sorle does find me attractive. Perhaps he'll invite me to become his mistress between conferring infants on Priscilla.

Lord Ashby requests the pleasure of Miss Tibbetson in his bed to celebrate his thirtieth birthday. RSVP.

'Hah!' she shouted into the wind. 'How can I ever look him in the eye again!'

Sorle would have laughed if Gerald Batterby hadn't been quite so serious.

'Gerald, you've reached the wrong conclusion about this matter. You're right in that Geneva came back to the manor after the ball. Your cousin had mistakenly thought that one of my guests was about to do me harm. So she locked him in his chamber. When she alerted me of what had been done, we talked for a while, then I escorted her home.'

'She cried herself to sleep.'

Guilt filled Sorle. 'I was worried about her being out so

late and was harsh with her. She was embarrassed. I'm pleased you didn't alert your father to any of this.'

Gerald nodded, then said uncertainly, 'Sir, you wouldn't harm Geneva in any way, would you? I mean . . . well . . . I'm sure you know to what I refer.'

The concern for his cousin's welfare was expressed clearly on Gerald's face. It was unbearable, for Sorle knew that his control had been on so thin a thread that he doubted it would hold if another opportunity presented itself.

It had taken Gerald a great deal of courage to approach him on this, and he was filled with warmth for him. 'If I ever have a son like you, I shall be very proud,' he murmured. 'Your cousin is lucky she has you to care for her. There's something I should like to tell you, but I cannot at this moment. Will you keep your counsel and trust me for another day?'

When Gerald murmured in assent, Sorle nodded. 'I want you to know that the doubts you've raised are groundless, but, as one man to another, I admire your courage in approaching me. Rest assured, Geneva will never come to any harm with me.' He mounted his horse and gazed down at the lad. 'I must go now. I have an appointment with the squire.'

When Gerald gave a defeated sigh, Sorle smiled at him. 'It's on the personal behalf of another.'

Gerald's head jerked up.

'I'll be calling on your father tomorrow. No doubt I'll see you then.' Clicking his tongue, Sorle set his horse in motion.

The next morning, James Batterby and his wife went out early. He made one or two purchases then went to see the dress-maker.

'Is it ready?' he asked.

'Yes, Reverend Batterby.' The woman uncovered a long-sleeved pink gown, the bodice and hem decorated with deli-cately embroidered white daisies.

James felt pleased with his choice and headed back home with it as fast as he could.

'It's a waste of money. If she hadn't been so silly, Geneva could have kept the gown Priscilla Hunter gave her,' Maudine snapped.

'She is ill dressed when set against other girls of her age.

237

Her allowance entitles her to some consideration. If you wish to save money that badly, perhaps you should go and beg clothes from Mrs Hunter for yourself.'

'As if I would lower . . .' Maudine shrugged, said grudgingly, 'I never thought of it that way. You're right of course, James.'

He placed the box in her hands. 'Go and present it to her as an early Christmas gift from both of us. Tell her it would please me if she wore it today. Now, I must get on with my Christmas sermon.' A wide smile crossed his face. 'The earl has an appointment for eleven.'

Her eyes sharpened. 'I heard that Lord Ashby went to see Squire Hunter after church yesterday. Do you think he's asked for Priscilla's hand? She'd be the most obvious choice.'

'Yes . . . I imagine she would be.'

'Perhaps he's come to ask your advice on calling the banns.'

'Perhaps he has. Rest assured, Maudine, you shall be one of the first to know. Send one of the maids in with a cup of coffee, if you please.'

'You know the maids are not here, since you sent them on an errand yourself – and just when I needed them to help prepare the ingredients for the oxtail stew.' She sighed. 'I shall bring you some coffee myself. There's something odd going on in this house, James Batterby. I can feel it in my bones.'

'That must be uncomfortable.'

'Oh, you can laugh. Geneva is too distracted for words. I think her ideas have risen above her station since she was given that ball gown. No doubt she'll come crashing down to earth after the earl has wed – and she'll be spending her days moping about like a sad miss.'

Smiling to himself, James escaped into his study, where a fire was crackling in the grate. Soon his hands were clasped warmly round a cup. Forgetting about his sermon, he watched the hands click slowly around the dial of the clock.

There was a knock at the door and Geneva slipped through. 'I hope I'm not disturbing you, uncle.'

How lovely she looked in pink, and the soft white shawl about her shoulders would add extra warmth. 'I'm always delighted to see my niece.'

'I've come to thank you for the gown. It's so pretty.' Holding her skirt, she twirled around, just as she used to when she was

238

a small girl. 'Everyone is being so kind to me.'

'There's no reason why things should be otherwise. Did you enjoy your first ball, my dear?'

Her eyes suddenly filled with dreams. 'It was wonderful, and so kind of the earl to present me with a gown to wear ... though extravagant.' She gazed at the floor for a moment. 'I should have consulted you, but didn't have the time, since the gift was a last-minute surprise.'

'To refuse would have been churlish.'

The breath she inhaled indicated she had something more difficult to express. 'I did something rather silly afterwards.'

'And you want to tell me about it?'

'It's the last thing I want to tell you about, for it's of a personal nature,' she said honestly.

'Geneva, my dear, you're no longer a child. Sometimes it's wiser to keep your counsel. Such matters often resolve themselves, given time. This could be one of those occasions, perhaps? And I really don't think I want to be confided in just at this moment.'

She nodded.

'Think over your problem for a while. If you feel you must reveal what's on your mind, perhaps a female ear would be more suitable. I'm sure your aunt Maudine would be only too happy to advise you.'

Her eyebrow gave an unbelieving upward twitch. However, she nodded. 'I feel superfluous now my job at the manor is finished. But I've left some of my clothing in Mrs Ashby's rooms, and I must go and collect it.'

'I'd prefer it if you went this afternoon, since Moth and Edward both need supervision. I can hear them in the hall, and do believe they're sliding down the bannister.'

'I'll take them into the drawing room and ask them to write an account of the ball if they're disturbing you.'

'As long as Timothy can keep his observations under control. He seems to have picked up some rather peculiar expressions of late.'

'He's very astute in what he hears and sees around him.'

'Too astute at times, and his powers of observation can result in some very uncomfortable moments.'

'Moth has a vivid imagination and the sounds of words

impress him.' She gave a faint smile. 'He can read well for his age and will probably be able to combine the two and put them to good use when he's older.'

'Always your cousins' champion.' A wry smile appeared on her uncle's mouth and his eyes twinkled. 'I can see you envisage a glorious future as a great orator for Timothy. Prime minister of England, no doubt. Or perhaps he'll take to the stage, since he has a certain flair for performance and drama.'

She chuckled. 'Would you mind very much if he did, Uncle?'

He shrugged. 'No doubt he'll do what the Good Lord has seen fit to suit him for, as we all do ultimately.' Her uncle's eyes widened as he gazed at the clock. 'Is that the time? Goodness, I'm expecting my visitor at any moment. Perhaps you'd remove those noisy creatures from the hall. I can't hear myself think, let alone carry on a sensible conversation.'

Her cousins were all in the hall and there was an air of excitement about them.

Odd, Geneva thought. The twins should be at the church practising their Christmas music, and Michael and Robert were supposed to be fetching milk from the farmer. It was a wonder her uncle hadn't chased them off.

'Have you fetched the milk?'

'Papa sent Hannah and Essie for it today.'

Moth and Edward were rolling around on the floor. They stopped to grin up at her, and nodded when she said, 'Have you collected the eggs?'

'Well, come into the drawing room. I'll find something to occupy your time, for your father is expecting a visitor and the noise you're making is disturbing him.'

Gerald and Matthew came down the stairs, pulling on their gloves. Gerald's voice seemed to have deepened overnight, for he said with great authority, 'Sorry, Gen, we've got something planned. Right, off you go, you lot.'

Before Geneva knew it, the hall had emptied as they poured out into the garden and the door closed behind them.

Well, she thought, baffled by their strange behaviour. I shall go and find something to read, and enjoy the peace while I can.

Sorle had taken his time dressing. He'd tossed up on whether to wear his comfortable black dittos, and had finally asked his man to advise him.

'It's best to show a bit of dash, while retaining a look of dependability, on such an auspicious occasion, My Lord. I'd advise you to wear grey pantaloons with your hessians, a black, double-breasted jacket, and your burgundy waistcoat.'

Sorle gave the man an even glance. 'What auspicious occasion? I'm merely going to visit the Reverend Batterby.'

'Quite, sir. A man of the cloth deserves respect.'

'Hmmm,' Sorle rumbled, thinking, *Everyone seems to know a man's business before he knows it himself, in these parts.* Glancing in the mirror, the thought crossed his mind that he should take a personal gift to present Geneva with.

He went to his strongbox, unlocked it and inspected the Ashby jewellery collection. 'The very thing,' he murmured. With a pleased smile he extracted a ring set with a heart-shaped ruby surrounded by small diamonds, which he slid into his waistcoat pocket.

'Sorle, my dear, you look quite splendid,' his mother said as he crossed the hall. 'Are you going out?'

'I'm off visiting.'

A grin spread across her face. 'Oh, may I ask where? If it's to the rectory, you could deliver a parcel to Geneva.'

'Best if you send a servant with it.' He kissed her cheek and strode off, leaving her gazing after him, open-mouthed. She'd not stay there long, he'd be bound, but would rush off to find Elizabeth and discuss her suspicions.

Indeed, when he looked back, the pair of them were standing at a window watching him. He grinned to himself as he cracked the whip. Horse and phaeton picked up speed, with Florin and Shilling streaking behind him.

Edgley had an unusually large crowd of people gossiping in groups, despite the cold. He slowed to a walk to give the dogs time to catch him up.

Among the rumour mongers was Priscilla Hunter, who was holding court to a small group of young females. She talked and laughed in a spirited fashion, using her hands to emphasize a point. She would get what she'd always wanted, a title. In exchange, Tobias would get what he'd always wanted, heirs and a fortune. The match had worked out well, but he doubted if the couple would remain faithful to each other.

His ball seemed to have given the rumour mill plenty of ammunition, he thought.

Arabella Pringle was with her mother. Her eyes widened and she gave him a hopeful smile and bobbed a curtsy as he passed. Another year would mature her a little, and another ball would secure her a suitor, no doubt.

Jane Whitmore and the corpulent major she'd been dancing with passed him at a walk in the opposite direction. Their horses snickered at each other.

'Good morning, Lord Ashby,' she honked. 'You'll be joining us for the hunt on New Year's Day, I imagine.'

'I'll probably give that new mare of mine a run, see how she performs.'

'How very droll.' She turned to the major. 'You should see the bag of bones he intends to ride, Freddie.' The pair went off, noisily convulsed with laughter.

Gerald and Matthew were sitting on the church wall. Gerald smiled at him and the pair began to follow after. A little way along, he came across Adam and Simon.

His eyes narrowed. Geneva's guards were out in force today, despite his talk with Gerald – or was it because of it? It seemed he was to have an escort, so he slowed down to accommodate them.

Michael and Robert joined them further up, then when he reached the rectory, Moth and Edward dashed forward to greet both him and the dogs. There was a melee of brotherly dog greetings, then Florin, Shilling and Bandit headed off across the countryside towards the manor.

'Do I meet with your approval?' he asked the Batterby boys as they gathered around him with questioning expressions on their faces. He smiled gently when the answer was in the affirmative. 'I'm here to see your father.'

'I'll tell him you're here,' Gerald said when they went in, and he preceded him to the study.

It didn't take Sorle long to gain the reverend's permission. They talked a short while, enjoyed a glass of sherry together, then shook hands.

242

'Geneva should be in the study, Lord Ashby.'

The boys were sitting on the stairs when he crossed the hall, as quiet as mice. He nodded to them, whispered, 'I'll let you know what her answer is.'

Geneva was surprised to see the earl enter the drawing room. Colour flooded to her face and she placed her book aside, for the sight of him, elegant in his pantaloons and hessians, was somewhat overwhelming, and she suddenly had a vision of them gloriously naked, embracing on the bed, and her hands . . . ? She averted her eyes, and blushed. 'I hadn't expected you to call, especially after . . .'

His wicked grin told her he was remembering it too. 'Your narrow escape? I enjoyed every single moment of it. Such passion in a maiden so innocent is rare.'

'A gentleman wouldn't remind me of it.'

'This one would, and I expect I'll always remind you of it. I was totally shocked by your unladylike behaviour. A woman in breeches.' He grinned. 'But, ah . . . how well you looked in them . . . so round a handful.'

Hurling a cushion at him, she covered her boiling face with her hands. 'It's cruel of you to measure me against others, then mock me.' Her eyes gleamed at him through her spread fingers as she rallied. 'Exactly how many maidens have you seduced, Lord Ashby?'

'Your tongue is barbed.' He chuckled. 'My dear Gen, neither of us are the least bit ashamed of our conduct, and coyness really doesn't suit you. How becoming you look in pink. It matches your cheeks.'

She decided she could stand his teasing, and smiled. 'The gown was a gift from my uncle, just this morning. Why are you here?'

Sorle shuffled from one foot to the other. 'There's something I wish to tell you.'

How formal he was being, and how splendid he looked. Though her heart sang at the sight of him, it began to sink as she realized what he was here for. Catching her breath, she sought to make it easier for him. 'You've chosen a wife for yourself, haven't you?'

'That's so.' He cleared his throat. 'Although there was

243

nothing wrong with any of the young ladies presented to me, I believe I've selected the most suitable.' A tiny smile played around his mouth. 'She's fair of body and face, kind-hearted, intelligent and filled with fire. I love her dearly and I'd give up my life for her.'

'Oh, Sorle,' she whispered. 'I'm so pleased you've found someone who will make you happy.' Though she thought his assessment of Priscilla was a little far-fetched. Nobody was that perfect. 'Am I to understand that you've chosen Priscilla?'

'Priscilla? Good God! Are you insane? None of those fancy words describe Priscilla Hunter. They are a portrait of you, my love. I have loved you from the first moment we met.' Falling to his knees, he took her hands in his. 'I adore you, Geneva Tibbetson. I'll cherish you for every day of my life. Will you do me the honour of becoming my wife?'

Moth's voice came through the keyhole in a frantic whisper. 'Say yes, Gen. I've got thruppence wagered on it.'

'Yes,' she said.

They exchanged an amused glance when there was a scuffle on the other side of the door. 'Come away from the door, you pest.'

'Ouch . . . let go of my ear.'

Maudine's voice. 'What is going on here?'

'Geneva's going to marry Lord Ashby.'

There was a loud scream from Maudine. 'There, I knew something was going on. Didn't I tell you so, James?'

'Yes, dear, you most certainly did. Now, shall we all go into my study so the earl and Geneva can have a little privacy.'

Heaving a sigh of relief, Sorle fished in his waistcoat pocket, brought out his gift of love and set it on her finger. He rose to his feet, then, pulling her up after him. His arms circled her and pulled her close, his mouth sought hers, and she was kissed until she thought she'd die from the heaven of knowing he loved her.

'We must go and tell my mother now,' Sorle said when the hubbub in the Batterby household had died down. 'Perhaps you'd bring the family over for dinner tonight, Reverend, so we can celebrate properly.'

Handing his lady love into the phaeton, he tucked a fur rug

around her knees and affixed bells and streamers of red ribbons to the horse's bridle.

The journey back through the town was pleasurable. He smiled and nodded to the townsfolk as they watched them pass with the bells jingling and the ribbons streaming. If the good citizens of Edgley had any lingering doubts, the kiss Sorle gave Geneva halfway down the main street would have laid them to rest.

From their position at the window, Sarah and Elizabeth watched Sorle guide the carriage up to the front door.

Sarah smiled broadly when she saw Geneva sitting next to Sorle, and the glance the pair exchanged brought tears to her eyes.

'Red ribbons and bells, no less. Who would have thought my son would display such flair when it came to courting a girl. He wears his heart on his sleeve for all to see.'

'I'm so glad it turned out to be Geneva. She seems to be so right for him.'

'I never had any doubts over who he'd choose to be his countess.'

Mother and daughter went down the stairs to greet the couple.

Sorle's face shone with happiness when he saw the approval in his mother's eyes.

Nineteen

It was spring, the air was sweet, the sun shone, the birds sang and the ground was covered in a festivity of daffodils.

The banns had been called for the past three Sundays.

The Edgley church was filled to bursting. Sorle stood calmly at the front waiting for his bride to arrive. In attendance was Gerald Batterby, self-conscious in his new dress suit.

Having won the toss, Simon was playing his father's new

cantata, the one James had finished especially for Geneva's wedding day. The choir's song rang joyously to the rafters.

There was a murmur of voices from the congregation. Sorle turned, smiling at the sight of his nieces, as pretty as buttercups in golden gowns, with white flowers in their hair.

Behind her came Reverend Batterby, proud, with Geneva on his arm.

Sorle's heart turned over at the sight of her. She was wearing a simple cream-silk gown that shimmered through a layer of golden tulle, which was caught up at one side into a blushing silk rose. Her pale hair was swept up, cascading ringlets from a matching trio of roses. Around her neck she wore a simple gold cross, a present from her uncle.

Geneva's expression was slightly anxious. He placed his hands together in an attitude of prayer, kissed his fingertips and inclined them slightly towards her. Her smile came then, and it was full of love. He felt blessed.

When she reached his side, he took her hand in his and gently squeezed it.

The music ended, the bishop stepped forward and the service for the solemnization of marriage began. *'Dearly beloved, we are gathered together in the sight of God . . .'*

How sweet and serious she was as she listened to him promise to love, comfort and honour her for the rest of his life.

'I will.'

Her bottom lip gently quivered.

'Wilt thou have this man to thy wedded husband . . . ?'

He could have drowned in the blue of her eyes, and kissed her shy, grave smile when she murmured, 'I will.'

'Who giveth this woman to be married to this man?'

'Me,' Moth said loudly.

'Acting as head of the Batterby household, and also on behalf of my sons, I do,' the reverend said, remaining unperturbed. 'You may proceed without further interruption, My Lord Bishop.'

Geneva giggled softly when Sorle took her right hand in his. He slid her a grin and repeated after the bishop.

'I, Sorle William Ashby, take thee, Geneva Mary Tibbetson, to my wedded wife . . .'

246

Soon they were back at Welford Manor, welcoming the guests who were to celebrate their wedding at the nuptial feast.

'Mrs Emma Mason,' Duncomb announced.

Geneva gave a small gasp and gazed up at him, her eyes slightly wounded.

Sorle, his voice reminiscent of melted sugar, murmured, 'Thank you for attending our wedding, Mrs Mason . . . May I present, my wife, Countess Ashby.'

Emma Mason turned a dark shade of red as she remembered the beating she'd subjected the girl to. 'My Lady.' She bobbed a deep curtsy, then passed into the room.

Mr Bowers was subjected to the same punishment. The man bowed over her hand and gave her a sickly sort of smile. 'Your servant, Countess.'

When she smiled graciously at him, Sorle chuckled.

And so it went on, a procession of people who had once scorned her, now being obliged to defer to her. While part of her deplored the necessity of it, the other part found the poetic justice of the process exquisitely enjoyable.

The day had been too long. Arms around each other's waists a little later, the earl and his lady watched the last of their guests depart.

Sorle gazed down at her. 'It's all over, at last.'

Geneva grinned at that. 'No, My Lord. I think it's just beginning.'

'And there's some unfinished business between us, as I recall, for your cousins were too vigilant.' He laughed as he scooped her up in his arms and headed for the stairs. 'We'd best make a start on it, I think.'

Geneva did, by snatching a kiss that lasted until the chamber door closed gently behind them.